DATE DUE			APR 04
7-13-04			
9-24-04			
GAYLORD			PRINTED IN U.S.A.

Southern Living

This Large Print Book carries the
Seal of Approval of N.A.V.H.

Southern Living

Ad Hudler

Thorndike Press • Waterville, Maine

Published in 2004 by arrangement with
The Ballantine Publishing Group,
a division of Random House, Inc.

Thorndike Press® Large Print Americana.

The tree indicium is a trademark of Thorndike Press.

The text of this Large Print edition is unabridged.
Other aspects of the book may vary from the original edition.

Set in 16 pt. Plantin by Al Chase.

Printed in the United States on permanent paper.

Library of Congress Cataloging-in-Publication Data

Hudler, Ad.
    Southern living / Ad Hudler.
      p. cm.
    ISBN 0-7862-6165-X (lg. print : hc : alk. paper)
    1. Women — Georgia — Fiction. 2. Festivals — Fiction.
  3. Georgia — Fiction. 4. Large type books. I. Title.
  PS3608.U5416S68 2004
  813′.6—dc22   2003063981

To the fine people of Macon, Georgia,
for their grace and civility

As the Founder/CEO of NAVH, the only national health agency solely devoted to those who, although not totally blind, have an eye disease which could lead to serious visual impairment, I am pleased to recognize Thorndike Press★ as one of the leading publishers in the large print field.

Founded in 1954 in San Francisco to prepare large print textbooks for partially seeing children, NAVH became the pioneer and standard setting agency in the preparation of large type.

Today, those publishers who meet our standards carry the prestigious "Seal of Approval" indicating high quality large print. We are delighted that Thorndike Press is one of the publishers whose titles meet these standards. We are also pleased to recognize the significant contribution Thorndike Press is making in this important and growing field.

Lorraine H. Marchi, L.H.D.
Founder/CEO
NAVH

★ Thorndike Press encompasses the following imprints: Thorndike, Wheeler, Walker and Large Print Press.

Acknowledgments

This book could not have been written without my friends in central Georgia, where we lived for five years in the late nineties. Space does not allow me to mention everyone — and indeed there are hundreds — but special thanks goes to Tom and Tricia Bass, Pamela and Charles Richardson, Joni Woolf, Carey Pickard, Josephine and Gordon Bennett, and the Macon *Telegraph*.

For their expertise and advice, thanks to my agent, Wendy Sherman, Beverly Bremmer, Gary and Marlene Price, Cindy Long and the Vance Publishing Corporation, and Carol Fitzgerald of Bookreporter.com, who understands online marketing better than anyone. For friendship, keen eye, and judgment, I thank Karen Feldman, Joann Haley, Mary Ellen Eagan, and Leah Barr.

Thanks to everyone at Ballantine Books who works so hard to sell my novels and connect me with readers. Special thanks to Maureen O'Neal, my brilliant, fun editor whose thoughtful critiques make my job much easier.

Thanks to my daughter, Haley Joy, for brainstorming during the morning drives to school, and to Carol, my supportive wife and frontline editor whose smile can still make my heart melt into my stomach.

Lastly, thanks to my supportive readers, who can always reach me at ad@adhudler.com.

Prologue

"This is a letter from your mother," said the attorney, reaching over the desk to hand Margaret an envelope the color of stoplight red. "She wrote this a month before she died."

Margaret noted her name in her mother's craggy, impatient handwriting, which looked like the line of ink on an erratic EKG. She tore open the sealed flap, pulled out and unfolded the letter, then began to read:

I wish there was more to give you, Margaret; you will be surprised at how little there is. I'm sure you understand why Planned Parenthood gets the bulk of my money. With eight years of a Republican administration in the White House, they are under fire and underfunded. You also can sell my clothes if you want to, though I'm guessing it will be hard to find a buyer for an all-red wardrobe.

I might already have told you the following, but I'm also writing it down be-

cause it is critical information, and I'm not sure how bad dementia will set in during my final days.

I've been less than forthcoming about a few things. I do know who your father is, and the trustee of my estate will divulge his name on your fortieth birthday should you wish to know the name of this sperm provider. I'm sorry I can't be more free with this information, but there is a time and place for everything, and I'm thinking you'll be able to better handle this news when you're forty. Emotionally, forty was a watershed year for me, and I'm hoping the same is true for you.

Secondly, I own a home in Selby, Georgia. It was given to me by an old college friend as a gift of gratitude. (You remember all the Jeannie stories, don't you?) Her daughter was impregnated by some Bubba, and I offered the girl a free, far-away-from-home abortion because she came from a well-known medical family in Selby. I have never seen this house, nor have I ever seen Selby. The South has never interested me. It frightens me for obvious reasons.

Lastly, you have bothered me in the past about old family photographs, and I actually do have a few. These you will find

10

with the keys to the Georgia house in a manila envelope in the safe-deposit box at the Erie Community Savings Bank on Clifford Road. (Key is in the pair of brown house slippers on top shelf of my closet.) They are pictures of me as a child and your grandmother and grandfather. It was best they died when you were young. (Cancer STINKS! Don't forget to get a Pap smear EVERY YEAR!) I don't know what potent demons my father had, but his need for control over women was strong enough to blow me out of the house at seventeen. I remember a brief period during my early teenage years when my mother seemed to find strength, and she began planting her feet in preparation for a War of Independence. It was then that my father decided to stop drinking and enlist the help of the Almighty. Suddenly, every order was backed up by the fire of the Bible. In his world, it was God's will for women to suffer. So it is no mistake that we never went to church. It is no mistake that I approach all men with suspicion and dread, and that I have no patience with meek women. Sometimes I fear you are too much like your grandmother, Margaret. Your reluctance to judge and make waves is sweet, but if you choose to be a gentle breeze for most of your life,

11

also remember there will be times that call for the roar of a hurricane — and you must blow the bastards away. *History does not remember the "good girls."*

Mom

Ruth

I never know how to sign my notes to you.

One

By her own choice, Margaret's workday began at five a.m., about the time that Louis, the janitor, began buffing the terrazzo floor of the lobby of the *Selby Reflector*. Her job, transcribing four to five hours of thick, middle Georgia patois, required great concentration, and the daily arc of life in the newsroom did not begin until around nine o'clock, when the first reporters, still puffy-eyed from indulgences of the night before, began to mill in. Clutching brown-stained, steaming coffee mugs from Starvin' Marvin's, they would walk into the darkened room and find Margaret sitting at her computer, headphones on, her face ghostlike from the glowing, gray light of the monitor. The only sounds were an occasional squawk from the police scanner and the whispering clickety-clack of Margaret's keyboard.

For three months, Margaret had been editing the new phone-in-and-vent column named Chatter, and in that time it had grown to be one of the most popular features in the *Reflector*. People quoted it on elevators in the Perry County Courthouse downtown and on the benches outside Johnny Chasteen's Seafood Shack. Local disc jockeys called it the redneck Internet, quoting it daily with a whoop and a holler. One day, when Margaret was picking up a pair of leather slides she had had resoled at The Peach Cobbler, she overheard a woman say, "Y'all treat me good or I'm gonna call Chatter."

Anywhere from fifty to two hundred people called the Chatter hotline each day to leave a comment or query at the sound of the beep. They wanted recipes for homemade fried pork rinds. They wanted to know who stole the sofa off their front porch or who could tell them where to find the best barbecue in Perry County. They called to condemn the owners of the new We-Bare-All that had opened up in the old Stuckey's building on the interstate west of town.

Lonely alcoholics would call in the middle of the night, verbally stabbing at anything that might make them angry: news anchors who talked too fast, teachers' vacation time, a neighbor's barking dog, an editorial that frightened them, dishonest refrigerator salesmen, Dillard's underwear ads. As the first and only Chatter editor,

Margaret felt like Selby's psychiatrist. Despite her newcomer status, she had a feel for this city's collective values and paranoias, a verbal patchwork quilt composed of nonmatching yet oddly compatible sound-bite squares: Jane Fonda and guns and smoking and Jesus Christ and rude cashiers and chitlins and birth control and kind strangers on the corner of Mulberry and Second.

" 'Mornin', Margaret."

Harriet Toomey walked up and set a pile of manila folders onto her desk, then patted the back of her impeccably tamed silver beehive. Even after three months, Margaret still could not stop staring at Harriet's hair, voluminous and oblong like the cotton candy she remembered from the Erie County Fair. When she first saw it, she thought, "So *this* is why it's called a beehive!" It was easy for Margaret to imagine something going on inside.

The *Reflector*'s food editor for sixty-one years, Harriet appeared to be about eighty, and she produced on her own an entire page of food news for central Georgia readers every Wednesday. Her column, *Thanks for Askin'*, answered readers' questions about the food in their lives, even though for lunch each day Harriet ate Wheat Thins topped

15

with processed cheddar cheese from a can she kept in her desk.

Margaret took off her earphones. "You're here early today," she said.

"I'm fixin' to leave town," Harriet answered. "I'm goin' down to Valdosta to see my great-granddaughters, and I got to get these pork recipes done."

Harriet sat down in the cubicle next to Margaret's, the only other cubicle in the newsroom free of rebellious, visual declaration. Most journalists seemed to have a burning desire to be noticed and unique and irreverent, and they used their desks to make statements about themselves. Some had pinned up cutouts of comic-book strips with disparaging remarks about some authority figure. There was also a dancing porcelain hula girl on springs, and a bust of Shakespeare entwined with a feathery purple boa. Jason Nohr, the education reporter, kept a headless Barbie on his desk to use as a stirring stick for his coffee. The doll's legs, permanently stained, appeared to be covered in suntan-colored pantyhose.

"You look tired, Margaret," Harriet said.

"I was up late, Harriet. My cat's stuck in a tree behind my house."

"Oh, no!"

"He's been up there for five days."

"Five days!"

Margaret nodded.

"Five?"

"Shouldn't I be worried?"

Overnight, while dusting Harriet's desk, Louis had nudged a bookend of gold-painted plaster hands in prayer from its position, and the cookbooks had fallen over and lay on the desk like a row of expired dominoes. Harriet set about pushing them back into place and aligning the spines so they were flush.

"Well," she said, "everything's gotta come down some time or other."

Harriet then shook her head and looked into the air with a quizzical expression, an index finger on her closed lips, as if she were searching for a book on a high shelf. Suddenly, her face lit up.

"Did you call the fire department?" she asked.

"Do they really do that kind of thing? I thought that was a myth."

"Ben Tuckabee's cat got up in a tree and they got him down."

"Good morning, ladies."

As Randy Whitestone approached, Harriet quickly turned her focus to the pile of folders before her. Margaret realized early on that the new executive editor, with his un-Southern, brusque delivery and the impatient, staccato manner in which he chewed his gum, made Harriet nervous. He also bombarded her with constant requests to add an international flavor to the food page. Randy was a foodie. Harriet would come to work two or three days a week and find hurriedly-torn-out clippings on her desk from *Cook's Illustrated* and *Saveur*, recipes for kimchee and Vietnamese beef soups and low-fat pad Thai. Harriet responded by pinning to the gray fabric walls of her cubicle certificates of appreciation from the Middle Georgia Muscadine Growers Association and the Georgia Pecan Board, among others.

"What deep-fried delicacy are we planning for this week's food page, Harriet?" Randy asked. He leaned forward, resting his arms on the top ledge of her cubicle.

"Well . . ." Her hands, usually as steady and fluid as a heavy door on hinges, shook slightly as she looked at a press release from the Peach State Pork Council. "See, next week is National Pork Week. I was gonna write up some recipes for pulled pork."

Randy ignored her, turning his attention to Margaret. "Have you had the barbecue here yet? It's incredible. Tangy, not sweet like you'd expect it to be. Why is that, Harriet?"

"Sir?"

"What's the story behind the barbecue in central Georgia? How did it get so tangy?"

"Just always been that way," she said.

"No, no, no, there's got to be a reason for it. It's got to do with ingredients or influence of some culture or something. You need to call a food historian."

Harriet wrote on her yellow legal pad — *Call food historian* — in slow, curvaceous letters that reminded Margaret of the young, delicate tendrils of a vine.

"What about next week's page?" he asked.

For the first time in the conversation, Harriet looked up at him. "I was gonna write a story about an artist in Vidalia who's makin' fake food."

"Fake food?"

"Yes, sir. They call it faux food. He makes polymer fruits and some desserts that look real as can be."

Randy laughed and started to shake his head. "Why would anyone want to use fake food, Harriet?" he asked.

"For decoration," she explained. "People

like to use fake food in their decoratin'. Like a bowl of fruit out on the counter."

"But why not use real food?"

"Because it'll spoil," she answered.

"That's okay, Harriet. Never mind. It must be a cultural thing. . . . Did you get that article I put on your desk yesterday?"

"Yes, sir."

"And?"

Harriet stared at the blinking cursor on her screen for a moment. Her chin began to tremble slightly, and her eyes grew shiny with a coating of tears. Finally, she looked up at Randy.

"Mr. Randy," she blurted. "I just don't think my readers are gonna wanna read about raw fish."

"It's sushi, Harriet."

"I already write about fish."

"There's only so much you can say about fried catfish."

"There's no need to get ugly with me."

"I'm not getting ugly, Harriet. I just know that three hundred Japanese families now call Selby, Georgia, their home. We've got to diversify our food coverage to meet their tastes."

Just two months before Margaret arrived in Selby, the Toyota Corporation opened its newest North American auto assembly plant southeast of town. Along with the executive families relocated from Osaka, nearly twelve hundred workers from a closed plant outside Camden, New Jersey, followed their old jobs south. Shortly thereafter, the rest of the world discovered Selby, Georgia.

In these tumultuous, post-Toyota days — Randy referred to them as A.T., After Toyota — a Japanese grammar school moved into the abandoned Ponderosa Steakhouse on Cusetta Road. Walgreens bought out a local four-generation drugstore chain named Ringleman's and not only stopped home delivery but replaced the adjacent Hallmark card shop with liquor marts. Natives were boycotting their banks because the new out-of-state owners fired the receptionists and installed voice mail. Selby's first X-rated video store opened in the old post office on Pio Nono Road. New Yankee parents at Ronald Dunwoody Elementary School started a petition to fire the principal because she refused to abolish the moment of silence that followed the Pledge of Allegiance each morning. Four sushi restaurants opened in the affluent, northern part of town, and the Selby roll was born — a marriage of barbecued pork, tempura-fried Vidalia onions, and rice wrapped not in nori but in a ribbon of steamed collard greens. And, for the first time ever, it was possible for Selbyites to get their hair cut and car washed on the Sabbath.

Two months after the Toyota plant opened, the *Reflector*, a family-owned newspaper that had seen just six publishers, all with the same last name, in its one-hundred-eighty-year history, was sold to Granite-Peabody Communications of Washington, D.C. On the day the sale was announced, they brought in Randy Whitestone, a Pulitzer Prize–winning editor from the *Philadelphia Inquirer* who, unfortunately for Harriet Toomey, knew the difference between a serrano and jalapeño chili. It was Randy who took the daily Bible verse off the front page. He cut the society column that featured monied Selby enjoying themselves at Sugar Day Country Club. He directed the features editor to include a men-seeking-men and women-seeking-women section on the personals page in the weekend entertainment guide. He started Chatter and hired Margaret, despite his concern that she was vastly overqualified with her master's in women's studies from SUNY-Buffalo.

After extracting a promise from Harriet

that she would ask the consumer test panel to weigh in on rice cookers, Randy wheeled a chair into Margaret's cubicle and sat down. Lanky, six-foot-two, with brown eyes, an omnipresent beard shadow on fair skin, and black hair parted on the side, Randy reminded Margaret of Alan Alda's *M*A*S*H* character of Hawkeye Pierce, with an opinionated voice that seemed to babble on like a brook after spring thaw. Randy seemed incapable of practicing verbal restraint, and Margaret could imagine him talking back to the television at home, in the dark: "The peanut you are referring to in your ad is pronounced BOY-uhld . . . not bold. It is BOY-uhld peanuts, not bold peanuts! BOY-uhld peanuts are cooked in hot water. Bold peanuts would be peanuts that are flavored with Cajun spice."

"I'm loving that Chatter, Margaret," he said. "Are they still howling about food?"

The first shot had been fired that Monday, when a newcomer to the city called in to complain about the paucity of salads in local restaurants.

Dear Chatter: Only in Selby does a vegetable plate include macaroni and cheese and mashed potatoes with gravy.

No wonder we have so many doctors in this town — you're all doing a great job giving them business. Spinach salad, anyone?

Dear Chatter: Y'all don't like the food down here? Just go on back to New Jersey or wherever you come from. God gave man fire to cook. Cows eat raw greens. I went to Atlanta and saw "Cats" last week, and if that's Yankee entertainment, well then, y'all can just have it because it was just about the stupidest thing I've ever seen.

Dear Chatter: I've got a bucket of used chewing gum. Has anybody got any use for it? It's gotta be good for something.

"I was wondering," Margaret said. "Should I keep the 'y'alls' or write 'you all'?"

"Keep it raw and real," he answered, "just like you're doing. That's the charm of the column."

"You don't think it parodies the natives?"

"What's not to parody?"

"Be nice," she said.

"Be real," he countered.

Randy seemed to have an addiction for throwing the final volley in a conversation, and though everyone else in the newsroom would quickly disengage from him with a "Yes, sir," a verbal shutting of a door on his face, Margaret would often counter his remarks because she thought that someone had to tame and corral this man, and the Southerners were too polite to do so. Randy seemed out of control, brilliant but wild and arrogant, and Margaret enjoyed watching him exhaust his oral firearm, shot by shot, until the only bullet he had left was an "Okay, then" that would humbly trickle from his lips.

But not now, Margaret thought. At this very minute, she had a cat stranded more than thirty feet up a sweet gum tree in her backyard on Kimes Place, and she wanted to quickly key in the last of the typesetting commands, send her column to the copy desk for editing, run by Kroger for ginger-root and fennel bulbs, then get home and try, again, to coax him down.

"Yes, sir," she said to Randy.

Two

Dear Chatter: I don't believe one word of that story in the *Reflector* that talked about pig guts bein' just like human guts. Maybe your editors need to read the Bible more. God created Adam, and it's Adam's job to eat that pig. Remember that.

Dear Chatter: I just wanna say thanks to the man who told me I left my eggs on top of my car at FoodMax. God bless you. Those eggs are expensive.

Suzanne opened the door to find John David swinging a grease-spotted white bag of Krystal hamburgers. "I'm here to tempt you, Suzanne," he said. "How 'bout an early lunch?"

Suzanne looked at her silver Bulgari watch, which she had bought two weeks earlier at Neiman Marcus in Atlanta. "It's ten-forty, John David. We can't eat lunch right now."

"But it's not too early for a highball, is it,

Suzanne?" he asked, raising his eyebrows and looking at the glass in her hand.

"I'm working extra hard, you know that, John David. This house has got to be perfect for Boone's office Christmas party, and I'm copin' the best way I can."

"And we're gonna eat outside," he said. "On the patio."

"No, John David, we're not eating outside. They'll see us."

"I know."

Suzanne already had started back toward the kitchen.

"I want mine in a Waterford tumbler just like yours," he yelled after her. "And get us some napkins, too. You know how messy Krystals are."

John David had shown up almost daily since the roof work began on the addition next door. For the past seven days, three young men with broad, tanned backs had been working to shingle the steep, plywood slopes of what would soon be the largest home in Red Hill Plantation, ten thousand square feet. With the addition of the third story, the house was so tall it required a crane, which cast a shadow that throughout the day crept across Suzanne's property like the hour hand of a clock.

The tag on the truck indicated the crew

27

had come from Marietta, and it was obvious this was their first Selby job. The unwritten rule for service workers in Selby, even the young men who cut the grass, was that they wear a shirt on the job.

Suzanne and John David sat on the patio, eating the burgers and drinking vodka and ice from their tumblers.

"I don't care what you say, John David, I think it's awful."

"If that's awful then you've got problems, girl."

"I'm gonna call the number on that truck and complain."

"Suzanne, if those roofers put their shirts back on I'm leavin', and you're gonna be here to drink this luscious Ketel One vodka all by yourself."

He took a drink. "Look at those backs, Suzanne. Brown and hot! Don't you think they look like loaves of bread fresh outta the oven?"

"I think it's tacky, John David."

"I'll bet you butter would melt on those backs."

The roofer John David had named Sven looked down, and John David gave a wave.

"Y'all are doin' great work up there!" he shouted, holding his glass in the air in a toast. "Keep it up!"

He turned toward Suzanne. "I want Mr. Mediterranean," he said. "You can have Sven."

"John David!"

"Oh don't get your panties in a wad, Suzanne."

"John David," she said, "we gotta talk about the master bath and that tub. You gotta find me a claw-foot tub with Jacuzzi jets."

"What do you want a Jacuzzi for, Suzanne? You're too uptight for a Jacuzzi."

"There's gotta be a way to get one."

John David took a drink of his vodka. "I've told you there's no way to hook up a freestanding tub to Jacuzzi jets, there's just no way," he said, his eyes focused on the roof. "Besides, Jacuzzis are tacky. When are you gonna learn that?"

John David popped the last corner of a Krystal burger in his mouth and followed it down with a wash of vodka. "Did you get the wallpaper up in the foyer?" he asked.

"Ronnie didn't show up today," Suzanne said. "He said his momma was havin' a coughing fit, and that he might could do it tomorrow. I do not want to sleep another night in this house with that old wallpaper."

"It's not even a year old, Suzanne."

"But it's not right, John David. It's never been right since the day it went up."

John David had seen this before; Suzanne would pick a new bed or painting or carpeting or wallpaper and be satisfied with it until she saw something she liked better in a catalog or store or someone else's house. When she decided it was time to replace something, the older version immediately repulsed her, and the once-cherished item suddenly became as undesirable as a stinking vagrant asleep on the front porch.

John David had anticipated this passionate and urgent desire to redecorate, fueled, in part, by the castle rising next door. (Until the renovation of this house, Suzanne's had been the largest in the subdivision.) There also was the feature in *Metropolitan Home* of her new next-door neighbors from California. The San Francisco row house with wooden floors was sparsely decorated with Persian rugs, Mexican antiques, and a combination of Louis XIV and Bauhaus-inspired furniture. John David's favorite feature was the collection of different-sized, perfectly round, Calder-red rugs whimsically placed around the house. It looked as if a giant had cut his finger and bled in random spots.

John David was inspired, Suzanne was repulsed, and she dreaded the outcome of the renovation taking place in the California couple's new home in Red Hill Plantation. She was not alone. John David, who decorated most of the homes in Red Hill, had noticed that the women of the north Selby neighborhood had been slowing down as they passed the house in their Suburbans and BMWs and Mercedeses, scrutinizing the fruits of demolition piled in front — splintered wood, appliances, shower stalls, tile, carpeting, and Sheetrock broken into pieces like giant soda crackers. Passing by one day in her black Lexus sedan, Suzanne was moved to the point that she felt compelled to call John David.

"You are not gonna believe what's layin' outside Claire Penrose's old house," she told him. "All those gorgeous window treatments piled up there like dirty clothes. Just tossed out with the trash!" (Hidden by the dark of the following night, John David and his housemate, Terrance, snatched them all up and stowed them in his garage.)

Unbeknownst to Suzanne and his other clients, John David had grown weary of the Southern, let's-pretend-we're-in-England

31

decor that had paid his bills for so long, and Lord help the next woman who asked him to find another oversized gilt mirror, or to paint another dining room red, or to commission one more portrait of the lady of the house, or to purchase one more lamp with a monkey or pineapple on it. John David had begged Suzanne to let him loose on her house. He'd had a vision of something he called Spouthern, a combative, Spartan-Southern elegance that mixed Scandinavian minimalism with French antique furniture and gold and floral accents. He'd pictured Suzanne's mahogany French-Colonial bed flanked by cylindrical, brushed-chrome nightstands.

Yet she and her peers would not budge. No one dared stray from the Southern School, adding ornate to the already ornate, layer upon layer of tassels and pillows and rugs and brass and gold-leaf until the home felt like a Baroque chandelier.

After reading the feature in *Metropolitan Home*, Suzanne had Virgil, her hired man, install two new weather vanes on the garage roof. She added gold bows to the front-porch topiaries and hung another set of framed botanical prints in the foyer. She found two life-size brass pineapples at Big Peach Antiques and set them on each side of the parlor entrance.

John David refilled his tumbler with vodka. "If you wanna get your home in *Selby Magazine*, you gotta get brave," he said. "You're puttin' on lipstick, Suzanne, when you need plastic surgery. Let me put those chrome cabinets in the kitchen."

"You know Boone won't go for that, John David. He doesn't like that modern look."

"Oh, Boone can go to hell."

"John David!"

"But you suck his little Boonie enough and he'll let you do whatever you want."

"John David!"

As her laughter melted away, Suzanne lay her head back and slowly swayed it back and forth with eyes closed, reminding John David of Ray Charles. She breathed in then exhaled sharply, as if to wake herself from a trance.

"I gotta get dinner thawed, John David."

"What casserole are we havin' tonight?" he asked.

The biggest fund-raiser for the Selby/Perry County Museum of Arts and Sciences was the frozen casserole sale held every September. Suzanne would buy thirty casseroles, the maximum number allowed. She then would give money to John

David and Virgil to buy thirty more apiece, and all of these would go into the deep freeze in the garage, where they would hibernate until pulled out, then thawed, microwaved, and paired with a tossed green salad from a bag.

"Boone likes the one with noodles and cream cheese," she said. "Maybe I've got another one of those left."

John David stood up from the table. "None of that cat vomit for me, Suzanne. I gotta go."

"Are we still goin' to Atlanta tomorrow?"

"Why?"

"You said you'd take me to the merchandise mart to find that lamp."

"I'm way too busy tomorrow, Suzanne."

"John David, you promised."

"Suzanne, I gotta spend all day with Mona Beckner."

"Mona Beckner!"

"You got a problem with Mona?"

"Is she doin' that dining room over? 'Cause I could have told her beforehand you just don't paint a dining room yellow. That's tacky, anybody knows that."

"I'm doin' the master bath."

"Doin' what?"

"Doin' it all. They're even gonna have a steam shower."

Suzanne, still sitting, poured herself another finger of vodka. "What kinda countertops is she gonna have? Granite?"

"I don't know yet."

John David pulled his keys from his pocket and started dropping them from hand to hand, back and forth, as someone plays with a Slinky. He had keys to some twenty upscale Selby homes, including Suzanne's, and they occupied a ring as big around as an orange.

"I gotta go," he said. "Where's that throw pillow you want me to take back to Jeppeson's?"

"Are you sure I don't need it?"

"I told you what I think, Suzanne. You need to work a fourth color into that living room, and that blue pillow is perfect."

"But it's just so plain, John David. Can't you find one with fringe or tassels or somethin'?"

"Damnit, Suzanne, not everything in the house has got to look like Cinderella's ball gown."

"I just don't think Boone'll like it."

"That's bullshit, Suzanne. Boone doesn't care a thing about this house."

"You don't have to get ugly with me, John David! I'm just askin' for tassels and fringe."

She stood up to walk him to the front door. Unlike the plumber and the exterminator and the other service workers, John David always used his clients' front doors. He would park his Toyota truck in the driveway instead of the street and was even known to pull into the garage if there was a space.

Having watched his truck disappear around the bend of Red Hill Drive, Suzanne walked into the foyer, shut the door, and leaned back against it. When she opened her eyes, she flipped on the chandelier overhead and glared at the walls, which had been stripped of all adornment in preparation for the project. Had Ronnie Dipson shown up as promised, these would now be covered by a Schweitzer print of magnolia blossoms on vanilla background, ninety-eight dollars a roll.

Suzanne walked up to the wall and felt for a seam. With a red-painted fingernail she picked at the line until she pried an edge loose. Suzanne then pulled, expecting to remove from the wall a large scroll of old paper, but instead tore off a disappointing two-inch scrap. She continued to pick at this unwanted scab on her house, piece after tiny piece, until a pile of paper formed at her feet.

"Do you like your dinner?" Suzanne asked.

Boone wiped the corner of his mouth with a cotton napkin, golden fleur-de-lis on a burgundy background.

"You already asked me that, Suzanne. Yes, the dinner's fine."

They each sat at an end of the dining room table, separated by ten feet of polished mahogany that held a long, scarlet silk runner, two lit candles in sterling-silver holders, and a porcelain serving dish filled with something named Tokyo Surprise, which was a mixture of soba noodles, canned water chestnuts, baby corn, cubes of chicken, and cream of mushroom soup. Suzanne had found the casserole on the table marked "foreign." She had wanted to avoid this table but was late arriving at the sale, and most of the traditional fare had already been sold. Not all of it was awful, however; Boone had enjoyed the dish named Mount Olympus that she served one day the previous week.

"I don't know," she said. "I'm not sure I like it. What kinda spaghetti is this?"

"You made it, Suzanne. Don't you know?"

"Maybe I put in a wrong ingredient or somethin'."

Boone rarely finished a meal in less than forty-five minutes. To slow herself down, so she would finish after him, Suzanne would watch her husband and try to match his pace. He cut his food in the steady, methodical manner one would expect from a neurosurgeon, setting the knife down on the edge of the plate — *clink* — after every cut. Thanks to vigorous scrubbings each day at the hospital, Boone's hands were immaculate and pale pink, the color of cooked salmon. His fingernails were trimmed and filed into perfect crescent moons. Boone engaged in no activity that would endanger his hands. He would not pick up a hammer or try to open an obstinate jar of pickles.

"I see the dogs of Red Hill are at it again," he said, setting down his goblet of water. "Didn't you call the pound?"

"Are they doin' it again?" she asked.

"There's another spot down by the mailbox, Suzanne. I don't see how you could miss it."

It seemed as if every house in Red Hill Plantation had one or two purebred hunting dogs, and shortly after moving to this part of town, Suzanne discovered that few people actually trained or disciplined these dogs, let alone hunted with them, so they roamed in packs, like bored teenagers in a mall, through the curvy streets and cul-de-sacs of Red Hill Plantation.

A group of Labradors had begun using Suzanne and Boone's front yard as a bathroom. The turds were bad enough, but what bothered Boone even more were the more permanent, random yellow stains from the urine. "It looks like we don't take pride in ourselves, Suzanne," he had said. "Please find a way to get rid of those dogs."

Obviously, she could not call animal control; these creatures belonged to her neighbors. After calling Chatter to leave a complaint, Suzanne tried simple verbal intimidation at first. Then, when no one was looking, she would pelt them with the brick samples she'd been carrying around in the trunk of her Lexus. Exasperated, Suzanne finally placed behind the potted dogwood topiary a tastefully aged-and-green copper bucket that held squirt guns filled with gasoline or Tabasco sauce. The problem was, the dogs would saunter in, do their business, and be on their way before she could even get to the front door.

"I just don't know what to do about 'em, Boone," she said. "I've tried everything."

He pushed his plate away from him, finished. "You're smarter than a bunch of dumb dogs, Suzanne."

"Maybe Virgil knows what to do."

"I sure hope so. I didn't pay to plant winter rye just to have it look like that. I'm wanting that yard to look nice for the Christmas party, and that means green grass without doggie stains on it."

Suzanne stood up with her plate in hand. She walked over to Boone's end of the table, picked up his plate, and disappeared into the kitchen with the dishes. Boone had not eaten but half of his salad for the third straight night — or was it four now? Five? How could he suddenly not like the salad? It was the exact same salad she had served for months, even the same Wish-Bone Lite Caesar dressing. If he didn't like the salad, why didn't he tell her? Or had he? As Suzanne crammed lettuce down the garbage disposal with a wooden spoon, she tried to reconstruct the hazy, brusque conversations of the past several nights.

Suddenly, she heard a dog bark. Grabbing a dish towel, Suzanne walked quickly to the front door, drying her hands along the way. She looked out the window, clicked on the outside light, then opened the door. On the porch, Suzanne reached into the bucket for one of the guns and pulled out an orange one filled with gasoline. It had "Avenger" written along the barrel in blue letters that were slanted to give a feeling of movement.

She ran out toward the street until she reached the most favored spot in the yard and stood there in the darkness, somewhat out of breath, smelling the dank ammonia odor that wafted up from the moist grass, waiting there, with her finger on the blue trigger. Across the yard, Suzanne could see Boone inside, watching the news from his leather wing-back chair. He had moved the floor lamp again to the left side of the chair, which put it too close to the lamp on the desk. John David had said the two light sources needed to be farther apart, and Suzanne would return it to its proper spot before going to bed.

Three

Dear Chatter: Is it true that Toyota's giving health insurance to homosexuals? The Lord did not want men to be with men, and that goes for white or yellow men, too. It doesn't matter. We're all the same in God's eyes.

Dear Chatter: Can anyone tell me how to get rid of moles? Please respond in Chatter.

Ruth and Margaret Pinaldi first found Susan B., emaciated and nearly unconscious, under the juniper bushes behind Ruth's practice on Shornwood Avenue. Short-haired and all white, she appeared to be a ghost even though alive. Though Ruth had strong opinions about dogs — "They lack courage and individuality, and they run in packs because they don't have the skills or confidence needed for solitary journeys" — she had no life experience with cats. Ruth assumed the animal was female; she had no idea that a cat's testicles were neatly tucked up close to

42

the body, discreetly covered in fur. She named their cat after the famous suffragist and decided to keep the name even after the true gender was revealed when she brought him in to be spayed.

Susan B. loved to climb trees. Often, when the back door was opened, he would dart outside, leap onto the nearest cylinder of bark, and pull himself skyward, his claws clicking and crackling like static electricity all the way up.

Sometimes he would stay up there for two or three days. This time he had climbed higher, at nearly fifty feet now, and since it was the first time he had gotten stuck in a Georgia tree, in a backyard still unfamiliar, Margaret was more concerned than usual.

After four days she opened a can of Friskies Elegant Entrée and smeared it on the bark of the tree, hoping the aroma would tempt him downward, but the food just developed a dark crust and attracted yellow jackets. Margaret wondered how he could survive. She guessed he was licking the dew off the leaves, but when had he slept? And how could he just shut down his bowels like that?

On the eighth day, she took Harriet's advice and called the fire department. Margaret was standing beneath the tree, trying to coax Susan B. down, when two firefighters with postlunch toothpicks in their mouths walked up to her. Their ample bellies pushed at the blue material of their shirts, reminding Margaret of newly upholstered easy chairs. She'd never seen overweight firefighters. The ones back home, in Buffalo, were known for their buff, tough appearance, and the *Buffalo News* had even published a beefcake calendar featuring the finest twelve specimens as they posed half-naked. Margaret looked at the men before her now and wondered: How could these guys climb ladders or shimmy across a floor on their stomachs?

The older man, with curly brown hair and a mustache with a few gray invaders, appeared to be in charge. He looked skyward, using his hand to shield the sun from his eyes.

"That cat's pretty high," he said. "We ain't got a ladder that goes up that high, not one that'll fit back here in these trees."

"He's been up there eight days," Margaret said.

The man looked at his silent partner, who was younger, about Margaret's age, with ruddy cheeks and blue eyes shaded by long lashes. His stomach, she realized now, was not nearly as robust as his partner's.

"Eight days?" the older firefighter asked.

"Yes."

"Nah — that cat's been down and gone back up."

"I can assure you he hasn't been down," Margaret said.

The firefighter looked at the dried cat food on the tree trunk, then down at the blue plastic bowl of water and the folding beach chair Margaret had been sitting in for occasional vigils.

"You're payin' too much attention to that cat. You just forget that cat and he'll come on down."

"How do you mean?" she asked.

Again, he looked at his partner, wiggled his toothpick with his tongue then smiled.

"Ma'am, there ain't no cat that's ever not got down from a tree."

"You're sure?"

"You know how I know that?" he asked.

"How?"

"You ever see any cat skeletons up in a tree?"

Margaret shook her head.

"Well, there you go."

"Okay . . ."

"You a Bills fan?" he asked.

"Excuse me?"

"Your jacket. Buffalo Bills."

Margaret looked down at her chest.

"Oh, no. I don't watch football. I won it in a radio contest."

"I don't watch the pros, just the Dogs."

"Dogs?"

"Bulldogs."

Margaret shook her head.

"Georgia Bulldogs! You ain't from around here, are you?"

"No," she answered.

In so many other locales, the next question would have been "So where are you from?" But Margaret already had learned this was not the Selby way. People here did not pry, and she liked that. Instead, they stood there quietly, waiting for you to toss another morsel of information onto the floor in front of them, and if you didn't, they simply turned around and wandered away, which is exactly what happened with the two firefighters.

Margaret watched them amble across the grass, back to their long ladder truck at the curb. As she had noted several times before, there was a softness to the men here, and it was more than the doughy, unexercised appearance so many of them had. Their gaze was not as steely or sharp or invasive as the Northern male's. They seemed to look at women more with the curiosity of a boy than with the hunger of a man.

Perhaps it was the haircuts that made them less threatening, those seventies lengths with bangs, parted on the side like a Ken doll or Watergate-era heartthrob. Randy called it Bubba-Bowl hair. For weeks, Margaret had stared at the men in Selby. Something seemed out of proportion and unnatural, reminding her of the time she transposed the heads of two similarly sized dolls. She was getting her hair cut in the Selby Mall when she finally realized the source of the visual discordance: It was a boy's hairstyle atop a man's body.

Most likely, however, it was the bellies that put Margaret at ease. These half-moon appendages were indicative of leisurely grazers, not predatory carnivores — she could outrun them if she had to. Yet there was something appealing about these bellies, and more than once Margaret had found herself wanting to reach out and pat or stroke a Southern man's stomach as she would pet Susan B.

From the truck, the younger firefighter looked back at Margaret.

"Ma'am, don't worry 'bout your cat," he yelled across the yard. "He's gonna come down. . . . He's up there 'cause he wants to be."

He waved good-bye, grabbed the bar up near the door handle, stepped onto the running board and pulled his broad body up, into the cab. When the door was shut, the window came down and the elbow of the young man's tanned forearm poked out and rested on the edge. As the immense truck inched forward, gaining speed, Margaret watched the arm bend outward and then the large palm pop up into a halt-there! position. He then repeatedly opened and closed his fingers, feeling the resistance of the warm, moist air.

Even this late in September, the air outside seemed as thick and fragrant as the air inside a greenhouse. Margaret wondered what the atmosphere was like right now on the outside, in places other than this deep bowl in which Selby sat. She thought back to her drive down to Selby and how surprised she was at the differences in the last seventy miles, from Atlanta to her mother's house. Somewhere between the two cities palm trees began to appear — not the tall, slender coconut palms of postcards but the squatty, hardier varieties that look like survivors of the Mesozoic era. She saw vines of blooming wisteria that had climbed and smothered the Georgia pines on both sides of the highway so that at times Margaret found herself driving between two fragrant, purple walls. And the kudzu — in spots it covered every tree, every telephone pole until it seemed as if she were driving through lumpy, chlorophyll-green cumulus clouds. All this time, Margaret noticed herself descending, soft dips followed by long stretches of coasting, as in the final stages of an airplane flight when the seatbelt sign pings on to indicate initial descent. During the seven-hundred-foot drop between Atlanta and Selby, Margaret felt as if she were driving into water, a great lake with a long, gradually sloping bank. Even the air changed, sunny clarity replaced with humidity so heavy it gave an appearance of still-life steam. Margaret had not been outside the car since Chattanooga, and when she opened her door and stepped onto the driveway of her new house that very first time, the warm, wet air instantly fogged her glasses.

The firefighters gone, Margaret returned to the tree for one last plea to Susan B. She then looked at her watch and noticed she had thirty minutes before her meeting with the office manager of the Middle Georgia Heart Clinic. Finally, it looked as if she would snag her first contract. For five months, Margaret had run an ad in the *Reflector* classifieds for her heart-healthy catering business named Georgia on My Plate, which was proving to be as popular as crudités at a toddler's birthday party. Plenty of potential customers had called to inquire, but after receiving a copy of her menu they seemed to instantly lose interest, and Margaret was perplexed. Was it the prices? Was it the food itself? Who could resist gorgonzola cheese grits with grilled shrimp or collards sautéed in garlic and extra-virgin olive oil and topped with grated Romano? Margaret was not making the connection with Selby palates, and it concerned her. Though she loved her job at the *Reflector*, it was barely enough to get by, and Margaret needed furniture in her empty house. She wanted an overstuffed chair and ottoman for reading and an antique kitchen table to replace the black card table from Target and an honest-to-goodness bed instead of the red futon she'd found on clearance at Pier One in Atlanta.

Ruth Pinaldi, much to Margaret's surprise, had left her daughter with a debt of nearly $320,000, which ate up every cent of the life insurance and more. Unknown even to her attorney, she had taken out a second mortgage on their small Tudor on Linden Street to finance the addition at the ob-gyn clinic.

Margaret not only had to sell the clinic but also the house and most of its contents, leaving the home in Selby as her only option for shelter. Reluctantly, four months before her thirtieth birthday, she bid good-bye to friends, packed her mother's Tabasco-red Mercedes with books, clothes, and a cat box for Susan B., and headed south. It almost seemed too perfectly choreographed. The debt. The revelation of the second home. More than once, Margaret wondered if her mother had master-planned this odyssey for her daughter's personal development. It was not beyond her to do something like this. Over the years, Ruth had accused her daughter of handling confrontation like a possum, claiming that she scaled the nearest tree and hid in the foliage until the tension ebbed away.

At the clinic, Margaret had been her mother's patient-care counselor, the woman with whom anxious patients would speak when first calling for an abortion. Margaret would talk them through the process and be there for them on the appointed day with kind words and a day-spa certificate and, if needed, a ride home. She shared the office with Greta, the brusque, buxom Norwegian who ran the office and tried to collect on unpaid accounts.

Occasionally, Ruth would send Greta home for a few days of vacation time and force her daughter to secure the money herself. One time, after a young man screamed at her on the phone, Margaret ran into the bathroom and vomited into the toilet. When she lifted her head, she saw her mother leaning against the doorjamb in one of her red pantsuits. Her hands, in white latex gloves, were folded across her chest. "Are you finished?" she asked. "Because you have three other calls to make."

Margaret left Susan B. in the tree, climbed the stairs to the porch of her brick, bungalow-style home and went inside, to the bathroom. First, because she was just five-foot-two, Margaret had to pull out the white Rubbermaid stool from beneath the sink. She stepped up, looked in the mirror, and unlocked the bun on the back of her head, letting her black hair fall to its full length, just above the curve of the hips. As she brushed it through, she wondered why and how it ever got this long. It made no sense to have long hair because she always wore it up. Yet the more her mother complained about it — and why — the more she quietly resolved to leave it be. As far as Margaret could tell, this had been her sole successful method of rebellion.

And it would stay, she decided, at least for now . . . because even in death, Ruth Pinaldi was proving to be an impressive force. Wedged between the hours of missing her mother were newer, swelling nuggets of anger that Margaret likened to the cardamom pods in Indian food — crucial for the depth of the sauce but, if broken open by teeth, causing a turpentine taste to flood forth and contaminate the tongue for the rest of the meal.

In these flashes of anger, Margaret realized she had plenty to be mad about, most notably being forced into exile and poverty, away from her friends and the only home she'd ever known, to a place that had no good bread boutiques or independent booksellers or Planned Parenthood. Her roof leaked. The window frames were starting to rot. She needed a microwave. Everyone in Selby seemed to be blinded or hypnotized by church and Jesus, and even the few smart liberals she'd met attended

53

adult Sunday school classes with their well-thumbed, worn Bibles in hand. Other than Randy, Margaret had met no one who could offer truly secular, challenging dialogue.

She missed humor tinged with cynicism and found herself staying up late to watch David Letterman for a fill of it. She missed the smell of garlic in restaurants. She missed efficiency. Speed. People were always letting her cut in the line at Kroger because, in their eyes, she appeared to be in a big hurry to get someplace. Margaret longed for Wegmans, her supermarket in Buffalo, and she wanted soppressata and passion fruit and soba noodles. She wanted some interesting, pro-choice couple to invite her to dinner for tabbouleh and grilled eggplant. She wanted the Persian rugs that she had to sell before she moved here. She missed seeing bumper stickers that had nothing to do with Jesus or guns or the Confederate flag. She wanted her cat down from that tree.

"Stop it!" Margaret chastised herself in front of the mirror. She set her hairbrush down on the vanity. "You will make a home here, Margaret Pinaldi," she said. "You have no alternative."

Four

Dear Chatter: I was eating at Red Lobster last night and someone blew their nose right at the table! I can see doin' that at a McDonald's but not a nice restaurant like Red Lobster.

Dear Chatter: I pulled out my new boss's chair the other night at dinner and you woulda thought I'd pinched her by the way she looked at me. Now you tell me what's wrong with a man who wants to help the weaker sex.

Reclined in her father's brown, crushed-velvet La-Z-Boy, Donna Kabel was reading but absorbing little. She had lingered on page one hundred sixteen of the Produce Manager's Guide to Successful Merchandising — the section on bulb onions — for a good ten minutes, and the only bit of information that had truly stuck with her was the paragraph that said onions had less tear-producing effects if you chilled them before cutting. The cordless phone lay in her lap.

Donna had not spoken to or seen Robbie in five days. In the first few weeks after the car accident, he had been good about stopping by on his way home from work at Fall Line Chevrolet-Buick. Yet Donna was worried she had soured him on his last visit. Robbie had surprised her with a box of six red roses and news that he'd been named July's salesman of the month, winning a free weekend at the Days Inn on Tybee Island and some coupons for dinner at the Olive Garden in Savannah.

"When you get better we can go," he said, looking at the scar that ran up the side of her cheek. It was the first time he'd seen Donna without a bandage. "How long's that gonna take to go away?" he asked.

"Robbie, I can't do that," Donna replied. "That's an overnight trip. Daddy wouldn't like it one bit."

"You're twenty-two years old, Donna. He can't tell you what to do." As he spoke, Robbie kept shifting his head, looking at the scar from different angles, as if he were trying to see beyond an object that blocked his view.

"If I went off and did that, even if all we did was hold hands, my daddy would think he'd failed as a Christian parent.

Don't you understand that?"

"No, Donna, I don't," he answered. "Your daddy's kinda crazy when it comes to Jesus."

In south Selby, Frankie Kabel was known as the Plywood Prophet because of the Bible verses he painted on large sheets of wood in fluorescent green paint and displayed in the front yard, leaned up against the trunk of a weeping willow. He also moderated a Bible study group for older Christians who had lost a spouse to cancer. On Saturdays, Frankie rented a space at Happy's Flea Market, sandwiched between a vendor of camouflage clothing and a woman selling clear plastic bags of deep-fried pork rinds. He handed out rainbow-colored vinyl bookmarks imprinted with Bible verses as he preached to passersby.

It was a man from her father's cancer group who helped Donna find the job at Kroger. Buddy Wright, the perishables manager at the store on J. B. McDonough Road, knew that Donna had been the main Lancôme sales associate at Dillard's in the Selby Mall; he remembered her from the time he went shopping for his daughter's birthday gift. Intending to drop by and purchase a single tube of lipstick, he left, thirty-five minutes later, toting a black

Lancôme bag filled with two hundred dollars of moisturizing creams, perfumes, lip liner, a nighttime rehydrating mask . . . and respect for a beautiful, enthusiastic young woman who not only had a knowledge of her products but also a natural ability to sell.

Yet Buddy also knew that Donna would no longer be wanted in a high-profile cosmetics sales job. Her scar began at the right corner of her mouth and ran across the entire cheek before stopping and turning northward, creating a perfect right angle and continuing all the way to the outside point of her right eye. The lines were remarkably straight and geometric, underscoring the wound's presence, and people often stared because it appeared that someone with a ruler and red pen had drawn something on her face.

Urged by her daddy to take the job, Donna agreed, because in her heart she knew she would never return to the job she loved, in that glorious, invisible cloud of perfume beneath the bright halogen lights.

From the La-Z-Boy, Donna reached over and grabbed the compact that was sitting on the side table, on top of her father's Bible, which appeared to be titled *ible* because Frankie, when he was reading scripture, liked to caress the gold embossed *B* with his left forefinger. With a click, she opened the compact to look in the small, round mirror.

Each night, Donna had covered the scar with a thick, mint-green coating of NurishMasque and a bandage. Every morning, she would slowly peel it away, hoping to discover that the fault across her face had faded into her skin, as would an overnight hydrating lotion.

After a few weeks, when the wound was not as sensitive, she began to try covering it with various foundations and concealers, even her competitors' potions, but they just seemed to highlight the problem, turning the rose-colored line into a beige river with tiny but noticeable ripples.

Donna set the phone on the end table and got up to go to the bathroom. She sat on the toilet, flipping through her stack of produce flash cards that showed a colored photograph of each apple and a brief description of characteristics. There were Empires, Crispins, Cortlands, Cameos, Pink Ladies, Ginger Golds, Galas, Gravensteins, and Ida Reds. Fujis were the most predictable in crispness. Granny Smiths and Empires were the best for use in salads because they were more acidic and didn't turn brown as quickly. *A useful tip for all varieties: When unloading apples, never hurriedly dump them; despite their tough appearance, they can easily bruise then break open. Be sure to remove all apples with broken skin as they will cause other apples to rot and perish.*

Donna set the cards on the floor and looked at the wall before her. There used to be a mirror in this spot. Donna had hung it so she could multitask and apply makeup when she was in a hurry, but before the accident her father had removed it and the other mirror as well and stowed them both in the hall closet behind the extra pieces of plywood that he used for his signs. She asked him about it, and he reminded her that vanity was a sin, and that neither she nor anyone had a good reason for looking at themselves in a mirror. "You gotta look on the inside," he said. "A mirror don't show the inside." Donna knew that arguing with her father would do no good. When challenged about anything, he had a way of roaring up like oxygenated fire. She would have to put her makeup on in the car. And that's what she was doing when a man named Bruce Toland, drunk and barreling down Truman Parkway, slammed his red Toyota pickup into Donna's passenger-side front door at sixty miles an hour.

Donna opened the bathroom cabinet and reached for the handheld mirror she kept hidden beneath the pile of clean towels. She squinted as she looked at herself, trying to make the scar disappear. Donna tried to remember what kind of lighting grocery stores had. Fluorescent, wasn't it? That cool, gray light was generally so unforgiving to most skin tones, but wasn't it better at filling in the shadows of the face? Surely the brown uniform would help . . . it was one of her better colors. (The trainer at the Lancôme school in Charlotte had said that Donna, with her dark-brown hair and skin reminiscent of creamy, white eggplant, was a perfect example of someone with "summer coloring.") Donna was certain a hair net was mandatory on the job. . . . If only she could wear her hair down! That extra vertical line created by hair meeting flesh could be a helpful distraction. (Donna had frequently made this tactful suggestion to women who had prominent noses. "Your hair is so pretty," she would say. "Don't hide it behind your head!")

Wait! How about a completely different look? What if she increased the width or color of liner on the tops of her eyes? For her most needy clients, after all, those with a truly challenging facial feature, Donna would always try to create some sort of distraction on the face, in hopes of drawing people's eyes away from the unsightly mole or overbite . . . or huge scar that could make someone want to stay home and eat potato chips all day in front of the TV.

"Lord, give me strength," Donna whispered, her breath fogging the lower half of the mirror.

Five

Dear Chatter: To all the people who broke the hair-bow chain letter we sent: I just wanna say thanks for ruinin' my little girl's day. We were countin' on those hair bows.

Dear Chatter: I don't know what's going on but my dog dropped dead in my driveway, and he wasn't old — he was a pup. Whoever hit him is gonna have to answer to God because your soul is in danger.

In these days of transition, from insular, family-owned newspaper to "real" newspaper, as Randy Whitestone put it, he called frequent impromptu meetings in the newsroom to share his vision. There was a steel trash can beside the sports editor's desk, and he would turn this upside down, step on top, and speak to his people.

"Okay, two big changes to announce today," he said, rolling up one of his shirt sleeves. "First, from this moment forward, there will be no such thing at the *Reflector* as an off-the-record comment. If a source or public official offers you a nugget off the record, and if you agree to it, you immediately incriminate yourself as a puppet of that politician, and you are guilty of hiding the truth from your readers. Remember, we are the only institution empowered to seek truth and provide enlightenment for the common man, and you should never, ever take this responsibility lightly. Any reporter who accepts an off-the-record comment is lazy. And my advice to you is that you get off your fat ass and find that information in another way.

"Second, there has been a change in legal counsel for the *Reflector*. Thanks to the questionable wisdom of the previous owners, this newspaper actually shared the same attorney not only with the police department and Perry County, whom we frequently cover in controversial issues, but also this city's two largest employers, who also happen to be unbridled industrial polluters. We need independent counsel to be a strong voice, and that's why I've retained a kick-ass Atlanta firm named Boyes, Hersch and Howard.

"Oh, and one more thing. If I get one more anonymous complaint about the sports department having to take down their *SI* swimsuit calendars I'm going to take away the watercoolers. There's this thing called sexual harassment, people. Hello? Welcome to the twenty-first century? We cannot have anything in the work environment that makes either gender feel uncomfortable or threatened.

"Okay, any questions? None? Great. Until next time."

Later, Margaret stopped by Randy's office before going home.

"Hey," he said. "Come on in. Shut the door."

"I really admire the changes you're making and the things you're standing up for," Margaret said. "But they don't make you very popular, you know that."

"It's not my job to be liked, Margaret. If I'm reviled it means I'm doing my job well."

Margaret leaned against the doorjamb and crossed her arms. "Don't take this badly, but when you're up on that trash can you remind me of one of those toothless prophets on the street corner . . . the ones who hand out leaflets as they yell out to passersby?"

"Which reminds me," he said. "I have something I want to show you. You are not gonna believe this. Shut the door."

Randy reached beneath his desk and brought out a wrinkled paper sack, and from this he pulled an eighteen-inch-tall Jesus flocked in blood-red felt, standing with head bowed, looking at a large heart he held in his hands.

"Is this rich or what? And look!" he said, turning it around. "It's a piggy bank!"

Margaret quickly looked out the large office window to see if anyone else in the newsroom had witnessed the unveiling.

"I am so jealous," she said. "Where did you get it?"

"A friend from Philly bought it at an Urban Outfitters. He also sent me this Jesus action figure — like a GI Joe? — and when you push a button on his back the arm goes up and down . . . like he's blessing you."

"This is most sacrilegious, Randy Whitestone," she feigned in a parental tone. "You need to ask yourself: What would Jesus do?"

"Okay, I'll ask him right now. Jesus, what would you do?"

Randy bent down to the figure and pretended to hear a message that was being whispered to him.

"He wants fifty cents," Randy said.

"Jesus is hungry." He dug into his front pocket for some change. "Excuse me while I feed Jesus."

Margaret was laughing so hard she fell backward into a chair and hugged her midsection to help restrain the spasms in her diaphragm. "You are awful!" she said, finally catching her breath.

"It's hard not to rebel," Randy said. "Everywhere I go there's a prayer before a meeting, and it's always 'In Jesus' name.' I was at a Chamber of Commerce seminar on diversity in the workplace, and they schlepped up some Baptist minister before it began . . . and what did he do? He prayed to Jesus. I looked over at these two Japanese guys and shrugged my shoulders."

Margaret nodded. "I'm not comfortable with the religiosity in this place either. I know there are good Christians, but I've mainly been exposed to the very worst."

Randy looked at her, quizzically.

"My mother was a hell-raising abortion provider," she said. "The Christians I remember are the ones who would spit in my face when I went in to work every day. And even then —"

"Holy shit," Randy interrupted. "I can't believe I didn't connect the two of you before. You're Ruth Pinaldi's daughter. Margaret, I used to be the medical writer at the *Inquirer.* I came to Buffalo when that asshole tried to gun her down in front of her clinic."

"You were in Buffalo?"

Margaret instantly began probing her memory for clips of Randy during that awful day four years ago, when Leo Rush of Marion, Indiana, stepped out of his rusty white Dodge Caravan and began walking briskly toward Ruth Pinaldi as she pulled into her parking spot. Suddenly, he yanked the crinkly tan Walgreens bag off his black revolver and opened fire. Ruth, the world soon would learn, was a better shot, and in the time it took Leo to pierce the back door of the Mercedes with three bullets, she managed to pull her own forty-four from the console between the front seats and, crouching behind the open door of her car like a gangster, render him impotent for the rest of his life. The wounds on the car remained to this day. Ruth preferred to leave them as an intimidating reminder to the picketers who visited her clinic almost daily. Even now, when Margaret stopped or started quickly, she could hear the bullets rolling around in the metallic guts of the door, like marbles in an old biscuit tin.

"I respected the hell out of your mom," Randy said.

"You remind me a lot of her," Margaret said.

"With testosterone."

"My mother had plenty of testosterone."

Randy picked up the red-velvet Jesus. "I'm going to keep him in the passenger seat of my car. I'll buckle him up and he'll protect me from these moronic drivers."

He held it at arm's length to take it all in. "I think Elvis would have bought one of these, don't you?"

Six

Dear Chatter: This is to the jogger who jogs every night around six o'clock going west on Thomasville Road: You need to be joggin' south, so when you get hit by my car you will be closer to the cemetery.

Dear Chatter: To explain something to our new Yankee residents: If you've got the name Bubba it does not mean you're stupid. Bubba comes from Brother, which is the word we use for Junior. If you've got the name Trey it means you're the third. Trey's a French word that means three. Guess they didn't teach you that in New Jersey.

"It's a contemporary painting," said the salesclerk. "You're probably gonna want a more contemporary frame. Like maybe this white one."

"I don't think so," the customer replied, her tone drawing raised eyebrows from the women within earshot. "I have a clear vision of what I want here."

She wore no makeup, and her long, blond hair was pulled back in a high ponytail. Though very pregnant, the woman wore metallic-purple running tights and an oversized white T-shirt with "Bay Area AIDS Walk 1992" printed on the back.

"I'm looking for a juxtaposition," she said. "I want a frame with that Old South look. You know . . . chunky and gold. Very overdone and over the top."

"Ma'am?" she asked.

"Exaggerated," explained the woman. "Like Liberace."

Suzanne Parley, waiting in line behind the woman, could not take her eyes off the painting, which was leaning against the cash register on the counter. Rendered in blues and earth tones, it was an oil of a human baby suckling a pig's teat. The newborn, naked and male, had mud on his face and stomach. Milk dribbled down his chin. Most of the patrons who had walked into the store immediately spotted the painting then looked away, as if they'd caught someone in an embarrassing act and wanted to preserve her dignity.

"Okay. So how 'bout this one?" the salesclerk asked.

"Yes, I like that. But do you have one

71

that's even more voluminous?"

"Ma'am?"

"Fatter? Even more gold-y."

"Yes, ma'am." She turned and pulled from the wall another L-shaped gilded frame sample, then gently set it on the top corner of the painting. Suzanne had this very frame on the oil of the hydrangeas in her master bedroom, and she was surprised that this very woman who had thrown out more than a hundred thousand dollars of exquisite window treatments would want such a beautiful frame.

"How's this?"

"Perfect," said the customer. "Fabulous. That's exactly what I need."

As she wrote up the order, the clerk leaned to the left, to address Suzanne, who still stood behind the woman. "I'll be right with you, Miss Suzanne," she said.

"Oh, no, that's okay," Suzanne said. "I'm not in a hurry."

The owner of the pig painting turned to Suzanne. "Don't you live in Red Hill Plantation?" she asked. "Black Lexus sedan?"

Suzanne smiled. "There's lots of black Lexus sedans in Red Hill."

"I think you're my neighbor," she said, holding out her hand. "I'm Jodi Armbuster . . . at twenty-four eleven?"

"Well, we sure *are* neighbors!" Suzanne looked at Jodi's purse — or was it a purse? It appeared to be a black canvas backpack from L.L. Bean or some other outdoor catalog. On the strap was an elastic sleeve that held a cell phone, and on the side a net pouch occupied by a half-full bottle of Evian. Suzanne was almost certain it was the same kind of bag she'd seen Melanie Griffith carrying in a photograph in *People*.

"I haven't seen you over there," Suzanne said.

"We're still at the La Quinta out on the interstate. The house is a war zone right now."

"Oh, I know what it's like to redecorate."

"We're trying to get everything done by Thanksgiving. I'm really sorry about all that mess out front. We basically had to perform an abortion on the house."

"I see . . ."

"We needed more room."

"Do you have more children?"

"No," she answered. "Just one hellish, out-of-control art collection. We needed storage space. . . . Do you have any kids?"

"Oh, no," Suzanne said. "Boone keeps me too busy for kids. You know how men are."

Suzanne moved aside so another woman

could go before her. "Did y'all find a good decorator?" she asked Jodi.

"Actually, I'm an interior designer. I'm doing it all myself."

Suzanne unconsciously leaned back and looked at Jodi, noting the absence of makeup and the freckles and sun spots that blemished her overtanned skin. She noted that Jodi didn't even wear a diamond, just a simple gold band, and then recalled her car, a royal-blue Volvo station wagon that had to be at least seven years old.

"I'll bet you save some money that way," she said.

"I'm sorry . . . I didn't catch your name."

"Oh, I'm so sorry. I'm Suzanne Parley."

"As in Parley Road?"

Suzanne nodded. "That was named after Boone's great-great-granddaddy."

"Really."

"The Parley family's had four generations of doctors in Selby. Boone's a neurosurgeon. What does your husband do?" she asked, already well aware that he was the new president of WSEL. Boone had told her with concern one evening that the television station had been bought out by a company based in Sacramento, and that Billy Thieber, the president and their neighbor, had been asked to retire at fifty-six.

"Marc's the new president and general manager of WSEL," Jodi said.

"I think I remember Boone sayin' somethin' to me about that."

"Here it is, Miss Suzanne," interrupted the clerk, lifting onto the counter a large oil painting, surrounded by an imposing gilded rectangle so ornate and thick it seemed more sculpture than frame. "Lord, is this heavy!"

As a surprise for Boone, Suzanne had commissioned an artist to paint Journey's End, the Parleys' historic family beach house on Sea Island. She had given the artist photographs and swatches of all the fabrics and wallpapers in the dining room so he could do his best to make it match.

"It sure is pretty, Miss Suzanne," said the clerk.

"You sure you don't think the frame's too much?" she asked the clerk. Suzanne looked over her shoulder to engage Jodi, but she had already left.

"Oh, no, ma'am. It's a beautiful frame."

"Can your man help me out with this? Is he around?"

"Yes, ma'am."

The clerk disappeared into the back

room and returned, followed by a sixty-something black man with a close-cropped gray beard who was permanently bent at the waist. His tan work pants were wet from the water outside, where he'd been washing the store owner's car. He leaned over to pick up the painting and stopped short when Suzanne spoke.

"You got to wrap that first," she said. "Don't go grabbin' that frame until it's wrapped."

"Yes, ma'am," he answered, his eyes never leaving the floor.

On the way home from the frame store, Suzanne stopped at Enright's Jewelers and had them install a small brass plate on the bottom of the frame that said *Journey's End: Our home away from home!* for the benefit of those who did not know about their house on the sea.

At home, Virgil had already put in the screw. Suzanne gently pulled off the paper and hung the painting on the wall.

Thrilled with the outcome, she poured herself a glass of chardonnay and stood back to admire the wall. It was not the painting that pleased her most, but the entire setting, which she had orchestrated without John David's help. Two wall sconces, which were large, gilded scallop shells, flanked the painting, adding to that overall nautical theme. And she was especially pleased that the artist managed to work in some spots of the yellow from the vase on the table beneath the painting.

Suzanne left the dining room and began her late-afternoon ritual of walking the house and turning on all the lamps, twenty-eight at last count. In the den, she closed the drapes to admire how the forty watts of yellow light bathed the Chippendale secretary, which lay open to show a feather plume and bottle of ink and two sheets of expensive vellum. Josephine had dusted the day before, and Suzanne quickly saw that she had moved the plume so it lay parallel with the edge of the paper. Suzanne quickly returned it to its correct position, laying it diagonally across the top of the paper, as if someone had been penning a letter and left it unfinished.

Suzanne could spend hours enjoying the company of her house, walking from room to room, switching lamps on and off, depending on the position of the sun at that time of day. She moved vases and pictures to different spots or transposed throw rugs and pillows. She would move and remove and replace until she felt that satisfying but imperceptible click that occurs when the eye, for inexplicable reasons, decides it is happy.

Yet in an instant the house could turn on her, revealing a void that would scream until she filled it. A corner, perfect the night before, would suddenly be in desperate need of attention. Why hadn't she noticed it before? Perhaps she needed a silk fern, bursting upward like a fountain. Another table? But what would she put on it? Suzanne would sit down with magazines and catalogs and search out ideas. Horchow. Ballard Designs. *Southern Living.* She would buy and return, buy and return, buy and stick it under the bed until John David found the right place for it or took it away to resell to somebody else.

Suzanne heard the rhythmic beeping of a truck in reverse and went to the window to investigate. She saw a white box truck with an Atlanta tag backing up to the third garage bay of Jodi Armbuster's home next door. Jodi emerged from around the side of the house to meet the driver. After briefly talking, he and his partner unloaded three huge panels covered in white plastic, each about the size of a twin-bed mattress. Once they were leaning against the truck, they removed the covering.

Lined up, side by side, the paintings

showed the entire life span of a human female, starting on the far left as a baby, then moving right, growing older and taller and reaching the full height of a twenty-something woman in the very center, then descending again, painfully chronicling that age-old relationship between gravity and human flesh, falling into motherhood, then middle age, then on down to an old lady, hunched over in a wheelchair with a toothless smile on her face. Each figure, from the newborn to the crone, was naked.

She picked up the phone and dialed her neighbor's number.

"Mary Nash, go look outside your front window right now. . . . I know! . . . I *know!* Can you believe that? I mean, what is it? You think it's for the baby's room? I just can't imagine a baby sleepin' next to somethin' like that. . . . Uh-huh. Just today. I met her at the Frame Game. She had on purple tights. . . . I am serious as I can be. . . . Yes!"

As she spoke, Suzanne watched Jodi and the two men looking at the panels, each of them occasionally stepping forward to point out a new discovery, then standing back to absorb them as a whole. She scanned the painted characters and estimated that she was closest in age to the career woman with pearls and a black-leather briefcase clutched in her hand. She was at the highest point in this chronological arc of humanity, midway through the life cycle, and, oddly enough, the petite woman looked a lot like Suzanne, who was nearly thirty-four with small facial features, plucked, fermata-shaped eyebrows, breasts that Suzanne considered too small, and black, shoulder-length hair, just long enough that she could pull it back with a bow on Sundays for church if she wanted to.

As Suzanne listened to her friend describe a dining room sideboard at the Lakewood Antique Mart, she focused on the squealing baby, evidently fresh from the womb, all wrinkled and glistening and pink-red. And then, as it had done countless times before, Suzanne's mind traveled into her own body, visualizing the inside of her congenitally half-formed uterus. She saw a hopeful, naive egg, fresh from its journey down the fallopian tube, jump into the deep-scarlet uterine sea, then get sucked out a hole the size of a grapefruit. Since her senior year in high school, when she learned of the deformity that would leave her childless forever, Suzanne had imagined these eggs the size of caviar, hundreds of them by now, maybe thousands, floating up and down her arteries and capillaries, all of them lost, all of them looking for some safe harbor where they could drop anchor.

She had married Boone, the last male heir in the Parley family, without telling him. There was always hope, she thought — bodies healed themselves all the time if it was God's will. Let's not have children right away, she'd told her new husband. Let's have some fun and travel and then settle down and be responsible and boring. Suzanne was certain he'd change his mind about kids once he saw how wonderful life could be with just the two of them.

For four years, this was true. Then, in a Delta 757 somewhere over the Atlantic, on their way home from Ireland, Boone announced it was time to start a family, and he focused his energies on this endeavor until a Saturday when one of his golfing partners was called out of town for a brother's funeral. His replacement for the day's game was Rossie Nolan, a stranger to Boone but not his wife, whom he'd seen naked once every twelve months for the last five years, his head and hands probing between her thighs as she lay on the crinkly white paper liner of his examination table.

"I think your wife's a patient of mine," he said.

"I thought so," Boone answered. "I wasn't sure, but I thought so."

"Suzanne . . . right?"

Boone nodded. "You'll be seein' a lot of us pretty soon," he said. "We're fixin' to start a family."

To hide his bewilderment, Rossie took a long drink of his Diet Coke. He pushed on the pedal with his cleated foot, instantly filling the silence with the mosquitolike whine of the electric motor as their cart climbed a hill.

"I'm hopin' for sons," Boone said.

"Sons," Rossie echoed.

"I'm the last of the Parleys," Boone said. "It's gotta be boys or nothin'."

He would reveal the truth to Boone later, at a corner table in the lounge of the clubhouse, the backs of their necks red and warm from the sun, a third round of bourbon buzzing through their veins. Oh, how to tell a man he's been fooled by his wife! And that his family name will perish when he takes his final breath on this sweet Earth.

Seven

Dear Chatter: To the person who wanted to get rid of moles. Just pour gasoline and broken glass down that mole hole and it's see-you-later-alligator.

Dear Chatter: To the lady who wants to get rid of the deer eatin' her hydrangeas in her backyard: Just set out a bowl of urine and that'll scare those deer away. It's got to be male urine because those deer aren't afraid of women.

Margaret was halfway through transcribing Chatter when she decided her ears needed a break. Too much of the Georgia drawl created an uncomfortable discordance in her mind because it differed so greatly from the collective societal voice she'd absorbed as a child. Taking in too much Chatter at one time had the same effect as someone banging away on the black keys of a piano. She removed her earphones and walked back to Randy's glass-walled office.

Margaret was the only person in the newsroom who seemed comfortable in Randy's presence, and indeed people would look over with wariness when they heard the two of them cut up in laughter, as if they were suspicious of being made the butt of a joke.

This was the first time in Margaret's life that she had had a boss other than her mother, but authority held no mystique or power in a household that questioned its every motivation and move. And Ruth Pinaldi, whose like-minded, messianic famous friends would drop in for weekend visits, taught her daughter to hold no one on a pedestal. Margaret's eggplant Parmesan was loved by Jane Fonda and Paul Simon. Betty Friedan would call a day ahead with her request for Margaret's Puerto Rican asopao, a rice dish flavored with green olives and capers, smoked ham hocks and dark-meat chicken.

"Hey," Randy greeted her. "You want to have lunch?"

"I don't think I have time for lunch."

"Sure you do. Come on. I need a Waffle House fix."

"Waffle House?"

"You haven't been to Waffle House?" he asked. "Oh, man, you haven't had scattered, smothered, and covered?"

Randy had tried his first Waffle House restaurant on the initial trip down to Selby. He saw his first one outside Louisville, and as he sank deeper into the South, the brown-brick-and-yellow restaurants grew in frequency, with one and sometimes two at every interchange. Randy liked the aggressive retail presence and the retro appearance: the white orb lights suspended like yo-yos over yellow Formica tables, the counter stools upholstered in orange vinyl, the walls covered in what looked like wood-grain Contac paper, the waitresses' hair hidden by yellow-and-orange kerchiefs tied at the napes of their necks. Later, he would learn that what appeared to be an effort to look fifties actually was nothing more than a refusal to evolve and match the aesthetic whims of the outside Yankee world. Fact was, the privately held Waffle House Corporation had intentionally never changed — it remained true and loyal to Southern sensitivities. The iced tea was sweet as Life Savers candy. The salad was made exclusively of iceberg lettuce with some token shavings of carrot and red cabbage. There was a constant tug-of-war between the smoke from frying pork and unfiltered cigarettes for dominance of the airspace, and after eating at a Waffle House you carried in your clothes for the rest of the day the smells of a culture not concerned with preventive health.

Randy and Margaret took stools at the counter. A waitress whose name tag said *Nancy — Nineteen Years!* set white coffee mugs down in front of them. Around her neck hung a gold cross the size of a circus peanut. Her glittery, aquamarine eye shadow reminded Margaret of the contraband Barbies she used to play with whenever her mother was at work.

"How y'all doin' today?" she asked.

"Very well, thank you," Randy answered. He turned to Margaret. "Do you trust me to order? You like spicy, right? Okay, then, two orders . . . no, two double orders of scattered, smothered, covered, chopped, diced, and peppered. And two sweet teas."

"Y'all want chili on those hash browns?"

"Absolutely," he answered.

After scribbling down the order, the waitress stepped up to a line of brown tape on the floor, about five feet from the grill. "Okay, boys!" she yelled, bringing her pad out to arm's length as if she were farsighted and reading a song book, and she began to bark out the order. "I need two scattered-smothered-covered-chopped-diced-peppered. And drown it all!"

The two cooks before the open grill, both of them middle-aged men (*Lonny — Twelve Years!* and *Warren — Seven Years!*), wore the pup tent–shaped paper hats Margaret remembered from *American Graffiti*. Their faces were pinched in focused scowls of concentration, and it took Margaret a few minutes to understand why. Each waitress shouted out her order, and, like tape recorders, the cooks absorbed the words and repeated them back, all the while their hands reaching for rubbery orange squares of cheese and flipping circles of red, raw meat and dumping piles of shredded potatoes onto the sizzling grill.

"My God," Margaret said. "How do they remember everything?"

"It's like that in every single Waffle House," Randy replied. "Is that the weirdest damn thing or what?"

"But why?"

"You're asking me to interpret Southern culture? Hell, Margaret, I don't know why. Why do the grown men here keep the *Y*'s on the ends of their names? You tell me why."

Within five minutes, Margaret had before her a steaming mound of hash brown potatoes speckled with chopped tomatoes, onions, diced ham, American cheese, jalapeños — all of it awash in a big ladle of chili. The waitress suggested she try a few shakes of Tabasco to top it all off, and Margaret agreed.

"I had two more calls about dogs today," Margaret said to Randy as they ate. "Where's Red Hill Plantation?"

"It's the newer McMansion neighborhood around Sugar Day. The docs and lawyers and children of Old Selby. Why?"

"Someone's black Lab was found dead in the middle of a neighbor's driveway. And then there was a different dog found in someone's yard. Or at least it sounds that way."

"You mean in addition to the ones from last week?"

"Yes."

"Hit by cars?"

"I don't know. I can't tell from what I've heard in the calls."

"So that makes what? Five now?"

"That we know of."

"My guess is death by monster truck," Randy said, speaking with his mouth half full. "The teenagers in that zip code know no limits. North Selby is so fucking weird. They think they're English aristocracy over there."

Despite being the editor of the news-paper, it was obvious to Margaret that Randy had no intention of ever integrating with Selby; he had divulged to her that the president of the newspaper division of Granite-Peabody told him that if he did his job well they would rescue him from his exile deep in the heart of Georgia and re-ward him with the managing-editor posi-tion at the *Enquirer.* As a result, Margaret thought he was more anthropologist than journalist, except that his observations were always tinged in judgment — funny and accurate, yes, but oftentimes mean-spirited.

Randy had not even bothered to search for a house. He lived in the new Residence Inn, an extended-stay, faux-Tudor motel off I-75 on the west end of town, and, even after half a year, the warranty tags still hung from the grill inside the oven. As if he were a guest, Randy continued to use the free, miniature soap bars, even though they seemed to dissolve as quickly as a loz-enge on the tongue, and he was always cursing at the diminutive size as they slipped from his grip like a wet goldfish. He flavored his take-out meals with the paper packets of salt and pepper that the maids refreshed every day. He unconsciously refused to change the AOL access number on his laptop from Philadelphia to Selby, requiring a long-distance call each time he wanted to retrieve his e-mail. In fact, the only thing Randy Whitestone had added to feather his new nest-in-exile was the black Krups espresso machine in the kitchen, which he used morning and night.

Randy kept a journal of what he called his "travels," filled with the details of life in central Georgia that he found unique, and he would pull out this palm-sized leather-bound notebook and his yellow Mont Blanc fountain pen whenever anyone started telling him something that he feared his friends on The Outside, as he called it, would never believe.

He focused his attention and wrath on the affluent northern half of town, the environs of Sugar Day Country Club. These were the people, the power brokers and agenda setters, whom he had to deal with in his job, and he despised their air of exclusivity and attempt to create an identity of British landed gentry. He did not like how they drove to Atlanta for shoes or T-shirts instead of shopping with the working class and blacks at the Selby Mall. He scoffed at their perfectly symmetrical, oversized, hollow-pillar homes with the circular driveways and boxwood topiary hedges. He did not like how they had all but abandoned the public school system.

"I swear they seem more consumed with class than race in this town, especially north Selby," he said. "Have you noticed the weird little stickers in the back windows of all the cars?"

Indeed, Margaret had noted the cryptic adhesive patches, always in the lower left-hand corner of the back windshield of a Chevy Suburban or Mercedes or Lexus SUV. She'd seen a red *P* on a white circle; a yellow *T* rimmed in black; a blue star with a curvacious, plump white *C* that was reminiscent of the *S* on Superman's chest.

"It's taken me forever," Randy said. "But I've got it all figured out now. Okay, so the red *P* is for Montezuma Presbyterian Day School. It's expensive but very, very conservative, so you don't see many docs' kids there. Certainly no Northerners. Basically it's where the rich white-supremacists go.

"Now, the yellow *T* is for Traemont Academy. Tuition is half of what it is at Presbyterian Day, so these people can't even really hang with the *P* people, and they're more likely to drive teal-colored cars and luxed-out pickup trucks. The *T* says 'I might not have graduated from college but my kids are going to.' I'm sorry: 'fixin' to.' Oh . . . and a lot of them smoke. And it's obvious that a lot of the moms dye their own hair."

Randy took another bite of hash browns, swallowing after just three chews.

"Now the *C*," he continued. "The *C* is the signature of royalty in the kingdom of Selby. It costs twelve thousand a year for your kid to go there. The *C* in your window means you belong to Sugar Day or are on the waiting list to belong. It means you own your own tuxedo and that you probably retain a poor older black guy around the house to do things like wash your sidewalk. Canterbury's acceptable to the transplant Yankees because it's the only school in Perry County where Emory and Duke recruit. And it's where the Japanese kids go. Oh, and the *C* moms will find something at Target and lie and say they bought it in Atlanta."

Margaret smiled.

"Now get this," he said. "The other day I saw a Suburban with four *C* stickers on her windshield. Four! Now what the hell would she need with four of them? What's she trying to say? 'Hey, I'm at the top of the food chain in this Cesspool of the South!' . . . It's like some African tribal branding thing, isn't it?"

Randy's cell phone rang, an electronic chiming of "Yankee Doodle Dandy," which turned heads every time it went off. He retrieved it from his breast pocket, looked at the display window, and answered.

"What is it, Pearline?"

Buckner Meeks, a local oncologist and owner of several dilapidated inner-city houses, had caught wind that Randy's new investigative reporter was researching an exposé on substandard housing. It turned out that Meeks, along with a dozen or so other wealthy, old-Selby families, moonlighted as slumlords who rented their decrepit properties to inner-city black families. Already the reporter had uncovered two cases in which people had been killed by antiquated wiring and a collapsed roof, and the families were paid ten thousand dollars to keep their mouths shut.

"I've got to take this one," Randy said to Margaret. "I'll be outside. Here." He pulled his white-leather, Hugo Boss wallet from his pocket and tossed it to her from across the table. "Go ahead and pay."

As Randy left, a young man on his way inside held the door open for him, watching Randy with a bemused smile on his face. He then walked in, looked at the counter and nodded in the manner of a cowboy at Margaret, politely staying back until she nodded and smiled in return.

Obviously off-duty now, he wore a tan, crew-neck T-shirt tucked into a pair of blue jeans that were clean and pressed but faded at the knees. On his feet were square-toed, broken-in boots that were clean and polished, a brown the color of dark chocolate. A blond cowlick on the top of his forehead reminded Margaret of Dennis the Menace, yet he was a big man, with shoulders that could fill a doorway and hands that could conceal the identity of a can of Coke.

"Hey," he said.

"Hello," Margaret replied. "You were right. My cat came down when he wanted to."

"How long was she up there?" he asked.

"Till that next day. I woke up and he was curled up like a shrimp on the front porch. I thought he was dead — he looked so skinny."

"She gonna be all right?"

Margaret nodded.

"You keepin' her inside now?"

"I try to," Margaret said. "But he's fast."

"I thought she was a girl. I thought her name was Susan."

"No, it's a boy. It's a long story, but it's a boy."

"I didn't catch your name."

"Margaret."

"Margaret."

"Yes. Margaret."

"Margaret what?"

"Margaret."

He ran his hand through his short, thick hair, then pursed his lips and nodded as he looked out toward the parking lot. "Well, I'm sorry," he said. "But I was fixin' to ask you to a movie or somethin', and I sure can't call you if I don't know your last name."

"I'm not comfortable giving it out," Margaret said. "I'm sorry, but I'm not."

"Okay, then," he said. "Well, have a nice day."

"Good-bye."

He turned and headed for a booth where a uniformed firefighter awaited him. Margaret wondered if he walked this slowly all the time or if he was lingering as long as possible, hoping she would change her mind and call out to him. She noticed how the hair on the back of his head grew in a circular pattern with the cowlick at the very center, giving it the appearance of a blond hurricane.

Once more, he turned to her. "Don't you even wanna know my name?" he asked. "It's Dewayne."

"Duane."

"No, you say it Dee-wayne, like that."

"Dee-wayne."

"Yes, ma'am."

Margaret stood and picked the bill up from the table. "Well, I've got to get back to work, Dee-wayne. Enjoy your lunch."

"Yes, ma'am."

Margaret pushed open the glass door and walked into the sunshine and the smell of Confederate jasmine, which mixed with the lingering odor of microscopic pork grease particles that had come to rest in the fibers of her shirt. Randy disengaged from his cell phone as she was smelling the sleeve of her arm.

"You smell everything," he said.

"Not everything."

"Yes you do. Why?"

"I don't know. I get pleasure from smells."

Over the years, many people had remarked on Margaret's predilection for smelling the things she invited into her personal space. She smelled each fresh handful of toilet paper. She smelled a clean coffee mug before filling it. When Margaret grocery shopped she unconsciously sniffed each item before setting it in her cart, not just apples or eggplant or a grouper fillet, but even a box of tampons or toothpaste or a lightbulb in its cardboard packaging.

"It's like you're looking for clues or something," Randy said. "Like a bloodhound."

"Very flattering, Randy. Thank you."

"So what was that all about inside?"

"What?"

"Mr. Refrigerator."

Margaret smiled. "That was Dee-wayne."

"You know him?"

"Not really."

"What did he want?"

"Nothing. . . . Nothing that's your business, anyway."

From the sidewalk, Randy scowled at the two men sitting in the booth beyond the window.

"Don't be so sure of that," he said.

When it was time to build Selby's first cemetery in the late seventeen hundreds, founding father Reginald Flanders, who did not much like the idea of being lowered into the ground and forgotten forever, found the inspiration for Rosemont. He traveled the world in search of unusual flora that would thrive in this middle Georgia latitude, and he planted them all on these thirty-six acres that consumed four hills.

He told the *Selby Reflector*, "I want young couples to come here and proclaim their love beneath these glorious oaks as the sun sets. I want a leafy respite from the heat of the day, where a lady can take her hat off and ponder life from her bench overlooking the majestic Muscogee. I want to see families here, with picnic lunches spread out on the grass, feeling the wisdom and warmth emanating from their loved ones who lay beneath. . . . In essence, a cemetery in a park."

In Margaret's opinion, the word *majestic* was a stretch as a modifier for the river that ran the entire length of Selby. Sluggish and thick from cutting through miles of clay, it reminded her of a pot of bean soup that had been simmering and thickening for hours. Yet its heavy, tortoise pace, which mirrored the speed of the people who lived here, comforted her.

Margaret had never lived so close to a river and was surprised at what a wonderful meditation tool it was. Watching the water flow eastward, she would let a thought bubble to the surface of her mind, and then she would set it into the current and imagine watching it float away, ridding herself of item after item that crowded and clambered in her mind until she was empty and calm. Somewhere in the Atlantic Ocean, or perhaps even farther away now, were nuggets of anger and grief with Ruth Pinaldi's name on them. Margaret mused that psychics might say she was polluting the environment with toxic waste.

Margaret parked her car at the cemetery entrance, grabbed her journal and began the walk to her favorite concrete bench at river's edge. She had just forty minutes before dark, when the resident pack of wild dogs that lived beneath an old magnolia tree would awaken and claim the cemetery's cobblestone streets as their own.

Margaret passed the Victorian gazebo where Robert E. Lee reassured Selbyites more than a century earlier that their sacrifices would not be made in vain. Beyond this lay row upon row of Confederate soldier graves, the identical, arch-shaped headstones so dense and plentiful they reminded Margaret of magnified, white beard stubble. It had rained earlier in the day, and the water gathered in holes and puddles in the red clay, making it look as if the earth were covered in fresh wounds.

Finally at her destination, Margaret sat down to write:

> *I actually have two man friends!*
>
> *RANDY: Randy is the type of man I've always thought I should/would be attracted to. Smart — brilliant, really — and confident with a passion for excellence that rivals my mother's. (They say girls marry their fathers, but since I don't know mine I guess I'm destined to marry my mother.) I enjoy his company, but is it smart to date someone at work even though he's not my direct supervisor? He seems to have no concern for appearance or rules. I suppose that's one thing I like about him.*
>
> *DEWAYNE: His wonderful scent. Smells like warm peach scones. How and why can one of the natives be attracted to me?*
>
> *At Waffle House I kept fighting the urge to lean into him as you would lean into the shade of a cabana in the desert.*
>
> *Does he drive a truck?*

Eight

Dear Chatter: To the lady who wanted to stop her gums from bleedin': All you gotta do is rub some kaolin clay and baby oil on those gums every night. Also stop eatin' potato chips and carrots because there's somethin' in potato chips and carrots that makes your gums bleed. Thank you.

Dear Chatter: This is to the person who is messin' with my husband. I know it. God knows it. You know it. And I am gonna leave it in the hands of the Lord. But I say unto you, "Woe to you."

In a span of ninety minutes, Koquita paged Donna eleven times. It got to the point that whenever Donna heard the electronic *ping* that preceded every announcement she would roll her eyes, drop whatever produce she had in her hand, and start walking toward the line of registers.

"What is it now, Koquita?" she asked.

"Don't get ugly with me, girl. What's

this?" she asked, holding up a bag. Donna squinted, trying to distinguish the mass of green beyond the wrinkles of clear plastic.

"Sunflower sprouts. I already told you that yesterday."

"I thought you said it was watercress. Looks like watercress to me."

Donna opened the bag and looked inside. "No," she said. "Sunflower sprouts are puffier, see? And smell it — smells like a sunflower seed."

"I ain't smelling nothin', girl. What's the code?"

"Four nine six."

Carefully, because of her inch-long orange fingernails with tiny rhinestones glued on in the shape of a *K*, Koquita keyed in the numbers.

On the way back to her section, Donna recognized two girls who graduated from Southeast High a year after she did, Class of '97. One of them was Raymie Sisson, who was on the junior varsity cheerleading squad with Donna her sophomore year. They were picking out snack food in aisle twelve, Donna's usual path from produce to the front of the store.

"Great," she sarcastically whispered to herself. The last thing Donna wanted was for anyone under thirty to see her in this uniform. She hated her Kroger uniform; she hated everything about it. She hated the polyester knit that rubbed against her skin like the nylon scratchie she used to wash the dishes at night. She hated the flared pants with the elastic waist. She hated the brown-colored smock that buttoned down the front and the white accents on the lapels that were so wide they reminded Donna of aircraft wings on the F-16 fighters that landed at Robins Air Force Base east of town.

Donna detoured through frozen foods, undetected, and returned to her work. She had been packaging broccoli rabe in green foam trays with cellophane and decided that she would take some home that night. Donna had been trying to get her father to sample and embrace the new vegetables and fruits she was discovering at work.

"What kinda dessert is this?" he'd asked the night before.

"They're prunes, Daddy."

"I know what they are," he said. "What about some cobbler? Or some cookies and ice cream?"

"Daddy, you're overweight. You shouldn't be eatin' like that. Besides, prunes slow down the aging process in the brain, and they got lots of antioxidants."

Frankie Kabel leaned forward, toward Donna, who sat across the rectangular oak table. "Food ain't supposed to make ya live longer, Donna," he said. "It's just supposed to make ya live."

Since her mother's death five years ago, Donna's father had gained four to six pounds a year. Donna, who learned to cook from her mother, prepared every meal for her father, and it seemed to her now that he was using this food to help him remember something he had lost, and instead of burying his nose in a perfumed hanky, he held on to his wife through the flavor of glistening brown gravy with a hint of nutmeg. Since his wife's death, Frankie always wanted the same Sunday-dinner foods every night of the week, and he would stuff himself with cheese-and-squash casserole and stewed okra with tomatoes and smothered chicken and biscuits with butter, stuff himself until he was overcome with the fuzzy, warm dizziness of a carbohydrate overload, and he had to lean back and close his eyes and rest his hands on his belly as if it were a shelf. And then, after a minute or so, with the taste of his wife's food in his mouth, he would take one deep breath and slowly open his eyes as if returning from a dream, and Donna would see a look of bewilderment and disappointment on his face, and she would feel guilty, albeit briefly, because she was not whom he wanted to see sitting at the other side of the table.

Finished with wrapping the rabe, Donna carried it out to the display case and saw Mr. Tom standing in front of the apple case, his hands on his hips with a furrowed-brow look of concern on his face.

"Mr. Tom," Donna said.

"Hey, Donna. We've got a little problem here."

"Sir?"

"These bananas . . . they're too close to the Fujis. We've got to get them farther away. That banana gas is going to ripen those things in a few days, and we'll have all that waste."

"Oh, Mr. Tom, I am so sorry."

"That's okay, but you've got to isolate your bananas, Donna. They really should go on an end cap. Here," he said, beginning to roll up the sleeves of his blue shirt. "Let me help you move them."

"Oh, no, sir, I can do this."

"It'll be my pleasure. There's something I want to talk to you about, anyway."

The store manager, Tom Green, had been transferred from a Kansas City

Kroger two weeks after Donna started work. Aghast at the condition of the perishables sections of his new store, he quickly fired the produce and meat managers, which left Donna all alone with no boss. So three or four times a day, Mr. Tom, as his new Southern employees called him, would breeze through and stop to check on Donna, the smell of his Polo cologne lingering in the air until she would break open a carton of fennel bulbs or ripe bananas. In snippets of conversation he'd learned of her job at Lancôme and noted the sadness and regret and reluctance she'd carried with her to Kroger.

"I want to talk to you about Adrian," he said, gently placing bunches of bananas into a box on the stock cart.

"Yes, sir?"

"You've got to exercise more patience with him, Donna."

Though she would never divulge this to Mr. Tom, Donna remembered Adrian Braswell from Trafalgar Weaver Middle School. Of course they were not friends, and he most likely would not remember her, but Adrian Braswell was one of those hard-to-forget people Donna always saw and stared at from afar. A five-foot-tall African American, Adrian had one arm that was half the length of the other, and instead of a hand there appeared to be a flesh-colored mandible, two thick, Snickers bar–sized stubs that he worked like a hand puppet. A small, limp pinky finger hung on the underside, dangling like a piece of jewelry. Adrian was a roving stock clerk at Kroger, and because Donna was short-handed in produce Mr. Tom had placed him there to help her out.

"He dropped a whole flat of kumquats today," Donna said. "They were rollin' around this place like marbles."

"No harm done, though, right?"

"And it took him two hours to refresh those nectarines."

"Donna, the boy has one arm. Would you cut him some slack?"

"It's just not very efficient havin' him around, Mr. Tom. I feel like I have to baby-sit him."

"Just try harder. That's all I'm asking. Okay?"

"Yes, sir," she answered. "I'm gonna try. But, Lord, does that boy try my patience."

"Good . . . Oh, I forgot to tell you. I took a message for you today."

"Sir?"

"Somehow the call came through to my office. Jackee called and said she'd pick you up at ten. Outside the store. Do I have the name right, Jackee?"

"Yes, sir. Jackee Satterly. That's my best friend."

"Donna, please don't call me 'sir.' I'm forty this year and I feel really, really old."

"Forty's not old."

"Forty's old."

The bananas safely segregated, Donna retrieved her purse and sweater from her locker in the employee lounge then went to wait outside. She was leaning against the Coke machine when Tom Green came out of the store, carrying his dinner for the evening in a crinkly, tan Kroger bag — some Fritos and an Italian deluxe sandwich with extra mayo from the deli.

Donna watched him as he walked to his silver Mazda pickup truck with Missouri tags. While Robbie was a stalk of broccoli, bulky floret muscles atop a lean sinewy torso, Donna thought Mr. Tom was more the shape and texture of a ripe Bartlett pear. He wore the same two striped ties over and over again, alternating each day, and neither of them appeared to be silk. His brown hair, starting to thin on the crown of his head, made it look from afar as if he wore a flesh-colored yarmulke. And, Donna thought, he really should drop the mustache — some guys needed to realize they just didn't have the follicle density necessary for attractive, full facial hair.

Still, he was one of the kindest men she'd ever encountered. Donna noted how Tom Green would carry out the twenty-five-pound bags of dog food to senior citizens' cars, and when he found money in the parking lot he always put it in the March of Dimes box at the customer service counter. When Louise in deli lost the end of her index finger in the slicer, it was Mr. Green who, in the midst of the bloody chaos, remembered to find the tip among the fleshy sheets of honey-glazed ham and set it in a plastic cup of ice he quickly scooped from the fish case . . . and then drove Louise to the emergency room in his truck.

"Good night, Mr. Tom!" Donna yelled out, across the parking lot.

He turned to the voice. "Donna? You need a ride somewhere?"

"Oh, no, sir," she yelled back. "That's my red Camaro over there. I'm just waitin' for Jackee. We're goin' over to Rio Cantina for a margarita. We go every Friday. Here she comes now."

"Okay, then."

Jackee pulled up in her blue Geo Prizm. Donna heard the engine's cooling fan click on as she opened the door and sank into the velour seat.

"Okay, okay," Jackee said, shifting the car into park and clicking on the dome light. "Let me see."

Donna turned toward Jackee and lifted her chin toward the light.

"Turn a little that way," Jackee said, pointing to the windshield. "I think you're right," she said. "I think it's gettin' better."

"You don't think I'm tryin' to fool myself?"

"It's been a week since I saw you. Things can change in a week. God made the whole world in a week."

Donna pulled down the visor to look at herself in the mirror.

"Why aren't you wearin' foundation?" Jackee asked.

" 'Cause it only looks worse," Donna answered. "Looks like tire tracks on a dirt road after a rain."

With her tongue, she pushed on the inside of her cheek, enlarging the scar for a better look. Though the redness of the line had faded somewhat, the width of the scar, which was straight and wide as a piece of uncooked linguini, had not changed, and

Donna was certain now that when the emergency room doctor sewed her up he did something to the corner of her mouth. It felt tight and forced and unnatural, like the time she went to a costume party dressed as a geisha girl and her father had used duct tape to hold back the skin around her eyes to make them look slanted. And while she thought such a subtle, perpetual smile might be sexy on Dennis Quaid or Kevin Costner, Donna wondered how a girl could act aloof and mysterious when she couldn't stop grinning like a clown.

"I need to get plastic surgery, Daddy," she said one evening.

"No, ma'am. Nosiree. Not my daughter," Frankie Kabel replied.

"The doctor said a glass cut would leave a bigger scar. Look at me."

"No, missy. We are not messin' with the plans of the Lord. You are already the vainest creature on this planet."

"But look at me, Daddy!"

She was lying in bed that night, staring at the sprayed-on ceiling that looked like cottage cheese, when she heard her father's knuckles rap against the outside of her door, then the cool whisper of paper sliding across tile. Donna left the note until morning and read it on the way down to breakfast: *When Judah saw her, he thought she was a prostitute, for she had covered her face. Genesis 38:15.*

Jackee turned down the volume of her stereo, and Faith Hill sank into the dashboard. "So how was your day?" she asked.

"Horrible," Donna answered. "I got in trouble from Mr. Tom."

"What for?"

"He says I was talkin' mean to Adrian."

"Flipper Boy? Oh, he gives me the creeps."

"And you don't have to look at him all day, Jackee. You just don't know what it's like to be washin' lettuce and look up in that mirror and see that little thing wigglin' around. It just about makes me want to throw up. I don't know how much longer I can take it."

She often saw him from this perspective. Whenever Donna heard the timed, recorded sound of thunder that foreshadowed the simulated rain shower that drenched the leafy vegetables, she stopped whatever she was doing and moved to a spot near the refrigerated case along the wall. In the line of mirrors behind the produce, she saw an image of herself as she used to be, protected by the gauze of mist

112

that hid the details of her face.

"I like what you're doin' with your eyeliner," Jackee said. "It's heavy, but that's the look now."

As they drove through the parking lot, Donna looked out the window. She saw a Japanese couple, about her age, holding hands as they walked from their Mercedes toward the red door of Mount Sushi, the new restaurant two doors down from Kroger. On the man's nose were perched silver-frame glasses with lenses no bigger than a quarter, and both he and the woman wore retro, striped turtlenecks and black, square-toed boots — items that, just a year ago, would have flagged them as outsiders. Everywhere in Selby, Donna now saw people who, in her mind, belonged in the Range Rover zip codes of Atlanta.

"You ready for a margarita?" Jackee asked.

"Can we go by the dealership first?"

Robbie had not spoken to Donna in two weeks. It most likely would have been longer, but Donna finally called him from a pay phone so he wouldn't recognize her number on caller I.D. Flustered and guilt-ridden when he discovered the caller's identity, he made plans with her to go to lunch that Saturday, but when the day arrived he called in the morning to cancel, saying his boss had changed his schedule, and he had to work the lot. Donna had not seen him in person for four weeks. Robbie said he was working overtime, but Donna did not believe him. The previous week she had seen his car in the parking lot at Whiskey River two nights in a row, and Jackee had heard thirdhand that he'd been seen riding the bumper cars at the Fun Tree with a redhead.

Jackee turned north, onto Columbus Road. "I'm thinkin' I don't care much where Robbie is tonight."

"What do you mean?"

"There's a new restaurant out on Milledgeville Road," Jackee said. "It's food from Vietnam or some place, but Brittany says there's a cute little bar, and that the bosses from the Toyota plant like to go there . . . not the Japanese ones but the Yankees."

"What about Robbie?"

"Donna . . ." With the heels of her hands on the wheel, Jackee shook out two white Tic Tacs and popped them into her mouth. "Is he really worth us chasin' him all over town every Friday night? Let's go meet us some cute guys."

"Let's just go see where Robbie is, and then I'll go with you."

"Donna."

"Just help me find his truck, Jackee, and that's all I'll wanna do. I promise. I just wanna see where he's at."

It was an easy truck to spot, a cherry-red Chevy 4X4 pickup with white lightning-bolt decals down each side. Robbie had sold Donna her Camaro in the exact color almost a year ago to the day, when they met as salesman and customer. They had their first date the following week, on the night after Robbie brought his sister, Lynn, to the Lancôme counter for a makeover.

"I wanna know somethin', Donna," Jackee said. "All your life, cute boys have followed you like a dog chasin' a bone. Why are you so set on Robbie when he treats you so bad?"

"I don't know, but there's his truck," she said, pointing to the lot of Fall Line Chevrolet-Buick where row upon row of new cars gleamed beneath the bright lights. "Don't park by the window or he'll see us."

Jackee hid her Geo between two new Suburbans. From the darkness of the car, they looked across the empty guest parking spaces and through the large plate-glass windows and could see the idle sales staff laughing and talking as they leaned on the receptionist's round, gray Formica desk, their feet tired from pressing hot asphalt all day.

"I feel like I'm watchin' TV without the sound," Jackee said. "Who's that cute guy with the black mustache?"

Robbie wore his trademark long-sleeve, white Polo dress shirt and the Jerry Garcia tie Donna had bought him for Valentine's Day. Donna remembered how her mother always said that men were as easy to read as a Dr. Seuss book, and she focused on Robbie's face, searching for clues as to whether he was happy or guilty or anxious or oblivious . . . or a sign, any sign, that showed he had simply moved on without her.

"You gonna go in?" Jackee asked.

"Shush," Donna said, not losing sight of him. "I'm fixin' to look into his heart."

Another three minutes passed, and Jackee noticed that her friend's eyes had begun to well with tears. She watched Donna bring an index finger to her lips and unconsciously begin gnawing at her unpainted nail. Jackee had never seen her friend do such a thing — feeling so low and empty and hungry that she would actually eat herself.

"I'm thinkin' we need some margaritas," Jackee said. She shifted her car into drive and pulled out from the valley created by the towering Suburbans. White light from above suddenly filled the car, and shadows crawled up Donna's lap then torso then face.

"Where we goin'?" she asked her friend.

"Rio Cantina," she answered.

"I wanna go home," Donna said.

"I'm not lettin' you."

They headed down Bass Road, flanked on both sides by established, live oaks, all with large yellow ribbons as thick as twisted beach towels tied around their trunks. In the glare of the headlights, they popped out at them like the fluorescent strips on a fireman's jacket. These trees, whose branches reached across the road to form a canopy, had been naively planted just off the shoulder, back in a time when even a two-lane, paved road seemed luxuriant and unnecessary. Leaning against one of the trees was a white-painted plywood sign the size of a card table. In crudely drawn red letters someone had written *SAVE ME!*

Donna leaned her head back and looked up through the tinted sunroof. Through the leafy ceiling, she noticed that the moon was three-quarters empty.

Nine

Dear Chatter: I get more wrong-phone-number calls in Selby than anywhere I've ever lived up North, maybe five or six a week. Can someone explain this phenomenon to me, please?

Dear Chatter: Is it true that Jimmy Allred got fired from Channel 12? If it is then that's a shame because the new weatherman talks too fast and I can't understand anything he's sayin'. I am also tired of his stories about New Jersey.

After two hours of waiting, Suzanne could finally push a fork into the once-frozen piece of Mount Olympus casserole. It had been built in layers, this casserole; from the side it looked like a cutaway of the earth from some geologic formation in Arizona, and the lumpy layer of freezer-burned white cheese blanketed the top like old, crusty snow.

Suzanne had agreed with Boone that it was one of the best dinners she'd ever prepared, and at the end of the meal — How long ago was it? Three months? Four? — she'd had the foresight to freeze a cupcake-size portion. And now, God bless women's intuition, she needed it. That morning, before exiting the kitchen door, Boone had told her that he was bringing home for dinner a new prospect for the neurological clinic, and that they would be home for cocktails at six, dinner at seven. "Can you make that Greek casserole?" he had asked. "The one with the mashed potatoes on top?"

No, this was cheese, Suzanne was certain, but what kind? Cottage cheese? Feta?

Suzanne reached for her wineglass but stopped short when she discovered it was empty. She picked up a fork and slowly scraped the cheese off half the piece of casserole, revealing a blond lasagna noodle. Then, with a paring knife, as if she were dissecting some brine-soaked creature in biology lab, Suzanne made a V-shaped slit into the noodle and pulled back the flap, revealing a brown mixture of ground beef with cubes of carrot and tiny, randomly shaped nuggets of something the color of yellowed teeth. She smelled. Was it garlic? It was garlic. Wasn't it garlic?

"Oh, Boone . . ." she whined out loud to

herself. "Why on earth have you gotta have this one?"

With a spatula, Suzanne returned the casserole to the Rubbermaid container then snapped the lid shut. She would take it to Kroger, not what north Selbyites called the "social Kroger" near her house, where it was impossible to shop without bumping into the buggy of someone she knew, but to the Kroger in south Selby, next to the Silk Flower Warehouse on Truman Parkway, where she frequently went to buy her wine, always in liter size, always a Clos du Bois chardonnay. Suzanne had chosen this label because it was the same wine served by the most expensive caterer in town, Touch of Class Catering, whom she would use for the Dogwood Festival party.

Until last year, north Selby's unofficially official Dogwood Festival Party had been thrown by Giles and Georgia Griffin. Old Selby's signature event, it exclusively included everyone who wielded power in town, and this included not only the big bankers and Realtors and business owners and politicians but, by nature, any wealthy family that had bred for three or more generations within the Perry County limits.

When Georgia died of breast cancer in

July, there was a silent scuffling and posturing among the women who fancied themselves as the likely hostess to carry on the torch. Perhaps because he had no legacy of children to leave behind, Boone embraced the Dogwood party as his raison d'être, and he granted Suzanne unbridled purchasing power to groom the candidate, their six-thousand-square-foot, redbrick Georgian Revival home.

Four women who aspired to be the new hostess, including Suzanne, began to drop hints around Sugar Day and in the wallpaper stores and antiques shops of north Selby. In the end, it was Suzanne and Ginny Cuthbert on the jousting field, and it appeared that neither would swerve from the path of the other. Each woman placed strategic calls throughout the day, asking friends their opinions of decorations and invitations and caterers and musicians. Each began first-floor renovations in earnest.

And then, just when an ugly confrontation seemed inevitable and north Selbyites would be forced to declare their loyalty, there came a call from Ginny.

Suzanne, who had not spoken to Ginny since Georgia's funeral, had taken pains to avoid her because she feared comparison with this woman known as the Martha Stewart of Selby. She feared that, should they ever be found standing side by side, those around them could not help but weigh one against the other, and they would remember that Ginny's yard had been featured in that year's Mother's Day Secret Gardens Tour, and that Ginny was the first north Selby woman to use goat cheese in an appetizer dish, and the first to install granite countertops, and the first to put colored marbles (pink for Easter; red and green for Christmas; red, white, and blue for July Fourth) in the bottom of her flower-filled vases. Conversely, they would remember how Suzanne had set out her decorative hay bales and pumpkins too early for Halloween, and that a neighbor anonymously called animal control after spotting two large rats feasting on the rotting, orange flesh a few weeks later.

"Oh, Ginny!" Suzanne exclaimed on the phone. "Where have you been hiding? You been down at Sea Island?" Carrying the cordless phone, Suzanne walked over to the refrigerator and retrieved the wine bottle from the freezer. She preferred her wine ice-cold, and often, before scurrying away to answer the phone or help Josephine or Virgil with a task, she would stow the bottle in the door of the freezer, returning to find it in optimum condition, flecked with tiny shards of ice that would melt on her tongue. Suzanne had developed a habit of pooling the icy liquid around her bad, back right molar, providing three or four seconds of repetitive but tolerable penance for her vice.

"I've just been busy," Ginny said. "I've been doin' some things to my kitchen."

"You're not replacin' those gorgeous countertops, are you?"

"No, no, just puttin' in new flooring."

"You usin' Pergo?"

"Pergo's what I'm gettin' rid of."

Suzanne looked down at the simulated-oak Pergo floor of her own kitchen, just two years old.

"I'm getting one called Zeelis."

"Zeelis?"

"It's from Switzerland. It's like Pergo but nicer."

Suzanne reached for a pen on the counter and spelled out *Z-E-E-L-U-S* on the front page of the Southern Bell phone book.

"Did you hear about Kathy Hollander?" Ginny asked.

"No."

"About the dog?"

With the phone tucked in the crook of her neck, Suzanne carried her wine out to the dining room. She stood in the doorway, looking at her new lamp on the sideboard, a crouching, cloisonné monkey that was holding some kind of red fruit in its hands. She walked over and clicked it on, then stepped back to admire the warm, yellow-beige glow from the rectangular silk shade whose bottom and top edges were outlined in gold leaf.

"Oh my gosh, no," Suzanne said. "What?"

"She was walkin' out to get the mail, and she couldn't open the front door, so she went out through the garage and came up front . . . and you are not gonna believe what she saw."

"What?"

"A dead dog!"

"No!"

"Right there on the porch. Right between those cute rocking chairs she's got. It was Buck, the Matthews' golden retriever."

"I can't believe it," Suzanne said. "That little dog was so cute."

"Just six months old."

"You know, I've seen that little dog in my yard. I just can't believe it."

"That's seven dead dogs now in Red Hill Plantation, Suzanne."

Buck, in fact, had been one of the principal artists in the ever-changing work of art that was the yard of Boone and Suzanne Parley. Suzanne was glad the little mongrel was dead; now maybe her grass could begin to heal from its acidic burns, and Boone would be happy.

"Do you think we should have a meeting at the club?" Suzanne asked.

"The police have been out here, Suzanne. They just don't know what's goin' on."

"The police? Who called the police?"

"I don't know. And Lord knows I don't like what's happening, but I don't have time for anything like that. Not now."

Suzanne bit: "You been busy?"

"You haven't heard my little secret?"

"No."

"I'm pregnant, Suzanne. I'm gonna have a baby!"

"You are kiddin' me!"

"At my age! Can you believe it?"

Suzanne's eyes opened wide, far enough that she was conscious of stretching facial muscles that had long been in hibernation. She immediately remembered to add specially printed coasters to the list for the printer: *Welcome to the Parleys' — One of Selby's Oldest Families and a New Dogwood Tradition.* Or would it all fit? Maybe she would simply put *Parley Dogwood.*

"June twentieth's my due date. Of course I'm gonna have to drop everything to get that nursery ready. There's just no way I can do the fund-raiser dinner for the symphony this year. I can't be hostin' anything, Suzanne."

"Oh, no. I understand."

"I was even playin' around with the idea of havin' the Griffins' Dogwood party, but that's off for sure."

Suzanne almost laughed out loud. Their posturing for the party had been officially clandestine but known to all.

"You know," Suzanne said. "I was thinkin' of havin' that party."

"Then you better get goin'."

"Why?"

"Because that new neighbor of yours from California is fixin' to do the same thing."

"No!"

"Yes!"

"She's not even from Selby!"

"I know, I know. It's so tacky. And can you imagine what her decorations are gonna look like?"

After telling Ginny about the huge, strange painting she'd watched being unloaded outside her new neighbors' house, she got into her Lexus and, after debating for a moment on whether she should go anywhere in this state of drunkenness, she carefully backed out of the garage and drove to the Kroger in south Selby.

Greater Selby (population 146,400) straddles what is known in Georgia as the Fall Line, the spot where the Appalachians finally peter out and the coastal plain begins its long, subtle slope out to the sea. The higher, northern half of the city feels more like foothills, and gardeners need pickaxes to penetrate the compacted, red clay of their backyards. Yet in south Selby, one can effortlessly push a spade into sandy soil that yields an occasional fossilized whale bone, shell, or shark's tooth left over from two million years ago, when the southern half of Selby was ocean floor and the northern half was prime beach-front property. Two lands, two types of people, and Suzanne was one of the few who could claim both sides of town as home.

Home to the Armstrong ceiling-tile factory and the Little Debbie's bakery and Happy's Flea Market, south Selby was segregated from north Selby by Truman Parkway, and the only reason a north Selby woman would venture south of that line was to pick up an aging relative who was afraid of the immensity and mad-ant pace of the Atlanta airport and had hopped one of Delta's shuttle flights that landed four times each day at the Warren "P. J." Reynolds Municipal Airport.

Suzanne was born and raised in south Selby in a house on Kottrell Avenue, where her parents still lived.

Her father, an oven supervisor at Little Debbie's, was the mastermind of a now-famous, two-block Christmas decorating endeavor that pulled visitors from as far away as Birmingham and Jacksonville: a dense, polychromatic milky way of Christmas lights that not only covered every house and tree and chain-link fence but also crisscrossed the street like the laces of a corset. One neighbor had constructed life-size aluminum-foil sculptures of camels, made of an accumulation of the silvery squares from thirty-four years of sandwiches he ate while working the graveyard shift at Armstrong. And each year, on the day after Thanksgiving, Suzanne's uncle Marlen, who lived across the street, would denude his living room and porch of furniture to display his collection of three-hundred-plus mechanical Christmas characters: a Santa checking off his list of good girls and boys, Snoopy striking a hockey puck, carolers in plaid berets who leaned back and forth in unison as they sang "We Wish You a Merry Christmas" — all of the machines humming with electricity and moving in a repetitive, sleepy, predigital manner. For a donation, visitors could tour the Christmas wonderland, and as they milled about, Uncle Marlen, dressed in a Santa suit, sat on a chair in the corner with the beard pulled down, the elastic bands stretching out from the ears as he smoked cigarettes and welcomed guests into his house.

Suzanne was always caught off guard when she walked into this Kroger; it was set up differently, the floor plan inverted. Intending to inquire at the deli, she found herself in the produce section, and because traversing the entire length of the store seemed impossible at this point — she felt light-headed and numb in her fingers and cheeks and above her eyes, and it was already noon, and her breath felt as shallow as a puddle — Suzanne walked up to a young woman who was unloading and stacking lemons. Her name tag said *Donna*.

"Can I help you, ma'am?" she asked.

A beautiful girl, Suzanne thought, and then: What has happened to this poor girl's face?

"I hope so," Suzanne said. "I've got this dish here — it's a casserole — and I need to make one but I don't know what's in it."

Suzanne held it out with two hands, as if it were a present of gold or frankincense, and the young woman took it from her.

"All I need you to do is taste this and tell me what's in it," Suzanne said.

"Ma'am, I don't think I can do that," the girl answered. "I mean I'm just the produce clerk."

"I'll pay you," Suzanne said.

"Ma'am?"

"I'll give you twenty dollars if you tell me what's in this. Please, you've just got to. I don't know what I'm gonna do if I can't make me one of these."

The young woman unsnapped the blue plastic lid and peered inside.

"It's some kind of casserole," Suzanne said.

"Yes, ma'am. You know, you can buy some Hungarian goulash — they make it here in the deli — and sprinkle some breadcrumbs on it. Or you could melt some cheese on top if you want it to look like this. That'd be good."

"I need *this* one!"

The young produce clerk noticed the tears welling in Suzanne's eyes, the tremble of her chin. She reminded her of a child who had just broken her mother's precious vase and was panicked and wanted to set things right, to turn back time, before the mother returned from her errands.

"Are you okay, ma'am?"

Suzanne reached into her Louis Vuitton handbag and pulled out her wallet. "I'll pay you a hundred dollars if you make this casserole for me."

"Ma'am?"

"You can do it at home, I don't care. What time do you get off work?"

"Ma'am, I don't think I can help you."

"What time do you get off?"

"At two, but I don't think . . ."

Suzanne plucked a second hundred from her wallet and held it out.

"I gotta have it by six. Can you do that?"

The young woman looked at the bill. "Ma'am?"

"I need this casserole. I gotta have it to-night. How about a hundred now and a hundred when I pick it up?"

"To make this here casserole?"

"That's right."

131

The young woman held the Tupperware container beneath the lights over the Brussels sprouts. "It's got a pie crust, but I can do that. I make good pies."

"Can you bring it to my house?"

"I might could do that."

"No. I'll come pick it up. Where do you live?"

"Dahlonega Road, down by Happy's Flea Market."

Suzanne fished for and found a pencil and a Pasta To Go receipt in her purse. "Two sixty-five Dahlonega Road," continued the woman, watching Suzanne write it down in tight scribbles. "Little green house with white trim. My daddy's got a Bible message on a big board in the front yard. It's kinda hard to miss."

Suzanne handed her a hundred-dollar bill then turned to walk away.

"I can't accept this much money, ma'am."

"It's worth every penny to me," Suzanne said.

"You want me to bake it, too?"

"I want it all done, everything. Like it's gonna go right on the table."

On the day Suzanne O'Neal married Boone Parley in Tattnall Christ Church on

Cotton Avenue, her father showed up fifteen minutes before the ceremony was to begin. He was wearing one blue sock and one black, with Jack Daniel's and cash register mints on his breath and a speeding ticket poking out of the breast pocket of his tuxedo like a kerchief. His wallet had been emptied, once again, that morning at a roulette wheel in the Creek Indians' Big Peach Casino south of town.

Suzanne, expecting the worst — expecting exactly *this* — intercepted her father at the front door and yanked him by the arm, pulling him into the pastor's study. Her mother, seeing this from the room across the vestibule, followed them inside then shut the heavy walnut door behind them.

Suzanne pushed her father into a wooden chair. Drunk, he fell back easily, and he looked at her, hurt and bewildered. "What's all this about, young lady? You better get to talkin' and you better get to talkin' fast!"

Suzanne bent forward at the waist, got her hands around the base of the veil and came back up, flipping it, like long hair, to the backside of her head. She wanted nothing in the way that would soften or filter her anger.

"No, Daddy," she said. "You listen to me, you sorry, sorry man."

She spoke in a hushed tone, just a few degrees stronger than a whisper, but the words were born from someplace so deep within her that by the time they reached her lips they seemed to pack the power of an untethered, primal scream.

"Look at you! You look like somethin' the cat drug home and the kittens refused. My gosh, Daddy, can't you even shave on your own daughter's wedding day?"

"You got some nerve to —"

"No, you've got the nerve. I can't believe you, I just can't believe you. You know, Daddy, I've been wantin' to say this for a long time, and I'm gonna say it now. You are a worthless man. You are a drunk. You're a gambler —"

"Honey, don't be ugly to your daddy," her mother interrupted.

"You have ruined Momma's life, and you sure as heck have tried to ruin mine, and if I hadn't won the Miss Selby pageant and gotten that scholarship to Athens my life would still be a livin' hell."

"Suzanne, now watch your language," said her mother.

Suzanne jabbed her rigid index finger onto his chest as she spoke. Both her

134

mother and father watched her, wide-eyed with mouths open. "Momma and me are sick (*jab*) and (*jab*) tired (*jab*) of you makin' our lives junky and poor, and I promise to you right now that the rest of Suzanne O'Neal's life is gonna be rich and sweet — I am never gonna eat canned beans again — and if you mess this up for me today I truly think I could find it in my heart to kill you, 'cause you've already just about killed Momma, and you've tried to kill me, but thank the Lord we are both stronger than you."

Suzanne stood up straight again and took two deep breaths to calm down. The veins in her neck twitched and pushed at the surface of her reddened skin.

"Momma," she said, "can you help me with this veil?" Her father sat there, looking at the floor with his shoulders slumped, deflated as a burst balloon.

"Now," Suzanne commanded, "you need to walk me down that aisle without fallin' down . . . if you think you can do that. And then I want you to turn right around and walk right back up that aisle and out that door and I never wanna see you again."

It was five-thirty. Suzanne had half an hour before she was due to pick up the casserole from the pretty girl with the scar on her face. Already in south Selby, she found herself drifting toward her old neighborhood — down Bloomfield Road, left onto Jennifer Drive, right onto Carson Street. The once-familiar homes, most of them single-story ranches, seemed so small to her now.

Suzanne drove by a house where an old woman was rocking on her front porch, and she slowed down to watch. In north Selby, front-porch rocking chairs were ornamental, like stone lions or urns, and in the five years she'd lived in Red Hill Plantation Suzanne had not seen one person use those rockers, always immaculate and painted cruise-ship white.

There was so much to learn in the beginning. (Christmas alone was overwhelming. You had to buy white lights, not multicolored, and you wore a Christmas sweater from Talbots or Neiman Marcus; only south Selby women wore the Yuletide sweatshirts with iron-on appliqués.) Like an immigrant in a new land, Suzanne watched and absorbed, struggling to emulate the north Selby lifestyle and behaviors. People didn't forget where she came from. They didn't ask her "Who are your people?" because they all knew. But as long as Suzanne smiled and sent the right bread-and-butter notes she remained a welcome thread of the tapestry. She was, after all, a Parley.

Still, Suzanne frequently found herself confused. Why could you paint your dining room red but not your car? If gold and diamonds and Rolex were so wonderful then why was it considered tacky to combine all three? And if her mother-in-law stressed that a foyer set the tone for the house then why did she not like Suzanne's Wedgwood, crystal, and gilt-bronze twelve-light chandelier?

Every time she came to visit her mother — and only during the day, when her father was at Little Debbie's — Suzanne was surprised at how people left things out for the world to see and judge. Wet clothes lay over porch railings to dry. Dead appliances sat outside the garages, as if they'd been granted some leisure time in the sunshine after all those years of toiling in a dark corner of the basement. Children's toys — bicycles and bright pink balls and Tonka trucks and forts made of cardboard boxes — were not seen as junk to be hidden out of sight. Suzanne remembered the saw-horses her mother kept on the driveway for her painting projects, and how she pretended they were balance beams after watching Mary Lou Retton in the Olympics on TV.

Finally, she pulled up to the curb in front of her house. No one was home; her mother was probably delivering one of her wedding cakes. Suzanne noticed that another of the green shutters — there was just one left — had fallen from the house and lay on the ground in the untamed ivy that had been allowed to roam free in the front yard. Like water flooding a room, it had run across and smothered much of the grass and, now out of room, had begun to rise, scaling the walls of the house and every tree in the front yard.

"I hope it eats that house up," Suzanne said to herself.

After sitting in the car for a few minutes, Suzanne decided to walk around the side of the house, to the backyard. The tractor tire was still there, standing on end and half buried so it rose then returned to the ground like some junkyard rainbow. Suzanne remembered standing and hiding in here; if you squeezed inside and made your body follow the contours of the tire, arms over your head as if you were flying like Superman, you could elude any grown-up for hours. This was Suzanne's refuge when her father would come home on a rampage after losing his week's wages in a poker game.

Someone, probably her mother, had pierced the inside edge of the tire and hung plastic pots of petunias and geraniums. Plastic — it seemed so foreign. She thought of the clay pots and concrete statues of her own life. The glass measuring cups and mixing bowls. Steel flashlights. Sterling-silver goblets. Why was everything so heavy now? When had she stopped using plastic? How could something so much lighter and easier be considered tacky? Suzanne nudged one of the hanging plants and watched it swing like the pendulum of a clock: *Plas-tic. Plas-tic. Plas-tic. Plas-tic.*

She unhooked two of the plants and set them on the dirt. Bending forward, Suzanne then backed into the tire, one buttock at a time, chafing the rim, leaving black smudges on each side of her pale-yellow linen dress. Once inside, eyes closed, she became aware of her breathing and the beating of the blood in her ears. The tire had absorbed the day's sun, and Suzanne found comfort in the warmth of the rubber that now hugged her.

Ten

Dear Chatter: Whoever changed the Selby Mall to no-smoking has sand for brains. I'm not going anymore. I'll spend all my money at the flea market instead.

Dear Chatter: The reason there are so many wrong-number phone calls in Selby is because everyone's fingers are so fat from all the greasy food. That's the problem.

Dear Chatter: What are cheese straws? Translation, please.

It had rained earlier in the hour, and as Randy and Margaret emerged from the air-conditioned lobby of the *Reflector*, they saw steam lazily rising from the asphalt of Cotton Avenue. Margaret quickly remembered a call she'd received in Chatter, from some man who truly had too much to say, too many voices in his head wanting to be heard. In between snippets about smothered pork chops and ATM user fees and the new no-smoking policy at Selby Mall, he managed to drop in an exquisite line explaining how steam was the spirit of dead rainwater, rising up to its home in heaven. Margaret was so excited about this revelation that she quickly pulled off her headset and placed it on Harriet's head, accidentally denting her silver beehive. Harriet politely listened, smiled, said "Well, isn't that nice?" and then quickly disappeared into the ladies' room for fifteen minutes.

Randy reached into the breast pocket of his navy blue blazer and pulled out a pair of gray titanium, aerodynamic Oakley sunglasses, which he put on as they crossed the street. Margaret thought they made him look like an insect.

"Jesus! This humidity! Look at my glasses — it looks like I'm in a fucking sauna."

Margaret internally flinched. Seven months of residing in Selby had already eclipsed twenty-eight years of living with Ruth Pinaldi — her ears were now sensitized to such language. For the most part, all four-letter words used to denote body parts or human waste were absent from the aural landscape of middle Georgia, and hell was verboten because it was a true place and destination people feared. Locals frowned upon damn because it was a root word from the Bible. In fact, Margaret had learned that the word *damnation* occurred eleven times within this book whose thick yet floppy composition reminded her of a raw porterhouse steak.

Shortly after moving to Selby, Margaret bought her first Bible at the New Way Christian Books and Music next to Kroger, where she found twenty-three varieties to choose from, including a downloadable version for Palm Pilots and a liberally abridged Bible for children with attention deficit disorder. Margaret selected a cheaper, burgundy, faux-leather, New International Edition from Dentwirth and Sons Publishing in Grand Rapids, Michigan, and took it to the checkout counter. A twenty-something woman in braces was reading a comic book titled *The Rapture*, whose Roy Lichtenstein–like cover showed jumbo jets falling from the sky and exploding into fireballs on downtown streets full of screaming people.

"Do you want a concordance with that, ma'am?" she asked.

"A concordance?" Margaret asked. "I don't know what that is."

"You . . . uh . . . you don't know what a

concordance is? What do you use in Sunday school?"

"I don't go to Sunday school."

For a few moments, the woman looked into Margaret's eyes with an empathetic, solemn expression, as if someone with a horrible secret had just confided in her.

"Well, but you're startin' now, and that's what counts," she said. "You know I met a man in here the other day who didn't find Jesus till he was sixty-nine. A concordance is a reference book. Tells you everything that's in the Bible."

"Can you show me one?" Margaret asked.

She disappeared between two aisles of books and returned with the cornflower blue, two-inch-thick *New Strong's Concise Concordance of the Bible*. Margaret thumbed through it and was immediately pleased with this discovery: Some patient, fastidious man named James Strong had dissected and cross-referenced by key word all seven hundred plus pages of the Holy Bible! According to Mr. Strong, palm trees were mentioned thirty-five times. Human feet, ninety-two! Foreskins, a mere five. Scabs, seven. Righteousness, two hundred and twenty-six. Horses outranked dogs, forty-three to fifteen. And, curiously, the number six was mentioned one hundred ninety-one times.

Margaret had learned there were two things that Southerners sprinkled over much of their daily lives — sugar and church — and she wondered if these ingredients were what made this culture so gentle. Margaret could always tell the newer Yankee transplants in Chatter calls not only by accent but also by the delivery of their censure. A Yankee would call someone a fat slob. A Selbyite would say, "Now there's a lady who likes her cheese straws and biscuits."

Sharing foul, aggressive language in Selby was no different from lighting up a cigarette in a vegetarian restaurant; in their respective cultures, both acts released fleeting but potent environmental toxins that left a lingering unpleasantness.

"You really shouldn't talk like that, Randy," Margaret said. "It's not acceptable here."

"Okay, then, how's this: Well, bless her heart."

"That's better."

"Do you even know what it means?"

Margaret shook her head.

"It means 'she's a bitch and I don't like her and I'm fixin' to say something ugly about her.' "

"Have I complimented you yet today on your translation skills?"

"No, really. It's like this: Well bless her heart, she's got the fattest ass on the planet and her taste is all in her mouth, but she does the best she can."

"Where are we eating?" she asked him.

"The Forsyth Room. You been?"

"Are you kidding me? On my salary?"

"I got the membership as a bennie with the job. It was that or a golf club membership, and I'm not fat enough to play golf in Selby, Georgia."

"I've heard the grumbling in Chatter about the new chef," Margaret said.

"Oh, he won't last long," Randy replied. "He's raising absolute hell with the natives, but his food is unbelievable." He walked five more paces before adding, "Dixie meets Napa Valley."

The Forsyth Room was a private club with a facade of ionic columns in front, tastefully worn Persian rugs in the elevators, and a ladies' lounge with a tapestry-covered Chippendale sofa. Since 1923 the club had served lunch to the business elite of Selby, and though women were allowed as guests of their men, they could not become members. Then, in 1993, Georgia's new assistant state attorney, Pat Reinhold, received in the mail an invitation for "A Social Gathering of Men," which was the Forsyth Room's annual Christmastime, male-only eggnog party for the power brokers of Georgia. Unfortunately for members, the Forsyth Room's new (and now former) secretary that year, Jennifer Hebovsky, was not a regular follower of current events, and she did not know that five years earlier Ms. Reinhold had made history by successfully suing the University of Georgia for the right to participate on the Bulldog crew team.

With invitation in hand, Pat Reinhold drove down to Selby for the party, accompanied by Marvin Cornish, the Atlanta correspondent for National Public Radio. Cornish recorded an impressive verbal tussle between the six-foot-tall Reinhold and a diminutive Sigmund Rollie, the chairman of the board of trustees, who, earlier that morning, as he did every year, personally delivered porcelain cups of eggnog to every powerful woman in middle Georgia so they would not feel excluded from the fellowship.

Yet the dinner club's biggest changes and challenges were to follow. The principal investor died shortly after Toyota came to town, and his children, all of whom had severed their Dixie roots and lived in Connecticut, sold the Forsyth Room to TasteMark, Inc., of Charlotte, North Carolina. (A Chatter caller had begged, "Couldn't they at least sell it to someone from South Carolina?")

The new chef, snagged from the Ritz-Carlton in Laguna Beach, had made a name for himself in Latin-Asian fusion, and upon his arrival in Selby began integrating Southern ingredients into his repertoire, casting grits and collards in what some locals considered to be undignified roles.

"The catfish in the ginger glaze is incredible," Randy said. "He puts it on a bed of wasabi grits."

Though he was speaking to Margaret, Randy had been watching and eavesdropping on the two couples dining a few tables to the south. They had ordered iced teas, and the waiter had just set down four glasses of what was now the restaurant's house tea, an unsweetened, lychee-flavored oolong served with a stalk of lemon grass.

"What *is* this?" asked one of the women. She pulled the lemon grass from the glass and held it up to her nose. "You think it's sugarcane?"

"No, darlin', sugarcane's brown."

"Could be baby sugarcane."

The second woman took a drink: "There is *no* sugar in this tea! Do y'all think they forgot?"

"Smells like Lemon Pledge."

"The new cook's an Oriental," said the other man.

"Oriental?" asked the woman.

"Is this Oriental tea?"

"I don't know, darlin'. I just know it's not sweet tea."

"I expect this in Atlanta, but things are gettin' bad when you can't get a glass of sweet tea in Selby."

"Maybe they think you're sweet enough, Sugar."

Randy quickly pulled from his pocket the small spiral notebook and Mont Blanc pen, and he began to quickly scribble down the dialogue. "Sometimes I just can't believe I'm hearing the shit I hear."

The waitress came to take their drink orders.

"Do you like olives?" Randy asked Margaret, who nodded.

"Gin?"

Before she could respond, Randy said to the waitress, "We'll have two dirty martinis."

"I don't think I like martinis," Margaret said.

He waved the waitress away with an impatient fluttering of his fingers. "Have you ever had one?" he asked.

The answer was no. A size four, Margaret had a metabolism she once compared to a child's pinwheel; one glass of wine provided enough breeze to send it merrily spinning in the sun. She could not imagine the effect of the gale-force winds from an all-gin drink.

"You're done for the day, right?" he asked. "I am, too. I told Pearline to call me if she needs me."

The martinis arrived, clouded with olive juice and laced with ice crystals.

"I had someone ask me again today if I'd found a church yet — for the millionth time," Randy said.

"So have you?" Margaret asked.

"Ha!"

"I've been to a few churches."

"No way. Why?"

"How can you live here and not be curious about church?"

Margaret shared her stories about her visits to both white and black churches. She mused that the latter tended to be less up-tight and infinitely more stylish with a stronger emphasis on fashion than architecture. She recalled a women's choir dressed in asymmetrical, off-shoulder, gray silk dresses. She described heads wrapped in turbans the colors of turquoise and fuchsia and lemon yellow and orange, often paired with a gown that unpredictably swirled like a vortex around the torso. The men wore tailored suits that fit like driving gloves and dress shirts of colors and patterns that Margaret had not seen in the white-world retail landscape.

Next came the Helen Brown Baptist Church on Tifton Road. Drawn by its personal, intimate name, she was surprised to find a mammoth four-story structure that looked like a convention-destination Holiday Inn with a steeple glued on top. They strategically built the church near an undeveloped exit of I-75, and a computerized marquee with rolling blood-red letters pulled potential worshipers off the freeway.

Got God? Come in for breakfast and daily morning worship! ONSITE day care and dry-cleaning drop-off! We will shine your shoes while you shine with the Lord.

Inside, Margaret found an imposing circular information desk like those in the baggage claim areas of large airports. The greeters, all of them sitting before computer terminals, wore matching lavender polo shirts and cordless headsets like the ones on salesclerks at Old Navy.

On her way to the sanctuary, Margaret passed four nurseries with large windows. In one she counted sixteen rocking chairs all in a row, each of them occupied with a woman snuggling a worshiper's baby.

Margaret was late, and they had run out of bulletins, so a kindly usher gave her his. "Now this has some things on it that you don't need to pay no attention to," he said, "but it'll let you know what's goin' on. Welcome to Helen Brown."

Margaret noticed that the previous week's offering and tithing amounted to $67,466.87. She also noted a disclaimer on the bottom of page eight: *Ushers, this is only a guideline, not a program. The HOLY SPIRIT is in charge — be prepared to change gears!! You NEVER KNOW!!!!*

The sanctuary held eighteen hundred people, a half-scale orchestra, and two choirs whose lavender robes matched the upholstered pews. Hymnals were not necessary because of two minivan-size screens up high on the walls that showed inspirational photographs of landscapes when they were not providing lyrics, which were delivered with help from a bouncing white ball, à la "The Mickey Mouse Club," guiding worshipers syllable by syllable through the songs.

Midway through the service, the lights in the sanctuary dimmed, and behind the minister, a hundred feet up, near the ceiling, curtains parted to reveal a secret room behind a wall of glass. Two women in white terry-cloth bathrobes took turns being guided into a white Lucite chair and dipped backward for full top-body immersion in what looked like an extra-large shampooing sink from a beauty salon. Margaret was surprised at how clinical and unemotional it was. Each woman leaned back for a second, into the water, then perfunctorily sat upright again, where an assistant quickly wrapped her head in a white towel to help each woman avoid getting any wetter, as if there was something wrong with the water and they had to minimize exposure.

Margaret compared the experience to a baptism she'd witnessed the previous week at a smaller, all-black church south of downtown. There, after an African American woman was submerged, she stood before the congregation, dripping wet in her metallic, kelly green dress, and after wringing out her long hair as if it were a sopping towel, she leaned back and thrust her arms into the air and screamed "I'm here, Jesus — and I'm yours!" And then, as the standing congregation clapped and swayed with the music from the choir, she hugged the minister, turning his black suit even blacker, and then walked out into the congregation, where she hugged her children and her husband, all the while leaving a trail of holy water in her wake. Margaret had never been baptized, but she decided then that if she were going to be, it would happen at a black church where they did not worry about getting the carpet wet.

Randy caught the waitress's attention. "Two more martinis, please," he said. Already, Margaret's head had begun to slowly spiral like an emerging whirlpool, and she began to drink water in hopes of slowing it down. She promised herself not to finish the second cocktail.

"I want to talk about your work at the *Reflector*," Randy said. "You know what I think of your work. I think it's brilliant."

"I transcribe people's thoughts, Randy. They are the authors. I'm just the secretary."

"No," he said, shaking his head. "You

can't get away with that, Margaret. You have an ear for voice and an eye for irony. Those inane ramblings are strategically, artistically strung together. And I want you to try some other things." Randy sipped his martini. "I want you to do some writing of your own . . . with a byline, of course."

"I'm not trained for it."

"My undergrad was in English and anthropology," he said. "My master's psychology. You're more qualified than most of those stupid people I've inherited in my newsroom."

"I like the anonymity of Chatter," Margaret said.

"But you're wasting your talent. I'm just asking for a few profiles."

"I don't think so," Margaret said.

"I'm thinking of a series that has your name all over it. Profiles of the storybook, quintessential Southern characters — the endangered species of the Middle Georgia ecosystem."

"I don't know, Randy."

Suddenly, one of the women from the table they'd been eavesdropping on bumped into, then slid against the back of Randy's head. She wore a pale yellow cocktail dress, a large diamond ring, and a triple-strand choker of pearls that reminded Margaret of a dog collar.

"I'm so sorry, 'scuse me. I was just tryin' to take a shortcut to the ladies' room."

She looked at Randy, then at Margaret.

"I think I know you, don't I?" she asked her.

"I don't think so," Margaret answered.

"Are you sure?" she asked. "Don't you work at Silk Flower Warehouse?"

"I work at the *Reflector*."

"Oh! Are you a writer?"

"Yes," Randy interrupted. "She's a writer. A fabulous writer."

"Oh, I just love writers 'cause they're so interested in people, and I never finished school but I've been fixin' to go back for a long time to get me an interior decoratin' degree."

She was drunk, and as her brown eyes locked onto Margaret's with vigor she fell into the chair beside her, and the words, never stopping, began to flow from her mouth like water running down a playground slide. "Let me tell you that bartender over there with the muscles out to here he stopped me and said I looked like one of Charlie's Angels and I thought that was really sweet to say and he said I was about the prettiest lady he'd seen in here for a long time and I had to tell him I'm a married woman and that's my husband sittin' right over there."

From the corner of her eye, Margaret saw one of the men at the table, shooting quick, inquisitive glances toward them while pretending to listen to his friends.

"Did y'all order the tea tonight? That's what you should write a story about is that tea. It's got a little stick in it and it looks like the bamboo on the wallpaper in one of my bathrooms, and I just can't believe they don't have sweet tea anymore."

Suddenly, the woman stopped talking and took a deep breath with eyes closed, as if she were meditating. Her tongue glided across orthodontically straightened teeth. She then leaned sideways, toward Randy, with eyes partly closed, and just when it appeared that she was going to pass out on his shoulder, she reversed direction and weaved the other way, then back and forth again, drunkenly but gracefully and with a rhythm, as if she were remembering a love song from her past. Margaret looked at Randy. He shrugged his shoulders.

"Suzanne? Sweetheart?"

The man from the table had walked up behind them. "I was wonderin' where you went to," he said. "Come on back to the table, honey, we're missin' you."

She opened her eyes and looked at him. Saying nothing, she reached into her purse and pulled out a tube of Bermuda Sunset lipstick, which she twisted open and applied with a look of childlike concentration. When she finished there was a light blip of red that escaped the clean boundary of her top lip, reminding Margaret of the messy, northeast corner of Kansas on a map.

"I'm gonna have a baby," she said, looking at Margaret.

"Suzanne?" the man said. "Honey?"

She then looked up him. "I said, Boone, 'I'm gonna have a baby.' "

"Darlin', you've had a little too much to drink. 'Scuse us, please," he said to Margaret and Randy. "Y'all have been too kind. Come on now."

"In July," she said. "July fourteenth."

First, thinking he hadn't heard her correctly, he lowered his eyebrows and pushed his chin forward a few inches. When his wife nodded, the look of agitation and puzzlement melted into one of surprise, and Margaret suddenly detected a quick, inexplicable change in his attitude toward this woman. Gently taking her arm, he helped her to her feet then guided her back to the table, his manicured thumb caressing a spot on her lower back.

"But how can that be, Suzanne?" he whispered to her.

"I was fixin' to tell you, Boone — I had an operation. It's a surprise."

"But your doctor said it couldn't be done."

"I found me a new doctor."

"Who?"

"One in Atlanta."

"When did you do this?"

Pausing for a moment, she finally said, "Last year. When I said I was goin' down to St. Simon's with John David for that antiques show. That's when I did it."

"And you're really pregnant?"

"Why won't you believe me?"

After seating her, he took away her half-empty glass of chardonnay and ordered a cup of coffee. Margaret noticed that the ice had melted in the four glasses of untouched lychee tea.

Randy pushed a fork into his guava cobbler. "Do you think it's something in the air?" he asked Margaret. "Do you think it comes from a lifetime of breathing in that acrid smell of the paper mill? I don't know how much more weirdness I can absorb."

Randy dropped Margaret off at the *Re-*

flector to get her car, and as she emerged from his BMW she saw, leaning against the building with his hands in his pockets, Dewayne.

Somewhat self-conscious because of her martini buzz, Margaret began walking toward him, and as she grew nearer he pushed himself away from the tan-brick wall and brought his hands behind his back, locking his fingers.

"Miss Margaret?" he said, nodding his head. He wore a white shirt and a too-short, blue-and-white striped tie that sloped down and outward, over his belly like a ski jump.

"Hello," she said.

"Ma'am."

"Have you been waiting for me?"

"I have."

"How'd you know where to find me?"

"Oh, I know a lotta people who know a lotta people."

"That sure makes me comfortable," Margaret deadpanned, repositioning the strap of her purse on her shoulder. Reminiscent of Indian moccasins, it was a tan, leather child's purse with fringe made of turquoise beads, which she had bought at the Salvation Army thrift store on Anthony Road.

Dewayne looked over Margaret's shoulder, toward the street, as Randy's car suddenly sped away. After disgorging Margaret, it had idled there in the middle of Cotton Avenue, the driver hiding behind dark green, tinted windows as he watched the two of them converse.

"I haven't seen you at Waffle House lately," she said.

"I've been workin' at the station down on Houston Road. They're short-staffed this month. Some guys got called out on reserve."

"Where do you usually work?"

"In the north Selby station. Right there on Vineville."

As he talked about his work, Margaret snatched glances at his body — arms, shoulders, his neck and lips — whenever his eyes would look upward or sideways or down for a second or two, and this did not give her much opportunity because he stared at Margaret in the eyes more than anyone she could remember, other than a salesperson or pro-lifer, and it made her feel simultaneously vulnerable and treasured. He was so reverential and polite and unthreatening, the way he kept his voice soft and arms behind his back.

"So I was wonderin'," he said. "Would

you like to go out with me?"

"Oh, I don't know," Margaret said.

"You don't know?"

"I mean I don't know what to say."

"How about yes?"

"I just don't go out on dates," Margaret said. "I just never have. It's just . . . something I don't do."

"Well, if it makes you feel any better, I don't do this much either."

"Why not?"

He shrugged his shoulders. "Shy, I guess. So don't make me beg like a dog here. How about you let me take you out for a nice meal. I mean, I'd pay for it and everything."

Margaret laughed. "How old are you?" she asked.

"Twenty-four."

"I'm four years older."

"Is that a problem?"

Her defenses and verbal skills somewhat numbed by two martinis, she sighed in resignation, took a pen and Kroger receipt from her purse, and scribbled down her phone number.

"Don't be expecting some experienced older woman."

"Ma'am?"

"You're going to be disappointed," she

said. "I'm sure we have nothing in common."

"Do you like to eat?"

"Yes."

"Then we'll do just fine."

Once inside the building, she watched him through the window as he crossed the street and climbed into a clean, blue Ford pickup. Never in her life had Margaret imagined she would be going on a date with someone who drove a pickup. She wondered if it had bucket seats and what kind of stations were programmed on the radio. And why did they call them pickup trucks?

Too drunk to drive home just yet, Margaret walked upstairs, into the newsroom, to get some coffee and sit awhile at her desk. She noticed her voice mail light blinking and slipped on her headset to listen to her messages.

There was only one: "Miss Pinaldi," said the voice, mispronouncing the first syllable like the ubiquitous conifer that lined every highway in Georgia. "This is Lieutenant Nordy Thorpman of the Perry County Sheriff's Department. Could you please call me back? I've got somethin' I need to talk to you about."

Eleven

Dear Chatter: I just called my bank, Selby First Federal, and I had to talk to a computer voice. I say no thanks to that. I want hometown service, and I'm takin' my money out of there and into a bank where the president is right here in Selby and not in some place up north like Charlotte.

Dear Chatter: Why should I care about what's going on in the public schools? Maybe you didn't know it but thirty percent of the kids in Selby go to private school. So I say bring back the society page and don't waste that newspaper space on school news because most of those people can't even read. Thank you.

Arms akimbo, Donna stood on the loading dock behind Kroger, looking at the seven-foot stack of crated South American bing cherries that would prove to be her challenge of the day.

Donna looked over at the truck driver, perched upon the seat of the yellow fork-lift. "What am I gonna do with all of these?" she yelled over the sputtering and revving of the piston engine and rhythmic beeping of a service vehicle in reverse.

"Eat 'em!" he yelled in return, smiling, and then he shifted into forward and dis-appeared into the dark, aluminum cave of the truck. With his square jaw, blond flattop, and tanned arms attached to lean torso, he reminded Donna of her cousin Ricky. Donna liked watching how confi-dent he was with the lift, as if it were an appendage of his own body, zipping back and forth with the speed of a carnival bumper car, often coming within inches of the concrete edge of the dock.

"Very funny," she yelled. "I'm dyin' laughin' over here."

Donna looked down at the clipboard in her hand. At first she'd blamed the supply boys in Atlanta for misreading her fax as they had done with the Granny Smiths and tangelos, but after scrutinizing her hand-written order, Donna admitted to herself that her ambitiously curvaceous threes did somewhat resemble eights. Mr. Tom would not be happy. He'd warned her twice to slow down when filling out her orders.

And, to make matters worse, this came one week after she'd injured a customer.

Needing New Mexican chilis for a casserole but realizing Kroger was out of them, a middle-aged woman asked Donna if she could use habaneros as a substitute. Busy with a box of Swiss chard, Donna didn't want to take the time to consult her book or the corporate website, and she said, "Oh, no that's fine. They all taste the same."

Two days later, Mr. Tom, looking very serious in the face, appeared in the break room where Donna was snacking on a bag of barbecue-flavor Lays and Diet Coke. Laying in his hands, open like a large Bible, was the store's sole copy of the four-inch-thick, three-ring *Kroger, Inc., Guide to Produce Care, Display and Marketing.*

"Donna," he said, "did you recommend habaneros in place of New Mexican chilis the other day?"

"I'm not sure, Mr. Tom. I might have. These customers are always botherin' me about somethin'."

"The customers never bother you, Donna. They may distract you at times but they never bother you. It's your job to answer questions."

"Yes, sir. That's what I meant to say."

He laid the produce manual on the table before her and pointed to a Scoville-unit chart, which ranked the heat of twenty-two peppers from first to last.

"You see where New Mexicans are?" he asked.

"Yes, sir. Nineteen."

"Now look at number one."

Donna's eyes grew wide. She gasped. "Oh, Mr. Tom!"

"Hottest pepper on the planet," he said. "And our customer, Mrs. Thornley . . . she asked her husband to help cut these chilis . . . and he did . . . and then he did the unfortunate thing of going to the bathroom without washing his hands."

"Mr. Tom! Oh, no!"

"They went to the emergency room, Donna. The man panicked because he had blisters on his penis."

"Oh! Mr. Tom! Oh, my Lord! I am so sorry!"

"Don't tell me you're sorry. I want you to call the Thornleys and apologize."

"Yes, sir. Yes, sir, I will."

"And then I want you to read the section on Scoville rankings. Okay?"

"Yes, sir."

"And Donna. I know you're mad at the world right now. But you've got to be a professional and rise above all your troubles and do the very best you can. And please remember: What people eat can make a huge difference in how they feel and live. That's a big responsibility, and I don't want people on board who accept it lightly. Understand?"

Donna looked at the surfeit of cherries on the loading dock and realized she had to act quickly or risk losing her job, which didn't sound too bad at the moment except she knew she'd have to go home and tell her father.

"Well," she said to herself. "I suppose this is God's will. And if this is a test, I'm gonna pass it."

A fruit or vegetable's march to death begins at the moment of harvest, and Donna was amazed at the disparity of life spans among picked produce. Unchilled citrus could last three weeks, but in two days' time a peach could turn from firm, blushing maiden into a dying, overripe crone with oozing bedsores.

Misting the cherries would not help; though their skin appeared to be impermeable as Scotch tape, they actually absorbed water, which hastened their rotting. Donna knew the best thing she could do was wrap them tightly in cellophane.

That Friday would be Valentine's Day, and Donna decided to cut green foam produce trays into the shape of hearts, fill them with cherries, then finish it up with a good, tight shrink-wrapping and contrasting white bow around the middle. Today was Tuesday, so she would be sure to include only cherries with stems because they had a longer shelf life than those without.

After getting permission from Connie, the front-end manager, she set up a display just inside the entrance to the store, in place of the giant foam football and Astroturf the Frito-Lay vendor had erected for the Orange Bowl. With the grocery markers, Donna made the sign herself: *"If you really love her, you'll give her these. Cherries — the heart-healthy valentine that will help her last FOREVER!"* The letters were black, except for the dots of the I's, which Donna made into oversized red cherries with happy faces.

The first thirty-six hearts flew out of the store by noon, and Donna hurriedly constructed another twenty-five, which were gone by three-thirty. Mr. Tom asked her to write up a merchandising diagram so he could fax the idea to the regional corporate office in Atlanta.

"Best Valentine's promotion I've ever seen," he said.

"Thank you!"

"And take a picture with the digital camera. We'll send that as well."

"But I've got some russets to stack."

"I need it by the time you go home tonight."

"Yes, sir."

Donna used to think new potatoes, with their clean, pinkish skins the color of a newborn baby, were the most beautiful variety, but lately she had been favoring the more weathered-looking russets. Just as someone could find pictures of objects in the clouds, to pass the time Donna found herself looking for shapes in the random, brown splotches left behind from a lifetime in the dirt. Unloading them two by two, she saw an . . .

Alligator . . . . Which reminded Donna that she needed a new purse. She'd not been shopping at the mall since her car accident, and Jackee accused her of avoiding the Lancôme counter, which had been taken over by Nadine Simmons. Donna had hired and almost fired Nadine because she did not understand eye shadow — she swore the girl was color blind — so Lord knew why they would promote her to such an important position.

The state of Michigan . . . or was it Wisconsin? . . . Whichever state it was that looked like a mitten. Donna remembered the puzzle of the United States she found with her mother at a garage sale when she was nine. She was drawn to it after hearing a grandma tell her little boy, "It don't have all the pieces, honey, it's no good." Donna walked up to the wooden puzzle and noticed the brown gap that should have been a yellow Alabama. She talked the owner into giving it to her for a dime because it was not whole, and Donna took it home, where she scraped up some red clay from beneath the magnolia tree, wetted it, patted it into a pancake, and pushed it on top of the void. With a butter knife, Donna cut out a replacement that fit perfectly, and after drying it in the sun she colored it yellow with the acrylic paints her mother used to personalize welcome mats with an airbrush gun at a booth in Happy's Flea Market. When she showed her mother, Doris Kabel kissed her daughter on the forehead and said, "Darlin', you will never go hungry in this world." Donna wondered now where her mother had put that puzzle.

Suddenly, Donna was yanked from her mental ramblings by something she pulled from the box. Not quite believing her eyes, she turned the potato over and over again in her hands.

"Oh, my gosh!" Donna whispered. "Would you look at this?"

Just as she said "this," the fake lightning and thunder tied to the timed produce sprayer came on. There was a flash, boom, rumble, spray. Donna got goose bumps, and she reached for the phone and dialed pound-fifty-five, the page for Mr. Tom.

Holding a large eggplant in his good hand, Adrian Braswell walked up to Donna.

"My Lord," he exclaimed. "Miss Donna, look what you got in your hand!"

"Can you believe this?"

Mr. Tom came hustling up aisle twelve, his keys jangling on his belt.

"What is it, Donna? Is something wrong?"

Donna noted that his breathing was labored. She estimated he'd gained at least seven pounds since moving to Selby, and he was already ten pounds overweight before that. More than once she'd thought of advising him against his frequent Kit Kat snacks and all the processed meat in his daily Genoa Italian deluxe sub from the deli.

"Mr. Tom, I'm sorry, but I was unloadin' these russets and look what I found."

He took it from her and rolled it over and over in his hands, the way a child quickly scans a baseball for an autograph.

"Wow," he said.

"Isn't that cute?"

"I've never seen anything like this, Donna. A red potato, sure. They mutate into some very strange shapes . . . but a russet!"

"That's what I was thinkin'," Donna said.

It was the perfect shape of a heart, not a human heart but a cartoon-land heart. Symmetrical with a perfect cleavage at the top, it required no imagination.

"You know what we're gonna do?" Mr. Tom asked.

"Sir?"

"We're going to call Channel Twelve."

"You think they'd really be interested in somethin' like this?"

"This is Selby, Donna," he answered. "Last night's news had a feature about some guy who decorates folding chairs with ribbons and bows."

Donna was surprised at how short Stephanie Reno was, and now she knew why they never showed her legs on Live at Five; her calves were beefy and round and grandmotherly like Hillary Clinton's.

"Are you ready?" she asked Mr. Tom.

"No, no," he protested, his hands going up. "Not me. It was her. She found it." He pointed to Donna.

"Oh, no, Mr. Tom, I can't do that."

"Oh, yes you can."

"Mr. Tom . . ."

"I'm the boss, Donna. It's your find. Now go claim your fame."

Donna groaned. "Can't I go freshen up? I look like I've been playin' in a sandbox."

"You look fine."

Stephanie turned toward her. Donna thought she was even more beautiful than on television, and her makeup was done well, not too much on the lower lids, and just a tiny bit on the outside corners. It looked like Estée Lauder, though she couldn't be certain.

"I'm Stephanie Reno," she said to Donna, thrusting out her hand.

"Donna Kabel. Nice to meet you."

Stephanie was less than discreet about looking at Donna's scar. She seemed to even lean a little to the right to see if she was missing anything, and it caused Donna to look down at her white canvas Nikes, which she really hadn't noticed for weeks, though they were the only pair of shoes she wore now. Like the purse, they needed replacing or, at the very least, to be washed. The right shoe looked as if she'd spent the morning working in E.R. surgery thanks to an avalanche of overripe raspberries that morning.

Donna then noticed Stephanie's dark-brown sandals with two-inch heels, very similar to a pair she used to wear at Lancôme. She took pleasure in realizing that her size-eight double-As were much prettier than Stephanie's feet, whose second toes were slightly longer than the big toes, like her father's and those of the chimpanzees she remembered from a sixth-grade field trip to the Atlanta zoo.

"Okay," Stephanie said. "I'll stand on her right, so we can get a good profile shot of her left. Got it, Billy? The left side?"

"Got it."

"Only the left side."

"Yes, ma'am."

"This is gonna be fast and easy," Stephanie said.

The light atop the camera popped on, and Stephanie brought the mike to her mouth.

"Donna Kabel was looking for love in all

the right places this afternoon when she noticed something unusual in her pile of potatoes."

The camera zoomed in on Donna's hands. She had not painted her nails in weeks, and now she wished she had. A deep-red tone would have contrasted nicely with the earthy tans and browns of the potato, and it would have added to that overall Valentine's Day feeling.

"What do you think of this, Donna? It is kind of strange, isn't it?"

The white lights felt hot, like the heat that rises from a glowing toaster. The sensation thrust Donna back to her senior year, when she was crowned International Dogwood Festival Queen. "Oh, yes, ma'am," she answered. "Russets are very predictable. Like my boss Mr. Tom was sayin' to me, if there's an unusual potato it's more likely gonna be a new potato — that's a red potato — but this is really strange for a russet."

"Don't you think the timing of this is interesting?" Stephanie asked. "I mean, Friday is Valentine's Day."

"Yes, ma'am."

"Do you think this is someone's idea of a joke? Maybe a secret admirer of yours?"

Donna looked down at her hands, which

she'd been tightly, nervously cupping as if the potato were water that could escape. She quickly flattened them, splaying her fingers, then slowly rocked them at the speed of a languid, hanging mobile, back and forth, the way the models did on Home Shopping Network or QVC when displaying a ruby necklace.

"Now you tell me how someone could make somethin' like this."

"Well, it certainly does look real!"

"It is real."

"Yes . . . well . . . Are you single, Donna?"

"Ma'am?"

"Are you married?"

"Oh, no, ma'am."

"Well maybe this is a sign. Maybe, Donna Kabel, this is your lucky day! From the Kroger on Truman Parkway, where Cupid — or somebody, anyway — seems to be mixing magical passion with the produce, this is Stephanie Reno."

The cameraman cut off the light, and Donna's world instantly grew again to its normal size. Rhonda from floral came forward with a holder she'd fashioned from a plastic rotisserie-chicken dish from deli, and she invited Donna to lay the potato down upon the nest of cut-up baby's breath surrounded by daisies and roses. Donna thanked her, even though she thought it looked too much like a casket.

After escorting the TV crew to the door, Mr. Tom returned to the produce section. "We'll need to keep it out," he said. "People will want to see it. How about up front with the cherry hearts?"

"I've got a better idea, Mr. Tom," Donna answered. "Wouldn't it be better if we put a sign at the front of the store, invitin' people to come back to see it in the produce section? I mean, that way we'd get them back there and there'd be a chance they might buy somethin' else. I'll get some potato recipes off the corporate website, ones that have lots of other vegetable ingredients, and then we can sell those, too."

Mr. Tom put his hands on his hips and smiled, revealing the nickel-thick gap in his two front teeth that reminded Donna of David Letterman. "You're right, Donna," he said. "That makes a lot more sense."

"Thank you, sir."

"Thank you, *Tom*," he corrected.

"Mr. Tom," she said.

After things quieted down, Donna returned to her job of stacking the russets. She could feel Adrian's stare as he sorted through nectarines, trying to pick out the spoiled ones. He'd been eyeing her warily ever since the TV crew left.

"Okay, Adrian, what are you starin' at?" she finally said. "You're givin' me the willies."

"Nothing, Miss Donna."

"No, Adrian, what is it? You're drivin' me crazy."

Adrian set down his nectarine and walked over. Unconsciously, he began taking deep breaths to lessen the pounding of his heart, which he could hear all the way up in his ears.

"So what is it?" she asked.

"It's your potato, Miss Donna."

Though he was just two years younger than Donna, Adrian always addressed her as an elder. And here was something new: He was now bowing his head in little Asian-like nods of respect. Donna wondered if he was trying to sneeze.

"Are you familiar with the scripture?" he finally asked.

She nodded.

"Jeremiah twenty-four seven?"

"No. Not by heart."

"It says, 'I will give them a heart to know me, that I am the Lord. They will be my people, and I will be their God, for they will return to me with all their heart.' "

"Yes?"

"Miss Donna, ma'am, I believe like all good Christians believe that Jesus is fixin' to come back any day now. And I believe He's tellin' us, through that potato of yours, that it's gonna happen soon, and it's gonna happen right here in Selby . . . and that you're part of His plans."

Donna laughed. "You've got to be kiddin' me."

He shook his head. "Miss Donna, I mean this from the very bottom of my heart and soul."

Donna rolled her eyes. "Adrian Braswell, you are weirder than a turban squash."

Donna was wheeling the produce cart back into the stockroom when she heard herself paged. She ducked into the employee lounge to take the call. Mr. Tom was at a table, talking in hushed, serious tones to Takeesha, who had called in sick three days that week, leaving Koquita to work double shifts each time.

Donna was expecting a return call from Lois at dispatch in Atlanta. This could be a long conversation; there had been problems finding Clementine oranges, and Donna needed three crates for a new

179

Italian restaurant down by Martha's Linens 'n Things on DeLeon Street. Lois had told Donna she should go ahead and sell him regular oranges, that he wouldn't know the difference, and though she was tempted to take her advice, Donna knew there was no comparison between the crude, thick-skinned California navel, whose rind had a slight petrochemical smell, and the more delicate Spanish sister, whose juice was sweet as green grapes and flesh as supple as well-hydrated lips. If four years at Lancôme had taught her anything, it was how to scrutinize then deconstruct a living, three-dimensional organism — only now the human head had been replaced by tangerines and artichokes and fennel bulbs. It was easy for Donna, and she did not have patience with anyone, especially Koquita and the other checkers, who could not grasp the obvious subtle differences between a Rome and Fuji apple.

Donna pulled a chair up to the phone on the wall and sat down as she answered.

"This is Donna Kabel. How can I help you?"

"Hey!" blurted a young man's voice. "I saw you on TV! Are you gonna make French fries outta that thing?"

Donna thought she had moved beyond

180

Robbie weeks ago, yet the second she heard his voice she felt herself begin to melt. Unconsciously, she'd been carrying inside her a morsel of hope, like a cash register mint in the bottom of a dark purse, lost and out of mind but *there,* and it would not decay and crumble for several months, and, subconsciously at least, she rested easier knowing about this emergency sustenance, a taste of something sweet and familiar in times of hunger.

"Robbie?" she asked.

"Yeah, it's me. Did you think I was dead or somethin'?"

Donna's eyes began to fill with tears. "I don't know what to say, Robbie," she said.

"I've been busy, Donna. I got top salesman again the last two months. I sold more Suburbans than anyone in the whole southeastern United States."

"You saw me on TV?"

"We had the news on in the showroom, and Leonard yelled for us all to come inside and watch. . . . You looked great."

"You think so?"

"You're all healed up, baby."

Donna unconsciously brought the receiver down to her chest and leaned her forehead against the wall. Feeling the muffled, electric buzz of Robbie's voice on her skin — "Baby? Baby? Donna baby? Are ya there, darlin'?" — she noticed someone quietly breeze past her and out the door. She smelled a fragrance that reminded her of sweetened peanut butter, some kind of candy bar or the oil that African Americans slathered in their hair to keep it moist.

Suddenly, Donna felt a hand on her shoulder. It was Mr. Tom, who had overheard Donna leaving messages on Robbie's voice mail time and again over the past several weeks.

He took the receiver from her and put his hands on her shoulders. Crying and wiping her nose with the back of her hand, Donna suddenly lunged for his torso and wrapped her arms around him tightly . . . as if she'd finally caught hold of a rock or log after being awash for days in a turbulent river.

As she cried into his shirt, Mr. Tom awkwardly patted her back, letting his other arm dangle at his side. Unbeknownst to Donna, he looked up at the security camera and rolled his eyes, a measure he hoped that would exonerate him of sexual harassment in case of a video audit.

"I'm sorry, Donna," he said. "But it's probably for the best, don't you think? It's time to move on."

He stopped patting and shifted his weight to indicate a desire for detachment, but Donna would not let go, and Tom Green soon noticed a warm, wet spot growing on his shoulder, a sensation he had not experienced since his youngest niece, Haley, was in diapers.

Twelve

Dear Chatter: That new Dilbert cartoon strip in the "Reflector" is just about the stupidest thing I've ever seen. If you don't bring back Mary Worth I'm cancelin' my subscription.

Dear Chatter: If a vampire can't see himself in a mirror, how does he comb his hair? How does he get to lookin' so nice?

His truck washed and waxed by hand, Dewayne arrived at Margaret's house thirteen minutes early. As he opened his door, Margaret emerged from the front door of the house then turned to lock it.

"I was fixin' to come get you," Dewayne yelled.

"You could have just honked," she said, descending the stairs of the porch. "I was watching for you."

Dewayne's eyes absorbed her as she came down the sidewalk. Margaret wore an orange, long-sleeve silk blouse, sandals, and a denim skirt short enough at mid-thigh that she'd tried on two pair of long pants, one pair of shorts, and two dresses in hopes of finding an alternative that would make her feel even prettier and not as naked.

Suddenly realizing she was almost to the curb, Dewayne scurried around the truck to open her door. He saw her already reaching for the handle and quickly pressed the remote lock button on his key chain. Margaret heard the muffled *thunk!* and looked up at him, surprised.

"Why did you do that?" she asked.

"I've gotta get your door," he answered. "You're way too fast."

"I can get my own door."

"No, ma'am. Not when I'm here you won't."

He opened the door and watched her step up into the cab.

"Is anything wrong?" she asked.

Dewayne smiled. "You look so good I wanna scoop you up with a biscuit."

"I can't say I've ever heard that one before, Dewayne."

He took her to Bellissimo, the restaurant on the top floor of the downtown Radisson that had recently metamorphosed from a Hawaiian theme to southern Italian. He ordered the cacciatore, she the Mediterranean spinach salad. The former had chunks of green pepper larger than the chicken pieces and so much oregano that the dish smelled like a cleaning agent. The salad, though it came with capers and calamata olives, had a dressing so sweet it tasted like candy, and the fake crab had been cut into clean, perfect cylinders that resembled sawed-off pieces of candy cane. Both of them made an effort to move the food around on their plates but very little went into their mouths.

"It's not real good, is it?" Dewayne finally said.

"It's fine," she answered. "Maybe we ordered the wrong thing. What do you usually get?"

"Oh, I haven't been here for a long time. We had homecoming dinner here in high school, but that was different. They had drinks you could light on fire in these big bowls that looked like volcanoes. I remember havin' a real good time."

"Where do you normally like to eat?"

"I usually eat at home."

"You cook?"

"I know a little bit."

Dewayne looked at her with wary eyes. He hesitated then said, "I'm the cook at the station."

"You're kidding me."

"But it's not exactly somethin' you wanna tell a girl you're tryin' to impress."

"You're wrong about that," Margaret said. "What do you cook?"

"Just home-cookin'."

"Can you make biscuits?"

"Course I can make biscuits."

For weeks now, Margaret had been tinkering with biscuit dough. As a signature dish for her catering business, she had a vision of warm biscuits with soppressata, thinly sliced canary melon, and a basil-infused olive oil. Yet despite experimentation with the amounts of butter and milk and the baking time, her biscuits continued to come out as dry and crumbly as the stale scones from airport coffee kiosks.

"My biscuits are a failure," she answered. "I'm trying to make those wonderful Southern biscuits I eat everywhere, and I can't do it."

"You usin' lard?" he asked.

"No."

"What are you usin' for fat?"

"Butter and vegetable oil."

"Why not lard?"

"But that's so unhealthy, Dewayne."

"I've never heard of cookin' good biscuits without lard."

"Where do you buy lard?"

"Kroger."

"You're kidding me."

"No, ma'am. Right there by the vegetable oil."

"You know," Margaret said, "I've got to go to the rest room. Would you excuse me?"

Dewayne quickly plucked his napkin from his lap and rose to his feet as Margaret stood up.

"That's not necessary," she said.

"Southern men know how to treat a lady."

On the toilet, Margaret recounted the conversations of the evening thus far: *Lady! I thought the word had dropped from the American vocabulary. . . . He's cute but seems too simple . . . his sentences sound like they're from a Dick and Jane book. . . . The longest eyelashes I've ever seen on a man . . . wouldn't they get singed on the job? . . . I could stare at his face all night. . . . He wants to scoop me up in a biscuit! . . . I want to put his fingers in my mouth. . . . What is wrong with me!*

When Margaret returned to the table, Dewayne stood up to pull out her chair.

"I can manage, Dewayne," she said.

"You're real resistant to this kind of thing, aren't you?"

"You should have seen my mother."

"Maybe I will some day."

"That's impossible. She's dead."

"Oh! Gosh, I didn't mean to . . ."

"No, no, that's okay. She died of cancer last year. She was a gynecologist and she died of ovarian cancer. Tops the irony scale, doesn't it?"

Wary of the Southern Baptists, Margaret had told no one in Selby about her mother. Despite her occasional interviews on National Public Radio and in the *New York Times*, most people here had no idea who Ruth Pinaldi was. And if they did, Margaret realized she most likely would never know because Southerners veered around controversy as if it were fresh roadkill. If they did know, Margaret was certain they were praying for her in a Sunday school class somewhere.

"You miss her?" Dewayne asked.

"I'm not sure," Margaret answered. "It kind of feels like my boss has gone on vacation, and I can do anything I want to."

She picked up her napkin from the table, smelled it, then put it in her lap. "Did you know we never once went to a movie together?"

"Maybe she didn't like the movies. My daddy doesn't."

"No, it's not that. I couldn't even get her to sit down and eat popcorn and watch TV. You know, if she just would have relaxed a little, I think we could have had some fun. We were always so serious in our house."

"You like movies?" Dewayne asked.

"Yes."

"Which ones?"

"Art films. Foreign films."

Dewayne shook his head. "You like Jim Carrey?"

"You know, Dewayne, I can say, with absolute certainty, I've not seen one Jim Carrey movie."

"Well then, I've got an idea. Let's go rent us *Ace Ventura: Pet Detective* and go to my house and cut up. Or your house. Doesn't matter to me. Whatever you're more comfortable with."

Margaret thought of the air-conditioning in her house, on its last leg, running nonstop even through the night as it tried to catch up with the previous day's heat. She knew it had to be replaced — that month's $289 Georgia Power bill convinced her of that — but in her fifteen months in Selby Margaret had managed to save no more than a thousand dollars. She was now buying generic cat food for Susan B. In lieu of blinds, African mud cloth from a garage sale was still tacked over the windows. Margaret had started reading and writing in her journal by candlelight to help keep the house cooler and whittle away at the huge utility bill.

"I'd be more comfortable at my house, honestly," she said. "But we can go to your house. I can't stay long. Just the movie, and then I'm going home."

Dewayne got up to go find the waiter, and Margaret closed her eyes and breathed in deeply his wake of air — okay, she thought, maybe his smell wasn't scones in particular, but it was definitely something baked. She wondered if she was smelling the salt from his pores, or yeast? — and there it was again . . . that top note of peaches or nectarines loitering in the background.

When Dewayne returned to the table, check in hand, Margaret was imagining herself leaning into him on his couch, her nose buried in his warm neck.

"On second thought," she said, "I think I'd just better go home."

On the way back to Margaret's house, Dewayne, never driving faster than thirty miles per hour, passed the entrance to Red Hill Plantation.

"Wait," Margaret said. "Can we turn back? I need to go in there."

He turned into a driveway without signaling. No one ever signaled in Selby. Margaret wondered if it was a lingering behavior from a rural past or because the public schools did not have driver's education . . . or was it heat-related? Was there a connection between the long, humid days and the economy of words and body movements that predominated behavior here? Southerners were stereotyped as being lazy — and they did indeed move very slowly — but Margaret wondered if this old-dog behavior was simply an ingenious way of normalizing the body temperature in a climate where both crayons and VCR tapes could melt in a parked car within an hour.

"What are we lookin' for?" Dewayne asked.

"I'm not sure," Margaret answered. "But this is the neighborhood where all the dogs are dying. I'm going to a meeting here next week."

The sheriff's department had been calling Margaret almost daily at the *Reflector*, wanting to know about any additional dead-dog phone calls into Chatter that she did not include in the column. Law enforcement in town had long enjoyed a cozy relationship with the newspaper, but Randy called them on her behalf to let them know that things had changed under new ownership and that real journalists did not provide such information, and that they'd have to sue the *Reflector* to get it. Instead, he told Margaret to cover the meeting as a reporter, something she'd been dreading the past five days.

The houses of Red Hill Plantation were the biggest in town, even larger than those in the historic district. Margaret was surprised at how the neighborhood seemed devoid of humanity, as if it were a space colony and there was no oxygen outdoors, and people had to shuttle back and forth from the stores and work and schools straight to their garages. No toys or children in the front yards. No occupants in all those immaculate, white front-porch rocking chairs. Only an occasional, uniformed maid coming out to retrieve the mail from postal boxes that looked like old-world brick ovens, which had been built in place of the metal-post mailboxes run down by the neighborhood boys in their monster-wheel pickup trucks.

"When I was a kid we used to drive through here on Sundays," Dewayne said. "My momma liked to look at the houses."

"I don't feel a pulse in this neighborhood," Margaret said. "I think it looks empty and sad. It doesn't surprise me that the dogs are dying here."

The clicking of Ferragamos on Mexican-tile floors. For twenty-eight years, it was the last sound Margaret heard at night and the first sound in the morning. Ruth Pinaldi was up by four o'clock every day, reading the *Buffalo News*, scanning her appointment book for the day, pounding out on her laptop an op-ed piece about pending pro-life legislation in Albany.

Now, the sound of those heels, as much a trademark of Ruth as her red suits, reminded Margaret of the ticking of a clock, and she wondered if her mother subconsciously knew very early on, maybe even as a child, that her days were numbered, and her goals were endangered, and she had to rush, rush, rush like Lewis Carroll's rabbit to get it all done, which she did not.

They had learned too late. Margaret walked in on her mother as she was scrutinizing a CAT scan on the wall-mounted light in her office. "Come on in, Margaret," she said. "Let me show you something. This . . ." She tapped the glass with her ballpoint pen bought at Office Depot because Ruth Pinaldi refused to accept any freebies from drug companies. "This is my left ovary. And this . . . this right here . . . this white mass that looks like a supernova . . . this is a six-centimeter necrotic mass with satellite lesions, and I am totally, irrevocably fucked."

Armed with all the self-prescribed painkillers she needed, Ruth Pinaldi rode out her last sixteen months at home under Margaret's care. It allowed Margaret to watch this glacierlike presence in her life drift away, and by the time her mother disappeared on the horizon, Margaret was already accustomed to her absence.

On the day before she died, Ruth lay on her side in the hospital bed they had brought home. Gaunt and pale, she still had her thick black hair because the cancer had progressed too far to consider chemo, but she had demanded that it be pulled up, out of her way, on top of her head in a pigtail that resembled a whale's spout.

She reached out for Margaret's hand and looked into her daughter's eyes.

"You've been a great roommate, Margaret," she said.

"Oh, Momma . . ."

Ruth's eyes widened. "You've never called me that."

"I have, too."

"No. You always call me Mother."

"I don't."

"You do."

"Mom!"

"Stop and listen to me, Margaret . . . I was never your mom. I was only your mother. You know that."

"Mother, please."

"I didn't mean to get pregnant — I've told you that before. But I want you to know something . . . honey . . . it has been such a pleasure watching you grow up."

A tear, which had been forming in the corner of Ruth's eye, suddenly grew heavy enough to break away and creep down her cheek. Margaret, too, began to cry; in twenty-eight years she had never seen tears on her mother's face.

"I really, truly think the reason I never got close to you was because if I did, I could not go on in my work."

As her mother spoke, Margaret reached to wipe the tear from her cheek with a corner of the bedsheet.

"Because don't you see?" Ruth asked. "How could I terminate all those pregnancies every day of my life if I'd bonded so closely with my own child? How could I rejoice in the fruits of my unwanted pregnancy and then turn around and advise all those young women to abort their fetus? It would have made me a hypocrite, Margaret. And all I can say now is, 'I'm sorry.' "

Thirteen

Dear Chatter: I've never seen so much litter thrown out of windows in my life. I saw a bag of McDonald's trash come flying out of a BMW! Selby, clean up your act! To paraphrase Richard Nixon: Such a strange creature is Man — one who will mess in his own nest.

Dear Chatter: This is to my neighbor, and you know who you are: Quit playing that gospel music so loud or you're going to be sorry.

"Can we see the manager?" John David asked the clerk at Barnes & Noble. "It's Faith somethin'."

The young man looked at him quizzically. With his wild, intentionally uncombed brown hair and extremely horizontal, thick eyebrows, he reminded John David of the line drawing of Beethoven over the cappuccino bar. Though John David was usually attracted to the type of men who had commercial charge accounts at the new Home Depot — and indeed he frequently lunched at the aluminum hot-dog stand in front of the home-improvement store on Byron Road — this young man had a brooding intensity he found intriguing and sexy.

"You must mean Hope Carswell," said the young man.

"Faith. Hope. Charity," John David said. "One of those flower-child names."

In search of his manager, he walked toward the back of the store. John David's eyes absorbed the back of his black jeans; his clinging, butterscotch-colored turtleneck; and the cocky strutting — *kuh-lump! kuh-lump!* — of his heavy, black Doc Marten boots.

"That boy is definitely not from Selby," he said to Suzanne. "He's so fierce-looking, don't you think so?"

"John David . . ."

"Like a Renaissance warrior."

Two days earlier, Suzanne told John David she wanted to transform the lilac-motifed guest room into a library before the Dogwood Festival party.

"We need to get to an estate sale to buy some books," he said.

"No, John David," Suzanne replied. "I

don't want some dead man's books. I want new books."

John David called the new Barnes & Noble on Ben Pond Jr. Boulevard and asked to speak to the manager.

"How much are your books by the yard?" he asked Hope Carswell.

"By the yard?" she said. "You mean like fabric?"

"Yes."

"Is this a joke? As in, Do-you-have-pop-in-a-bottle-then-go-let-him-out?"

"Sweetheart, I've got better things to do than make prank phone calls to bookstore workers. I'm the highest-paid designer in Selby."

"I've never been asked such a thing," she said.

"Can you get back with me on that?" he asked.

"Yes. I'll have to get back with you on that."

"I only want hardcover books," John David said. "None of those tacky paperbacks."

Hope Carswell, who would turn thirty-three Friday, stood six feet tall with a brunette, shag haircut and emerald-green, cat-eye glasses. She smiled as she approached them, showing strong white teeth with the dominant canines so common in the portraits of old-money, Northeastern families.

"Mr. Rush?" she said.

"Please, you're makin' me feel old as my daddy. It's John David."

"Very nice to meet you."

"And this here's Suzanne Parley. She's the lady who's gettin' the new library."

"I just love your bookstore," Suzanne said, offering her hand. "Those pictures of people over the coffee bar are so cute."

Hope, who had moved from Washington, D.C., to open and manage her first Barnes & Noble, was constantly amazed at how liberally the local women here used that word, and how they always stretched it, like a piece of fresh taffy, from one syllable into two: kee-YOOT. If something pleased the eye, a cover of a book, the piping on a chair, a sweater from Talbots, a pair of gilt pineapple bookends, they would alert their female compatriot shopper with a "Now isn't that kee-YOOT?"

And it did not take Hope long to learn that in order to make the numbers her bosses expected from a new store in a virgin, growing market, she would have to find more room up front for cute items that could suck these wealthy, north Selby women out of the antiques and silk flower and linen stores and into her doors.

Out went half the titles of Kurt Vonnegut and Carl Hiaasen and P. J. O'Rourke and Dave Barry and others whose needling, aggressive sense of humor did not seem to match the collective local sensitivity. In came an enlarged greeting-card section and leather-bound journals and pens topped with dyed ostrich feathers and a wooden book with hollowed out middle that held a TV clicker and any gilt object Hope could find in the supply catalogs: gold-coated monkeys and cherubs, busts of Shakespeare and James Joyce and Emily Dickinson. ("I could sell a bowl of Cheerios if it was painted gold," she told her supervisor.)

"So you gonna sell me books by the yard?" John David asked.

Hope shook her head. "I called my regional supervisor, and she said you would have to buy them book by book . . . and then we'll just ring everything up in the end with a twenty percent discount. Is that okay?"

"Are you gonna give us young Beethoven?" John David asked, pointing northward with his chin to the other side of the store.

"No," she answered. "I'm sorry, but

you're stuck with me. So, are we ready? Where should we start? Art books?"

"I like the color of those over there," John David said, pointing.

"Excellent choice," Hope said. "Biographies."

Standing, Suzanne watched them as John David pointed to and described a book — "The yellow one with the fern-colored letters" — and Hope would pull it from the shelf and show him the cover.

"I already told you I don't care what the front of the book looks like. Just the side. All we're gonna see's the side."

"Do y'all mind if I sit down?" Suzanne finally said. "I'm feelin' tired."

"She's in breedin' season," John David explained to Hope.

Hope set down a stack of books. She quickly walked over to Suzanne and took her arm. "I'm so sorry," she said. "You should have said something. Please, come sit in this easy chair. Let me get you some coffee."

"You're too kind," Suzanne said. "Maybe some sweet tea would be good."

"I'm afraid we don't have any sweet tea. But we have a really good mango tea."

"Oh," she said. "Well, then, I'll just take some water, thank you."

The past month had been glorious — everyone was waiting on Suzanne. Boone, who would not let her cook now, often brought home takeout from different restaurants, and he was surprised how much the lasagna from Café Amore tasted like his wife's homemade version.

Lately, Suzanne had been staying up after Boone went to bed, and she would drink a bottle of chardonnay as she leafed through catalogs and wrote down items for John David to order. At the end of her illicit evening, too dizzy to wash the wineglass and eliminate all evidence, Suzanne would turn off the burglar alarm, walk out onto the patio, across the yard, and up to the edge of the forest that separated their property from the eighth hole of Sugar Day. Then, awkwardly, like a presidential wife throwing out the first pitch of a baseball game, Suzanne would chuck the glass as far as she could into the trees. Some broke against the trunk of an oak or sweet gum or pine, but most of them landed in the thick quilt of decaying leaves and needles. In the morning, when the rays of sunlight penetrated the strip of forest, the glass sparkled like dew on spiders' webs. No one would ever know the difference. The only living creatures who ever went back there were those stupid dogs, and that problem was being taken care of.

Historically, Boone did not like Suzanne to linger in bed in the mornings, and he intentionally tried to rouse her. He would drop the toilet seat, shut the medicine cabinet door too firmly, or set his glass bottle of aftershave onto the granite countertop with an unnecessary amount of force.

Nowadays — and who would have thought that the possibility of a baby would change him so much — Boone slipped out of bed, tiptoed into the closet, then walked down the hall to shower in the guest bathroom so the running water and his Norelco did not wake her. Some days he even made coffee and set aside a cupful for her in the microwave. And better still, he was leaving her alone in the morning. It had been three weeks since she last heard the six a.m. rhythmic rustling of the 520-count sheets as Boone stroked himself in preparation, an audible warning of things to come, like the thunder of an approaching storm. And on those mornings, with her eyes closed, she would suddenly sense the mass hovering over her, bringing darkness for two or three minutes, until the cloud was spent and moved on its way.

Yet she would welcome him now; Boone

was sweet again. He was the man she remembered from ten years ago, and Suzanne had actually enjoyed him these past few weeks. For the first time in years he was sharing anecdotes and jokes from the hospital. He listened when she brought out fabric samples and paint chips from Lonnie's Color Wheel, and he even gave an opinion on the wood for the library bookshelves. Over breakfast, they laughed together at items from Chatter, and, briefly one day, she almost mustered enough courage to admit that she occasionally called the hot line herself.

Suzanne knew this could not last, but she was not yet ready to give it up.

At the Barnes & Noble, she reached into her purse and pulled out an alligator-skin Daytimer. With a royal blue ballpoint pen from the Amelia Island Ritz-Carlton, she began a list:

Gain weight!! Krispy Kreme trips *daily!* More Krystal burgers at lunch. Buy whole milk instead of skim.

In Atlanta: Maternity clothes. Nordstrom? Neiman Marcus? Stop by Aveda Salon for cleansing lotion.

Any new candle scents?

Find throw for caned recamier in downstairs hallway. *Must* have some of same cranberry color from mats in framed botanicals. NO chenille!

Ask John David: Who sells Italian marble faux fruits (like in the ad in Veranda)?

Gift for new TACKY neighbor.

Kroger list:
martini olives
bananas for Boone's cereal
those cute little tangerines
tampons

Like a spirit taking leave of its body, Suzanne's mind drifted into the cherry-wood cabinets of her kitchen, snaking among the cans and bottles and boxes, circling the peanut butter jar, peering within, and then on to the refrigerator, where it gauged the crispness of the baby carrots and counted the Stouffer frozen entrées that lined the freezer-door shelf like a set of miniature orange encyclopedias. What was missing on this daily tour of inventory and need? What could not wait until tomorrow, when Josephine would go to the store?

She clicked the ballpoint pen and wrote down one more item:

dog food

Jodi Armbuster answered the door in elasticized, maternity blue jeans and an XXL white T-shirt with a black-and-white photograph of a naked man. Muscular and young, with the creamy, hair-free skin of *GQ* models, he lay on his side, hugging his knees as if doing a cannonball off the diving board.

Yet what startled Suzanne even more was Jodi's exposed face, pale, sun-spotted and devoid of foundation or blush or lipstick . . . and her blond hair, pulled up into a ponytail on *top* of her head.

"Oh, I am so sorry," Suzanne said, already turning to leave, looking more at the redbrick sidewalk than at Jodi's face, as if Jodi herself had answered the door naked and Suzanne was doing her best to preserve her new neighbor's dignity. "I knew I shoulda called. I'm just so sorry. I'll just come back later."

"Don't be silly," Jodi said. "Please, come on in."

"Oh, no, no, that's okay," Suzanne said.

"I just had a little somethin' to give you, but it can wait."

"No, please," Jodi said. "I could use the company. I need a break."

She followed Jodi inside, this time noticing the back of her shirt: *Mapplethorpe: Good art is supposed to scare you.*

"I'm dying to show somebody around," Jodi said. "I've been working my ass off, and it has not been easy carrying around these extra twenty pounds. Let me get us something to drink. Come on back to the kitchen. Is Evian okay? I even might have some lemon."

The wood floors had been yanked out and replaced with terra-cotta Mexican tile, and Suzanne's heels echoed through the empty rooms, sounding like an amplified metronome. With sadness and revulsion, she inventoried the changes as she walked along. Gone was the mahogany paneling and coffered ceiling of the den. Gone was that gorgeous, marble faux fireplace in the parlor and the French doors that separated the parlor from the foyer. The windows, though covered with new, white plantation shutters, looked naked and vulnerable and cold without curtains. Holes had been punched into the ceilings of every room for recessed halogen lights — how many were there? thirty? forty? — evoking the feel of a department store. Everything was so . . . *white*. What Suzanne considered architectural rape Jodi called understated, elegant minimalism.

When they started hunting for a house in Selby, Jodi and Marc, her husband, quickly grew intrigued by the staples of affluent Southern decorating: Dark, beautiful hardwood furniture and fake fireplaces. Flawlessly crafted faux food, mainly desserts, on the sideboards in the dining rooms. Animal-print accents bought during a braver shopping moment and included in the decor only because it was the rage in Atlanta. Curtains that looked like voluminous Renaissance ball gowns, dripping with tassels and fringe like the Spanish moss on the live oaks outside. In some vacant homes, Jodi and Marc were surprised to find large family or living rooms whose oak flooring was interrupted by a huge expanse of crude plywood, which a Persian rug obviously once covered. "It's a mix between a movie set for a Dickens novel and Elvis's Graceland," Marc said.

When they signed on their house, the real estate agent said, "That's a good deal considering they're gonna leave all those gorgeous window treatments."

"The curtains," Marc said, "are outta here." And he brought up his thumb and jabbed it backward, over his shoulder, the way a basketball referee does when kicking a player off the court.

"Mr. Armbuster," she said, "those are very fine curtains."

"Yes, they are," Jodi cut in. "They're very well made, I can tell. I'll bet there's almost a hundred thousand in these curtains."

The agent leaned forward in her chair, raised her eyebrows and divulged in a hushed tone, "Ma'am, there's a hundred and *fifty* thousand of curtains in this house."

"In window treatments alone?" Marc asked.

Nodding her head, she leaned back in her chair. "Miss Ginny, the owner of this house, has very good taste."

Suzanne and Jodi sat down at the kitchen table with blue-rimmed Mexican glasses of Evian and lemon wedges.

"This is for you," Suzanne said, handing Jodi a wrapped present. After leaving the bookstore, she had stopped back home to rewrap the gift because the trademark Barnes-&-Noble-blue seemed too plain, and the clerk rolled his eyes and shook his head when she asked for a bow.

"It's lovely," Jodi said. "Look at this paper. Are these pansies?"

"They sure are."

"Oh, my God . . . look at these," said Jodi, pulling out a pair of gilt bookends, two fleurs-de-lis the size of grapefruits. "We have tons of books. These will be very handy." She set them on the mesquite, rectangular kitchen table that she and Marc had bought from an impoverished church outside Ensenada. Beneath the varnish on the top were several black marks from toppled candles that had been lit for troubled souls.

"So are y'all settled in yet?" Suzanne asked.

"Not too far away," Jodi answered. "Do you want to see the house?"

They began upstairs, in the nursery with the painting of the naked women that Suzanne saw being unloaded from the truck that day. Jodi pointed to the ceiling. "When Emma's born, we're going to paint her natal chart on the ceiling . . . you know, the planets and stars and how they're situated on the day of her birth. I found someone in Atlanta who can do it."

Like the downstairs, every room was painted white, the windows bare except for plantation shutters. The carpeting had been yanked up and replaced with light, maple-wood flooring. Navajo and Latin rugs were randomly scattered, like puddles after a rain, around the entire second floor. Folk art, in the form of sculptures and pottery and carved, painted wooden figures, graced the tops of bureaus and tables so big and blocky and nicked they reminded Suzanne of an ancient castle's door. And where *were* all the doors?

"Are y'all gettin' your doors repainted?" Suzanne asked.

"Oh, no," Jodi answered. "We took them all off and filled in the holes from the hinges. It's better feng shui without the doors. We like that open feeling."

In one bathroom Suzanne saw a yellow sink that looked like a big mixing bowl sitting on the countertop. There was a steam room as well, and a shower so large it did not need a door.

Jodi stopped before a five-foot-by-five-foot watercolor painting at the end of the hallway. "This is my favorite piece," she said.

It was an amorphous red, roundish mass, comprised of various chambers, some darker reds, other lighter, all blending into one another. Tiny white lines floated in the mass, resembling pieces of scattered rice floating in tomato soup.

"What do you think?" Jodi asked her.

Suzanne unconsciously twisted the four-carat diamond on her finger. "Looks like a tomato, right?" she answered. "Is that what it is — a tomato?"

"The artist is an ob-gyn in Oregon," Jodi said. "That gives it a slightly different perspective, doesn't it?"

"Well, it sure is cute," Suzanne said. "I've never seen anything like it."

She looked at her watch.

"Oh my gosh. It's almost four o'clock. I've been havin' such a good time talkin' that I lost track of the time. I sure like what you're doin' with it, though. You've been busy."

They descended the stairs, and on the way to the front door Suzanne noted that over the fireplace, instead of the traditional oil portrait of the lady of the house, hung a painting of a glowing orange square floating in a chartreuse-green background. She reminded herself to schedule an appointment to have her own portrait repainted in time for the Dogwood Festival. This time she would find someone outside of town, someone who had never painted a Selby woman before, maybe that artist whose ad she had seen in the back pages of *Atlanta* magazine.

"Oh," Suzanne said before descending the stairs of the porch. "I was fixin' to tell you about Dogwood. I don't know if you know this, with you bein' newcomers to Selby, but the Dogwood Festival's the biggest thing of the year in Middle Georgia, and Boone and me have the big party, so don't you be leavin' town during Dogwood. I want to see y'all there."

"I know about Dogwood," Jodi said. "I can't wait. It sounds glorious."

"You haven't seen anything till you've seen Selby in the springtime. And my party's gonna be somethin' you don't wanna miss."

Her territory claimed, Suzanne waved as she stepped into her Lexus for the twenty-yard trip home. Jodi, who followed her out to get the mail, watched her honk at a female black Labrador, squatting on the grass near the large magnolia tree. Unperturbed by Suzanne's car horn, she finished her business and ambled on down the street.

Fourteen

Dear Chatter: Put your bird feeder on top of a metal pole and smear that pole with Vaseline. I've never seen a squirrel that can climb a metal pole with Vaseline on it.

Dear Chatter: If you don't like gospel music then you must not love Jesus. I play my gospel music loud so I don't have to listen to all your cursing.

Dear Chatter: I'm wantin' to know who makes the best chitterlings in Perry County — and do they do takeout?

They had come to Kroger solely for collards, but Dewayne could not pull Margaret away from the produce section. He leaned against the end cap of dried fruits and nuts, his arms folded as he watched with amusement as she scurried from the key limes to the passion fruit, from yucca root to the herbs, picking everything up and smelling them before moving on.

"Dewayne, look at this!" Margaret said.

"What is it?" he asked.

"Lemon grass! I can't believe you have lemon grass! I haven't seen lemon grass since I moved here."

"What on earth you gonna use grass for?" he asked.

But she was off again. This variety of apples! It shamed the Kroger near her house . . . Jonagolds and Fujis and Empires and the hard-to-find Cortlands. Across the aisle, rectangular baskets nearly spilled over with Anaheim chilis, habaneros, dried chipotles, anchos, and gingerroot. Laying alongside the omnipresent collards were the more exotic escarole and kale and mustard greens. And the melons! Casabas and canaries and . . .

"That's the way to do it," said a voice.

Holding a melon in her hands, Margaret looked up and saw a beautiful young woman in a Kroger uniform standing beside her. On her face was an odd scar shaped like the letter *L*.

"I'm sorry?" Margaret said.

"You know how to pick produce. With your nose. The best fruits don't always look real pretty. Like these melons."

The woman — her name tag said *Donna* — scanned the pile of crenshaws then finally picked one up. "See," she said. "The shoppers who want the pretty fruit don't always get the good fruit. Like these crenshaws. I see 'em every time, shoppers come in here and they try to find a clean melon, and I try to tell 'em, you *want* that flat muddy spot because that means it wasn't picked early, and it was sittin' on the ground gettin' sweet and ripe."

Donna had been sampling every item she sold and learned that the most delicious and beautiful of God's creations often hid behind an imperfect epidermis. The sweetest, reddest pomegranates had dents and brown scabs. The mottled Fujis, not the storybook-perfect Red Delicious, were the sweetest and crispest and most predictable. And the kiwis! For years, Donna hadn't touched them; brown and stubbly, they looked like they'd dropped off an old man.

She took Margaret's melon and replaced it with the one in her hands. "Like this one, see?" Margaret looked at the smeared, brown spot that resembled a smudge on the knee of some pale-yellow pants that had slid into home plate.

"Is this your produce section?" Margaret asked.

"Well, not really," Donna answered.

"Mr. Tom — he's the store manager — he hasn't hired a produce manager yet so I'm kind of in charge. But, no, I'm not really the boss."

"It's beautiful," Margaret said. "I wish mine had even half these wonderful things."

"You think so?"

"Yes!"

Tom Green was not sure why — it might have been the heart potato sighting; it might have been the opening of the Target and Costco across the street — but the receipts in his store's produce section had jumped twenty-two percent in the past three weeks. Like an American spotting his first McDonald's overseas, these first-time customers were surprised and overjoyed to find bok choy or chilled, vacuum-packed soybeans between the collard greens and peanuts. It was Tom Green's guess that the growing diversity of Selby would warrant such a store, and if he could give the city a true urban market it would draw customers for miles.

And while Donna still did not like the insecticidelike smell of grapefruit or having to clean dirt each night from beneath her fingernails, she did enjoy the attention she was getting from the heart potato, which was now at home, safe in her freezer in a large Tupperware container that included other cherished and perishable mementoes: two snowballs from the time it stormed in Selby when she was twelve; a Three Musketeers bar that Billy Ray Cyrus had taken a bite of and thrown into the crowd at his concert in the Selby Civic Auditorium; a serving of the last peach ice cream her mother made before dying.

Even more, Donna enjoyed the exposure to a variety of people so unlike those she had lived with all her life. The Yankees and Japanese bought much more produce than native Selbyites, excluding collard greens and okra, and they did not seem to be as intimidated by the papayas and baby zucchini and enoki mushrooms. They asked questions, plenty of them, even more than her Lancôme customers did. And time and again Donna would have to find an answer from Mr. Tom or online and get back to them as they finished their shopping.

"Which Kroger do you shop at?" Donna asked.

"The one on Ben Pond Jr. Boulevard."

"We call that the gold Kroger."

"Because . . ."

"All the rich ladies shop there."

Donna then leaned into Margaret so she

could lower her voice and still be heard.

"And between you and me, the reason they don't have much produce up there is 'cause the ladies in north Selby don't cook. I even make meals for one lady . . . Miss Suzanne. I cook for her three times a week."

Margaret looked over her shoulder at Dewayne. "I'm Margaret Pinaldi," she said to Donna, holding out her hand.

"Donna Kabel," she replied. "I'd shake hands but mine are all sticky — I've been cuttin' watermelon. My sales of watermelon increase by three hundred percent if I cut 'em up. Can you believe that?"

Dewayne lived in south Selby, in a small, tan, ranch-style home with white ornamental shutters on the windows. A whitewashed, life-size deer stood in the front yard, something Dewayne inherited with the house when he bought it five years ago. The doe, her head and ears perked in alertness, had weathered down to the gray concrete, and the friend Dewayne hired to paint his house suggested he color the deer to match the shutters. Dewayne thought that would be just fine, though he later called him back to paint a black mouth and eyes on the face because Dewayne thought it looked too much like an animal trapped in some evil snow queen's spell.

With Margaret in the passenger's seat, he slowly pulled under his carport. The roof was made of corrugated, translucent green sheets of fiberglass, and when the sun was high it cast an Emerald City glow on everything below.

"Does he have a name?" Margaret asked.

"Who?"

"The deer."

"His name's Casper."

Inside was plain and utilitarian, the furniture mostly shades of brown or blue and most of it matching. Pictures of Dewayne's mother and father and two sisters hung on the wall over the television. A wooden cross with a shiny-gold, plastic Jesus was suspended on the wall over what looked to be Dewayne's TV-watching chair. From across the room, Margaret noticed two small black-and-white figurines on an end table. She left Dewayne's side to get a closer look.

"Oh, my gosh, these are so cute!"

She then saw another, this one a sitting Beanie Baby that leaned against a blue vase. She turned to Dewayne. "Dewayne . . . you have penguins in your living room!"

He lowered his gaze to the floor and rubbed the back of his neck. "Well," he said. "I collect penguins."

"You collect penguins?"

"Everybody collects somethin'."

"I've never known anyone who collects penguins, Dewayne. How interesting! Why penguins?"

"I don't know . . . I just like 'em. They look like they're havin' fun."

"Is this something you do to get women to go to bed with you?"

"Ma'am?"

"Because I'm sure it works."

Dewayne held out the paper Kroger sack to her. "I thought you wanted to learn how to make good biscuits."

"Show me the kitchen."

Over the next few hours, Dewayne not only baked the flaky, moist biscuits he promised but also cornmeal-and-vidalia-onion dumplings that simmered in ham hock–flavored collard greens. Margaret enjoyed watching his arms as he slowly sliced large, musky, beefsteak tomatoes that he would serve alongside the entrée.

As a cold, crisp complement, Dewayne included spicy okra that he had pickled himself with garlic, dill, and dried red pepper pods. And Margaret was surprised at the simplicity of his smothered chicken. All Dewayne used was the bird and its drippings, along with flour, butter, salt and pepper.

"No other herbs?" Margaret asked.

"Do you like chicken?"

"Yes."

"Do you like butter and flour?"

"Yes."

"Okay, then," he said. "Why glue glitter on a dog's fur?"

The only awkward moment of the date came early on, when Margaret opened the refrigerator and began rummaging through its contents. Dewayne, who was chopping onions on his butcher block, suddenly stopped, and Margaret looked over her shoulder to see on his face a look of amused bewilderment.

"Are you okay?" she asked. "Is something wrong?"

Dewayne resumed his chopping of the onion. "Do you always do that?" he finally asked.

"Do what?"

"Do they do that in New York — go into other people's refrigerators like that?"

"Like what?"

"That's okay. Never mind."

"No, Dewayne, please. I've obviously

done something wrong here. Please, tell me."

Again, he stopped chopping. "Well . . . it's just kinda forward. That's all."

"Opening the refrigerator?"

"That's how I was raised."

"Is this a family rule or cultural rule?"

"I thought everybody was raised that way — you just don't go into other people's refrigerators unless you're family."

"Wow," Margaret said. "That's fascinating. Why?"

He shook his head. "Just always been that way."

"So, it's the same as rifling through someone's panty drawer?" she asked.

Dewayne said nothing and looked down at his hands, which were still dicing the onion.

"You're blushing!" Margaret said. "My God, Dewayne you're a bigger prude than I am."

"I wouldn't know anything about that," he said.

"About what?"

He paused, letting courage accumulate like water behind a dam of mud so that it could gather in mass and finally burst through: "Panties," he finally said.

Fifteen

Dear Chatter: That girl findin' the heart potato is a sign from the Lord that he wants us all to shape up and get nice and start treatin' everyone like the Bible says we should. Love thy enemy. That's what that heart potato means.

Dear Chatter: Can anyone tell me where to find a good selection of imported beers? All I seem to find everywhere is Budweiser.

The turnout for the emergency meeting was so great that Margaret had to park her mother's Mercedes two blocks away. As she walked down Red Hill Drive — there were no sidewalks in this subdivision — Margaret smelled the paper mill south of town, an odor she likened to wet spitballs with slight notes of anise root and mint and sour milk. Almost weekly, newcomers to town railed about the odor in Chatter, worrying about airborne carcinogens. Yet natives swore the smell had actually improved over the years, and that every nose got used to it if it stuck around long enough, just as ears learn to ignore the ever-present buzz of fluorescent lights.

A man, presumably the owner of the house, answered the door. He smelled of a musky cologne and wore a blue, pinpoint-oxford-cloth shirt with the initials HDR on the pocket.

"I'm Margaret Pinaldi," she said, eliciting no response. "With the *Reflector*?"

Suddenly, his eyes widened. "Oh, yes, yes," he said, offering his arm to be shaken. "I'm Harnod Ristle. Pleased to meet you. Please, please come on in, come on in. Thank you so much for joinin' us tonight."

Margaret walked into the foyer of polished limestone floors and a wallpaper of blooming peonies. "What an unusual name," she said. "Is it H-A-R-N-O-D?"

"That's it. That's my momma's maiden name."

Considering the patriarchal leanings in Southern culture, Margaret was intrigued by this tradition that gave women's surnames one last leg to hobble on before they collapsed and decayed into the earth. She had encountered men named Haney, Verney, Walker, and Chalmers and women who went by Word and Tucker and Munnolin.

"I'm sorry," he said. "I didn't catch your name the first time."

"Margaret Pinaldi."

"Are you new at the *Reflector*?"

"Relatively new . . . yes."

"Well, come on in, make yourself at home. Everyone else is back here in the den. I sure do wanna thank you for comin'."

The den had a men's club feel to it, with an abundance of dark wood, broad leather furniture, a stuffed pheasant on the fireplace mantel, and a wildcat of some sort immortalized on a fake outcrop in a corner of the room. Next to that was a free-standing globe the size of a beach ball. Later, when walking by, Margaret would notice that each country — and not all the countries were represented — had been carved of semi-precious stones and inlaid into black-onyx seas.

Chardonnay and bourbon flowed freely in crystal tumblers and stemware. A black, uniformed maid offered cheese straws from a silver platter. To show solidarity, some of the women wore sweaters or vests with dogs crocheted or embroidered on them. Margaret noticed a uniformed Perry

County sheriff's deputy sipping a can of Coke. And holding court in a corner was an ebullient middle-aged woman with a flame-red, perfectly round bouffant that reminded Margaret of the halos in medieval paintings. From earrings to shoes, she was dressed in yellow so pale it almost resembled French-vanilla ice cream. Margaret had seen her around town, driving a Cadillac of the very same color.

Despite Margaret's objections, Randy had sent her to cover the meeting as a news story, and she knew she could not leave without quotes from people in attendance. Margaret began to work the crowd. All the while, she caught glances from the woman in pale yellow who, with her hand perpetually stuck out front like a campaigning politician's, seemed determined to interact with every person in the room.

"Hey, y'all!" yelled Harnod Ristle, clapping his hands. "I need your attention up here. . . . Y'all now! . . . Y'all now! . . . Everybody! . . . up here!"

The buzz in the room died down, quiet enough that Margaret could hear buoyant ice cubes tinkling in the glasses.

"I wanna thank y'all for comin' tonight, and I'm gonna hand the gavel here to Lieutenant Thorpman of the Perry County

Sheriff's Department. He's fixin' to tell us about this crazy mess. . . . Lieutenant Thorpman?"

Over the next fifteen minutes, Nordy Thorpman briefed the concerned listeners on what the department had learned. To date, thirteen dogs had been found dead, all in Red Hill Plantation. No puncture wounds. No bullet holes. No signs of trauma from being run over. They looked as if they had simply laid down and fallen into a Rip Van Winkle–like sleep.

A man's voice boomed out from the back of the room: "What about cottonmouths?"

"Not that we can tell," Nordy answered. "There's no swellin' anyplace."

"What about mushrooms?" asked another man. "You think they're eatin' mushrooms?"

"We ain't got no poison mushrooms growin' here in Selby," Nordy answered. "But I'll tell you this — we do think someone just might be feedin' 'em poison."

The comment drew gasps and whispers among the group. Suddenly, one man in a maroon polo shirt raised his hand.

"Sir?" Nordy acknowledged.

"Do you think they're eatin' my wife's cookin'?" he asked.

Nordy ignored the laughter. "Any other questions?" he asked.

Suzanne Parley, holding an empty wine-glass, raised her hand.

"Yes, ma'am?"

Her hand came down, and she nervously began twirling a section of her gold necklace around an index finger. "How do you know they're bein' poisoned?" she asked.

Lieutenant Thorpman, who had been leaning back on the edge of the desk, stood up and squared his shoulders, then hooked his thumbs in his belt.

"I ain't at liberty to say anything else about it, ma'am," he said.

"Why not?" someone asked.

"It's an ongoin' investigation. There's some things I just can't say right now. But y'all need to know that we're doin' every-thing we can do to figure this thing out. Sheriff Barnes knows this neighborhood is home to Selby's finest families, and he promises he's gonna get on top of this. The sheriff wants your dogs to be safe. No man should have to worry about his dog dyin' young."

Unbeknownst to Margaret, Randy had snuck up behind her to read from her screen.

"Holy shit!" he blurted, jolting Margaret in her seat. "This reads like a Johnny Cash song. Did he really say that?"

"I can't write a news story, Randy," she whined. "Besides, nothing happened. It was interesting, but nothing happened."

"Bullshit," he said, "you're doing fine. Just keep going. I need it in twenty minutes."

As she did in her journal entries, Margaret selected those details that tickled and fascinated her the most, and they were the type of fictionlike details Randy had been trying to get his staff to include more of in their reporting, such as Lieutenant Thorpman's sad, basset-hound eyes and his habit of scratching his left forearm when he answered a question . . . and the oil portrait of the owner's golden retriever who had succumbed to cancer (*"Radar" 1982–1996 . . . Gone huntin' in heaven,* said the brass plate beneath) . . . and, flanking the Ristles' driveway, identical sandstone sculptures of Irish setters, each with a paw on a basket of stone flowers . . . and, Margaret's favorite detail of the evening, the tuxedo cat who attentively watched the entire meeting from the window ledge outside.

She finished just before ten o'clock.

After sending the story on to Randy, Margaret went to the bathroom then to the lounge to retrieve her purple, plastic Hunchback of Notre Dame lunch box that she'd found at a garage sale in her neighborhood.

On her way out, she stopped to see Randy. He leaned back in his chair and put his hands behind his head. "You're right," he said. "It's not a news story."

"I told you so."

"It's really, really great, but it's not a news story. It's an essay is what it is."

"Pass it on to whoever can use it as research."

"Still, it's really good. Hilarious."

"It's not meant to be — that's your perception of the culture — but thank you."

"New lunch box?" he asked.

"Yes, it is."

"Nice."

"And look." Margaret opened the lid and pulled out the thermos. "It's a castle turret. Isn't it fun?"

Everywhere Margaret turned she'd been finding irresistible items of whimsy that had been absent from the home she shared with her mother all her life. It's not that Ruth Pinaldi disapproved of a child-centered environment, she just never really thought about it. Margaret was ten when she lost her eighth baby tooth one night while munching corn on the cob. Her mother, upon noticing, gasped and said, "Oh, my God! I forgot the whole tooth-fairy thing. I owe you" — she paused, calculating in her head — "a dollar and seventy-five cents."

Ruth Pinaldi's life was filled with battles — raising a daughter alone, scurrying to shore up the eroding foundation of abortion rights, struggling to keep open a clinic that did more than its fair share of pro-bono work — and, as in the military, her tools in life needed to be easily recognizable and plain and sturdy, which gave their house on Linden Avenue the feel of a spartan bachelor's apartment. She banished throw rugs from the house. ("They are obstacles in a necessary path.") And why, she asked her daughter one day, should they place a bowl of colorful fruit on the center of the kitchen table when it needed to be moved for each meal?

"Have you been avoiding me?" Randy asked.

"No."

"I get the feeling you've been avoiding me."

At two minutes before seven, Margaret

was roused from bed by an energetic rapping at the back door. Somewhat groggy from staying up until one o'clock to finish a collection of short stories by Flannery O'Connor, she hurried into her aqua chenille bathrobe and scuttled out of the room.

Holding a white paper bag and the day's *Reflector*, Randy blew in like cold air.

"There's hope for this town yet. Look: Bagels! And the *Times*! Today's *Times*."

"It's seven o'clock, Randy."

"I've got something to show you."

He set the bag on the kitchen counter and pulled out two bagels and a clear, plastic dish of cream cheese. "I've never seen you with your hair down," he said, looking at her. "It's longer than I thought."

He looked around at the spartan furnishings — an orange beanbag chair, a card table and chairs, and a lava lamp that Margaret had found at Second Hand Rose. "Nice place," he said. "Who's your decorator?"

"You're here this early to show me bagels?"

"No. This," he said, tossing her the *Reflector*, still folded in its plastic bag, which Randy called a condom. "On the op-ed page."

Margaret unfolded the paper and turned to the editorial page in the local section, which Randy had renamed *Metro* from *Mid-state Report*. She scanned the two pages . . . Ellen Goodman . . . William Raspberry . . . a guest-opinion column about the new Planned Parenthood that was scheduled to open that month in Selby . . . and then she saw it and gasped. Randy had taken her notes and run them as a guest editorial column . . . with her photograph!

"Randy! What is this?"

"It's brilliant. That's what it is."

She scanned the essay — he had run it almost verbatim — and at the bottom was an italicized tag line that said, *Margaret Pinaldi, a "Reflector" writer and editor, earned her B.S. in anthropology and master's in women's studies at State University of New York at Buffalo. She is covering this issue for the "Reflector."*

"Where did you get that picture?"

"It's from your photo I.D. H.R. had a copy."

"You didn't tell me you were going to do this."

"I didn't ask."

"I would have said 'no.' "

"I know."

"Youuuu!" She shook the open paper in his face like a voodoo rattle and let it fall to the floor. "God! I feel so . . . violated!"

"I don't understand what you're so mad about," said Randy.

"You've exposed me," Margaret answered. "Don't you understand that?"

"Most people cream their jeans if they get on the editorial page."

"I'm not most people, Randy. I am a very private person. It is why I like doing Chatter."

"Would it help if I told you the publisher loved it?"

"No, it would not."

"Here," he said, handing her half a bagel slathered with cream cheese.

"I don't want any, thank you."

"Oh, quit pouting, Margaret. Come on, let's celebrate brilliance. Yours and mine."

"Sometimes I think your arrogance might even dwarf my mother's."

"It's called confidence."

"That's exactly what she used to say."

Randy set down the bagel and walked up to Margaret. He put his hands on her arms and dipped his head down, trying to see into her eyes. "Hey," he said in a voice softer and lower than she had ever heard. The tone startled Margaret, and she felt the tension ebb from her body. "I thought you said you were drawn to confidence," he said.

"No," she replied. "I said I was drawn to brilliance."

He leaned into her. "So am I."

A good eight inches shorter than Randy, Margaret had to tilt her head back as he moved in over her like a cloud, and as they kissed Margaret kept her eyes open. Overhead, a moth banged against the lit bulb again and again and again, despite the warnings of the corpses of her burned brethren that littered the glass of the fixture. She seemed slower each time she returned to the bulb . . . dazed and burned and weaker but inevitably unable to resist such brilliance. And for what in return?

"No," Margaret mouthed beneath his lips. "Stop."

And when he rose with a quizzical look on his face, Margaret, too, was perplexed, uncertain if she was addressing Randy . . . or the moth . . . or herself. But one thing she knew for sure: It was not Randy she was kissing here — it was her mother.

Sixteen

Dear Chatter: When I talk to a Southerner why do they look at me with a blank smile? It's like they don't understand what I'm saying or asking. Can someone enlighten me here?

Dear Chatter: The only way to keep a squirrel from eatin' your bird seed is to shoot it.

Dear Chatter: I'm absolutely amazed at how you Southerners can find Jesus and God's hand in everything. Let's get some things straight: God has nothing to do with you winning the lottery or the raise you get at work, and he sure as H--- doesn't do magic with potatoes. I've lived in Selby for six months now, and sometimes I feel like I'm living with wild natives of some third world country.

In the Rand McNally atlas, cities are represented by pale orange, ragged stains that grow with each census, creeping outward like a drop of water on a paper towel. In the center of the orange mass that was Selby, Georgia, floated a strawberry-shaped white spot, and therein lay Sugar Day Country Club and its affluent environs, a boldly gerrymandered island in the Sea of Selby created long ago so the leaders in town wouldn't have to pay city property taxes on their sprawling brick homes. For this reason, some locals called it The Reservation.

Sugar Day was host to everything that mattered in affluent, white Selby. It was where a stripper could still perform at an all-male cigar party for the birthday of a prominent banker. It was where Hickey Freeman and Talbots sponsored their annual, regional trunk shows and where a wife would debut her newest, Austrian-crystal Judith Leiber handbag.

It cost eighty-five thousand dollars to join, and golfing privileges were another twelve hundred a month from initiation till death, but Sugar Day had a five-year waiting list. And young, climbing couples would brood and worry and feel like the fat kid on the playground as they awaited sweet inclusion and sipped their chardonnay and bourbon with the masses in no-name bars and restaurants throughout town.

Lately, though, cracks had formed in the foundation of the venerable golf club. For the first time in the history of the one-hundred-and-sixty-year-old institution, both the publisher and editor of the *Reflector* had declined invitations to join, as did the general manager of WSEL, middle Georgia's oldest and farthest-reaching television station. Not wanting to anger the local advertisers, the publisher and TV executive tiptoed around the issue. ("Oh, we're not the golfing types.") But editor Randy Whitestone was not as diplomatic. He'd been heard in a local Mexican restaurant, slamming an empty Tecate bottle down on the table and proclaiming in Yankee volume, "It has no black or Latino or female members. That's why we're not joining your stupid club!"

Boone Parley, head of the membership committee, sat in the daytime dining room of Sugar Day, awaiting his mother and talking with Comer McDonald, the club's manager. Though neither would say it out loud, both men had spent much time pondering the significance of the three powerful Yankee men's snubbing of Sugar Day, and just that morning, as if someone had been reading their minds, an item in Chatter gave them extra gristle to chew on.

Dear Chatter: To all you Old Selby families: Your names are fading just like Norma Desmond and the silent film stars. You are outdated and out of touch. You're losing your grip on this town. See you at the bottom of the food chain.

Boone wondered: What was it about the privileges of membership that these men could not understand and appreciate? Who could not like Sugar Day? Who could not embrace Bulldog Saturdays in the bar, when the men of The Reservation would gather to eat boiled peanuts and drink bourbon as they cheered on their alma mater? Who could not like the Fourth of July with their private fireworks display and low-country boil, a stew of crawfish, spicy sausage, tomatoes, potatoes and corn served poolside, with corn bread and champagne in sterling-silver goblets? Who could not like the fellowship and sanctuary from their wives that Sugar Day provided? Boone lived for his Saturday mornings when he would meet Donny and Langston and Dunill on the crest of the tee-off for hole one, the toes of his brown-leather, saddle-style golf shoes darkened by cool morning dew; his aluminum, insulated cup of morning coffee warm in his hands; the verdant, rolling landscape enshrouded in a light morning haze; the mockingbirds that cockily swooped and darted from magnolia tree to Georgia pine to the top of the Greek Revival clubhouse, chirping their schizophrenic collection of sounds that hadn't changed since Boone was a child growing up in the white Italianate on the sixth green.

"Here comes your momma," Comer McDonald said. He and Boone stood up from the table to greet her.

"Miss Evelyn." Comer leaned in to air-kiss her cheek. "You're lookin' beautiful as ever."

Wearing her cobalt-blue St. John knits and a simple strand of pearls, her gray hair pulled back into a bun, Evelyn Parley had just come from a board meeting at the Telbottom House, which was not only regional headquarters for the Daughters of the American Revolution but also Selby's only architectural casualty of the Civil War. After burning Atlanta, Sherman, for unknown reasons, marched right on past Perry County and Selby, ignoring her, as if she had nothing to offer and was not worth his soldiers' trouble. It created in Selbyites an odd inferiority complex that lingered to this day. Indeed, when the Olympics came to Atlanta, Selby was the only second-tier Georgia city that did not have a sporting venue; it never even occurred to local leaders to ask for one.

Because of Sherman's snubbing, the city could now boast of more historic structures on the National Register than even Savannah or Charleston or Macon, but it also had turned the town into the crippled man who gets left behind while his compatriots go off to fight then come back with war wounds and bravado and stories of valor. Instead, all Selby had to show was a single, accidental wound from an errant cannonball that Sherman's troops had intended for a passing munitions barge floating down the Muscogee River. The black orb flew across the watery divide, over the granite and marble mausoleums of Rosemont Cemetery, almost grazing a second-floor gable of the historic courthouse before arcing downward and into an open window of a wealthy textile merchant's home where it unceremoniously landed with a thud at the base of the stairs in the vestibule. Within days, it was soldered into place and became a bittersweet landmark for what old-Selby families called The War Between the States.

"I hope I'm not interrupting you boys," Evelyn Parley said.

"Oh, no, ma'am," said Comer. "I was just fixin' to go to a meetin'. Y'all have a good lunch. The lobster bisque is pretty good today." He winked and walked away, disappearing through the swinging stainless-steel door of the kitchen.

Boone helped his mother with her chair. He then instinctively unbuttoned his navy blue blazer and seated himself.

"How was your meeting?" he asked her.

"Well, it got a little ugly today."

"What happened, Momma?"

Evelyn looked at the painted turquoise fingernails of the African American waitress who leaned over to fill her glass with sweet tea. "There's a new girl on the board who thinks we need to rewrite the little cards that go with the exhibits."

"From Selby?"

"From California. The wife of the new president of WSEL. She says that the exhibit's funny, can you believe that? She says the writing sounds paranoid. And I spoke up and tried to tell her that those cards were written a hundred years ago, and even if you don't agree with 'em, we should not be messing with history. And anyway, she starts to get ugly with Marlyn

Finstrom who's trying to keep control of the meeting. And this woman, Boone, this woman started pointing her finger at everyone like it was a gun, and she was saying how we were the laughingstock of the South. And I'll tell you what, we just sat there and didn't say anything. There was just no need to yell at the board like that."

"No, ma'am."

"And on the way there, to the meeting, someone honked their horn at me for no good reason. I can't remember anyone ever honking their horn at me."

Evelyn took a drink of her tea then wiped her mouth with a pink linen napkin that was the signature of Sugar Day.

"Anyway, I'm not here to tell you about my day, Boone. I'm here to talk about Suzanne. I'm concerned about her."

Evelyn thought Suzanne seemed manic of late, rushing to and fro like Holly Golightly in *Breakfast at Tiffany's*, as if a door were going to slam shut any second, and happiness would vanish as quickly as it appeared. Convinced that Suzanne had been avoiding her more than usual — indeed, Suzanne screened her calls through the answering machine — Evelyn Parley called Boone the previous week to ask about his wife, pitching at him question after question that he could not answer: Who was Suzanne's ob-gyn? Had she found a pediatrician yet? Was she sick in the mornings? Which bedroom were she and John David remodeling for the nursery?

"Well, I did find out about the pediatrician, Momma," Boone said. "She's going to her momma's pediatrician in south Selby."

"Do you know him?"

Boone shook his head. "I've seen his name pop up a few places, but, no, I don't know him."

"What's his name?"

"Madison. She doesn't know his first name."

Evelyn shook her head. "Why did she choose a south Selby doctor?"

"I don't know, Momma."

"You know I called and offered her Dr. Stinson. He's not taking new patients but he agreed to see Suzanne."

Evelyn sighed. "You know I've tried with your wife, Boone. I've tried very, very hard."

She thought back to the time she took Suzanne to pick out her pattern at Beverly Bremmer's Silver Shop on Peachtree Road in Atlanta. Just as Evelyn feared, Suzanne immediately turned toward the overly ornate Versailles pattern and then, even worse, to the Edgemont, a new Queen Anne–inspired pattern from Gorham that featured highlights of gold that twisted upward around the handles like a serpent.

Evelyn excused herself and Suzanne from the salesperson and walked away from the glass counter, leading Suzanne with her hand around her arm, to a corner of the store where the julep cups and sterling frames were on display.

"Darlin'," she whispered to her future daughter-in-law. "It's called *silver*ware for a reason."

"What do you have at home?" Suzanne asked.

"Chantilly," she answered. "You can't go wrong with Chantilly, Suzanne. It's dignified but not fussy. You want something that cleans up easily but looks nice. Always look for things that are both practical and beautiful but not tacky. Versailles is overdone, and it's hard to get polishing paste out of those tiny crevices."

Despite her coaching over the years, Suzanne continued to disappoint her mother-in-law. Evelyn did not like her having two cars, both the Lexus and the matching black Suburban, and she thought a three-car garage was vulgar. She did not like the china with Fabergé eggs painted on the gold-rimmed plates. She did not like the quail-and-pomegranate-motif, Lacy-Champion rug that was custom designed to match the colors of Suzanne's dining room. She did not like how Suzanne went out of her way to buy only clothes and accessories that were easily recognized or specifically branded, mainly the interlocking C's of Chanel on her shoe buckles and lipstick and compact. Nor did she like how John David had taken pictures of every table in Suzanne and Boone's house so that Josephine, whom Evelyn shared with Suzanne, would know exactly where to return things after dusting.

Evelyn shut her large black menu and handed it to the waitress.

"I don't know why I even bother looking at this," she said. "I'll have what I always have — the niçoise salad."

"Sir?"

"I'll have the fillet, medium rare."

"You want the house béarnaise sauce?"

"Please."

Methodically, habitually, like a flight attendant serving drinks in slow motion, Evelyn carefully pulled her reading glasses from her face, folded then pushed them back into their floral-patterned sleeve. She then picked her purse up off the floor, clicked it open, and gently set her glasses inside. She had carried this brown-leather purse for sixteen years, needing only to replace the buckle on the strap after a frightening encounter with the unforgiving automatic doors of the train in the Atlanta airport. Once each month, Evelyn had Josephine nourish the leather with mink oil.

"Now," she said, folding her hands on the table before her. "Boone, as I was saying, I'm worried about Suzanne. She doesn't look well."

"Momma, she's pregnant."

"No, darlin', it's more than that. She looks like she's living on the edge . . . like she's fixin' to fall out of a tree house."

Boone thought of the weathered, wooden tree house still perched in the live oak behind his parents' home, where he used to hide his *Playboy* magazines in a cardboard Chiquita carton he and Reilly Conover found in the Dumpster behind Sugar Day. He wondered now: Could they still be up there after fifteen years? It was possible; the two lowest boards, which ascended the trunk of the tree like buttons on a shirt, had long ago rotted and fallen away. Boone told himself that before his baby boy could climb, he'd need to replace those boards and retrieve the contraband literature . . . and the old, navy blue, Sunday school sock he would use to wipe off the pages.

"She's under a lot of stress, Momma. She's got that Dogwood Festival party on her mind. You know we're havin' the Dogwood party."

"Yes, I know," she answered. "Everyone knows, Boone. Suzanne's made sure of that."

"Well, aren't you happy about that? It's an honor to have that party. I'm glad it's staying with an old Selby family like ours."

"Is she taking prenatal vitamins, Boone?"

"I don't know, Momma. How would I know that?"

"Because you're her husband."

"She's been sleeping in. I don't see Suzanne many mornings now."

"If she was taking vitamins she'd have that healthy, rosy glow that pregnant ladies get, and she doesn't have that glow, Boone. She looks malnourished and all deep-eyed. She isn't still drinking, is she?"

"No, Momma, she's not drinking."

"Suzanne likes her chardonnay, Boone."

"She's not drinking, Momma."

"Well, I don't know what it is, but she just looks frantic to me. Bless her heart, that girl has never been a happy one."

Evelyn cocked her head and looked beyond Boone's shoulder, at a gilt-framed watercolor of two sailboats.

"But then again," she said, thoughtfully, as if speaking to herself and not her son, "she seems happier now, like she's not as lost. Like she's found something she's looking for."

"Momma, I don't understand what you're sayin'."

Evelyn exhaled loudly and looked at her son. "I just can't shake this feeling that something's going to happen. Something's not right, Boone," she said, spearing a vinaigrette-coated olive. "Something's not right. Mothers know these things."

Years ago — how much of this was his fault . . . and how much hers? — Boone had exiled his wife to a deserted island in a sea of the mind to which he'd never return. It was nothing he'd done consciously, as is so often the case with marriages that take a wrong turn, but he slammed shut a door in his mind on the day he learned that Suzanne had lied to him about her ability to conceive. She trapped him for personal gain knowing very well that the Parley name would die in his hands. It was murder on her part, and she had made him an unwitting accomplice.

And through these dry years, though they still had sex and dined together in the evenings, Suzanne had become as vague and indistinguishable as the furniture in the house she had commandeered. Though she took his arm at social functions and dinners at friends' homes, though she would ride next to him on the way to Christ Church every Sunday, he had ceased to see his wife, and she him. That Thanksgiving, looking at Suzanne from across his parents' dining room table, he noticed her hair looked shorter and asked her when she'd cut it. "Labor Day," she said. "Do you like it?"

It was a marriage of motions, a cohabitation similar to sitting through a mediocre movie in a pleasantly cool theater on a blazing August day, neither happy nor stimulated but not upset enough to leave and face the sweltering heat outside. And by the time Boone finally reached the summit of his anger and began to ponder his descent to détente, Suzanne had retreated into her own world, wherever it was she went, whatever it was she did every day with John David. The timing of their personal evolutions, he realized now, had been awful.

But then, this miracle. And this resurrection of feelings akin to the smell of freshly overturned soil. What did it mean when a man's opinion of his wife could change overnight just because she was carrying his child? Was she happier because he was being nicer or vice versa? Suzanne no longer complained when he kissed her before shaving. She'd been letting him leave the floor lamp on the side of his wing-back chair that he preferred. And one night last week during dinner, she smiled coyly and slipped down her chair as if it were a slide, submerging herself beneath the table and coming up for air at his crotch, where the sound of giggles intermingled with the clinking of his belt buckle as she undid his pants.

"No, Momma," Boone said, trying to contain a smile. "Things are just fine."

The Mediterranean-looking man standing at the entrance to the Prada boutique had wavy, black hair shiny with pomade and teeth that were white and strong and carnivorous looking. His thin but muscular torso appeared to be shrink-wrapped in an ecru silk T-shirt.

"Great top," he said to the woman passing by.

"Thank you," Suzanne Parley answered. "It's Pucci."

"Of course," he said. "Not Prada, but I'm sure you already have some Prada."

"No," Suzanne answered. "I don't think so."

He raised his eyebrows, slowly, flirtatiously, as if they were a piece of clothing he was peeling away from his coffee-with-cream skin. "Would you like some Prada?" he asked.

"Well, I don't know," Suzanne answered.

"Please," he said, standing aside and motioning with his arm to enter the boutique. "Come in. Let me show you some beautiful things. Would you like some champagne?"

Finally, someone in a chi-chi boutique on the second floor of Neiman Marcus in Lenox Square was offering Suzanne champagne! For years, in her weekly trips to Atlanta, she had watched this from afar and always wondered why other women, most of them not as attractive as she, were chosen for special treatment, and she was not. But why today? She was certain it had to be the Pucci, which she'd bought on her last trip to town.

Thrilled, Suzanne leaned back in the blocky, black-leather chair with chrome legs and reached for a crystal flute that he presented to her on a silver tray. She had never seen such a flute, tall and triangular and sharp, like an elongated, upside-down pyramid.

Piece by piece, he brought out his wares, and as Suzanne absorbed this personal parade of haute couture and drank this handsome young man's expensive champagne, she was distressed to discover that she did not like clothes from Prada; they were so bleak and dark and mean looking.

"What about somethin' lighter?" she asked.

"Ma'am?"

"Somethin' more colorful," she said. "Like this Pucci top."

"Ahh, yes. I have exactly what you're looking for."

He disappeared through a doorway and returned a few minutes later with a clear plastic raincoat trimmed in black. Suzanne thought it looked no different from the plastic, taffy-thick raincoats her mother used to buy at Walgreens.

"These came in today," he said. "I haven't even put them out on the floor yet.

This," he said, draping it over his arm, "is the rage of Manhattan. No one in Atlanta has one of these. Not yet, anyway. Can I help you with it?"

Suzanne stood, and he slipped the raincoat onto her back, and when she turned around to face him Suzanne saw his hands coming toward her. Without asking, he began to click shut the round, black snaps of the coat, starting at her breasts and slowly moving downward.

"Oh, no, I can do that," Suzanne said.

"It is my pleasure, madam."

He continued downward, past her stomach . . . her waist . . . her knees . . . gently brushing the back of his hands against her with the randomness of a windsock in a breeze. Suzanne looked down at the back of his neck and admired the way the curls of his black hair crested and broke over his skin, reminding her of waves on a deserted beach. And then she tried to imagine this man lying on this beach, and, unlike Boone, he would have no hair on his chest or stomach or back. Instead, the surface of his body would resemble the Sahara from five hundred feet up, a smooth landscape with ripples and rises formed not by sandstorms but ribs and muscles. And then, she would trace these undulations with her fingers, dragging them across his sun-warmed skin.

Suddenly Suzanne noticed her lips; they were dry from unconscious, deep, open-mouth breaths, and she moistened them with her tongue.

"There," he said, standing up and backing away to look at her. "When you've got a figure like yours why hide it under an opaque raincoat? This way, you can show off your beautiful Pucci and strut around in your Prada at the same time. It's brilliant, really."

"How much is it?" Suzanne asked, now feeling awkward as she tried to look him in the eyes.

"Does it matter, really?"

"Of course not," she said, recovering. "I just wanna know how many Skymiles I'm gonna get today."

He handed her the receipt, and she folded it without looking at the price. "Wait," he said, reaching into a drawer. "This is my card."

With exaggerated slowness, he set it into her hand then looked at her for reaction, as if he'd just slipped her a hotel-room key. "I would love to help you again," he said. "Nothing would please me more."

Nothing would please *me* more, she

thought, and Suzanne caught herself staring at his hands, which led to his arms, which led to his chest, which led to the flattest stomach she'd ever seen on a man his age. Wasn't he over thirty? Maybe not. He *had* to be over thirty.

Suddenly realizing she had ogled for too long, Suzanne severed her stare and put the receipt and card into her Louis Vuitton pocketbook. "Well, thank you so much," she said. "I just loved that champagne. Bye now."

"Good-bye," he answered. "I will see you later, I'm sure."

As the heels of her leather Chanel loafers clicked across the marble floor, Suzanne fought the urge to turn and see if he was watching. She hoped the two glasses of champagne did not make her appear wobbly or insecure.

All the way down the escalator, through the north wing of the mall, across the parking lot, Suzanne kept closing her eyes for seconds at a time and reliving the snapping of the coat and the brushing of his hands against her skin. A chill spread through her body, as freon fills a compressor, producing a tingling sensation from her cheekbones that traveled up, behind her eyes and over her scalp, down the spine and into her extremities — her wrists, her breasts, the bottoms of her pedicured feet — and then back up again, where all this energy seemed to collide at the base of her skull, causing Suzanne to shake her head.

And then, once in the car, the heat of the Lexus's interior reminded Suzanne of that beach in her mind, and there he was again, not naked but in white, loose-fitting Polo swim trunks, the ones she'd bought Boone that he had never worn.

Surprised at these sensations, Suzanne tried to remember another time she'd felt this way and she remembered Boone's room in the Beta house at UGA. Only it was not Boone she saw. It was his roommate, Dixon Satterfeld, an ag engineering major from Waycross with brown eyes that appeared to be perpetually dilated. He, too, had this inexplicable, electrical effect on Suzanne, which caused her to stay clear because she had already chosen the promising future neurosurgeon from her hometown.

Dixon used his hands in a slow, thoughtful manner that reminded Suzanne of an aged woodworker, always seeming to savor the texture of whatever it was he was touching — a pencil, a shiny doorknob, even the braided shoestrings of his boots. She remembered a time when a splinter from Boone's desk chair lodged in her flesh. Dixon took her hand, set it in his blue-jean lap and slowly, repeatedly stroked his index finger over her palm, as if he were telling her fortune, looking for but not finding the penetrating intruder. And Suzanne, experiencing an intensity of physical pleasure unknown to her, and embarrassed by her reaction, and desperately seeking a polite exit yet wanting to linger right there forever, closed her eyes in confusion and fell backward, into darkness, just as she nearly had again minutes ago in the Prada boutique.

In contrast, Boone's gentleness with his hands was a learned behavior that surgeons adopt early on, not a natural one, and when he did touch her it seemed as empty of human energy as a mannequin's appendage. Over the years Suzanne had witnessed the metamorphosis in Boone and all his peers: As their hands evolved into valuable, precision tools, surgeons seemed to grow away from them, just as she imagined prostitutes abandoning their breasts. Indeed, when Boone's hands were idle during conversation, he would set them in his lap, palms up, as if they were delicate machines no longer attached to his body. They appeared to be items for which he was not responsible.

Leaning her forehead on the top of the leather-clad steering wheel, Suzanne looked at the Prada receipt that had fallen out of the bag and onto the floor. She picked it up and discovered she had just paid $1,600 for a new raincoat that she did not even like. But no one in Selby had one, and that made it priceless.

With Miss Suzanne in Atlanta for the day, Josephine decided to finish deodorizing the carpets and leave a half-hour early.

In her baby blue Chrysler New Yorker, she headed downtown on Linella Road, feeling a tinge of relief after passing beneath what her people called "the bridge," which was nothing more than a railroad trestle next door to Talbots yet it was the symbolic dividing line in African Americans' minds between the land of Sugar Day and the integrated city of Selby.

She turned onto Pio Nono Road, named for a pope who visited the city a half-century earlier, into the parking lot of a brown-brick strip mall whose original tenants fled the inner city long ago. What used to be a Piggly Wiggly was now Econo Carpets Plus. Ellington's Lad and Lassie clothing store had evolved into Middle Georgia Pawn and Gun, whose owner had bolted lemon yellow steel bars over the large windows. Next to that was Eunice's, whose only signage were the words *candles and soap* painted in white letters on the window.

A small, homemade anteroom with the look of a lean-to had been constructed of painted, magenta plywood, and hanging from its low ceiling were hundreds of strings of ceramic beads that reached down to Josephine's breasts. Eunice had hung them to caress her weary, beleaguered patrons and to help brush away tensions created by the injustices of the day. Josephine felt the cool glass beads gently wipe across the skin of her arms and face and neck, and she soon entered a plain, small store with an island counter in the middle and four walls filled with different-colored bottles.

"Josephine!" Eunice cried, setting down her fried-fish-and-yellow-mustard sandwich. She raised her arms in the air in a hallelujah manner, her hands aquiver. "Where you been, girl? Horace!" she yelled toward the back of the store. "Horace, Josephine's here!"

Horace and Eunice Meeker had run a Popeye's Chicken franchise, a hat and wig shop, and a car-detailing business downtown on Broadway, but their latest endeavor was this low-rent storefront filled with the entire line of Mama Louise's Potions. Clearly marked with the word *alleged* on their labels, they came in little rectangular bottles filled with different tints of clear liquid that purportedly cured or alleviated the ills and hurdles of daily life, including poverty, a bad boss, a mean boyfriend, an unfaithful wife. There was the emerald-colored *Do as I Say*, the scarlet *Road Opener Oil*, the orange *Go Home*, the purple *Bend Over*, the sapphire *Win Lottery*. If patrons had an aversion to oil, they could purchase the same remedies in candle form or in a colorful cream body wash that looked like tempera paint.

With her purse in her lap, Josephine sank into the soiled, tan recliner that Horace had found at the curb two blocks from his house on trash pickup day.

"Lord have mercy," Josephine said.

"Miss Suzanne givin' you trouble again, Josephine?" Eunice asked.

"It's days like today when I'm just hopin' and prayin' that the good Lord decides to call me home."

She shook her head in disbelief. "You know what she done yesterday? You not gonna believe what she done yesterday."

"No?" said Eunice.

"I come into the kitchen and she's got on her yellow Playtex gloves and right there on the counter's a gallon jug of anti-freeze, and she's mixin' it into some smelly dog food. And I come up and I say, 'Miss Suzanne, what are you doin'?' And she just takes off those gloves and walks right over to her purse and gives me a hundred-dollar bill!"

"Girl!" Eunice exclaimed.

"Uhm-hmm. And, Lord, I know right then and there that she the one killin' all those dogs, and she say to me, 'Josephine, just don't say nothin' about this. I'm doin' this neighborhood a favor.' And I tell her I can't take her money. Jesus would frown on me for takin' a bribe for such a crime. Killin' some of God's creatures. Oh, and did she yell at me? Uhm-hmm. Lord, did she yell at me."

"Now why would she wanna be killin' all those dogs?" Eunice asked.

Her fingers stroking the padded, velour arms of the chair, Josephine shook her head. "Miss Suzanne do a lotta things I don't understand . . . you know she's pregnant with child? Well, she still drinkin' wine like she just won the lottery."

Horace took a bite of his wife's now-cold, fried-fish sandwich. Despite having the appetite of a teenage boy, drinking full glasses of whole milk with every meal and constant snacks of pecans roasted in butter and salt, he still had a lean, tall figure reminiscent of a Giacometti sculpture. With his mouth half full, Horace said, "I think you'd better call the police."

"Nosir, Horace, I need that job. Lord, do I need that job. I'm just gonna mind my own business. You know what happens when we don't mind our own business. What I'm hopin' is that you can find me some kinda potion to use on Miss Suzanne. She one sad, sad girl. I know that 'cause she mean. Mean folks is sad folks."

Horace, like his wife, wasn't certain that the potions they sold had intrinsic, benevolent properties, but they viewed their products in the same light as the Scripture; they were tools of empowerment their people needed to help them believe they had control of their daily lives and destinies. The makers of Mama Louise's Potions also sold a line of more negative tonics — *Have Affair, Go Crazy, No Sex, Lose Money* — but the Meekers considered them mean-spirited, and they would rather their patrons use positive change to overcome the problems in their lives. Yet, Horace reasoned in his mind, Josephine was kin, his first cousin on his mother's side, and it sounded as if Miss Suzanne had altogether abandoned inner peace and was too far gone to reform. This time, he would make an exception.

As the two women talked, he shuffled to the back storeroom and returned with a small, wrinkled paper sack, its top rolled down like a scroll to conceal the contents.

"This is on the house," he said, handing it to Josephine. "You be careful with this now, you hear?"

She opened then reached into the sack and pulled out a small bottle of tonic the color of orange Kool-Aid. Josephine read the label, smiled, and returned it to the bag.

"Well, God bless you, Horace," she said, sharing a tired smile. "You a good man. I think this just might do the trick."

Seventeen

Dear Chatter: To answer your question: When a Southerner looks at you with a blank smile and doesn't answer you right away it's because he doesn't trust you and he's lookin' you over to see how much damage you can do as a human being. Southerners are good listeners and we take in a lot. Why do you think all the great writers of this country come from the South? Have a nice day.

Dear Chatter: To that Nixon lover who called I just wanna say he wasn't no poet, he was a crook. It's not up to you to tell me where I can throw my trash. God put man on this planet to do what he wanted to do, so there.

Sipping their peach daiquiris through foot-long straws, Jackee and Donna had been exchanging frequent glances with the table of guys beneath the TV on the other side of the bar at Rio Cantina.

"I think they're fixin' to come over," Jackee said. "How's my hair look?"

"For the forty millionth time your hair looks fine, Jackee."

"You got your lipstick on you?"

"You know I don't carry lipstick anymore."

In her months at Kroger, in the wake of the accident, Donna's use of makeup had tapered down to almost nothing. And on most days now, if she wore any at all, Donna allowed herself some blush and a single coating of lipstick every morning, mainly because she missed the smell and it helped keep her lips hydrated in the dry, cool air of the produce department.

"What is wrong with you?" Jackee asked. "Why don't you wear makeup anymore?"

"It's a waste of time to wax a rusty Chevy, Jackee," Donna answered.

One of the guys, handsome, lean, and dark-haired, stood up from the table, drained the last of a Bud Light, then turned and started to walk toward the girls. It was Donna whom he connected with at fifty feet away — a smile, a nod — and as he got closer she began the countdown in her mind . . . *forty feet* . . . he sees something now . . . *thirty* . . . he thinks it might be hair in my face . . . *twenty* . . . a

slight startled, inquisitive look in his eyes
. . . *ten* . . . he is panicking now; he has
come this far and must do something . . .
any second now . . . any second . . . *click!*
Just in time, the magnet in his mind flip-
flopped, and what was once attractant became repellent.

"You wanna dance?" he asked Jackee.

And as she got up and walked with him
to the dance floor, his friends back at the
table looked at each other in confusion.
*What the hell happened? He's got the wrong
one.*

"Where on earth did you get tomatoes so
red and juicy this time of year?" Frankie
Kabel asked his daughter.

Donna had already finished her meal, a
low-fat stir-fry of broccoli, Napa cabbage,
and, in a compromise to her father, sliced
skirt steak. At the last minute, she realized
the plates of food needed a splash of red or
orange, and she hurriedly sliced the tomatoes and lightly drizzled them in olive oil.
She had learned this trick from her new
friend Margaret, who'd switched to her
Kroger even though it was six miles out of
the way. Margaret was an excellent cook,
and she shared with Donna plenty of recipes for her meals for Miss Suzanne, in-

cluding a white-bean, garlic, and rosemary stew over polenta that she'd been requesting nearly every week.

"You like 'em?" Donna asked her father.

"Real good, darlin'. Real good. I s'pose they're from South America some place."

"No, Daddy, they're American-grown. Outside Orlando."

"Well, praise God."

"They're hydroponic tomatoes. They're grown hangin' up in the air without any soil."

His fork in midair, he frowned. "I've never heard of such a thing."

"It's a cleaner environment 'cause they're not in the ground. And they don't catch as many diseases that way."

Frankie set down his forkful of tomato and took a drink of sweet tea. "It's just not right, though, Donna," he said. "It's not natural. God intended fruits and vegetables to be grown in the ground."

"Daddy . . ."

"Daddy nothin'," he said, his voice growing louder and more agitated. "This is the same thing as happened last week. The same thing, and I am not gonna agree with you. They are just dead wrong to be messin' with God's creations like this."

He was referring to their argument the

previous Tuesday about genetically modified crops. For their nightly dinner conversation, Donna made the mistake of sharing with him the highlights of a special edition of *The Packer* that featured genetic advancements in the produce industry. And what seemed to frighten Frankie Kabel the most was her example of scientists introducing the antifreeze gene from coldwater fish into potatoes so they would become more cold-resistant.

"I'm worried about you, girl," Frankie said. "I'm worried about your soul."

"My soul is fine, Daddy."

"I thought that accident of yours would push you closer to God, but it just pushed you further away."

"How can you say that?"

"See? By that way you're talkin' back to me now. That's how. You never used to do that."

Donna threw her wadded napkin on the table. "You know what, Daddy? You know why you think the Devil's got ahold of me? Because I'm not actin' like a scared little puppy dog around you anymore, that's why. And you know what? Momma might've acted that way around you, but I'm not goin' to."

Frankie quickly leaned across the table,

the corner of it pushing into his large stomach. Shaking his finger at his daughter, he said, "If your momma, God rest her soul, heard you talkin' to me like this she'd die all over again. That heart potato was a sign, Donna Louise Kabel. You are gettin' too big for your britches. Psalm twenty-five, nine: *He guides the humble in what is right and teaches them his way.*"

"And you know what, Daddy?" Donna's voice grew louder, as if she were yelling at someone who was rolling up his car windows as she spoke. "Genetic engineering is gonna make it so more people can have fruits and vegetables. They're gonna cost less and taste just as good. And the more fruits and vegetables we're gonna eat the less cancer we're gonna have. Maybe Momma'd still be alive today if she got her antioxidants. The Southerners' diet is killin' us off. We gotta change it."

"We got no control over such things, Donna."

"She died of cancer, Daddy. Quit treatin' her death like it was the will of God. People die of cancer, and there's some things we can do to help prevent it."

"Cancer is the Lord's tool for callin' his people home. Why don't you think they've been able to find a cure? Because it's

God's secret tool — he don't want us to figure it out. He needed your momma. He called her home."

Abruptly, Donna pushed herself back from the table, her chair leaving two black skid marks on the white linoleum, then stormed into the living room. She sank into the couch but got up after a few seconds to walk across the room and turn on the light in the bleached-oak china cabinet that held her mother's collection of Hallmark Precious Moments figurines. Frankie had built and given it to her for their twenty-fifth anniversary.

Donna opened the glass door and reached inside for the porcelain girl in overalls holding a violet umbrella and standing in a puddle up to her ankles. She picked it up and wound the silver knob on her back. The tinkling notes of "Singin' in the Rain" poured forth. Donna carried it with her to the couch and held it in her cupped hands as if it were an injured bird. In the background, she could hear her father mumbling in prayer at the kitchen table.

"All I want is someone to hug me and say everything's gonna be all right," she said, crying. "Is that askin' too much?"

Donna squatted down to pull out a

carton of green bananas from beneath the display case, and when she rose again to her feet, the heavy Del Monte box in her hands, she saw him again — Question Man, the name she'd given this new shopper because he asked her something every single visit: How can I tell if a pineapple is ripe? How do I grill an eggplant? This time he was holding two bell peppers, a red and a green.

Seeing he had Donna's attention, he held them in the air as if they were torches. "Okay, so what's the difference here?"

Donna stole a glance of herself in the mirror behind the cucumbers and green onions. She wished she at least would have put on some blush that day.

"Hey," Donna greeted him. "Bet you didn't know they're the same pepper. They come from the same momma."

"But they're different colors."

"The red ones used to be green ones," she explained. "But they got left on the vine longer so they could ripen. And the longer somethin's on the vine the sweeter it gets. That's just a fact with produce. Same with tomatoes and melons. I'd buy the red one even though it costs more; I don't think the green ones are fit for a horse. They give a lot of people gas."

He favored Armani suits and Jerry Garcia ties, and Donna had mistaken him for a lawyer until he came in one time wearing surgical scrubs that were nearly the color of her uniform. She thought he looked like Matthew McConaughey with darker hair, and his voice, soft and buzzing, reminded her of the skin of a peach or the fine hairs on an okra pod. What intrigued Donna most was how he always seemed to look at her scarred cheek for a moment or two and then just keep right on talking. And he returned again and again, always connecting with her through the fruits and vegetables.

Bagging three red peppers, he said, "You did something different in here, didn't you?"

"I sure did," she answered. "I moved things around quite a bit."

"It looks really nice. Like something you'd see in Atlanta."

Donna watched him walk away, toward dairy. She knew he always bought a quart of refrigerated, vanilla-flavored soy milk and then went on to meats, where Sabrina usually sold him some variety of fish, usually a salmon or grouper fillet — and always just enough for one.

Warmed by the compliment, Donna

stood back and surveyed her work from the previous day. Even she had to admit that, in recent weeks, she had lifted the produce department to a new level. Warren Jalowski, the perishables manager who had been uncomfortable with Donna's drive and barrage of daily ideas, had been promoted to manager of a store in Montgomery, and the day he left Donna worked through the night, completing a vision she'd been forming in her mind for months. Somewhere along the way, she had realized that a produce section, like a woman's face, should be considered as a whole, and the beauty lay in the harmony of its parts. There was a code to be cracked — arranging these creations of God into an uplifting, glorious scene while still following the practical rules of produce care and merchandising. And finally, at seven a.m., her arms and face dusted and smudged with the dirt of thirteen states and seven countries, Donna went to wash up in the bathroom. When she returned she found Mr. Tom standing before her pièce de résistance, the corner of the main refrigerated case that she had transformed into a scene from a Tuscan marketplace. Large overturned baskets lined the top of the case, their contents spilling downward, toward the customer, each with a vegetable that contrasted perfectly with its neighbor, purple eggplant next to the orange-and-green turban squash, green cabbage intermingling with yellow summer squash, carrots with the greens attached, red stalks of rhubarb, artichokes and radicchio and Brussels sprouts and yellow wax beans, all lying in a state which straddled that fence that separates natural chaos and man-made order.

"See?" she said to Mr. Tom, pointing to an article on page twenty-six of *The Packer*. "It says here, 'The spill effect from bushel baskets gives a fresh feel and movement without the need for laborious fruit hand stacking.' And I just didn't do it by looks either. I mixed the more popular items . . . like the yellow squash, which is almost all water with hardly any nutritional value . . . with the ones they won't buy . . . like this vitamin-rich acorn squash . . . because maybe they'll try somethin' foreign if it's lyin' next to somethin' they're comfortable with. That's human nature, don't you think?"

That afternoon, Donna found a note in her mailbox in the break room, hand-written on a piece of paper with the blue Woolite logo on top.

Donna: At Lancôme you helped women find beauty they had lost. At Kroger you have an even higher calling. You are successfully helping to change the unhealthy eating habits of an entire city. You are helping people live longer, healthier, and happier lives. You've come a long way since the day you tried to sell plantains as bananas. Keep up the good work.

T.G.

Eighteen

Dear Chatter: My little girl's fixin' to go into kindergarten next year and she's still wearin' a diaper. Can someone tell me how to get my little girl into panties? I'm at my wit's end.

Dear Chatter: This message is to the person in Lake Hillary who reported me to the police because my dog accidentally got loose for about ten minutes Wednesday night when I was at church. Thank you for such a warm welcome to the neighborhood. Since it'll probably happen again in the future — stuff does happen — I suggest you stop bein' petty and get a life. Or put the Perry County Sheriff's Department on speed dial, because you will need to call them again.

A Danielle Steel paperback in one hand, a cream-and-sugar sandwich in the other, Harriet sat at the table in the *Reflector* newsroom, her chin lifted high so she could see through her cat-eye glasses. They were plastic frames, cloudy gray with a thread of Dijon swirling throughout, and what younger female reporters mistook for expensive, trendy eyewear from an Atlanta boutique was actually the result of five decades of cautious, thrifty living. Harriet had changed these lenses seventeen times.

"Do you mind if I join you, Harriet?" Margaret asked.

She looked up and smiled. "Course I don't mind — I've been missin' you. They've got you off runnin' all over Selby."

Margaret sat down and began pulling the contents from her paper bag — a hunk of extra-sharp cheddar cheese, an orange, eleven blanched green beans, a heel of sourdough bread, and a piece of sweet-potato pie Dewayne had baked the night before. Dewayne worked ten straight days at the station, where he slept and took all his meals, then got seven days off. And though he never stayed the night, most of that time was spent at Margaret's house. He cooked for her and she for him, each eating things they'd never sampled — pork-and-rice casserole for Margaret, and kashi and seared, rare tuna steaks for Dewayne. He taught her how to stew collards and make pimiento-cheese-and-Wonder-Bread sandwiches. When she was at work for the day, Dewayne would clatter around the house with his bulky red toolbox, replacing rotten wood on the porch, planing the bottom of a swollen door, hanging wire shelves in the closet so Margaret no longer had to store her clothes in the plastic milk crates on the floor. "It looks like you're not plannin' on stickin' around here for long," he had said.

Harriet wiped the corner of her mouth with a paper napkin. "I sure did feel sorry for that poor man and his family," Harriet said. "The rocking-chair man?"

Under pressure from Randy, Margaret had started her series of profiles on local natives, and the most recent was the life of Bernie Pinshew, who, Randy thought, best illustrated Selby's recent transition from an insular mom-and-pop economy to one owned and run by anonymous corporate accountants in the windowed high-rises of another city.

A Selby native, Bernie lost his job as gate guard at the region's Budweiser distributor when it was bought out by an Atlanta company. The new owners quickly installed a computerized I.D. scanner and electronic gate, replacing Bernie and his outhouse-size, white wooden structure, where he sat all day with a little fan and radio tuned to

Peach Country 105.6 FM. But what Randy liked even more was what transpired during the course of reporting the story. "This man's life is a country-western song if I've ever heard one," he said.

On her fourth day of shadowing him, Margaret was scheduled to tag along with Bernie to interviews at the Delco battery plant and a new Kroger distribution center on the south side of town. Yet she knew something was wrong when she drove up to the house in south Selby and noticed his metallic gold Ford pickup truck missing from beneath the rusty carport. His wife, Melinda, answered the door, crying, and Margaret quickly discovered that Bernie had landed in jail. Evidently, he'd been driving up and down I-75, snatching the rocking chairs from the fronts of Cracker Barrel restaurants and successfully selling them to the housewives of Red Hill Plantation.

When Randy read the transcripts of Margaret's jailhouse interviews, he busted open two full pages for the story. "This deserves the space," Randy lobbied his publisher. "This man speaks in that misleadingly naive but piercingly accurate and succinct and insightful, sad voice of the South. Just listen to this."

He pushed the play button on Margaret's tape recorder.

. . . You can bet I was nervous the first few times, but that didn't last for long when I learned how easy it was. I just acted like this was somethin' I was supposed to be doin' . . . don't be lookin' over your shoulder and act like a dog who's just got caught messin' on the rug or you're gonna get caught. . . . Anyway, I backed my truck up to the Cracker Barrel porch, and I laid a tarp out on the floor of the truck, then I loaded them up, and I closed the tailgate and drove away real slow. I always took more than one rocking chair 'cause no one's gonna think that someone would be stupid enough to steal two at a time.

Sometimes I'd even stop and tie my shoe or light up a cigarette after I loaded them up. That way if anyone was watchin' me and thinkin' I might be stealin' them, they'd think "Nah, he's too relaxed and he's takin' too much time." That's what they think, but they don't even know they're thinking it. You know how that is. People do that all the time . . .

They're real easy to sell, these chairs. Everybody has to sit down some time, and when they do they'd just as soon be rockin'. Makes 'em wish they was babies again without a care in the world.

As Harriet listened to Margaret, she was pleased to note changes in the girl's appearance. Her black hair was still rolled up in a tight bun, but Margaret had started wearing some makeup, and, as she spoke, Harriet fought the urge to wet her thumbs and reach across the table to better blend the rouge into the skin at the outside of her cheek.

"Are you likin' writing those other stories?" Harriet asked. She had taken out her processed cheese in a can and squirted a gob onto a Ritz cracker.

"It's very interesting," Margaret said. "But I feel guilty for exposing these people to the whole world."

"You're still doin' Chatter, right?"

"Oh, yes, ma'am."

"I was worryin' that you wouldn't be doin' Chatter anymore. I don't like Chatter much."

"I didn't think so."

"I think it makes us all look our very worst, like a child talkin' when he's mad.

But if it's gotta be done then I want you to do it 'cause you got a kind heart and you don't judge people. You can't be doin' Chatter if you judge people."

For a few minutes, they ate in silence. Harriet looked up at the television atop the refrigerator, at a CNN segment on cosmetic facial surgery for men. Margaret listened to the comforting clickety-clack of people's coins descending through the dark, metal interior of the Coke machine.

"You sure are lookin' happy, Margaret," she finally said. "Good things must be happenin' to you."

"Yes, ma'am."

"Are you makin' new friends?"

Finished with her beans, Margaret dragged her thumb and forefinger across the blue seam of the Ziploc bag. "Yes," she answered. "A good friend."

"Is it the Case boy?" Harried asked. "Dewayne? Don't look alarmed, sweetheart. I know his grandma. She and I went to high school together. Dewayne's a good boy. We think you're just about the sweetest couple in town."

"Why haven't you said anything to me?"

"It's none of my business. Have you met his momma?"

"It's not that serious, Harriet. We're just going out."

Harriet began to refold her clear baggie, which she would use again the next day. "Ronna bakes the best pies in south Selby," she said.

Margaret dug her unpainted thumbnail into the rind of the orange and leaned over the fruit to smell the microscopic explosion of citrus oils.

"The truth is, Harriet, I'm spending way too much time thinking about him. When he's in the house I don't even turn on NPR. I don't read. I feel so stupid for saying this, but I just like to sit there and look at him. When I'm around him I feel like a cat lying in the sun."

Harriet nodded. "He's got the longest eyelashes I've ever seen on a man," she said.

"We cook a lot together. We do have that in common. But we really don't talk about anything of substance. It's just not what I envisioned in a relationship."

Using her wadded-up napkin, Harriet began to brush together the crumbs of the Ritz crackers that had fallen onto the wood-veneer table.

"You know, Margaret," she said. "Lorn and I don't talk much. We're one of those couples you see at McDonald's who's sittin' there not sayin' anything. But that doesn't mean I don't love him. It just means we're comfortable with each other."

"But is that enough, Harriet?" Margaret asked.

She shrugged her shoulders. "It is for me."

The crumbs gathered, Harriet used the edge of her hand as a food scraper and pulled them into the open paper bag on her lap. She then reached into her purse and pulled out a compact and tortoiseshell tube of lipstick. Margaret had never seen anyone reapply lipstick so often, and it was probably due to the shape of her mouth. Harriet's thin lips raced across her face like a straight, hurried brushstroke, and to create curves that nature forgot Harriet would stray northward of her top lip, boldly coloring outside the line, creating two symmetrical, red waves that cleanly crashed into each other at the center.

"You don't wanna talk too much with your man, darlin'," she said. "That's what girlfriends are for."

Their stomachs stretched from large bowls of *pho*, Margaret and Dewayne emerged from the new Vietnamese restaurant on Truman Parkway and walked to Dewayne's truck. Margaret waited for him to open her door and let her in, then watched him walk around the front to his own. She was inexplicably drawn to and fascinated by Dewayne's belly-in-progress, amazed at how every ounce of weight a man added to his body could congregate in that one single spot, causing it to grow and grow as if a fetus were inside. Margaret was surprised at how hard it was, not gelatinous but dense and springy, like a woman's stomach in her last trimester.

Dewayne got in but did not start the car. Margaret looked over to find him looking at her.

"You know," he said. "I'm not gonna bite you."

"What?" Margaret asked.

"Why do you always sit way over there?"

"As opposed to where?"

"Right here," he said, patting his thigh. "By me."

"You're kidding me, right?"

"No."

"Isn't that a Loretta Lynn kind of thing? It's awfully cliché, Dewayne. Where I'm from they do that in high school."

He shrugged his shoulders, the toothpick bobbing in his lips. "You always say you're cold."

"Yes . . ."

"Well, why be cold when you can be by me?"

Dewayne smiled, and Margaret felt a sudden zipper of warmth begin someplace behind her breasts and run down into her loins. Unconsciously looking out the windshield and upward, toward the clear sky, as if her mother might suddenly send some sort of missile down from the heavens, Margaret slowly slid over.

At Dewayne's house they sat on the glider beneath the carport as the sun was starting to set, eating pieces of Coca-Cola cake that Dewayne had baked the day before.

Suddenly, he pointed to the east; a buck had materialized from the wall of dark woods on the side of the house. "Looks like loverboy's back," he said.

"Oh, my God," Margaret whispered.

Dewayne explained how the buck first emerged that Monday and crossed the empty lot into his yard. He first sniffed at the doe's rib cage then followed a line along her back, leaving a moist, dark trail as would a snail, stopping at her hind side, which he smelled and poked at with his glistening black nose.

Then, a noise, maybe the Thornton boys shooting squirrels with their BB guns next door, or the whine and clatter of the trash truck down the block. The buck jerked up his head, looked eastward, then suddenly turned and bounded back into the dense woods, which swallowed him in one leap.

This time, with Margaret witnessing, there was no sniffing, no prodding. The buck strutted alongside the doe, surveying her as a sergeant would scrutinize a line of fresh recruits. When he got to her end, he turned and stood behind her frozen body then suddenly lifted himself onto his hind legs. He fell atop her back end, and he wriggled about, searching for entry and moist warmth, then finally hobbled backward and dismounted.

The buck walked ten yards to the south, as if taking time to contemplate his strategy. He returned, reared up and tried again. The scene was sad but strangely erotic. Any buck who mistook a white, concrete doe for the real thing was destined to be the end of his genetic lineage. Yet watching him mount the doe excited Margaret. Was it the juxtaposition of warm flesh and cold concrete? The sheer size of the lean, muscled creature as he tried to have his way with her? Still, it bothered Margaret that she was aroused by this arrogant, one-sided, forceful display of desire.

Margaret found Dewayne's free arm and squeezed his thick wrist. Dewayne looked away from the deer to meet her gaze. He'd stopped chewing at the end of the first mount and now had to swallow his bite of cake. Margaret watched his Adam's apple rise then fall like a light switch.

"You want some more Co-Cola cake?" he asked her.

My life with Dewayne is stuck in Donna Reed Land. We hold hands and snuggle, and we have kissed and kissed and kissed until my lips seem to lose their elasticity. His fingers sneak quick brushes over my bare skin when my shirt fortuitously rises above the belt line — but then he stops. So what is stopping me? I certainly was not raised to depend upon a man for anything. What is he waiting for me to say? To do? Am I sending a message of reluctance or is he as inexperienced and as scared of performance as I am? Perhaps he's not as attracted to me as I am to him.

The same was true with learning how to ride a bike. After the appropriate age passed me by, I was suddenly too embarrassed to let anyone know I could not ride one. And I have yet to try because I'm supposed to know how.

I must be the oldest virgin in North America. I have to be.

I didn't know how to kiss. I don't think he did either. (But we're both pretty good at it now!) Could I have met my match in inexperience? He may not be aware of it, but whenever we see a love scene in a movie he or I will try to emulate it — that is, anything that happens before the clothes come off.

Why haven't I bought any birth control?

I feel satisfied when I am with him. Why this man? Why now? Why have I never felt such stirrings?

Dewayne's metabolism radiates heat like a stone hearth, and I wonder — with my mother gone and father somewhere, be it dead or alive — have I simply sought out a comforting source of heat in this solitary journey in which I am all alone?

Or do I just need to get laid? I'm certainly overdue.

God, being a teenager is difficult. I wish I would have done it earlier.

Nineteen

Dear Chatter: I'm thinkin' you need to change the "Selby Reflector's" name to the "Ebony Reflector."

Dear Chatter: To the lady who went through my line at Winn-Dixie yesterday, I just wanna say I'm proud of my fingernails. They took a long time to get this way and you're just jealous.

Dear Chatter: If your kid isn't potty trained by four, they make pull-up diapers for big kids. If your kid isn't potty trained when he's ten, don't worry. You can buy Depends for them.

Suzanne had laid the sterling silverware out on the dining room table, each piece side by side like the rice-size pencil scrawls of someone keeping score in a card game.

"Every piece of silver?" Josephine asked her.

"You ask me that every time, Josephine," she answered. "Yes, every piece. I want it all polished and shiny, shiny, shiny."

Shaking her head, Josephine looked at the silver, nearly two hundred pieces in all, including the requisite forks, spoons, and knives but also a sardine server, olive spoon, asparagus fork, asparagus server, macaroni server, fish-serving fork, fish-serving knife, food pusher, chocolate spoon, cheese knife, cheese scoop, tea strainer, toast server, waffle server, jelly cake server, large berry spoon, small berry spoon, lemon fork, butter pick, ramekin fork, and bonbon spoon. Nearly every time Suzanne went to Atlanta for the day she would bring back with her a piece of silver. And four times a year, Josephine would have to polish it all and replace them to their black-felt sleeves and wooden cases, though a setting for two was left out for Suzanne and Boone's daily use.

"I need the tea tray polished, too," Suzanne said. "And the gravy boat."

"Miss Suzanne," Josephine said. "How you gonna use all this silver? You don't use all this silver."

Suzanne walked over to the sideboard, pulled open a drawer and retrieved a white pamphlet, now old and flimsy with creases worn to the point that they had started to leak light. Suzanne picked it up years ago when her mother-in-law took her to Beverly Bremmer's Silver Shop in Atlanta to pick out her pattern for Boone's and her wedding.

"Just read this," she said, handing the paper to Josephine.

Why sterling? Sterling says things about you that you simply couldn't say yourself. It reveals a graciousness and loveliness in your attitudes toward daily living . . . a quiet confidence in your own abilities and those of your family. Nothing celebrates success quite like sterling. Sterling silver tells the world, as few other material possessions can, that you know exactly who you are and where you intend to go. And that you intend to get there with dignity, elegance, and style.

Josephine scanned the pamphlet, as if she were looking at a photograph, and handed it back to Suzanne.

"All I know is I'm not gonna have time to go grocery shoppin' if I have to polish all this silver."

"You don't have to," she answered. "I've got Donna makin' me somethin' for tonight."

"Do I have to finish all this today?"

"Tomorrow I'm gonna need you to spray Clorox on the bricks of the patio. I'm fixin' to serve dinner outside on Friday."

"That mold adds some color to the bricks," Josephine said.

"That mold is tacky."

Suzanne had invited Madeline VanDermeter, the executive director of the International Dogwood Festival, in hopes of changing her mind. This year's official sister-country sponsors of the festival, named as one of the *Atlanta Journal-Constitution*'s top-ten events of the South, included Britain, as it did every year, as well as Japan (to please the new Toyota executives in town) and Botswana (a gratuitous nod to the majority black population who generally ignored the festivities anyway). And, much to Suzanne's displeasure, instead of getting the distinguished, white-haired, crimson-cheeked, parliament member from Wales, she and Boone had been chosen to host and quarter Ed Nwasu, the assistant attorney general for the Tswana-majority, south African country.

Feeling as if her status in the community was under siege, Suzanne called to complain to the organizers in the festival office downtown, a houselike, faux-stucco, Georgian-style building painted the creamy white of dogwood blossoms with shutters the color of the tree's foliage. In front of the building stood a new, specially commissioned, three-tiered fountain with dogwood blossoms and cherubs sculpted into the base. Unfortunately for Madeline VanDermeter, it had caught the attention of the new editors at the *Reflector*, who wrote an editorial critical of the extravagant purchase. Though the fountain remained, she no longer lit it at night.

"When I put my name in to be a host, I told you I specifically wanted Lord Benjamin," Suzanne said.

"It's an honor to host any of the delegations," the receptionist consoled her.

"But can't you change your mind?"

"No, ma'am. Everyone's already been contacted."

"Well, I am not happy about this," Suzanne huffed. "No, ma'am. I am not happy. Not one bit."

"Lord Benjamin's gonna be stayin' in your neighborhood. You can stop by and see him."

"Who's he stayin' with?"

"Someone new in town . . ."

"Who?"

Suzanne heard a ruffling of papers as the receptionist looked for the name she could not remember. "Armbuster?" she finally said. "Jodi and Marc . . . Now what a strange name that is."

Suzanne breathed in deeply and ground her teeth. "I can't believe this! I just can't believe this."

"Mr. Marc's the president of WSEL."

"They're not even from Selby!"

Unruffled, the young woman continued. "I guess she — Mrs. Armbuster? — she went to college in England or somethin'. That's probably why Miss Madeline put Lord Benjamin with them."

Suzanne thought of the new Yves Delorme bedding she'd bought for the guest room, an elegant mixture of satin off-whites and whites. When she put them on the bed the first time, it reminded Suzanne of a late-night TV commercial for an at-home teeth-whitening system — *before* . . . *after* — and, in front of the bathroom mirror, she held up an example of each color beside her open-mouth smile to make certain Dr. Pilcher was doing his job. She thought of Jodi Armbuster, and how she needed braces on her bottom teeth.

"Well, this just isn't gonna do," said Suzanne, on her third glass of chardonnay.

"It's just not gonna do. I don't even know what to feed someone from Africa."

As Josephine polished, humming along with the hymns on WHXK that she listened to on her paint-splattered transistor radio, Suzanne walked the house with her Daytimer, listing the remaining items John David needed to address before the Dogwood party. Along the way, she noted with pleasure all the changes they'd made, the additions they'd found on their trips to Atlanta and Charleston — the matching pair of Rose Medallion Chinese vases for the window table in Boone's den . . . the gilt, ram's-head finials for the living room curtain rods . . . the new fake fireplace they'd built in the living room, flanked by waist-high Imari vases from Jane Jarsen Antiques in Atlanta, even though John David had wanted to buy modern, black Tizio lamps for these high-profile spots . . . the Zuber and Cie wallpaper in the downstairs powder room, which featured scenes of Adam and Eve in the Garden of Eden, their genitals discreetly concealed by leafy flora that looked like banana leaves.

At seven-thirty — two hours after calling her husband to ask him to take the minute steaks out of the freezer — Josephine buffed to a shine the final piece of silver, a large soup ladle. She leaned back in her chair and looked at the seventeen spent rags on the table before her, all soiled with gray tarnish and the robin's-egg blue of Wright's Silver Polish.

After rolling her neck to relieve the tension from sitting so long, she gathered the rags and went to wash her hands in the kitchen, where Suzanne was using a rubber spatula to scrape the last of the mashed potatoes from a clear Rubbermaid container with *DONNA K.* written on the side in black marker.

"Did you get the bread plate, too, Josephine?" Suzanne asked. "The one on the small sideboard?"

"Yes, ma'am."

As Suzanne carried the Portmeirion botanical-print bowl of potatoes to the warm oven, she noticed from the corner of her eye that Josephine was staring at her.

"Is somethin' wrong, Josephine?" she asked. "Didn't I already give you your paycheck?"

"Oh, no, ma'am," she answered, diverting her glance to the floor. "No, no. Everything's fine."

Yet on the way out to her car, Josephine wondered if she should have put the potion in a different spot. Perhaps the oil that she had dripped into Suzanne's Playtex rubber gloves was laying, out of reach, in a small pool at the end of a finger. She had thought of rubbing a bit into one of Suzanne's prenatal vitamins, but she didn't seem to take them with any regularity.

Driving down Forest Lee Boulevard, Josephine pondered ways she could administer the drops secretly and effortlessly. She passed a billboard that featured a gigantic squeeze tube whose words were intentionally blurry and indecipherable. *"Toothpaste . . . or hemorrhoid cream? It's time for LASIK surgery from Dr. Marty Lanton."*

"Now why didn't I think of that before," she said to herself. "Lord, thank you for that inspiration."

Twenty

Dear Chatter: To the lady who was lookin' for a good manners class for their little girl: JCPenney's at the Selby Mall has a manners class for little girls called The Budding Magnolia. They teach you how to use the forks and how to put on makeup and talk to boys. I highly recommend this course on manners. Thank you very much.

Dear Chatter: If you don't like Halloween then you should come to the Judgment House at my church next year. It's a haunted house that shows what can happen if you don't do as the Lord wants you to.

For forty minutes, Margaret stood over the hot, gas grill on the patio, spearing with a fork and flipping sliced, marinated zucchini, summer squash, eggplant and Portobello mushrooms for thirty-two people. Though her eyes stung and her hair reeked of garlicky smoke, Margaret was ecstatic. This was her most lucrative catering job to date, and the first that actually called upon her knowledge and love of ethnic food. Jodi and Marc Armbuster, who tasted her bruschetta at a grand opening reception for a new Montessori preschool, called and ordered a Mediterranean buffet, including tabbouleh, hummus, a tossed salad of herb greens and baby romaine, grilled lamb and dark-meat chicken tossed with feta cheese and fresh mint . . . and the vegetables, all sliced by Donna Kabel, who offered to help when Margaret was shopping for supplies.

"We basically want a garlic buffet," Marc had said when they interviewed her.

"We're going through garlic withdrawal here," added Jodi.

"Put garlic in everything," Marc said.

"Even the salad dressing," said Jodi.

"What about your guests?" Margaret asked. "I don't know if you've noticed, but garlic isn't a favored staple in the native population's diet."

The husband and wife looked at each other in surprise. "I thought you were one of us," Marc said.

"What do you mean?" Margaret asked.

"One of *us*. You know — from the outside."

"We're change agents," Jodi interjected.

"We were brought in to drag this town's television broadcasting into the twenty-first century. They need garlic in their food here, you've got to admit it."

Not wanting to alienate herself and lose a potential client, Margaret nodded. Yet she fondly remembered the pre-Armbuster weathercaster on WSEL. Instead of relying upon computerized graphics, the balding, portly Billy Jeskins used maps of North America and Georgia that were permanently painted on a white dry-erase board, and with a black marker he would illustrate the easterly movement of the jet stream or an approaching storm. The daily highs across Georgia were recorded in his handwriting, the hottest temp written in red and the lowest in blue, and in winter months he sometimes added tiny icicles to the latter.

"Besides," Jodi continued, "they won't even know what they're eating. People always say they don't like garlic, but when they eat something with garlic in it, they always love it."

The Armbusters told Margaret that their trademark for entertaining was casual elegance, and indeed this was the case. A white, damask tablecloth covered the dining room table, and Margaret and

Donna served the food in a variety of bowls and baskets the Armbusters had collected in their years of childless travel. Red and white gladioli poked out of a vase fashioned from an old lens from a historic Canadian lighthouse. The only in-bad-taste outcast was intentional, a floral centerpiece in the middle of the glass coffee table in the living room. The International Dogwood Festival coordinator had commissioned Mattel to issue a commemorative Dogwood Festival Barbie dressed in green go-go boots, a beret with dogwood blossoms embroidered on the top, and a coat with genuine ivory-dyed mink collar and cuffs. It cost three hundred dollars, and though Jodi and Marc called to order one the day they read about it in the *Reflector*, they were already too late.

"Sold out?" Jodi asked. "How can that be? You don't have one left?"

"No, ma'am."

"None?"

"No, ma'am."

"Not one?"

"Well," she said, lowering her voice to a semi-whisper. "We do have five more, but they're . . . African American Barbies."

Jodi was silent.

"Black Barbies?" explained the woman.

"You're kidding me."

"We didn't order 'em but they sent 'em anyway. But we can put you on an order form for the next shipment of regular Barbies."

"Nobody wants the black Barbies?" Jodi asked.

"No, ma'am."

"I'll take three," she said.

Jodi took one of the Barbies to David Messenger Florists near her house.

"I want to speak with one of your gay floral arrangers."

The clerk looked puzzled. "Ma'am?"

"Do you have someone on staff who's gay? I need someone with a sophisticated Yankee sense of humor, and they're the only locals who seem to have it."

The young woman smiled politely and disappeared into the back of the store. After a hushed conversation between three or four people, out came a balding man in khakis and an L.L. Bean button-down shirt.

"Can I help you with somethin', ma'am?"

Definitely not gay, Jodi thought.

"I want this Barbie in a centerpiece," she said. "And I need it over-the-top. Funny."

He took the Barbie from her. "Well, she sure is cute."

"No, she's not. She's vulgar, and I want

to capture that somehow. I want something idol-like, something altarlike . . . as in, come and pray to black-princess dogwood Barbie. And make sure it has silk dogwood blossoms in it."

Disappointed with the tasteful outcome, Jodi disassembled the centerpiece, scavenged around the house for some other items and rebuilt the arrangement as she saw fit. The final result included Dogwood Blossom Festival Black Barbie rising from the middle of two antique mannequin's hands, set on their wrists so they flanked Barbie like large parentheses. On the fingers of the plaster hands were fuchsia Lee Press-on Nails, and the sprays of faux dogwood blossoms jutted out in all directions, as if to mimic a divine aura. Next to that, sitting in a plate holder, was a sign on a paneled card that Jodi had printed out on the computer: *Please join us for a celebration of the Dog Days of Spring, April 12. Watch for Invitations.*

With her bare hands, Margaret tossed the salad in an oversized stainless-steel bowl, coating the greens with a cumin-flavored vinaigrette. Suddenly, Donna walked through the swinging kitchen door. As it opened, the buzz of talking guests poured into the room.

"They're not takin' the grilled asparagus spears," she said to Margaret. "I don't think they know how to eat 'em."

"Just tell them they're like carrot sticks," Margaret said.

"I did. I even showed 'em how to do it." She set the silver platter on the butcher-block island. "I sure am gettin' lots of compliments on my tie, though."

At a caterers' supply store in Atlanta, Margaret had found bow ties made from a material of illustrated black-eyed peas floating in a violet background. Both she and Donna wore these, along with long-sleeve white shirts tucked into black pants.

"Miss Suzanne's here," Donna said. "The lady I do all my cookin' for? She wants me to cater a party she's gonna have in a few weeks."

"Do you cater?"

"No, but that's one reason I wanted to help you out tonight. To see how you do this." She picked up a tray Margaret had filled with circles of sliced, grilled Italian eggplant, each topped with a dollop of spicy baba ganoush. "And I think I could do it," she said. "If Jackee helped me."

"When is it?" Margaret asked.

"Friday week."

The phrase still caught Margaret off guard, one of the linguistic remnants of the English who settled Georgia three hundred years earlier. It was one of those wonderful, path-of-least-resistance, verbal shortcuts so common in the language here; *Friday week* was an impressive five syllables shorter than *a week from this coming Friday.*

"Let me help you," Margaret said. "I'm not doing anything that night. Dewayne's working that weekend."

"Oh, no, you're paid to do this," Donna answered. "You're a professional, Margaret. You shouldn't be givin' your work away for free."

"Then what if I don't pay you for tonight — and instead help you out at your party?"

Donna raised her eyebrows and nodded. "That would work."

"Let's get this salad out to the table," Margaret said. "I think that's everything. We're ready."

They stood back, watching the guests fill their plates from the buffet on the dining room table. "Now which one is she?" Margaret asked. "I'm curious."

"Petite with black hair . . . the black St. John's pantsuit."

Margaret recognized her immediately; it was the woman from the Forsyth Room.

Chatty and uninhibited from wine, she'd blown into Randy and Margaret's table, dropped into the chair and announced to them and her husband that she was pregnant.

By her own estimate, in her years at the clinic, Margaret had seen close to four thousand pregnant women at every stage of their nine-month journey. And though each carried the weight of a fetus in a way unique to herself, Margaret had never encountered an expectant mother who did not display an unconscious bewilderment at her condition. Even when engaged in conversation, each woman seemed to have a third eye, on her chin, that remained focused with fascination on the growing hump below her breasts: *Yes, yes, yes, blah, blah, blah, you talk about some interesting things . . . but would you look at this! Can you believe this! Look what's happening to me!*

Perhaps she was wrong, but Margaret thought this woman's third eye seemed more interested in the contents of Jodi Armbuster's built-in bookshelves.

Suzanne was the last to arrive at the party. She was alone; Boone had been called in for emergency surgery. Shortly after the sun went down, on the new I-75 bypass west of town, an eighteen-wheeler full of frozen, free-range chickens from Colorado had slammed into a local man's old, rust-colored Chevy Impala that was creeping down the busy concrete corridor at twenty miles an hour.

Jodi answered the door, wearing a black-knit silk tunic and matching pants that seemed to move like stirred crude oil when she walked.

"You look like you're fixin' to have that baby tonight," Suzanne said.

"Only in my dreams," Jodi replied. "She's a week overdue, and I'm ready to kill her. Is it true what I hear about you?"

"About the Dogwood party?"

"No, about the baby."

"Oh! Well, it sure is. It sure is."

"When are you due?"

"Oh, not till fall."

In one of her clandestine late evenings of chardonnay and phone-order shopping, Suzanne, realizing she was approaching the imagined third month, came across a catalog called Progressive Parenting, and in it she found a strap-on, weighted belly for curious fathers who wanted to know the sensation of carrying a fetus to term. She ordered the three-month, four-month, and five-month sizes and had meant to don the three-month prosthesis for this evening but in the end decided against it because it didn't look good beneath her St. John's knit.

"Y'all haven't forgotten about my Dogwood party, have you?" Suzanne asked.

"Actually . . ." Jodi said, looking sideways and downward at the Barbie centerpiece on the table. "Marc's bosses are coming out from San Francisco, and it just kind of grew into a bigger thing. I guess we're having one of our own. When is yours again?"

"April twelfth."

"Oh, no, Suzanne. So is ours!"

Suzanne faked surprise. "No!"

"I am so sorry, Suzanne. But Selby's a big town, and I'm sure we don't keep the same friends."

"Y'all aren't members of Sugar Day, are you?"

"That's correct," Jodi answered.

Suzanne glided onward, dismissing Jodi in her own foyer and moving into the living room, where she immediately noticed that the lovely gilt fleur-de-lis bookends she'd given for a housewarming gift had been painted stark white.

She saw a group of her neighbors — Alison Riner, Trevy Bates, and Jonnie

Newnan — huddled in the corner with their glasses of chardonnay. The three women seemed inseparable, and though they occasionally ran into Suzanne in Phipps Plaza or Lenox Square in Atlanta they had never asked her to join them. More than once, Suzanne had heard them recounting their adventures in Atlanta: at ladies' night at the Gold Club to see the Chippendale dancers . . . the time the women went to see the French Impressionism exhibit at the High Museum and got stuck in the elevator with the Federal Express man . . . drinking too much chardonnay at the Kudzu Cafe and, on a dare, riding a MARTA train for one stop before hurrying off and hailing a cab back to the safety of their cars. (The acronym of Atlanta's rapid-transit rail system, they joked, stood for Moving Africans Rapidly Through Atlanta.)

"Y'all now . . . y'all now, listen to this," said Alison Riner. Suzanne, recognizing no one else in the room, stepped up to the circle.

"We were fixin' to go up to our house in Highlands this weekend, in the mountains, and you will not believe what Robert asked me to do."

"What?"

"He wanted me to ride all the way up there on the back of that stupid Harley of his."

"No!"

"Yes! And what was I gonna say? You talk about tacky! So you know what I did? I wore my Sea Island T-shirt without a coat so people could see it on the back."

"Oh, Alison!" exclaimed Trevy. "What was your hair like when you got off that motorcycle?"

"You don't even wanna know. My lips were chapped like a sailor's hands. But I spent three hundred dollars at the day spa in Highlands when I got there."

"For pain and suffering," Trevy said.

"Suzanne!" Jonnie cut in. "Honey, that's chardonnay!"

Suzanne looked at the full glass in her hand that she instinctively picked up from the table as she approached the group.

"Oh, my gosh!" she said. "I thought it was water."

As Suzanne held the glass up to the light, the other three women exchanged quick glances.

"Let me get you some Co-Cola," offered Jonnie. "Now y'all don't say anything fun till I get back."

Standing so close to the women, all of

them mothers, made Suzanne nervous. Again, she chastised herself for not reading the *What to Expect When You're Expecting* that Boone's mother had given her. She did, however, keep it lying open and upside-down on her nightstand. Josephine had begun dusting it as if it were a vase or lamp or other permanent fixture.

"So you workin' on a nursery, Suzanne?" Trevy asked.

"It's gonna have to wait," Suzanne answered. "I've got Dogwood, and it's just killin' me to get everything done."

"I wouldn't have it," Alison said.

"Boone would have a fit if we didn't have that party."

It was true — at least partly true. Suzanne realized that Boone was still smarting from his exclusion from Selby's oldest and most exclusive palaver club. There were seven such clubs in Selby, all-male, monthly gatherings in which members would gather for dinner and listen to a fellowman's paper written exclusively for the group. Each man drew on his own experiences and connections, and the subjects ranged from the narcissistic (a travelogue of a bike ride through France) to the esoteric (a historical retrospective of the *Monitor*, the South's doomed, Civil

316

War–era ironclad ship) to the male-centered (an inside look at the University of Georgia's offensive line for the upcoming season). Boone had been lobbying to get into the palaver group for two years, but when one of the ten members finally succumbed to heart failure and new names were put up for consideration, Boone's was blackballed. And what bothered him most was that he considered everyone in the group a friend.

Alison used her napkin to wipe the lipstick from her wineglass. "I'd just tell him no," she said to Suzanne. "Sometimes you just gotta put your foot down."

Jonnie returned with Suzanne's Coke. She leaned into the group so she could whisper without being heard. "Did you see she's havin' a Dogwood party? Is it the same night, Suzanne?"

"I think so."

"That is so tacky," Jonnie said. "I can't believe that woman. I mean, have you seen that picture in the baby's room? Those naked ladies?"

"I saw it bein' unloaded," Suzanne said.

"That baby is gonna have nightmares like you've never seen," Jonnie said. "She is just too strange."

"And that floor . . . black-and-white tile?

They know it's a little girl. Why couldn't they make that room prettier? She said to me she didn't like pink. Now I just wanna know what's wrong with a little pink in a little girl's room?"

"You know, they're gonna send their baby to that new preschool out on John Morris Road . . . that Montessori?"

"Those Montessori kids act up. There's one in church, a new boy in town, and he gets up and gets a drink of water whenever he wants to — right in the middle of the service."

"You are kiddin' me!"

"There's lots of Orientals that go to that school."

"Is it true they let the little boys play with dolls?"

"I heard that."

"I did, too."

Sipping her Coke, Suzanne watched Jodi across the room speaking to John David. With sweeping gestures, she was explaining a large painting that was nothing more than messy, black, random lines on a white background, as if someone had been trying to clean the paint off their brush. When Jodi moved on, Suzanne excused herself and walked across the room to join him.

"What do you think of this, Suzanne?" John David asked, his arms folded as he looked at the painting.

"I think it looks like somethin' out of a nursery school," Suzanne answered.

"What you're supposed to do when you look at somethin' like this — Jodi just told me this — you clean out your mind . . . like wipin' off a chalkboard. . . . and then you look at the picture and see what thought comes into your head first. And then, see, that should tell you somethin' about yourself."

"So what do you see?" she asked him.

"I see skid marks from a motorcycle, and then I see a man on a motorcycle, and then I see me behind that man on the motorcycle . . ."

"John David!"

"And my arms are wrapped around that big, burly chest, and at the red light I slip my hand inside his shirt." John David turned to Suzanne. "What do you see?"

Suzanne sighed and looked down at the sweating, blue-rimmed, Mexican-glass tumbler of Coke in her hands.

"I see a great big cold glass of chardonnay."

"So go get some," he said, looking over at the table. "It's good chardonnay."

"I was fixin' to leave."

"Boone home?"

"No."

"He gonna be gone long?"

"I don't know. Probably."

John David jerked his chin toward the front door. "Then let's you and me go have some fun."

"Like what?"

"Meet me at my truck in five minutes."

"John David."

"Oh, come on, Suzanne. You don't wanna stay here in the Evil Queen's house all night. Let's go have us some fun."

For ten minutes, Suzanne stood in the dark beside John David's Toyota 4-Runner, ducking below the hood line whenever a car passed, letting the glare from the headlights sweep over her head and onto the front of the Armbusters' house. Finally, just as she was about to give up and walk home, she heard loud chatter on the porch and looked up to see John David walking backward, yelling out his good-byes. He arrived at the car rosy-cheeked and out of breath from the backward jog down the long sidewalk.

"How much have you had to drink, John David?" she asked.

"I brought you somethin', Suzanne." John David unzipped his brown-leather bomber jacket and pulled out two unopened bottles of the Oregon chardonnay, one from under the left breast, one from under the right.

"John David!"

"They musta had fifty bottles under that servin' table. They are not gonna miss two of 'em."

He opened his door and reached for a quarter-empty bottle of Knob Creek bourbon on the seat. "This is my poison for the evenin'. You can have all the chardonnay to yourself."

"Well, hurry up and open my door. I can't have anyone seein' me. It's not right for me to be with a man after dark like this."

"Oh, please, Suzanne. What about that overnight trip to Charleston?"

"That was a shoppin' trip, John David. Everybody knows that. But people are gonna think I'm goin' home with you."

"To do what, Suzanne, bake cookies? Come on. Let's go get us some Krystal burgers and go down and see Terrance. There's a corkscrew in the console there."

Suzanne opened then shut the console. "I shouldn't be drinkin' in my condition, John David. You know that."

"Oh hell's bells, Suzanne. I know you're not pregnant. And why the hell you'd lie about such a thing I have no idea. What were you thinkin'?"

"John David!"

"I saw those weird little strap-on bellies in your vanity. What are those all about?"

"What were you doin' in my vanity?"

"Lookin' for the silver polish."

"You breathe a word of that to anyone John David and I'm gonna have to kill myself. And you. You hear me? I mean it!"

He turned off Red Hill Drive and onto Knolton Avenue. With his open bourbon bottle between his legs and one hand on the wheel, he used the other to open the console and fish in the dark for the corkscrew, which he then handed to Suzanne.

"I guess if they can have strap-on dildos they sure can have strap-on baby bellies," he said. "Lord, I am feelin' more normal every day."

Venetian Village Greetings, owned by John David's housemate, Terrance Holiday, usually closed its doors at six o'clock, in time to get home for the habitual, six-thirty mai tais on the balcony of their historic downtown home. Yet two weeks ago, Terrance's most reliable salesclerk, Sally

Rubenstein, quit so she could enroll in the travel agent program at Middle Georgia Technical Institute. What that meant, of course, was that some things got set on the back burner, and this is why Terrance suddenly found himself faced with a microwave-size cardboard box beneath the counter that was so full of returned paper goods they appeared to be multiplying from within, rising up and falling over the edges like popcorn cascading from a theater popper.

"Hey, hey!" John David yelled from the door, the bell tinkling against the glass as it shut. "Me and Suzanne are here to say 'hey.' Terrance?"

"Down here!" Terrance yelled upward.

John David and Suzanne walked around the counter and saw him sitting on the floor amid the paper products he was sorting.

"Looks like a paper orgy," John David said.

"Hey, Suzanne," Terrance greeted his guest. "Did y'all come to help?"

"We came to provide immoral support," John David said, holding up the opened bottle of chardonnay.

"Go on back and get me my coffee cup," he said.

"No, this one's for you. Suzanne's got her own. I know you don't got a problem drinkin' out of a bottle."

Suzanne and John David joined Terrance on the floor, crossing their legs like children watching TV.

"You ever shrink-wrap, Suzanne?" Terrance asked.

She shook her head.

"Wanna try?"

"Don't know how. But I'm happy to just sit here with my chardonnay."

Terrance unrolled and cut off a clear, smooth piece of plastic, about two feet square. He then reached for a box of three-by-five invitations with a Mexican fiesta motif that Ginger Miller had considered too ethnic-looking and set it in the middle of the plastic. Terrance brought up the ends of the shrink-wrap covering and taped them together in the middle, as if he were wrapping a gift. He then picked up the shrink-wrapper, which was really nothing more than a steel, industrial-strength blow dryer, and pointed it at the note cards as if it were a gun. Suddenly, Terrance clicked on the blower, and in less than three seconds, the clear coating melted over the paper rectangle, hurriedly conforming to every edge and corner and plane. It reminded Suzanne of the time-lapsed Pillsbury cookie-dough ads.

"You wanna try?" he asked.

"Oh, no, that's okay."

Over the next half hour, they sat and watched and drank their wine. The loud, hollow sound of the blower reminded Suzanne of the color orange, warm and radiant and strong. She loved witnessing this rebirth of once-doomed consumer goods. Shrink-wrapping meant starting over even after you'd made a mess, a second chance for both buyer and seller, redemption of the sweetest, simplest form.

Terrance got up to go the bathroom, and John David was snoring, prone on the floor. Standing up, Suzanne looked down at her feet; her left was in the middle of a large sheet of unused shrink-wrap. She bent over, pulled it up from all sides, around her ankle, as if she were wrapping a bottle of wine in cellophane, and then held it in place with a piece of tape around her leg. As Terrance was walking back to the counter, she clicked on the shrink-wrapper and pointed it at her foot, and in seconds the cellophane warmed her toes and arch and hugged her foot like a blood-pressure machine.

"Very cool, Suzanne!" Terrance said.

"Let's do your legs."

"Terrance!"

"Oh, come on, Suzanne."

She lay down on her back and closed her eyes, drowsy and ambivalent from the bottle of wine. He worked his way upward, wrapping her legs together like a mummy's, then her round belly, her breasts, and, finally, her neck.

"What's it feel like?" Terrance asked her.

"Like nothin' can happen to me," Suzanne said. "Like I'm fixin' to be born, maybe."

"Can we finish it?" he asked

"You mean my face?"

"I just wanna finish what I started. Here," he said. Terrance reached over and pulled a red-white-and-yellow-striped straw from the lid of an empty McDonald's soft-drink cup. "Put this in your mouth to breathe."

He gently wrapped her head in the cellophane then lay it back down on the floor. Suzanne suddenly heard the forceful, scorching whine of the blower, and almost instantly her eyes were compressed shut, all smells and sounds disappeared as if she'd suddenly been thrown into deep water. With her only free, working sense, Suzanne felt John David stirring, then sitting up at her side. And then, a bright flash. A picture taken? An extra light being turned on?

She suddenly felt fingers pulling and tearing at the shrink wrap around her left ear, and it seemed more of an intrusion than a rescue.

No, she shook her head. No. . . . Not yet.

Twenty-one

Dear Chatter: I do not agree with the board of education for firin' that bus driver just because he was preachin' gospel to the children. There is nothing wrong with kids hearin' some Bible verses on the way home from school. It'll do them good.

Dear Chatter: Hey, you native drivers: Green means go! It doesn't mean fixing to go, it means go.

Convinced the heart potato was a sign of impending divine intervention, Adrian Braswell continued to shower Donna with inexpensive but thoughtful Christian gifts. He would set them among the russet potatoes, and they looked like some child's toy that had washed ashore, lying among the surf-polished, pale-brown rocks. The most recent offering was a small pair of white, painted-resin hands in prayer with an adhesive patch on the bottom.

"I've got mine on my medicine cabinet

at home, but you can put it anywhere you want to," he told Donna. "The kids at Piedmont Presbyterian Day School . . . they keep 'em in their lockers for good luck and to hang their car keys on. But I don't drive."

Donna had realized by now that Adrian was definitely borderline something. He constantly asked simple questions of physics and logic, the kinds of queries that bubble from children to help them understand the natural forces and relationships in their growing world: Why do raw collards feel like rubber? Why are the outsides of radishes red and the insides white?

"Why do you always keep the bananas so far away from everything else?" he asked.

"Because," Donna explained, "bananas give off this special ripenin' gas of some kind. If you wanna get something ripened fast just stick it in a paper sack with a banana and shut it up tight. Bananas are real good for that."

Adrian shook his head. "I can't get over how much you know about our Lord God's beautiful creations."

Yet Donna also learned that the young man, who still lived at home with his mother, had a gift that was both amazing and valuable to her and Mr. Tom and

Kroger. Like some guess-the-weight man in a circus, Adrian possessed a sixth sense for determining the quality and ripeness of any fruit that hid behind a mystifying, thick epidermis.

Donna spotted this gift first, and one night she and Mr. Tom stayed with Adrian after closing to test this sensory power. They lined up five honeydews, five cantaloupes and five mangoes. Adrian would hold a fruit in his hand, close his eyes then raise and lower the melon or mango as if he were trying to determine its weight, his right eyelid and the stubs on his other arm twitching as he did this. With his pocketknife, Mr. Tom would cut into the chosen fruits to see how he did, and every time Adrian picked the juiciest, sweetest specimen.

"Are you smelling them?" Mr. Tom asked.

"I don't think so, sir."

"It's gotta be touch," Donna said.

"But he's not using his fingers," Mr. Tom added.

For some reason, this ability seemed to intimidate or at the very least irritate Gary Scalamandre, the new assistant manager in the meat department who called Adrian "Fruit Loop." Fresh from Detroit, Gary was a barrel-chested man with thick mustache and beefy forearms covered in Marine tattoos, and to date he was Mr. Tom's sole bad hiring choice. Twice Mr. Tom had had to formally reprimand him for sexual comments made on the cutting floor, one about a salami and the other about fresh liver and how it reminded him of aroused women.

Adrian had gone for a break, and after thirty minutes Donna began to wonder what was keeping him. He was always on time, always dependable — slow as molasses but dependable.

She found him in the break room, crying in front of his open locker.

"Adrian . . ."

"Miss Donna!"

"What's wrong?"

With his good hand he pointed at the open locker. "Someone took my things, Miss Donna. These ain't my things."

Donna looked into the locker and recognized the Detroit Tigers baseball cap and the big blue jeans with a circle worn into the back pocket from a can of chewing tobacco. She then opened Gary Scalamandre's smaller locker and found stuffed inside Adrian's purple cardigan sweater and his bag of lunch and the pear-size

331

stuffed bear that had fallen off someone's red heart of chocolates in the parking lot that Valentine's Day.

"Come on, Adrian!" she said.

"Miss Donna."

Almost jogging to keep up with her furious pace, he followed her out of the lounge, through dairy and into the swinging metal doors that led into the meat department.

"Gary Scalamandre!"

Donna had to yell to be heard over the noise of the wrapping machine, which was covering mounded square gobs of ground chuck in cellophane and stamping them with white adhesive price tags.

"You need a goddamned hairnet to come in here, you know that."

"I'm not gonna be stayin'."

"What the hell do you want?"

"I want Adrian Braswell's locker back is what I want."

The five others in the room all stopped what they were doing to watch.

"He don't need that big-ass locker. Look at me, I'm the man here. I'm the one who needs all that room."

"For your information lockers are handed out based on seniority, and Adrian here has eleven years in this store. That's why he's got one of the newer lockers."

Adrian quickly tried to interrupt, tapping her on the shoulder with his good hand. "Ten," he whispered. "Miss Donna, I just got ten. It won't be eleven till August."

Gary stepped forward two paces and wiped his hands on the chest of his white apron, already smudged with the blood of lamb. "I run a whole damn department. I deserve that space. I ain't switchin' back."

"Then I'm gonna do it for you. And I can tell you right now you're not gonna like where you find all your things."

"You'd better stay away from my stuff."

"And you'd better start respectin' other people's property."

"Or what?"

"Or I'll tell Mr. Tom."

Gary folded his arms across his chest and started to nod. A smile grew on his face. "Oh, I get it," he said. "You think you can act like you're in charge 'cause you fuck the boss."

"What!" Donna screamed. "What did you say?"

"Come on, pretty girl. Who do you think you're fooling?"

Instinctively, Donna looked for a weapon within reach. From the roller conveyer she picked up an unwrapped, green-foam tray of hamburger meat and threw it at him. Gary dodged it easily, and it flew beyond him and landed, meat side down, with a moist smack on the red-tile floor.

"You're as low as a catfish, Gary Scalamandre! You need to jump right back in that muddy pond where you came from."

"You're turnin' me on, baby. Keep talkin' to me like that. I love it."

Donna breathed in deeply to calm herself down. She thought to herself: *Be professional, Donna. Use your brain. Hit him where it really hurts.*

She perched her hands on her hips, lowered her voice and smiled. "You know, Gary, you remind me so much of some of the boys I used to go out with."

"Oh yeah? Which ones?"

"These!" she said, extending her pinky until it was erect and pointing at the fluorescent lights overhead.

Twenty-two

Dear Chatter: My sister works at the Perry County school office and she tells me it's the Yankees who are callin' in to complain about the preacher bus driver. All I can say is we've got prayer and you've got New York City Murder Capital of the Universe.

Dear Chatter: I don't think it looks very professional for a Selby police officer to be driving a police car off duty wearing Bermuda shorts. Thank you very much.

The features department of the *Reflector* included Harriet, the oldest by thirty-two years; Margaret, the youngest and newest member; and a group of six women that Randy Whitestone referred to as "the henhouse," a name born from the warbling noise that would boil over and spill across the glass partition that separated them from the rest of the newsroom. Margaret secretly admitted to herself that the name fit — en masse, their laughter sounded operatic and shrill as a peacock's call — and sometimes would have to stop herself from putting her hands over her ears. This was true even outside the newsroom. Many times in Selby she had whipped her head around in alarm when she heard three or more Southern women cut up in laughter, just as one does when someone opens a door at the moment an ambulance is screaming past.

More than once, because she was now writing her popular profiles for the A section, Randy suggested to Margaret that she move to a desk on the other side of the glass wall, among the more cynical, male-dominant metro staff. Margaret did admire the earnest, Chicken Little nature of the news department, and she watched with interest each time they mobilized like fighter pilots after hearing a lead on the police scanner, which sat on a homemade plywood shelf over the metro desk, painted red and black to commemorate the Georgia Bulldogs football team.

Yet she still preferred the company of the women in her section. All of them mothers, the features women created an environment that was part coffee klatch, part slumber party, and Margaret, who had never experienced much of either in her life, soaked in this luxuriant, unmistakably female solidarity. They traded magazines back and forth — *Martha Stewart Living* and *Ladies Home Journal, Better Homes and Gardens* and *Southern Living.* They shared Web sites about parenting news and Hollywood gossip and horoscopes and ways to fight cellulite. They frequently brought in leftover desserts from their family meals the night before — cherry cobbler, peach cobbler, brownies, and pecan pie — or a surfeit of some backyard crop — cucumbers or tomatoes or peaches or muscadine grapes — and, most frequently, flowers in a vase — black-eyed Susans (June) or paper whites (January) or daffodils (February) or orange-red cannas (July), snipped from an editor's or writer's garden that morning. Margaret loved how there was no true dead of winter in Selby, no long dormant period when all smells other than chimney smoke would disappear in a freeze-dried landscape. Though it could briefly dip below freezing just before dawn, once the sun began to warm the ground you could smell again the subtle, green notes of chlorophyll from the cold-hardy live oaks and magnolia trees, ivy and sabal palms and yards of winter-rye grass. Though compact and hard as grape seeds, buds appeared on most trees by Christmas.

The green shoots of tulips poked out of the soil by Super Bowl Sunday.

It was seven o'clock on a Thursday evening, the newsroom eerily empty. Randy had dispatched every available news reporter to cover what the voice on the scanner said was a fire at Massey Hall.

Once the fifth-oldest Baptist university in the South, the block-long, five-story building had been left to decay since 1971, when the trustees moved the college to Atlanta. Though empty and dark, with windows punched out and graffiti covering the first eight feet of red brick, this was Margaret's favorite building in town. It reminded her of the original Smithsonian Institute building on the mall in Washington, the one that looked like a castle. Each time she walked by she would notice a new curve or line or angle of the rambling structure, whose turrets sprouted from surprising spots like oaks inadvertently planted by squirrels. It was so different from the rest of the historic structures in towns, most of them shrines to symmetry and order. Though immense, Massey Hall was subtle and challenging. It was not drive-by architecture, and therein lay the roots of its demise.

A new car dealer in north Selby, Ray

Dubose of Dubose Jaguar and Mercedes of Atlanta, Inc., decided that Selby needed a minor league baseball team, and he set about finding land for a stadium. Since all the larger parcels out by his dealership were too pricey, he looked closer in, on the edges of the depressed downtown area, and found two possible candidates. One was the decrepit Massey Hall and the other, at the corner of Second and Hanson Streets, was Mount Pleasant All People's Baptist Church and World Peace Center.

Over the last ten years, Dr. Recil Jackson, chief minister and CEO, had doubled the African American church's membership to just under two thousand parishioners. The redbrick building grew by a room or two nearly every year, giving the sanctuary the look of a large, rambling commercial bakery or candy factory. To counter this, Jackson built a new facade with soaring, white Corinthian columns and a stairway flanked by gold-painted lions lying atop homemade concrete pedestals decorated in a mosaic of broken glass from dishes brought by each family. Across the top of the facade, forty-seven plastic letters spelled out the name of the church, alternating in color from red to white to blue. Random-sized, immaculate, white-painted rocks outlined the entire yard of the church, like lights along a runway, as if to entice and guide spirits in for a perfect landing. And none of this hallowed ground, Dr. Jackson informed Ray Dubose, was up for sale.

So Dubose sniffed out and courted the blind-trust owners of Massey Hall, a collection of wealthy, north Selby businessmen who owned more than two hundred inner city homes, most of them rat-infested fire traps with leaky roofs that they rented to African-American families at inflated prices. The *Reflector* broke the story. And that next week, the Middle Georgia Historic Preservation Council, headed by the diminutive, white-haired Pixie Franklin, sued to stop demolition. She was just days from getting Massey Hall officially listed on the National Historic Register. And now this: obvious arson.

Margaret and Harriet stood at the second-floor window of the newsroom watching the blaze eleven blocks away on Massey Hill, the highest point in Selby. The sun had set, and the fire, which had climbed into every turret like ivy, cast an orange, quivering glow on every surface within a hundred yards.

340

The women noticed a long ladder, presumably one end of it connected to a truck, rising up toward the tallest spire of Massey Hall. On the end was a firefighter in a shiny, silver suit that reminded Harriet of a tented turkey in the oven. The extension ladder rose and rose, growing longer and longer, swiveled a little to the right, then rose again, and rose . . . and rose . . . and then, at some point near a hundred feet above the ground, it jerkily stopped, creating enough bounce that both women unconsciously held their breath until the fireman let loose with his hose, a stream of water that looked white and crisp as a laser beam.

Margaret suddenly felt Harriet's hand on her arm. "That man's too little to be Dewayne," she said. "Dewayne's a big man. I'm sure they've got him liftin' stuff down on the ground someplace."

Margaret touched her friend's hand. "I'm sure you're right, Harriet. He says he usually works the truck . . . whatever that means."

"I can't ever remember a fire this big."

Margaret could see minuscule, faraway firefighters in reflective yellow suits scurrying about the ground with the energy of mad ants. She thought of Dewayne and his sure but plodding way of navigating the planet. Did he move quicker on the job? Would he be able to dodge a rain of fiery debris? Margaret tried but failed to imagine him in adrenaline mode.

Harriet opened her purse, reached inside and pulled out a thick crescent moon of a mostly consumed York Peppermint Patty. She unfolded the foil, revealing the dried-out white edge cut by teeth a day earlier, and offered Margaret a piece. After they both finished their bite of candy, Harriet took Margaret's right hand in hers, bowed her head and closed her eyes.

"Dear Lord," she said, "please watch over these brave men tonight . . ."

The prayer caught Margaret by surprise, and for a moment she stared at Harriet as she spoke to her creator. Then, like a Sunday school teacher, Harriet peeked at Margaret to see if she had joined in, and Margaret quickly shut her eyes and bowed her head in compliance.

". . . and give them the strength to put out that fire and come on home safe and sound to their families . . . and close ones. . . . Amen."

"Amen," Margaret whispered.

"And what's all this about?"

They whipped around in surprise and

saw Randy leaning against a desk with his arms folded across his chest.

"Just givin' some support to those men out there," Harriet said.

"They're gonna need a helluva lot more than that," he replied. "They just called in some backups from Peachtree City."

"You don't need to sound so excited about it, Randy," Margaret said. "It's a horrible fire. That was a lovely, historic building."

"There's nothin' wrong with a little prayer, Mr. Randy," Harriet said. "It all helps."

"Harriet, do you really think God has anything to do with that fire?" he said.

"Sir?"

"I don't understand you people. Is this fallout from the Civil War or something? Is there some inferiority complex in the culture here? Do you guys attribute everything bad and good to God because you feel you have no control over your own destinies? Is that it, Harriet?"

"I guess I don't know what you're sayin'," Harriet answered.

"No," he replied. "I'm sure you don't . . . because it would involve deep, secular introspection."

"That's enough, Randy!" Margaret

yelled. "Or shall we deconstruct your tortured soul to discover the true roots of your blatant assholeishness?"

"God, what bug bit your butt?"

"Reserve some dignity for people, Randy, would you?"

"Boy, you've been pissed at me lately. Are you still weirded out over that kiss?"

"No. I've got other things to think about."

"I know you think I was rushing things."

"Please. Your brilliance is blinding me now."

"Let's go grab a bite to eat and talk about it."

"No. I'm tired. I'm fixin' to go home and go to bed."

"Fixin' to! . . . Margaret! God!"

Margaret pulled the sticks from the bun on the back of her head and let her hair cascade over her shoulders.

"You need to relax a little bit more, Randy," she said.

Just before three a.m., Margaret was awakened by a light knocking on the back door. She knew the knock; Dewayne had refused to accept his own key to the house, thinking it improper.

Wearing a faded, black SUNY-Buffalo

T-shirt over Power Puff Girl panties she'd found on clearance at Belk Lindsay, Margaret ran on her toes into the kitchen and flipped on the light. As she opened the door, she saw a paramedic's truck pull away from the curb.

"Oh, my God . . . Oh, Dewayne."

A bandage covered the left side of his forehead, from his hairline to below the eyebrow. His right cheek and chin had large scrapes that looked wet and raw, as if he'd been dragged across a roof of gritty asphalt shingles. His broad shoulders were in a perpetual shrug from the tops of crutches crammed into his armpits.

The cast ran from mid-thigh to the beginning of his toes. Unable to fit it into his jeans, Dewayne wore a pair of navy blue gym shorts with *SFD* embroidered on them, perhaps a gift from his mother. This was the first time Margaret had ever seen his bare thighs. They were full and muscular though pale from living beneath the boot-cut Wranglers he always wore.

"Oh, Dewayne . . . Oh, God . . . You must be exhausted."

Wanting to hug him but afraid she might hurt or throw him off balance, Margaret reached out, placing her hands on his forearms, and looked into his eyes, which had begun to fill with tears. She gently touched his uninjured cheek with the back of her hand and he leaned into it and closed his eyes, his chin falling, hydraulic-like, until it came to rest on his chest.

Both of them silent, Margaret led him into the bedroom. As he stood at the side of the futon, she took the crutches from him and leaned them against the wall.

"Can you put your arms up?" she asked.

Balancing on his good leg, Dewayne slowly raised them, and Margaret began pulling off his sweatshirt, stepping onto the futon to finish the task because she was so much shorter than he.

Dewayne sat down, and Margaret removed the one shoe, and then he leaned back, toward the pillows. After lifting and swinging his legs onto the futon, Margaret leaned over him and kissed his cheek, then his nose, then his lips, which were dry and salty. She then lay her head on his chest, feeling the beat of his heart on her ear, looking at the underside of his chin and noting, for the first time ever, blond beard stubble. "Are you okay?" she whispered. He nodded.

She felt a sudden, compelling need to touch him all over. Outside, the moon was full, and the lunar light coated much of the bedroom in a skim-milk white. Margaret could see herself as she traced her fingers over Dewayne's smooth shoulder blades, then across the twin mounds of his chest, dropping kisses, tiny like stitches, in the wake of her fingers.

She dragged her lips down to the rise of his stomach, then let them hop across the warm dense arc, and when she finally reached the end of this smooth beach of skin and the beginning of the undulating waves of his blue, nylon shorts, she lay down her head, floating on top, feeling him swell and stir beneath her cheek.

He moaned softly, and she leaned forward for a moment to connect with his face. Margaret smiled at what she saw: a look of naive, bewildered ecstasy, much like the expression she remembered from the time he first tasted her flan.

Twenty-three

Dear Chatter: In the days past, we kept sweet potatoes and sugarcane in a root cellar to keep them from freezin' during the winter. Also, when a bad storm came up, we would get in the cellar, and that's why we call it our 'fraidy hole.

Dear Chatter: To the person who doesn't like us blowing our noses at the table: It's either that or we drown in snot. Shots and pills don't stop it all the way. It's the paper mill; get used to it and get a life.

The UPS man delivered the day's packages just after three o'clock, and with an eight-inch butcher knife and highball of bourbon and soda Suzanne carried them out to the patio to open them.

From Ballard Designs, she had a French, fake-weathered, metal bread tin, which Suzanne would place on her kitchen étagère and fill with the faux baguettes she'd found at the Silk Flower Warehouse; from Williams-Sonoma, an eight-inch copper saucepan to add to the collection of matching, unused copper cookware hanging on the pot rack over the island in the kitchen; and from the Solutions catalog, the patented, goldtone-plastic Bracelet Buddy. *(An extra hand so you won't need someone to help fasten a bracelet around your wrist!)*

Anxious to try the latter, Suzanne disappeared into the bedroom and returned with her braided, gold-and-silver David Yurman bracelet and the Paloma Picasso from Tiffany, a circle of expressionistic, alternating, sterling-silver *X*'s and *O*'s.

Suzanne spread the David Yurman on the glass patio table then lay her forearm over it, upside down, as if she were preparing to be punctured for a blood sample. She was trying to attach the end of the bracelet onto the hook of her new tool when the doorbell rang.

Suzanne looked up, through the open French doors. From this vantage point she could see the foyer, and that someone was waiting on the other side of the narrow, stained-glass windows that flanked the front door. The glass was cloudy, for privacy's sake, and the person on the other end always looked like a witness on a true-crime show whose appearance is blurred to protect his identity, but Suzanne could tell this was a man by the heft of his belly. He was dressed all in dark green. And on the head, a hat with a wide brim. A service man? Had she made an appointment that she'd forgotten?

Immersed in her test of the new Bracelet Buddy, Suzanne ignored the door. He rang twice more before she saw him descend the steps of the porch and leave.

"Ma'am?"

Suzanne gasped and shot up, dropping the Bracelet Buddy, which fell to the flagstone and rolled toward the feet of a black man dressed in an Italian-cut suit, red medallion tie, and militarily polished, black, Cole Haan loafers.

"Who are you . . . and what are you doin' on my property?" Suzanne asked.

He pulled from his back pocket a brown wallet, well rounded from spending hours every day smooshed against a car seat. Men's wallets always reminded Suzanne of messy sandwiches, and this was no exception . . . all those layers of credit-card color and leafy, green notes and unruly, large receipts sneaking out of the side like errant slices of Swiss cheese — all pressed between matching slices of leather that snapped shut like a mousetrap.

He flipped it open, revealing a gold badge with the seal of Perry County in the middle, a shield of armor divided into quarters that featured a cotton bowl, a magnolia blossom, an Indian headdress, and a pair of peaches.

"I'm Lieutenant Crawford, Perry County Sheriff's Department. This here's Officer Piper," he said, motioning to the uniformed officer beside him.

Suzanne leaned forward to get a closer look. "What do you mean scarin' me like that?"

"I didn't mean to frighten you, ma'am."

"Well, that's exactly what you did. You scared the daylights outta me."

He bent down and picked up the Bracelet Buddy, which he handed to her. "When you didn't answer the door I was just guessin' that you were in the backyard gardenin'."

"Well I wasn't," she said. "I pay someone to do that for me. What is so important that you just about had to kill me like that? I'm not parked in the street. It's not the sprinklers, is it? I asked Virgil to fix the timer on those sprinklers."

The accompanying deputy's gold name

tag said *S. Piper.* He looked to be about forty, with freckles, a thick head of red hair, and a Teddy Roosevelt mustache. He was close enough, just on the other side of the table, that Suzanne could hear the fizzing and gurgling sounds of blossoming hunger emanating from his stomach. "Do you mind if we sit down?" he asked, wiping the sweat from his shiny forehead with a white handkerchief. The detective turned and frowned at him.

"How long's this gonna take?" Suzanne asked. "What's this all about?"

"Do y'all have a dog?" asked the detective.

Suzanne rolled her eyes and exhaled in impatience. "What does this have to do with anything?" she said. "No, we don't have a dog. I hate dogs."

Eyes only, with chin locked in place, he looked at the deputy, then again at Suzanne.

"You know about the problems with the dogs in the neighborhood . . ."

"You'd have to be livin' in a cave not to know about it. Why?"

The detective bit his lower lip and brought his hands to his hips, drawing back the lapel of his dress coat and revealing a gun in a black-leather shoulder holster. "Have you seen anything unusual in your yard?"

"Like what?" Suzanne asked.

"Well . . . any signs of somethin' that might be hurtin' those dogs."

"Now how would I know what's killin' those dogs?"

He looked away from Suzanne for a moment, at a mockingbird warbling atop the gable of the garage. "Miz Parley — It is Miz Parley, right? — I'll just be real straight with you, Miz Parley. There's folks who say they've seen you shootin' at dogs with a squirt gun at night."

Instantly, a picture of Jodi Armbuster came to mind, peeking from the plantation shutters in that side bedroom that faced Suzanne's house. If not her, then who? Suzanne had been so careful, shooting only after dark, always carrying a stack of envelopes with her so she could pretend to be scanning that day's mail when cars passed, their headlights illuminating her in her floral Christian Dior bathrobe.

"Is there any law against a little squirt gun?" Suzanne asked.

"No, ma'am."

"Well then . . ." Suzanne began to gather and crumple into a ball the brown paper from the UPS package. "It's no secret that the dogs of Red Hill Plantation are turnin' my front yard into a toxic waste dump," she said. "I've got a right to protect my property just like anybody else does. At least I'm not shootin' 'em with a real gun."

"Yes, ma'am."

"And my husband knows I'm doin' this. Dr. Boone Parley, the neurosurgeon? Have y'all heard of Parley Road? That's named after Boone's great-great-granddaddy — he was the mayor of Selby."

"Yes, ma'am."

Suddenly Suzanne remembered that she had not left the house that day, and she had no makeup on. She stood with the wad of paper beneath her arm, the bracelets and Bracelet Buddy in hand. "So if y'all don't mind, I've gotta go inside now and get dinner goin'."

The detective looked at the butcher knife and the untouched Waterford tumbler of whiskey and soda, which had started to sweat on the sides. "Yes, ma'am. Do you mind if we take a look around the yard?"

"What for?" she asked.

"Oh, I don't know — anything. You never know what you'll find. Me and Sergeant Piper been lookin' in everybody's yard."

"Well don't be trampin' in my pansy beds."

"No, ma'am."

From the windows upstairs, racing from room to room, Suzanne followed their progress around the house as they poked in the mature boxwood and holly bushes along the foundation. Luck was with her that day; just one hour earlier, Suzanne had retrieved the green, plastic dog dish and brought it inside to refill it with the Alpo and antifreeze. It was now soaking in the stainless-steel sink in her utility room, the flecks of deadly, stinky food loosening and rising to the surface of the sudsy water.

Still, the men seemed to linger somewhere on the southeast side, and Suzanne could not see what they were doing; her vision was blocked by the magnolia at the corner of the house.

She could not see Detective Andy Crawford on his hands and knees, pointing a powerful, yellow flashlight into the undergrowth of the shrubs. She could not see him reaching in, up to his armpit, firmly yanking as if to snag something free, then pulling out a small twig of holly. Suzanne could not see him hold it in the sun for a better look, smell it, raise his eyebrows and

355

nod at his partner, then pull out a Ziploc sandwich bag and stow the small branch safely in his breast pocket.

"Suzanne, honey, pass me that red."

"What's gonna be red?"

"This here's a woodpecker. His little crown's gonna be red."

"I haven't seen you do this one before."

"I haven't. It's my first time."

Known simply as "the cake lady," Carol O'Neal was one of the few reasons north Selby women ventured south of Truman Parkway. There was nothing on this planet she could not replicate in the form of a cake, and for years Suzanne had watched and helped her mother as she painted with frosting, tiny squirt after squirt, works of art that were nothing short of pointillism. She could create images of roses and magnolias and dogs, babies and pheasants and deer and lovers sitting arm in arm on docks. Once she'd been asked by the Perry County Commission to do a portrait of Madeline VanDermeter, the executive director of the International Dogwood Festival, and though up close it appeared to be a yellow-dominant piece of abstract art the cake did take on a striking resemblance of the woman when seen from across a room.

This time, on a huge, rectangular sheet cake covered in white frosting she had sketched out with eyeliner and diluted black watercolor a scene of Georgia forest with resident wildlife.

Once a week, when her father was bass-fishing at Lake Oconee, Suzanne would drive down and work for half a day with her mother.

"Why don't I come up there this week and let's us have lunch together," her mother had said on the phone that morning.

"Momma . . ."

"There's a new Italian restaurant on Gibron Road. I saw the ad for it in the *Reflector*. I don't think it's too far from your house."

"Really, Momma, I wanna come down there."

"I clipped some coupons for it, Suzanne."

"You know how I like helpin' you do cakes."

"You don't like helpin' me with my cakes, Suzanne. You just don't want me comin' up there."

"Now that's not true."

"I've stayed away from your north Selby life like a good girl, Suzanne. All I'm askin' is for you to have lunch with your momma in your own neighborhood."

"But there's somethin' I wanna talk to you about, Momma."

"We can do it over lunch."

"I wanna do it at home."

"Oh, Suzanne."

"Please, Momma?"

Carol sighed. "You are the most determined girl on the planet, Suzanne. I swear you would've driven me crazy by now. Okay, but you gotta bring us lunch. I do not feel like cookin' today."

After eating the casserole Suzanne had plucked from her freezer in the garage — something called Mexican shepherd's pie, which was written on the aluminum foil in black marker — they began the long task of filling in the woodsy landscape, creamy dot by dot.

"You do the trees," Carol said. "Now be patient, Suzanne. Stay in the lines. Please. This is my first cake for this lady and I want it to be good."

"Whose is it?" Suzanne asked.

"Her name's Alison Riner. You know her?"

"I know her. She just painted her foyer the tackiest green I've ever seen."

"Is she nice to you?"

"She's not ugly to me. How much you chargin' her for this cake, Momma?"

"Seventy-five."

"Seventy-five! They'd pay a hundred and seventy-five in Atlanta. You gotta charge more."

"How much do you think?"

"Charge 'em two hundred. Alison would pay that."

"No, no," her mother said, lightly swatting Suzanne's wrist. "That part's not supposed to be brown. That part's black. Here. Here's the black. Two hundred? Who'd pay two hundred dollars for a cake?"

"Any lady in north Selby would pay two hundred for your cakes, Momma. No one does 'em like you."

Unaccustomed to such praise, Carol smiled. "Now what was it you wanted to talk about?" she asked.

"Has Boone called you?"

"Boone never calls me, Suzanne."

"Well, he might be callin'."

"Why?"

Suzanne set her pastry bag on the table and nervously began to twist her diamond engagement ring. "Oh, Momma," she said, her eyes welling with tears. "Boone thinks I'm pregnant."

Carol lifted her pastry bag from its spot over the cake and looked at her daughter.

"Now how can that be?"

"It can't, Momma. You know that."

"What on earth have you done, Suzanne Denise O'Neal?"

"Oh, Lord . . . I don't know." Suzanne then pounded her fists on the table — the very same foam green Formica table she'd pounded her fists on as a child. "I was just so tired of him bein' mad at me all the time, Momma. And then I had too much to drink one night at the Forsyth Room and it just came runnin' out of my mouth like water."

"Suzanne, Suzanne, Suzanne. What on earth are you gonna do?"

"I don't know. I'm supposed to be three months pregnant, and I'm sure not."

"You gotta tell him, Suzanne."

"I can't! He's told his whole family. Evelyn keeps callin' the house, wonderin' why I'm not gettin' a nursery ready. She's even named the baby already! You know, Momma, that woman's gonna drive me crazy. She hates me. She's always hated me, and I sure don't know why."

"My Lord, Suzanne. Get ahold of yourself, girl. You're shakin' like a rattlesnake. There's no other way outta this. You've got to do the Christian thing and tell the truth."

Suzanne wiped her eyes with the back of her sleeve. "If I told Boone the truth he'd leave me," she said. "And then I'd be right back where I started."

"Well, what do you want me to do?"

"If Boone calls, Momma, you gotta say I'm goin' to your doctor."

"I'm not gonna lie for you, Suzanne. I just can't do that."

"You've got to. I'm your daughter."

"Suzanne."

"Oh, Momma, please."

"Oh, Suzanne. What is it you want out of life, girl? I sure wish I understood that."

Usually, when the little girls came with their mothers to pick up a cake, they stayed in the car or close to their mother, and they would look at Suzanne over their shoulder as if she were a dangerous temptation. From afar, Suzanne would admire their silk hair bows and patent-leather Mary Janes, and sometimes one of these girls would soften and melt away from her mother's thigh and enter Suzanne's world.

"What's your name?" Suzanne asked.

"Alison."

"My name's Suzanne. I like your shoes."

The little girl looked down at them. "You wanna try 'em on?"

"Can I?"

"Uh-huh."

"And you can put *mine* on!" Suzanne said, already standing on one leg, pulling off her slip-on, white-and-pink sneaker with a smiling Garfield on the heel and dirt and blue and yellow frosting stains on the tops.

When the mothers walked into the living room, the girls were sitting on the carpeting, leaning against the back of the couch with their legs straight ahead of them. Each gazed at their feet as if they were foreign objects, and indeed each little girl at that moment had fled into a daydream where such shoes could be worn at will.

"Mary Alison!" the mother exclaimed. "What on earth are you doin'?"

"She's just tryin' on my shoes, Momma. And I'm tryin' on hers."

"Well you get your own shoes back on right now — and I mean right now. Those shoes are brand new! Your daddy works real hard so we can buy those nice shoes, and you do not need to be lettin' every stranger in the world try 'em on."

As Suzanne drove home from her

mother's, she wondered if Alison Riner had matched the Suzanne of 243 Kottrell Avenue with the Suzanne of 2146 Red Hill Drive. She tried to imagine the two of them now, happy on chardonnay, doing the same thing on the floor of her living room in Red Hill.

Suzanne fled northward, uphill, back to the higher part of town, unconsciously leaning forward in her seat and depressing the accelerator further with each quarter mile until she was zipping down Pio Nono Road at sixty miles an hour, unable to shake the feeling that if she did not drive fast enough her black Lexus would creep to a stop and begin rolling backward, slowly at first, but then faster and faster, returning her to the world below.

Twenty-four

Dear Chatter: The Southern way is to live and let live, so for all you Yankees who don't like the way we do things down here, I've just got one thing to say: Delta is ready when you are.

Dear Chatter: Cats are not just stupid but also downright mean. One killed a squirrel in my yard, and why those creatures don't have to be on leashes I do not understand. God did not mean for man to have cats as pets. It's dogs who are man's best friend.

"Who's your friend, Donna?" asked Betty in bakery.

Donna carried beneath her arm the fruit of her labors from the previous night at home, a six-foot-tall Super Okra Man, which she had cut out from rigid, white cardboard and washed with light-green watercolor. With an exaggerated, toothy smile and oversized pupils, he was reminiscent of the giant, talking cigarette from the

Doonesbury comic strip, which Donna had recently discovered, and enjoyed, on the editorial page of the *Reflector.*

"Isn't he cute?" Donna said. She set him on the ground and posed with her arm around the giant pod. "You know how you can tell he's a guy and not a girl?"

"How?"

"Two ways. One: He's hairy."

"Yeah?"

"And that pointy little head ain't got room for much of a brain."

"Oh, you are nasty mean, Donna Kabel," Betty said, smiling. "No wonder they keep you back there with those vegetables."

Super Okra Man was created as a tool of subversive propaganda. For months, Donna had been scheming to get her native Southern customers to purchase and eat a larger variety of vegetables. And after the hugely unsuccessful taste demo of Thai coconut curry with broccoli and carrots, Donna conspired with Margaret, who devised a recipe designed to sneak healthier vegetables in with some old Southern favorites. Margaret's Piedmont pork stew included the local staples of pork and okra but also slipped in garlic, which could lower blood pressure and help prevent blood clots; red bell peppers (rich in vitamin C); and mustard greens (packed with vitamin A and folate).

Donna stapled Super Okra Man onto a wooden stake and stood him in the middle of the mounded okra pods. She then spent the next ten minutes with her colored chalk to create her tip of the day.

Did you know that your favorite Southern vegetable is related to a famous Southern crop? That's right! Okra is kin to cotton! In India and Egypt, okra seeds are roasted and ground for a coffee substitute! And right here in the United States they use okra to thicken catsup! We all know it's good in cornmeal and fried, but it's even tastier and healthier cooked outside on the grill. That's right! Why have FATTY chips when you can eat crunchy, delicious okra?

At eight o'clock, Nancy Gringle, the part-timer who served samples to customers, arrived with a pot of stew made from Margaret's recipe.

"My family loved this, Donna," she said, setting it on the hot plate that Donna had put on a card table beside the okra display. "Even Brother — but he still picked out the yellow squash."

Arms akimbo, Donna beamed.

"Are you just sayin' that to make my day, Nancy?" she asked. " 'Cause that's what you just did."

"I'm not kiddin' you, Donna. It's good stuff. I'm learnin' so much about food from you."

"Thank you!"

And then, from the corner of her eye, she saw Question Man approaching the end cap of bananas on the other side of the produce section. His black hair still wet from a shower, he was walking directly toward her, not even stopping to peruse the tropicals as he normally did. Sometime during the night, an avalanche of lemons had occurred, and some of the yellow fruit cascaded downward, into the limes stacked below. Donna quickly set about resegregating the fruits, yellow with yellow, green with green, yellow with . . .

"Good morning," he said.

She looked up, feigning surprise. "Oh! Good mornin'."

He smelled different today . . . fresher . . . because he normally came in the early evenings, toward closing. Donna detected some sort of variegated deodorant soap (Coast? Irish Spring?) and a cologne she did not recognize. It reminded her of passion fruit with black peppercorns mixed in.

"You're here early today," she said.

He nodded. "I've got business."

"Yeah?"

"I came to ask if I could buy you lunch."

Donna faltered for a second in her task of sorting fruit, as if a pair of internal, interlocking cogs had encountered a small stick then chewed it to pieces and continued their smooth rotation.

"Lunch?" she asked.

"Yes, lunch. Do you eat lunch?"

"Well, I bring my lunch to work every day 'cause I'm so busy."

"How about if we eat here in the deli?"

Donna smiled, watching her hands as she stacked the fruit. "You don't seem like a fried-chicken kinda guy to me. But you could get some sushi in fish and bring it over to deli. They don't care if you do that. Those tables and chairs are for all the customers, not just the deli customers."

"How about today?" he asked.

Donna set down the lemons she was holding in her hand. "I'd love that, I really would," she said. "But today's my big okra promotion. It's gonna be a crazy day. Mr. Tom even let me put something about it in the ad in the *Reflector*."

He frowned and looked away, biting on his lower lip in concentration. "I'm leaving town tomorrow for a few weeks. How about if I come in and see you when I get back?"

"That'd be fine," she answered.

He put his hands in the pockets of his dark blue, tropical-weight, wool trousers that were cuffed at the bottom. When he wore such pants or suits, he favored Cole Haan, oxblood-colored, tassled loafers, which were Donna's favorite men's shoe. "Good, then," he said.

Suddenly Donna was afraid that in her effort to sound calm she had come off as aloof and uninterested. "I like your tie," she blurted.

He looked down at his chest. "Oh . . . thanks."

"Those little polka dots are the exact color of mango flesh. Don't you think so?"

"Yes . . . I guess they are."

"Did you know that mangoes can be substituted for peaches in recipes?"

He looked at the name tag on her breast. Some time over the past month it had changed from *Donna* to *Donna Kabel, Produce Manager.*

"I am so sorry," he said. "You don't even know my name."

He stuck out his hand, whose creases and pores were free of accumulated grime, the fingernails coated in a satiny sheen and clipped and filed so the ends looked like perfect, white parentheses. Donna hoped he did not do the same for his toes.

"I'm Michael Kalcheski."

"Okay, Michael."

"Mike, actually."

"Mike."

"I thought you'd given up on guys," Jackee said, assembling a chicken fajita. "I thought you said you'd outgrown 'em."

"Oh, shush," Donna replied. "This guy is the world's cutest. And he eats so healthy! If I could just get all my customers to eat like him."

"I haven't seen you this bubbly in a long time, Donna. I was thinkin' your new job was turnin' you into an old lady or somethin'."

"Mike," Donna said. "I've got a theory about Mikes. You wanna know what it is?"

Over the years, from the halls of Southeast High, to the Sunday school building of Larry Drive Baptist Church, to the food court at the Selby Mall, Donna had noticed a curious pattern in men's names: She had never encountered a Mike who was not cute or sexy. Over the next twenty minutes, she and Jackee recounted the names of every Mike they'd ever known, famous or not, recording them with a green crayon on the back of a Corona Light coaster, seventeen in all, starting with Michael Bolton and ending with Mike Huckaby, a fellow high school graduate who was now a technician for Georgia Pride Heating and Cooling.

"Now you tell me," Donna challenged her friend, scanning the list before her. "Is there one of these who's hard to look at?"

"You proved your point," Jackee said.

"So it's not my imagination?" Donna asked.

"Doesn't look like it."

"You promise you're not just agreein'?"

"No, ma'am."

Donna circled her index finger around the rim of her empty margarita glass. "But now I've gotta wonder," she said. "Why is it true? I mean, don't you find that interesting?"

Jackee shrugged her shoulders and sipped through her long straw, and it occurred to Donna that her Friday margarita nights at Rio Cantina, sometime over the past month or so, had mysteriously transformed from recreation into obligation.

As Jackee complained about the new smocks they had to wear as receptionists at LensCrafters in the mall, Donna looked out the window and spotted a stray beagle in the parking lot, pushing his nose into a Taco Bell bag someone had tossed out a car window. He moved on, indiscriminately sniffing at the tires of cars, the beds of yellow and purple pansies in the median, at a Wendy's cup that rolled back and forth on the asphalt. Suddenly — and she felt a stab of guilt for having this thought — Donna found herself comparing Jackee's companionship to that of a dog's, loyal and true but content to sample and meander without thought or a plan of any kind. A dog would wag his tail and move on. Jackee, God bless her, would shrug her shoulders and move on.

Donna knew that Margaret, on the other hand, would have much to say about her Mike theory. They would spend an entire meal talking about it. They might even go to the Barnes & Noble and look at baby-naming books for clues. Donna loved Margaret's company, and she learned something new every time they were together, if not a fact then a peculiar perspective on things. To Donna, it seemed as if Margaret was always sitting up high somewhere, like a TV football commentator in the Georgia Bulldog press box, looking down at everyone and everything, far enough away that she could find connections and make conclusions that were impossible at ground level.

"I'm sorry about your smock," Donna said. "You need to say somethin' to your boss about it."

"I'm not gonna say anything to Mr. Wade about it."

"But if you wanna change it back to the old smock you've gotta say somethin'."

"Well, we all don't have the boss of the year like you do, Donna."

"Oh, you know what Mr. Tom told me today?" she said. "I can't believe I didn't know this — I felt so stupid.

"At home, see, I've always put my potatoes with my onions in the same plastic bucket under the sink because Momma always said that light would make 'em want to grow and the potatoes would get those little nubby things on 'em. You know what I mean, right? The eyes?

"So today, Mr. Tom comes up to me real serious like and says that I'm spoilin' the potatoes by keepin' 'em so close to the onions. Did you know that onions give off moisture that spoils the potatoes and makes 'em soft? Mr. Tom said they sweat like a marathon runner. And here I was all those years throwin' 'em in the same basket together . . . and under the sink with all that moisture. Can you believe that? My momma didn't even know that."

Jackee wiped a dab of sour cream from the corner of her mouth, admiring her new manicure as her hand sank back down to the table. "Donna," she said. "I gotta say I'm gettin' a little tired of hearin' about your job. I know it's important to you, but can't we just talk about makeup like we used to? I've got the new *Vogue* out in the car. You wanna look at it while we eat our fried ice cream?"

Twenty-five

Dear Chatter: The bigger corporations like Toyota are moving to Georgia because they're tired of paying the employees up North fourteen dollars an hour when they know the people down South are dumb enough to work for eight dollars an hour. Wake up, people! They didn't come here for the barbecue.

Dear Chatter: I am a white Southerner who has gotten over the fact that my ancestors lost the Civil War. What I would like to know is why black people can't get over slavery.

"Honey," Margaret said. "Honey? You'd better get up. We're gonna be late."

Dewayne opened his eyes and smiled at what he saw: Margaret stood beside the futon, wearing her flannel Miss Piggy pajamas and Alvin Chipmunk slippers, whose toes sported sewn-on, grapefruit-size stuffed heads of the buck-toothed rodent.

"You look like you're fixin' to go out and play," he said.

She fell to her knees on the futon and climbed across Dewayne's body until she was stradling his waist. "Good idea," she said. "Let's stay home and play."

Though Dewayne's cast somewhat limited their options, the two of them had been making love nearly every night when Dewayne was not at the station. Margaret had gone to Barnes & Noble and bought *The Joy of Sex* and *Art of the Female Orgasm*. She would try to read from them out loud as they lay on the couch, but Dewayne's neck and cheeks would flush and he would try to change the subject.

So much had surprised Margaret — the springiness and coarse nature of male pubic hair . . . the way orgasms could come in strings of different-sized beads . . . the striking similarities between semen and juice of fresh okra and how they both felt and looked the same and smelled almost identical, a fragrance of milk and earth and chlorophyll with a slight note of Clorox. Noting the penile shape of the okra pod itself, Margaret was certain there had to exist in some culture on the planet a story that somehow tied the two together.

"You sure you wanna go with me?"

Dewayne asked. "You don't seem like a church-goin' girl."

"And what do you mean by that?" she asked.

"I just mean you ask an awful lot of questions. People don't ask questions in church, Margaret. They just listen."

Every Sunday morning, Dewayne would slowly roll off the edge of the bed so as not to awaken Margaret, then patter into the kitchen and eat his breakfast of a strawberry Pop Tart and bowl of Sugar Frosted Flakes awash in whole milk. Afterward, as quietly as possible, he would shower, attempt to tame the cowlick on the crown of his head with water then put on his white button shirt, blue pants, boots and a red-and-blue-striped tie.

Wearing his *SFD* windbreaker, Dewayne would slip from the house, out to the curb, the sounds of mockingbirds and cardinals chattering in the cool morning air, and he would find the *Reflector*, thick and heavy with the Sunday inserts whose coupons he would clip and file away later that day, and return the paper to the kitchen table for Margaret. Then, as if he were going off to some secret men's club in the middle of the forest, Dewayne would disappear from her side for half a day.

But now, Margaret did not want him away from her side for that long, so she decided to join him.

Beulah Land Hills Baptist Church was a massive, modern, gray-brick structure whose sanctuary had reflective black windows on the front and a steep A-shaped roofline that gave it the appearance of Darth Vader's head. Connected to this centerpiece and jutting outward like airport terminals were sections that held a full-size gymnasium, day care, lodging for visiting clergy, a formal ballroom, two banquet halls, and an entire wing of Sunday school classrooms.

Like many predominantly white, conservative Selby churches, Beulah Land had abandoned its inner-city location to follow its white members, who continued to flee the city, into the northern, red-clay hills. Indeed, the affluent and upper middle class of Selby seemed to have unconsciously, unofficially seceded from the city to create a new community of their own on the edge of town, close to their beloved Canterbury Academy and Sugar Day. And the retailers seemed more than happy to oblige them. Target, Bed Bath & Beyond, Pier One, Borders, Orvis Outfitters all had signed letters of intent to locate in a new regional mall in north, white Selby. Nearly thirty years after desegregation, Margaret noted she was witnessing nothing short of a *re*segregation. The only whites who remained enamored with the inner-city architecture and fried-fish restaurants and hat-and-wig shops and Dollar stores and black, toothless men who pushed their shopping cart homes through the oak-canopied, redbrick streets were the newcomer Yankees, and they were snatching up historic mansions for a song, restoring them to their antebellum grandeur, then proceeding to "play" Deep South. They filled their homes with period antiques. They planted formal English gardens with topiary and fountains of cherubs and goats. They served their Jersey visitors cheese straws and pecans sautéed in butter and mint juleps in sterling-silver cups, accompanied by antique linen napkins monogrammed in the initials of some anonymous, fading Georgia family.

Dewayne pulled off Riverside Drive and into a parking lot the size of Wal-Mart's. Some urban planner had tried to lessen the immensity of this calm black sea by adding several skinny, curbed islands of yellow and purple and white pansies, each with a spindly, Bradford pear tree that would not shade a car for at least another five years.

"This is huge," Margaret said.

"Six thousand members," Dewayne said. "Course, they all don't come to church at the same time. The sanctuary wouldn't fit 'em all."

They entered through the Sunday school wing and began walking down a long, carpeted hallway with pale yellow walls. Above each door was a marquee with a computerized message running across in red letters, like the ones over the doors announcing the movie in progress in the theaters at the new Regal Cinema 20-Plex. Each revealed the name of the Sunday school class and the topic for the day. Margaret noted that every person they passed, whether fifteen or seventy-six years old, carried a Bible in his hands.

They passed twenty-two doors, and Dewayne finally stopped at one whose marquee announced *"Welcome to the Mountain Climbers! Today's topic is TOUCHDOWN FOR JESUS CHRIST!"*

Upon walking inside, Margaret immediately felt underdressed; she was the only woman wearing slacks. Dewayne nodded hellos as they worked their way to two chairs near the back of the room. Up front, the leaders of the group appeared to be a husband and wife, she with a large red hair bow in her blond hair and a bulldog-head pin on her lapel. With skin the color of cooked veal and military-precise brown hair, her husband reminded Margaret of Ralph Reed, the former leader of the Christian Coalition. He reached under his chair for a Georgia Bulldogs baseball cap and slipped it over his hair, then began waving his hands in the air, crossing them as a football referee does to announce the death of a play.

"Y'all now . . . y'all now . . . I need you to be quiet. I need you to look up here."

The buzzing quickly tapered off, and the man continued, telling his students about the coming week's activities, including the Tuesday night meeting of the Christians for John Grisham reading group and a diet-support group called Chocoholic! As he spoke, his wife looked at him, smiling, with hands folded in her lap.

"Okay, now we've got a fun day planned for y'all, but we're gonna start with some verse that fits in real good with what we're doin' today. Everyone turn your Bibles to one Corinthians fifteen, number fifty-five."

There was a shuffle of books as everyone reached for and opened the Bibles they brought with them. The husband began to read.

"Where, oh death, is your victory? Where, oh death, is your sting? The sting of death is sin, and the power of sin is the law. But thanks be to God! He gives us the victory through our Lord Jesus Christ."

He then looked at his wife, giving her a cue to speak. "Now," she said. "We know football season's over . . ."

"Go, Dawgs!" yelled a man. The room filled with laughter.

She forced a smiled laugh and continued. "We wanna talk about victory," she continued. "I mean personal victory. Bo and I wanna get y'all to think about what Jesus might think is a good victory. Like, for example, my victory is my children, Mary Margaret and Trey, and that they love God and accept Jesus Christ as their personal savior."

"If Jesus were here with us on this earth today, what would he think is a personal touchdown?" the husband asked. "Now I wanna hear your ideas. Speak up now."

A woman in a flowered dress raised her hand, and the man gave her a nod. "Giving some old clothes to Goodwill," she said.

"That's good," he replied. "Maybe some food to the Salvation Army, too, right?"

A red-haired man with wire-frame glasses and freckles on his arms: "How about stopping to help someone whose car broke down, like on the way to Atlanta?"

"Well, that's good, but you gotta be careful nowadays, too."

"Then how about callin' the police on the cell phone and tellin' them to go help," another man said.

"There you go. Now you're thinkin'."

Margaret raised her hand. Dewayne smiled to himself — he was not surprised that she wanted to speak up. One thing he loved about Margaret was her curiosity, and how she would stop a complete stranger to ask a question about something she wanted to know more about. To the clerk at the 7-Eleven: What percentage of customers use the pay-at-the-pump option? To the waitress at Fresh Air Barbecue: Do the Japanese like the spicy sauce? To the old woman sitting beneath her carport on Edna Drive: How did you choose the colors for your house (aqua and yellow)?

"Yes, ma'am, in the back, you're a visitor, aren't you?"

"Yes."

"Well, welcome to Beulah Land. You got a touchdown for Jesus Christ?"

"I do," she said.

"What is it?"

"How about holding the door open for an African American?"

Margaret noted the absolute, hold-your-breath silence of the room, not even a rustle of clothing from shifting weight or the rearranging of crossed legs. "What I'm trying to say," Margaret continued, "is that anything we can do to make an underprivileged class feel better about themselves is a good thing. A little bit of dignity will help us all in the long-run."

Finally, the wife leader shattered the quiet.

"Well now, that's real nice," she said, forcing a smile. "That sure is . . . Anyone else? Anyone got a touchdown for Jesus?"

Dewayne did not look at Margaret, and she wondered if she had embarrassed him. She looked at his hands — hands that had held hers through countless movies . . . hands that had minced onions and rolled out biscuits and tore romaine lettuce as if it were delicate skin tissue . . . hands that had created inside her body exquisite, neurological storms that she never dreamed possible. These hands were now holding, of all things, a Bible, turning pages that reminded Margaret of onion skins, dutifully following the scripture as did everyone in the room.

And as she sat there, recalling all the things they had not talked about in their thousands of hours together — Jesus Christ, her phantom father, the flap over redesigning the Georgia flag so it no longer bowed to the Confederacy, the new proposed stretch of freeway that threatened to wipe out a historic black neighborhood — Margaret looked at Dewayne's profile, those sensuous lips mouthing the words of Samuel 23:29, and she wondered to herself, *Who is this man?*

Twenty-six

Dear Chatter: In reference to keeping squirrels out of bird feeders: Take a post, stand it up about six feet high, put a hubcap on it and put the bird seed on the hubcap. No squirrel can get over that hubcap.

Dear Chatter: To the nasty man in the white Accord on Ridge Avenue on Thursday afternoon. Opening your car door and spitting tobacco juice on the street at 40 miles per hour three times while I followed you is even more disgusting than watching the lady digging into her ear with the Q-Tip.

The one-page menus at Joe Wren's changed each day of the week, except for Sunday, when the restaurant on Broadway Avenue was closed for the Sabbath. And though they had updated the kitchen with a stainless-steel Hobart dishwasher and new stovetop, little else in this rambling, low-ceilinged brick building had been altered in eighty-one years. Repainted and recarpeted, certainly, but customers sat in the same, uncomfortable Georgia-pine booths that their great-grandfathers had occupied. Pull chains still hung from the wall-mounted toilet reservoirs. There had never been a black hostess. There had always been a fried chicken plate, accompanied by a pimiento-cheese sandwich on white bread, three deviled eggs, pickle wedge, and a rounded mound of potato salad.

Every June, after the first of the peach crop had been picked, customers could savor Joe Wren's regionally famous peach ice cream until it ran out. The owners reminded their patrons each Memorial Day weekend with a small ad on the bottom of page two of the *Reflector*. The size of a business card, it said simply: *F.P.I.C.H.N.* There had always been debate in town on whether the acronym for "Fresh peach ice cream here now!" was a strategy to save money on advertising space or code to announce the precious, limited resource in a way that blacks and Yankees could not decipher.

It was Wednesday, and Boone Parley's choices for entrées were fried shrimp, red Alaskan salmon croquettes, or minced steak with mushroom gravy. Two vegetable sides came with each entrée, and Boone considered his offerings of boiled potatoes, lima beans, carrot-and-raisin salad, stewed tomatoes, fried corn, and macaroni and cheese.

Having eaten a filet with Suzanne at the new Longhorn Steakhouse the night before, Boone chose the shrimp.

"That carrot salad's got mayonnaise in it, doesn't it?" he asked the waitress.

"Yes, sir."

"Then give me the carrot salad . . . and the fried corn."

"Sweet tea?" she asked.

Boone nodded, the waitress walked away, and he snapped open the sports section of the *Reflector*. For the fourth day in a row now, the lead item was the ongoing saga of a local boy who was now the successful quarterback for the Atlanta Chieftains.

A graduate of north Selby's Canterbury Academy, Mike Relyea was known for his hot temper and love of speeding down the freeway at more than a hundred miles an hour. And in a bad-boy-does-good interview with *Rolling Stone*, he made the mistake of letting the reporter accompany him on the number-seven train through New York on his way to a paid public appearance in Queens, where he was to cut the ribbon for a new prototype AdidasLand shoe store. At one point, after getting peeved when a young Puerto Rican man refused to turn the throbbing bass down on his boom box, Mike Relyea let loose with a spit-producing string of epithets in which no minority group was spared — Jews, blacks, gays, Latinos, even New Yorkers themselves — a tirade that lasted for the duration of the ride.

All of this ran in the article, and Mike Relyea's world came crashing down. ESPN came to Selby to interview the city's new — and first — black female president of the city council. Boone was disappointed that even the *Reflector* lined up to punch him in the stomach, with a front-page essay from the new editor that asked "What is wrong with a community that can produce such a man?"

Boone could not deny that the boy was wrong in saying all those things out loud, at least the way he did, everything coated in bitter poison, but he spoke the truth. Yankees were so quick to judge Southerners on matters of race. Southerners were not racist; whites and blacks here simply had a longer history of living together, Boone reasoned. Civil and polite to each other, they knew and embraced those differences — it was okay to point them out. It was no different from saying women always changed their minds or worried too much about kids falling out of trees. Boone knew, for example, that black men liked their women with bigger butts while whites preferred ladies with a leaner frame. "They're different," his mother would say. "But we are not any better than they are — remember that, Boone Parley. They did not come to this country by choice, so we have a responsibility to take care of them."

Boone remembered having drinks at Sugar Day with his banker friend Leonard Woosely, whose entire staff at Middle Georgia Bank and Trust had to undergo sensitivity training after the bank was bought by an Ohio company. The new owners brought in Myra Gravenstein, a consultant who aimed to foster harmony between the races and hopefully curb the number of discrimination lawsuits.

Leonard recalled for Boone how she separated everyone by race, interviewed the groups separately, then brought them together to share the list of prejudices each of them came up with.

"What'd they say about us?" Boone asked, curious because he, like everyone else he knew, had no black friends.

"They think we're dirty."

"Come on, Leonard."

"No, man, really. They said they couldn't believe how we don't wash our hands after we go to the bathroom . . . like in a restaurant."

"Don't you wash yours?" Boone asked.

"Do you?"

"Only if someone's in there."

"Well, I guess black folks — excuse me, Af-ri-can A-*mer*-i-cans — wash their hands all the time. And they think our hair stinks."

"What?"

"I'm serious, Boone. One lady said that she could tell when a white man didn't wash his hair after two days. Said dirty, white-people hair smells like curdled milk. Sour."

The waitress brought Boone's fried shrimp, and since he found it distracting to read and chew at the same time, he took the time to recall the previous night's secret meeting of the Sugar Day membership committee.

Six Toyota executives had applied for membership into the club, five Japanese and one white guy, Norman Greenman.

Much to their delight and surprise, the

committee members enjoyed all five Japanese men and their wives. Through the interviews they discovered that their two cultures had much in common, including strong, dominant men, a distaste for overt confrontation, polite demeanors, conservative dress, quiet dignity and humility, a love of gardening and history and family lineage, and a gentleness and slowness that was missing in Mr. Greenman and his brethren from New Jersey.

Greenman was the most senior of the six Toyota men, the executive vice president of operations who reported directly to the CEO. And of the three open slots for membership it made good political sense to give one to him and his family. Yet no one liked him; he was as ugly as a Yankee could be. Norman Greenman corrected natives' grammar in conversation. He wore gold jewelry, a bracelet and rings on both hands, and the Mercedes he drove had the gold accents normally seen only in the black parts of Selby. Norman Greenman was loud, even louder after two Glenlivet scotches, and after three he donned the unbridled abrasiveness of Rodney Dangerfield. There was room for three new members at Sugar Day, which posed the problem for Boone and his committee.

Should they admit three of the Japanese and not Greenman, who basically was in charge of the largest employer in central Georgia? Or do they refuse them all and be labeled racist? Boone had no doubt that someone would call the *Reflector*, and, judging from their coverage of Mike Relyea, Lord knows what they would do with this news.

A lone pregnant woman, blond with a pink-flowered maternity top, entered the dining room. Boone quickly set down his forkful of carrot-and-raisin salad and got up to pull out her chair.

"Thank you so much," she said. "That's really kind of you."

"Oh, no, it's my pleasure," Boone replied. "My wife's fixin' to have our first child this fall."

"Mine's due in April." She rubbed her stomach with both hands. "Lord help me, sometimes I think this baby's standin' up in here."

He returned to his table and resumed eating, catching glances of the woman as she leaned back and read the menu, resting it on the shelf of her distended stomach. He realized now how much of Suzanne's pregnancy seemed secretive and out of reach. He had not seen her naked for the longest time. Saying she was tossing and turning most nights and that she didn't want to keep him awake, Suzanne had asked him to start sleeping in the east guest room. And his mother was right: Why didn't Suzanne have that sweet, rosy appearance and disposition of pregnancy? Was it the stress of the Dogwood party? Why hadn't she started putting together a nursery?

Boone had not even seen a sonogram of his new son — Suzanne was able to report the gender after her most recent visit — because Josephine evidently had mixed it up with the day's junk mail and tossed it in the trash on Thursday, which was rubbish pickup day in Red Hill Plantation. Somewhere in the putrid hills of garbage in the Perry County Robert "Robbie" Hines Landfill, mixed with his neighbor's moist coffee grounds and used Kleenex and the knobby tops of carrots and the silky, clear plastic from dry-cleaning and the past week's copies of the *Reflector*, was the first portrait of Boone Maston Parley IV, who, Boone's mother had already decided, would be called, simply, Maston.

Realizing that Suzanne was probably embarrassed about losing it, Boone made a note to himself to call the practice and get another copy. He knew the sonograms were all on disk nowadays, and they could send it as an e-mail attachment. He'd have Mylene, his secretary, call for it when she got back from vacation. He could wait a few weeks. He already knew it was a boy. That's all that mattered.

Twenty-seven

Dear Chatter: They took the cigar-store Indian out of the Applebee's restaurant on McDonough Road because someone thought it might offend real live Indians. Now, you tell me, how is it that that Indian never upset anyone for ten years and then all of a sudden it bothers someone?

With her mother's well-stained, crocheted hot pad, Donna pushed the roasting pan into the oven and closed the door.

"How much longer?" she asked Margaret.

"You don't want to overcook it," she answered. "Too many people overcook pork and it turns ugly and brown-gray."

"So what do you think? I don't want it too pink; people are scared of pink pork."

"Twenty minutes . . . No, fifteen. What do you want me to do with Dewayne's biscuits?"

"Put 'em in that bottom oven. You think they're gonna be okay turned on low?"

"How much time do we have? An hour?"

"Sixty-five minutes."

"I don't see why not."

Donna reached into a paper Kroger bag and began pulling out the fresh produce needed to make a tossed salad for eight — tomatoes and baby spinach; radicchio and hearts of romaine; a long, bowed, English cucumber and little plastic bags of Glencoe Farms fresh cilantro and dill and Italian parsley.

"You gonna make that dressing?" Donna asked.

"I don't want to overstep my boundaries, Donna," Margaret answered. "I'm your assistant tonight."

"I wish you would — I love that dressing. I want you to teach me how to do it. I gotta get my daddy off blue cheese. Did you know it's got eleven grams of fat per serving?"

Margaret left the kitchen and returned from the car, carrying a straw bag with handles made of skinny rope and a pink, poinsettia-shaped flower and the word *Mexico* embroidered on the side. She had found it in a thrift store on Inglewood Avenue, which was in the throes of a transformation from antiques row to a two-block-long Main Street for people who wear black. It began when a man named Sal Porpiglia, a restaurateur whose wife was a new executive at Toyota, moved to town and bought the Pleasant Peasant Tea Room. He covered the stenciled ivy patterns on the walls with indigo paint and began offering New York–style pizza and a two-page list of microbrew beers.

Next came a dank, basement coffee shop named Exquisite Buzz. Then, a tattoo parlor and New Age store, a Rastafarian clothing shop frequented by white boys in dreadlocks, an Andean-import store, and, finally, the Junkman's Momma, a thrift store whose owner seemed enthralled with inflatable furniture and affordable, mass-produced Christian icons. Margaret bought for herself one of the very same red-flocked Jesus piggybanks that Randy had shown her months ago. He now stood on her fireplace mantel, flanked on each end by a line of used McDonald's Kids' Meal plastic Disney figures (five cents apiece at Junkman's Momma), including Gaston from *Beauty and the Beast*, Snow White, and Simba from *The Lion King*.

"Your house," Dewayne said one evening. "It's lookin' like a toy store."

"I know," Margaret answered. "Isn't it wonderful?"

With her ingredients in hand, Margaret joined Donna at the island in Suzanne Parley's newly remodeled kitchen. With the side of her Joyce Chen chopper, she showed Donna how to use the plane of the knife to crack the skins of garlic cloves with a smack from the heel of the hand. Margaret then minced the garlic and, with help from some gritty kosher salt and olive oil, used a fork to mash it all into a paste right there on the counter. With a rubber spatula, she scooped it up and plopped it into a bowl, then began whisking in the Dijon mustard, the balsamic and raspberry-flavored vinegars, the extra-virgin olive oil, and fresh-cracked pepper.

"That's all you put in it?" Donna asked.

"I might add some chopped tarragon, but it's not necessary."

"Lord, I wish I knew half of what you know about food."

"It sure is doing me a lot of good," Margaret deadpanned.

Donna poked her finger into the dressing then licked it clean. "People in Selby just don't appreciate your kind of cookin'," she said. "It's fancy. You're the best cook I know, Margaret — and that's sayin' a lot because my momma was a great cook."

"Yeah?"

"Oh, yeah. We had preachers at our table every single night. I mean, it was food you probably don't like too much. You know, home cookin'. Smothered steak and fried potatoes and turnip greens."

"Dewayne food," Margaret said.

Hands on her hips, Donna began to pace around the room, absorbing the new kitchen — the gleaming, white Sub-Zero refrigerator . . . the Viking range and ovens, also white . . . the wallpaper of peonies and bluebirds on a golden yellow background . . . the gray-speckled granite countertops resting on custom-built cherry-wood cabinets, and on top of those, artfully arranged clusters of clear-glass vases filled with dried pastas and bottles of expensive decorator vinegars and oils, all dyed different colors and filled with layers of roasted red peppers and cherries, pepperoncini and olives and garlic cloves.

Donna thought of her own kitchen, which she was still decorating, and how the bottles would look nice on the windowsill with the light shining through.

Her new apartment was one of the new ones out on Lee Road, and she was pleased with the solitary life she had created for herself in this lovely new place, with wall-to-wall carpeting, a breakfast bar, and balcony off the master bedroom. If she got home in time, Donna liked to pour herself a glass of white zinfandel and sit on her green-plastic Adirondack chair from Target and watch the sun go down. There were days, entire weekends even, when she chose to see no one. Having visited Rosemont Cemetery with Margaret, Donna often went on her own now and hiked along the riverbank. Sometimes she stumbled upon wizened black men sitting on overturned buckets, fishing with bamboo poles, eating their cold fried fish or chicken from a crinkled tray of tin foil in their laps.

Donna was still surprised at how much she had grown to love the quiet. She passed on the CD option when she bought her new car — a black Saturn coupe with tan, leather interior. Though she did not need a new car — the one Robbie sold her was only two years old — her Camaro had started feeling like last year's skirt lengths. "It's really pretty," Adrian Braswell said one evening, sitting in the passenger seat as Donna drove him home. "No wonder you don't want me eatin' pork rinds in here."

She had started reading the books from the Oprah table at the new Barnes &

Noble. Lately, Donna had been spending most of her evenings trying to master her mother's air gun that she had used to paint the very popular, personalized welcome mats she sold at Happy's Flea Market. In place of people's names and a picture of a rose or magnolia or some other flower, Donna would spell out sayings that she had thought up and scribbled onto Post-it notes with the Chiquita logo that she kept in the pocket of her apron at work: *Lettuce Entertain You! . . . Caution: Active brain inside! Shallow men need not knock!*

"You gotta come see my new apartment," Donna said to Margaret. "How about this weekend?"

Margaret peeked through the window of the oven door, checking on the pork roast.

"Dewayne's off this weekend," she answered. "We were thinkin' of driving down to Hilton Head to the beach."

"Y'all are practically livin' together."

Margaret smiled.

"I still just can't believe Dewayne Case has got himself a girlfriend," Donna said. "That boy was always runnin' away from girls — and they was always chasin' him. He was the shyest boy in my high school."

"That doesn't surprise me."

"I don't even think he went to the junior-senior."

Margaret cranked the wooden knob of her pepper grinder, creating a pulsating black snow over the green salad. "He's perfect for me right now," Margaret said. "I've been afraid of men for most of my life."

"Why?"

Margaret plucked a leaf of arugula from the salad and nibbled on the rounded end. "They've been such a mystery to me. I lived with my mom until she died, Donna — even when I was going to college. I didn't date. I didn't go to slumber parties and call up boys on the phone and giggle and hang up. I just didn't do those things."

"Well there's nothin' to be afraid of," Donna said. "They're simple as can be."

During her months in the male-dominant produce field, Donna had learned a different side of men at her own store and at other Krogers when she went to fill in for someone. They were not as petty and competitive and nasty behind each other's backs as women were. They joked with Donna in ways she imagined them doing in locker rooms. It was so easy to be their ally. Simply sharing and getting lost in a consuming task — unloading a carton of lemons, coring and slicing fresh pineapples

— was all that was necessary to help define and solidify a friendship with a man . . . no talking . . . no sharing . . . just working toward a goal in the same aura of sweat and energy. Men did not seem as distracted around her nowadays. They did not waste their energy or her time with cocky, empty mating dances, and they seemed less interested in her lips than the words that came from them. And while she sometimes worried that all sex appeal had leaked from her body, Donna found great relief in this.

Suddenly, the door to the dining room swung open and in walked a woman with a red bouffant and red lips adrift in a pale, unblemished complexion. She wore a fashionable, ivory-colored, double-breasted knit pantsuit with square buttons and flared legs. Margaret immediately recognized her as Madeline VanDermeter, the executive director of the International Dogwood Festival, whom she'd seen at the neighborhood meeting she covered in Red Hill Plantation. Though Margaret had never spoken with her, the woman was a legend in town. In just nine years she had turned what used to be a simple pancake feed and parade into one of the largest, most lucrative festivals in the South that drew upwards of sixty thousand visitors.

Each year she allowed just five coveted corporate sponsorships for the event and as a result had collected an impressive array of gifts from CEOs who came to court. From Frito-Lay, she received a Tiffany sapphire ring; from Target, a dogwood-blossom-themed mailbox designed by Michael Graves; from American Airlines, lifetime Platinum AAdvantage frequent-flyer status; and from the CEO of Pepsi who tried every year, unsuccessfully thus far, to beat out Atlanta-based Coca-Cola, a case of Dom Perignon, a two-week trip for two to Tuscany, and an ivory Vera Wang gown, designed exclusively for Madeline in her busty size twelve.

Madeline VanDermeter hated the *Reflector*, especially since someone in her office had leaked to Randy Whitestone a detailed history of all these perks (which the companies denied giving, of course, throwing her honesty and integrity into question) and he ran a front-page story, including a photo of the mailbox outside her home.

"So y'all are the maestros behind those wonderful canapés."

"Yes, ma'am," Donna said. "I'm glad you like 'em."

"They're divine! They're just like

somethin' I once had in California — at the International Garlic Festival in Gilroy? I just love garlic, but it doesn't love me, if you know what I mean."

"Garlic's been proven to boost your immune system," Donna said.

"I'm Madeline VanDermeter," she said, offering her hand in an elevated manner that made it look as if she expected you to kiss instead of shake it.

"I'm Donna Kabel. This is my friend, Margaret. She's helpin' me out tonight."

"I work at the *Reflector*," Margaret said. "I remember you from the meeting at the house in this very same neighborhood . . . the one about the dogs."

"Why, yes! I thought I recognized you." She leaned back slightly to study Margaret. "I haven't read anything about those poor dogs for the longest time."

Margaret quickly intuited that the woman knew very well who she was, and that her reason for venturing into the kitchen was not to praise the salmon-garlic spread but to inquire about the story. The International Dogwood Festival was just three weeks away. The producers of the "Today" show had already promised to open their seven o'clock hour with a live feed from Selby, and both the *Chicago Tri-*

bune and *Dallas Morning News* had said they'd be in town to cover the festival as a live travel story. Of course, an epidemic of dying dogs — specifically, *murdered* dogs — in the land of dogwood blossoms, specifically during the International Dogwood Festival, of which Alpo was a sponsor this year, would be too irresistible for any irony-loving journalist to overlook. The result could be disastrous. And Madeline VanDermeter — whose beige, silk, stiletto-heeled shoe had just rendered a dropped raspberry into paste, splashing flecks of juice onto her toe and creating an impression that she was responsible for some small-scale roadkill — was on a fact-finding mission. Would the *Reflector*, which had taken on such an ugly face since the new owners bought it, break a story before the festival? How much did they know? And, most importantly, how much control could she exert over the situation?

Despite Randy's complaints, Margaret had been ignoring the story. There was good reason she had chosen to remain in the features department or, as news reporters called it, "fantasy island." Most news stories inherently implied fault and guilt, and where there was guilt there was conflict, and what she loved most about her job with Chatter and the profiles was its relatively conflict-free character. If anyone deserved a life free of conflict, she reasoned, it was she, especially after all those years on the front lines of reproductive rights with her mother.

Margaret pleaded with Randy time and again to give it to a reporter on the metro desk, but he refused. "It'll be good for your development," Randy said. "Now get on it."

For weeks, without lying, she could tell him there were no new developments in the case. Then, just yesterday, Margaret took a call from a veterinarian whose wife was a secretary in the sheriff's office. The tests were in. They'd found the poison (antifreeze) and the source of it (canned dog food set out by someone living in the neighborhood), but for some reason no arrests had been made, no press conference called.

"Actually, Ms. VanDermeter, I think they're close to finding out who's responsible for all the killings."

She laughed out loud. "Killin's? Darlin', we're talkin' about dogs here — sweet, dear things but dumb animals just the same."

"I've heard they're very close to making an arrest."

She leaned back, folding her arms across her chest. "And what if they do?" she asked.

"I'm sure my editor will want a story."

Every time Margaret had seen Madeline VanDermeter, both in person and on television and in the *Reflector* and in the colored snapshots on the "Smile!" society pages of *Selby Magazine*, she appeared to defy gravity, especially her face, which seemed to be held up at several points by marionette strings — the corners of the mouth, obviously, but also the active, high-arching eyebrows that reminded Margaret of cats stretching their backs. Margaret wondered how many calories this woman burned in an hour simply by having her face turned "on" at all times. It looked exhausting. Yet in an instant, just seconds after Margaret said "I'm sure my editor will want a story," Madeline VanDermeter's face collapsed, the strings all simultaneously severed, and everything that had pointed upward now pointed downward. Fascinated by this extreme, physical transformation, Margaret scrutinized her face. It reminded her of the before-and-after makeup shots she had studied in the window of Merle Norman at the Selby Mall.

"Would you excuse us, please?" the woman asked Donna. She gently took hold of Margaret's upper arm and guided her away from the island, over to the entrance to the butler's pantry.

"You do know, dear, that my festival's the biggest in the South. It brings more money and people into this city than anything else — except the tobacco plant."

"Yes, ma'am," Margaret replied.

"I just shudder to think what would happen if y'all ran that story before the festival. We'd be the laughingstock of the whole wide world, and all that hard work, all that money and all those jobs . . . they'd just go right on down the drain. You wouldn't want the *Reflector* to be responsible for that, would you?"

"It's not right to suppress news, Ms. VanDermeter."

"Please, call me Madeline. I'm not askin' you to suppress the news. I'm just askin' you to use good judgment."

"It's not my decision, Ms. VanDermeter. It's the editor's."

"Mr. Whitestone," she said.

"Yes."

Madeline paused a moment, recalling the many unpleasant conversations she'd had with him. "Mr. Whitestone hates

Selby," she said. "He hates Georgia. Did you read his column about the Bulldogs? I mean, what's wrong with likin' a football team so much? That's patriotism."

"He's a unique person," Margaret said.

"He's ugly," Madeline VanDermeter said. "Between you and me, Margaret, there's lots of people who've canceled their subscriptions because they don't like the *Reflector*. They feel like it's a friend who's turned on 'em."

"Ms. VanDermeter . . ."

"Listen to me, young lady!" she snapped in a whisper. "They know who's been killin' all those dogs, and let me tell you what — it would surprise a lotta people, and it's gonna be just too juicy to ignore. Tommy's agreed that we should just handle this on our own. Quietlike. All I'm askin' is for you to do the same. I know you got a phone call. You know about this."

"Tommy?"

"Tommy Barnes."

"The sheriff?"

"Of course."

Margaret looked over at Donna, who was stirring skim milk into the mashed potatoes. Margaret had tried to persuade her to use cream, at least half-and-half, but

Donna wanted to keep the fat content down. "I can't promise you anything, Ms. VanDermeter."

"What is it about you people!" she shot. "Don't you understand: sometimes . . . when you see somethin' wrong goin' on . . . you just gotta look the other way? Why make a big fuss and drag people through the mud just for a show? Sometimes you just gotta take care of things in a nice quiet way so people can keep their heads high. The *Reflector* used to do that, but let me tell you, those days are gone. No, ma'am. That newspaper of yours has gone to the dogs."

She stormed out of the kitchen, back to the living room, unaware of her comical choice of words that helped lessen the anxiety that was buzzing through Margaret's body like a double shot of espresso. Margaret looked at the floor, noting the red blotches left by Madeline VanDermeter's right shoe, evenly spaced and growing weaker with each step toward the door.

Twenty-eight

Dear Chatter: There is no justice in the world. A security guard who carries a gun is sellin' his sister's soul, and I have proof, but the law won't do anything. The person he sells it to has money — so can someone tell me what to do?

Dear Chatter: I don't know how many times I have to tell Yankees this but you should not plant any annuals until Good Friday. It will not frost, but the ground is too cold until Good Friday, and if you want your annuals to grow strong and big then you've got to wait. I don't know why y'all are in such a hurry to get those annuals in the ground. Maybe it's because you're so excited not to be shoveling snow in March.

It was late night, just after midnight, and Boone was snoring in the guest room. Suzanne set her glass of chardonnay onto a mahogany end table then focused her attention on the oversized wicker basket at the foot of her ivory-damask recamier in the bedroom. It was heavy, the size of an ottoman, with a load of at least three hundred mail-order catalogs, but she pushed slowly, alone, lifting one edge off the carpet until that point when gravity abandons the enemy and, sensing defeat, runs over to join the other side. Together, they overturned the basket with a weighty roll, and the catalogs, all cool and slick and shiny in the lamplight, flowed from the vessel like a load of freshly caught fish.

Happier in her marriage than she'd been in years, Suzanne was determined to make her man's thirty-third birthday the best ever, and she was pleased with her final selection of gifts. From the Horchow catalog, which was at the very bottom of the basket, a double, automatic watch winder that featured not only two rotating orbs that twisted and turned at night with the watches attached, but also a glass-topped display area that held up to six other watches, a perfect match because Boone had exactly eight.

From The Sharper Image, two items, including the Turbo Groomer 2.0 that trimmed unsightly hairs not only from deep inside the nostrils but also the ears. Made of black plastic and chrome with a laserlike light on the end, it reminded Suzanne of a weapon from *Star Wars*. Yet even more exciting, because Boone had started grilling again for them at night, was the combination fork/thermometer with ultrasensitive "fish" option, a long, two-pronged spearing device whose tines were actually thermometers that measured the heat of the meat and displayed the temperature on a lighted panel on the handle.

Unlike birthdays of years past, which she scrambled to fill with friends and noise, Suzanne decided this year's celebration would be an intimate affair. She had asked Donna to make beef filets with béarnaise sauce and to re-create the roasted asparagus with lime and garlic that had become a favorite of Boone's at the Forsyth Room.

After dinner, he would want to talk of the baby again, and to plan and dream ahead. Suzanne didn't mind this in the least because when he pondered the future of his son, Boone's blue-gray eyes seemed to dance, reminding her of moonlight on rippling water . . . or spinning bicycle wheels. She would watch him as he wondered out loud if his mother still had his baseball mitt from Little League and if they should start participating this year in the prepaid college tuition program at the

University of Georgia. He was so animated when he talked of such things! He twitched with playground energy she hadn't seen this late in the day for years, and Suzanne would fill to bursting and say "Kiss me." And as she felt his hands gently cupping her face, Suzanne would think, *How can I give this up? How can I ever live without this again?*

Suzanne got up, went into the kitchen and returned to the recamier with the Sugar Day directory and three felt-tip pens, one red, one blue, one green. Over the past month, she had been going through the roster of families, circling in red the ones she could count on to show up for her and Boone's Dogwood party, circling in blue those traitors who would attend Marc and Jodi Armbuster's party, and marking with green all the fence-sitters. These were the ones Suzanne had been scrutinizing the most, checking and rechecking the names to see if any of them had tottered to one side or the other. She based this on signs she observed throughout the week. For example, did someone choose to sit on the other side of the aisle from them that Sunday at Christ Church . . . or had she caught anyone wheeling their Kroger buggy directly to the checkout lane of the grocery store and then, after seeing Suzanne in line, suddenly but smoothly veer left, turning into the safety of aisle sixteen where they proceeded to read the labels on laundry detergent as if they were the backs of book covers.

Suzanne carried the Sugar Day directory with her as she went about town, and, like a politician on the stump, if she saw a chance to sway someone she would nab it. That Tuesday, Hal and Tiny Trane moved from blue to green. Emerging from the Aveda Salon, Suzanne saw that Tiny was searching for a rare, coveted parking spot, and as Suzanne pulled out she blocked a car with New Jersey plates long enough for her fellow native Selbyite to zip right in.

Tiny emerged from her bronze Cadillac sedan and waved. "Thank you, Suzanne," she yelled.

"See y'all next month at Dogwood!" Suzanne yelled back.

Twenty-nine

Dear Chatter: Thought y'all might get a kick out of this: Four guys are driving cross-country together. One's from Idaho, one's from Nebraska, one's from Georgia, and the last is a Yankee from New Jersey.

A little bit down the road the man from Idaho starts pulling potatoes out of his bag and throws them out the window. The Nebraska man turns to him and asks, "What in the world are you doin'?" The man from Idaho says, "Man, we have so many of these things in Idaho that they're laying around on the ground. I'm sick and tired of looking at them."

A few miles later, the man from Nebraska starts to do the same thing with ears of corn, throwing them out the window. The man from Idaho asks, "Why are you doing that?" The guy from Nebraska says, "Man, we have so many of these things in Nebraska that they're laying around on the ground.

I'm sick and tired of looking at them."

So the man from Georgia opens the door and pushes the Yankee out.

Yeah!

"Pass that casserole, Dewayne," Sonny Case said. "Your daddy's gonna have some more of that."

"I didn't know grits could taste this good," said his mother, Ronna. "You gotta give me this recipe, Dewayne."

Dewayne looked at Margaret and smiled. "I didn't make it," he said. "It's Margaret's doin'."

Margaret had made the entire meal in Dewayne's kitchen, where she'd labored since five o'clock that morning. At daybreak she baked a batch of Dewayne's biscuits. By noon she'd finished her homemade green-tea-and-lemongrass ice cream. She had planned on roasting a chicken in a Mediterranean marinade of citrus and bouquet garni but at the last minute was inspired by a piece of chorizo she found lying next to the cube of Velveeta in Dewayne's meat drawer. For the longest time Margaret had shunned the rubbery processed cheese as an ingredient in squash casserole, but after numerous, greasy, gloppy attempts with the firmer cheeses she finally relented and embraced it.

Tonight's popular casserole, now three-quarters gone, included layers of grits, four white cheeses, and a meat sauce of chorizo-infused ground pork with tomatoes, the tiniest hint of a chipotle pepper, cilantro, and adobo seasoning.

"What kind of meat is this?" Ronna asked.

"Pork," Margaret answered.

"Pork?"

"Yes, ma'am."

"Now we can't have garlic. I hope Dewayne told you we can't have garlic. This doesn't have garlic in it, does it?"

Margaret looked at Dewayne for guidance on the question.

"No, Momma," he said.

Margaret looked at him, surprised but secretly relieved that he would lie to his parents. Doing so put him on her side — for this evening, at least. She reached for and squeezed his hand under the table.

"Well, what tastes like garlic?"

"Probably the cumin," Margaret answered.

All evening — and Margaret found this peculiar — both Ronna and Sonny avoided asking Margaret anything about her pre-

Selby life. Instead, they talked about the *Reflector* and had many questions about a newsroom and how it works. Sonny shared his thoughts on Margaret's dilapidating roof and gave her pointers on quizzing the roofers when she would call for estimates.

Ronna was a homemaker, and though Dewayne was twenty-four she still bought his underwear and socks and did his sewing. Sonny was the assistant supervisor of elections for Perry County and worked in the courthouse downtown.

"Do you take lunch breaks?" he asked Margaret.

"Sometimes," Margaret answered. "Why?"

"You work downtown, right?"

"Yes, sir."

"Well there's this new program for executives at the Mulberry Baptist Church," he said, stopping to glance at his wife. "It's called Power Lunch with the Lord, and everyone takes their Bibles and gets a sermon every Monday from a different Baptist minister. Maybe you can go with me some time."

"Maybe so," Margaret said. "That sounds real nice."

"She's been goin' to Sunday school with me," Dewayne said, eliciting from both parents looks of surprise that melted into smiles.

The four of them stood on the sidewalk in front of Dewayne's house. It was obvious the elder Cases were waiting for something, but neither Margaret nor Dewayne could figure out what. So, as one looks for four-leaf clovers but in the meanwhile settles for interesting, exotic weeds, they exchanged empty items of chitchat.

Finally, after a long moment of silence, Ronna said, "Margaret, I don't see your car, honey. Did Dewayne drive you over?"

"Yes, ma'am."

"Do you want me and Sonny to take you home?"

"Dewayne can take me home."

"Well, he has work tomorrow, don't you, Dewayne? You probably better get goin' to bed."

"I'll take her home, Momma," he answered. "We've gotta clean up, first."

"I can have your daddy come back and pick her up later."

"No, Momma. I can manage."

"I'm just tryin' to help."

"Yes, ma'am. I know. Thank you." He leaned down to his mother and kissed her cheek. "Good night."

After they pulled away, Margaret walked over to the glider beneath the carport and sat down. "They hate me," she said.

"That's a pretty strong word," Dewayne replied.

"Okay, then, they don't like me."

"You can't be sure about that."

"I'm sure. I think it was the prayer."

Before the meal, Dewayne had had to ask Margaret to join hands to pray. When he offered his arm across the table, toward hers, Margaret simply thought he was being romantic; she didn't know she was supposed to grab Ronna's as well to complete the circle.

"They did not want to connect with me, Dewayne. They did not ask one thing about me."

"They did so."

"Not about my past. Not about anything that would have shed some light on who I am. For a culture that's always asking 'Who are your people?' they sure didn't seem interested in mine."

Dewayne sat down beside her and took her hand in his. Even after all these months, the juxtaposition of sizes made Margaret stare.

"They might've thought you didn't wanna talk about it."

"You mean the fact that I was born illegitimate?"

"No," he said. "I mean about your momma's job."

There was much about her mother Margaret had shared with Dewayne — the year of cancer, the alpha personality, even the anecdote of when Ruth Pinaldi gave her twelve-year-old daughter a *Ms.* magazine article with line-drawing illustrations showing masturbation techniques. Yet she had told him nothing about the clinic or what she did there. All he knew — or at least all she thought he knew — was that she had worked for her mother, the doctor.

"What are you getting at?" she asked. "What do you know about my mother?"

Dewayne gave a slight pained look as if he'd been caught in a white lie. "My momma's secretary-treasurer of Middle Georgians for Life," he said.

Margaret's mouth dropped open. "Oh . . . my . . . God. They know? You know? How long have you known?"

"Couple of months, I guess. Momma ran a Google search on her, and she gave me lots to read. It's not like your momma tried to hide behind a rock, Margaret."

"Well, then, I suppose you think of me as the Devil in the flesh now, don't you?"

"Why would I do that?" he asked.

"Guilty by association."

"That was your momma."

"Yeeeees. There's a connection here, Dewayne. Do you see it yet?"

"Don't get ugly at me. I might not agree with what your momma did, but that doesn't mean I'm gonna hold it against you."

"That's what pro-lifers do," Margaret said.

"No," Dewayne replied. "That's what Yankees do."

The sun had set, casting in the western sky a glow that reminded Margaret of orange sherbet. In anticipation of rain, the tree frogs had begun their tiny, whiny, seal-like barks.

"So you can honestly tell me," Margaret said, "that when you look at me you don't see the patient counselor of an abortion clinic who shepherded thousands of unborn children to their death?"

"No," Dewayne answered. "I see a girl who lost her momma to cancer."

While working at the clinic, Margaret received a version of the same phone call at least three times a week.

"There are two red lines," the woman

would say. "But how can I be sure?"

"Two red lines?"

"Yes."

"And this is from urine voided this morning?"

"Yes."

"Then you'd best set up an appointment to see Dr. Pinaldi."

"But how can I be sure?"

"Two red lines? Not one . . . but two?"

"Yes."

"A thick line and a skinny line?"

"Yes."

Margaret knew the reliability and indicator signs of every home-pregnancy test on the market — a thin blue line, a green circle, a blue diamond, two red lines. All meant yes. All would plunge the caller into either despair or guarded euphoria.

"It's positive," she would say. "I have an opening next Thursday, would that work?"

Now, standing before her own bathroom vanity, holding the disposable, white-plastic device in her hand, Margaret unconsciously repeated the words out loud.

"Two . . . red . . . lines," she said. "Oh . . . my . . . God."

And then she thought of the new Planned Parenthood on J. B. McDonough Road. She wondered if they simply doled out pamphlets and birth control pills or also had a clinician on staff.

"If not, there's always Atlanta," she said to herself.

Thirty

Dear Chatter: My friend and me went out for lunch the other day and we found a new restaurant that made sweet-potato milkshakes! It was so good I'm fixin' to go back and get me another one. Whoever heard of such a thing!

Dear Chatter: Okay, Selbyites, time for a driving lesson. There's this thing on your car called a turn signal. Use it! Also, we do not roll down the windows and chat with drivers of other cars on the freeway. It is for high-speed travel. Stop driving as if you're living in the country.

Donna was crouched before her easel in front of the tropicals, pieces of orange, yellow, and green chalk in her hands. From the corner of her eye she saw Koquita entering aisle eleven, coming into work, her purse around her shoulder and a McDonald's milkshake in hand.

"Koquita!" she yelled. "Can you come over here, please?"

Koquita ambled into the produce department. "Whatchu want?" she asked.

"Can you tell me what this is?" Donna asked, pointing to her easel.

"No, ma'am, I ain't takin' no produce test today."

"I just wanna know if you can tell what this is. I've been drawin' pictures on my daily tip board. People just notice 'em more if I do."

With her large, round, Garfield-like eyes, Koquita took in the drawing. "That's easy," she said. "That's a papaya."

"You are absolutely correct."

"That's good, Donna. You draw real good."

Donna stood back to admire her work.

Donna's TIP of the Day: Did you know there's a tropical fruit that can make your steak taste better? It's the papaya! Papayas, which are also called papaws, have an enzyme called papain, which is used as a meat tenderizer! Just rub some juice of the flesh onto that steak before cooking and then, mmmm-mmm, tasty, tender T-bone.

"I drew it cut open like that 'cause I wanted my customers to know what it looks like inside," she said. "Sometimes I think they're afraid of what's inside, especially if it's not the prettiest thing in the world. That's why I'm always cuttin' open a kiwi and layin' it out on a foam tray."

As Koquita left for the employee lounge, Donna bent down to pick up someone's crinkled shopping list and put it in her pocket. She'd grown to love the deep front pockets of her uniform that could easily accommodate the fallout from her entire day — broken rubber bands from broccoli stalks; crispy leaves that had dropped from a bunch of red grapes; a penny found on the floor in front of the apple bin; a blue Chiquita sticker that no longer stuck; contorted twist ties; lost buttons; a two-for-one coupon for nacho-cheese Doritos; Christian poems that Adrian would write and give to her.

Even more than the pockets, though, she had learned to appreciate how a uniform gave her so much more time in the morning. She no longer had to search for a combination of clothes that fit her budget, laundry schedule and mood of the day. Donna found she had nearly an extra hour each morning, and she could linger and drink her coffee and read Chatter and spend time with her new three-legged tabby, Miss Kitty, whom she'd found at the Perry County Humane Society.

Suddenly, Donna spotted Boone Parley standing before the lettuces. She had never seen him at Kroger. Slowly, with great effort, as if he were a patient undergoing occupational therapy, he used the chrome tongs to fill his plastic bag with the organic baby-lettuce mix that Suzanne usually picked up herself.

Something's not right, Donna thought. Maybe he thinks he's got the wrong greens. She started walking over to say hello and offer help, but the look of consternation on his face was so intense that she changed her mind in front of the plums, did an about-face, and retreated to the stockroom to fill out her orders for the next day.

Anyone who knew Boone Parley would recognize that something was indeed wrong. For starters, he was wearing his surgical scrubs, and Boone thought it unprofessional to leave the hospital in anything other than his jacket and tie and Brooks Brothers button-down-collar shirts. Also, he had not showered after surgery, as he always did, and his straight, brown hair was dented along the sides of his head from the straps of the surgical mask.

Seconds after emerging from surgery

that morning, Boone's secretary greeted him at the doors of the surgical suite with news that the sheriff was waiting for him in his office.

"The sheriff?" Boone asked.

"Yes, sir."

"Why?"

"Wouldn't say."

"Can I shower first?"

"He says he's kinda in a hurry."

"The Perry County sheriff?"

"Yes, sir."

"Tommy Barnes?"

"Yes, sir."

When Boone got to his office, Tommy Barnes was standing before a wall, his beefy hands crammed into his back pockets as his attention bounced from framed diploma to framed diploma.

"Mr. Tom?" Boone said, and he turned to greet him. "I haven't had the pleasure of talkin' with you for a long, long time. How's Timmy?"

Timmy Barnes, now a truck driver for Middle Georgia Budweiser Distributors, Inc., was Tommy Barnes's son and Boone's center when he quarterbacked for Canterbury Academy fifteen years ago, and Boone suddenly remembered many a post-football-practice steak dinner at the

Barnes's house. Normally a jocular man with dimples deep enough to hold a peanut (indeed, he would perform this trick for boys who came to the house), Tommy Barnes looked at Boone with the same sober expression a law officer uses to inform someone of a death in the family.

"I think you better sit down for this one, Boone," he said. "I've got some news gonna break your heart."

And by the time the sheriff finished divulging all that he knew about Suzanne and the dogs of Red Hill Plantation, Boone had leaned back in his chair, deflated, his chest sunken, his head woozy, feeling as if something had just sucked every ounce of oxygen from his body. So his mother was right after all — something *was* wrong with Suzanne. And before he could lift the lid off the pan of boiling anger within, Boone suddenly remembered how ugly he'd been with his wife, the mother of his son, about the pee stains in the yard, and how he hounded and hounded her to take care of the situation. Of course she'd poisoned the stupid dogs! What else could she have done?

Unconsciously, to help revive his senses and jerk him back into his body, Boone pulled open his top desk drawer, reached for a rectangular tin of peppery Starbucks mints, and popped four of them into his mouth. He breathed through his nose, and the vapors from the so-called turbocharged candies cooled his nasal passages like ice.

"Are you sure about this, Tommy?" he asked.

"Yep. I got lab tests and my best detective's word."

"I just don't know what to say. I feel horrible about this."

Tommy Barnes nodded his head in silence.

"Boone," he finally said. "Your momma says Suzanne's got a drinkin' problem. Maybe some depression."

"My momma doesn't like Suzanne, Mr. Tom. That's pretty well common knowledge," he answered. "Suzanne likes her chardonnay just like any other lady in Red Hill Plantation. But she's not drinkin' now, Tommy."

"No?"

"She's pregnant."

Tommy Barnes's jaundiced eyes opened wider. He pursed his lips and nodded his head again in thought.

"Well now, that might explain somethin'."

"What's that?" Boone asked.

"Women can do some crazy things when they're expectin' babies."

"Yes, sir."

"You almost expect 'em to do somethin' a little crazy. It's natural, don't you think?"

"Yes, sir, it sure is."

The sheriff, who was leaning back in the chair, sighed deeply, his great belly rising then falling again. His brown-leather belt creaked from the sudden expansion and contraction. "If these dogs was to stop dyin', I think people just might forget about all this. Then I could forget about it, too."

"Yes, sir," Boone answered.

"I'm assumin' those dogs are gonna stop dyin' here real soon?"

"Yes, sir. I'll see what I can do. You know I'll do my best."

"Problem is, I've got someone with loose lips in my lab."

Tommy Barnes stood up, placed his hands on the edge of Boone's desk and leaned forward. "If that newspaper finds out what's goin' on, I'm gonna have to do somethin', Boone."

"Sir?"

"I'm gonna have to do somethin'. I'm gonna have to make me an arrest."

* * *

On the advice of his doctor, twice each week Frankie Kabel got his blood pressure taken. And without telling his daughter, because he did not want to inflate her ego even further, the place he chose to do this was the machine at the pharmacy in the Kroger where she worked.

As the machine hummed and the stiff material inside the tube began to squeeze his arm, Frankie would look up at the pictures of the store managers on the wall and let the eight-by-ten color portrait of his daughter — *Donna Kabel, Produce Manager* — sink into him like butter on a hot biscuit.

Thirty-one

Dear Chatter: I wanna know why they're not givin' out Bibles this year in the middle schools when they've done just that for a hundred years or more. *To heck with the Constitution, right? — Editors.*

Dear Chatter: Is there any place in Selby other than The Gap where I can buy girl's clothes that do not have frills or lace or bows or cutesy appliqués on them? And while I'm at it, what is it with all the hair bows on grown women?

"Where are you taking me?" Margaret asked.

"It's a surprise," Dewayne answered. "It's not too much farther. Are you still feelin' sick?"

"A little."

"Is that Rolaids helpin' any?"

"A little."

"You're sure not happy this mornin'."

Dewayne paused, then smiled. "But I'm fixin' to change that."

They rode south on U.S. 41, the Dixie Highway — past the flea market, past the airport, past one dead armadillo on the road, past the shady pecan groves and the Badcock Peach Packing Plant and Visitors' Center, which was marked by a water tower whose roundish top was painted to be a peach.

Finally, Dewayne turned onto a red-clay dirt road, and a mile or so later they pulled up to a white trailer with hail-dented, blue-metal shutters, which seemed to be resting in the shade of a gigantic live oak.

"Who lives here?" Margaret asked.

"My friend Bobby."

"So what are we doing?"

"Just settle those ants in your pants and relax."

From the bed of his blue truck Dewayne pulled a large Igloo cooler and motioned for Margaret to follow him. They crossed a grassy field, sloping downward, and after a few minutes Margaret could hear water from a creek.

"There she is," Dewayne said. "She's always early — and here she's early again. This here's the first dogwood to bloom every year in Selby. And I'm the only one who knows about it. You ever seen one before?"

"No!"

Margaret walked up to the tree. It was relatively short, gnarly and twisty but with a wide canopy. "These flowers, Dewayne. They look like orchids."

He reached and plucked one from the tree then walked over, took Margaret's hand and set it in her palm.

"There's a story about this flower," he said. "About this tree. They didn't used to be short and squatty like this but big and mighty like that oak over there. And it was big enough that the Jews picked it to make the cross for Jesus, and the tree was so sad about bein' used to kill him that Jesus promised right there that dogwoods from then on would be short and squatty and crooked so no one would wanna use 'em for a cross ever again.

"Now, look at this." He pointed to the blossom in her hand. "These petals here — there's two long ones and two short ones, which makes it kinda look like a cross. And these little brown marks . . . Look at 'em real careful; they look brown but they're not. There's red for blood and rust for the iron, and these are supposed to be where the nails were in Jesus' hands. And in the very middle . . . see there? The little pollen things? That's supposed to be his crown of thorns. Course this probably isn't true, but it sure is a pretty story."

Margaret looked up from the blossom and into Dewayne's eyes.

"Darlin'," he asked. "Are you cryin'?"

She fell into him and buried her face in the denim shirt that covered his chest.

"Honey? Sweetie? What's goin' on? Are you okay?"

After a few moments, Margaret gathered herself and leaned back from his body. "Dewayne, I've got something horrible to tell you."

"What? What is it? Oh, Lord — are you leavin' me? Are you movin' or somethin'?"

"No," she replied. "But maybe I should so I don't hurt you. I'm pregnant, Dewayne."

His eyes grew large and round. "Oh, my gosh." He raked a hand through his blond hair and looked at the flowering dogwood. "I thought we were bein' careful," he said.

"We were," Margaret answered. "Sex is a game of chance, and we didn't beat the odds, Dewayne. We are now among the three percent who get pregnant on the pill."

Margaret reached for his chin and pulled

it toward her so she could look him in the eye. "I wasn't gonna tell you," she said. "I was just gonna take care of it and say nothing . . . because I know how you are and what you would want to do about this. And you and I have very different opinions. Children should be planned, Dewayne. They deserve it."

"Oh, no."

"Oh, yes."

On the way home they stopped for a red light at the corner of Tyville Road and Vineville Drive, at an overgrown lot with a large, professionally painted plywood sign pounded into the red-clay ground: "*Watch for us: Hersch Porsche-Audi. Atlanta's finest car dealer is coming to Selby.*" Beyond the sign sat what appeared to be an abandoned car of Cadillac length, consumed by a thick green blanket of kudzu. Margaret thought it looked like a piece of topiary that General Motors might commission for the front yard of its headquarters.

Everywhere in Perry County, bulldozers were felling trees; backhoes were digging trenches and laying pipe; two Atlanta concrete companies had moved in and set up temporary plants out by the new Holiday Inn Muscogee Convention Center because the local companies could not keep up with demand. It was hard to find a traffic light intersection in the outskirts of Selby that did not have some piece of earth-moving equipment snorting and clambering over the landscape like a tank sent in to occupy unfriendly territory.

Throughout the city, yellow ribbons had been tied to seemingly every tree and shrub whose trunk was thicker than a broomstick, and the group responsible for this had stapled hundreds of its printed cardboard signs to the bark of trees, featuring a grainy photograph of a traffic light on red with the letters H.A.L.T. underneath. Unfortunately, many motorists didn't know this was the acronym for the protest group who put them there — Help All Lovely Trees — and they immediately braked upon seeing these signs, mistaking them for official warnings of a new traffic light ahead. Such was the rate of change in this central Georgia city.

Margaret finally broke the silence. "They're ruining this town," she said. "I can't understand why the natives aren't jumping up and down screaming."

"They are. Look at all those signs."

"No. I mean ranting and raving and picketing and getting loud and right in the face of the zoning board and the county commission. What is it with Southerners, Dewayne? Why don't they fight? Why don't *you* fight? Why are you so passive? Why don't you try to change my mind about the baby?"

He continued down the road, both hands on the steering wheel as always. "We fought once," he said. "Didn't do a darn bit of good."

Thirty-two

Dear Chatter: I don't like those ugly comments you're puttin' on the end of some of the callers' words. They're mean and unnecessary. *And fun as heck to write! Comin' at ya! — Editors*

Using a sterling-silver pestle she'd ordered from the Frontgate catalog, Suzanne muddled the sugar cube, bitters and water in the bottom of a cut-crystal tumbler. In went the splash of Crown Royal, the ice, the maraschino cherry, even the twist of lemon she normally did not include.

The garage door had opened minutes earlier, and Boone's BMW, now inside, was still running. Suzanne knew he was finishing business on the car phone, and she rushed to make his old-fashioned so it would be waiting for him. She'd also removed the burgundy, tassled throw pillow from his chair that he complained about every night. And an hour earlier, Donna had dropped by with a casserole dish of veal piccata, Boone's newest favorite meal.

One of the better things about being pregnant, Suzanne had realized, was that she no longer had to lie about preparing the meals; suddenly, it was okay to be a slacker.

Suzanne wanted everything perfect, everything Boone-friendly this evening. She had been in Atlanta for the day and stumbled upon an immense, nineteen-thousand-dollar candelabra at Beverly Bremmer's Silver Shop and needed his permission to exceed the never-stated-but-implied limit of two thousand dollars for a single purchase. When Suzanne walked into Beverly's and saw it gleaming beneath the halogen lights on a pile of rumpled black velvet, she knew immediately that nothing else would do for the round table in the foyer for Dogwood.

Suddenly, Suzanne heard the alarm chime that indicated the door had been opened. With cocktail in hand, she checked her lipstick in the mirror behind the wet bar and turned to greet her husband.

"Hey, hey," she said.

"Hey."

Boone, normally a slow sipper, took the drink from her and downed a third of it in two swallows. "New outfit?" he asked.

"You always ask me that, silly," she replied. "No. This outfit's old as the hills. I've been tryin' to save money because of all the things we've been needin' to buy for Dogwood."

"Suzanne . . . we need to sit down. I need to talk to you about somethin'."

"Boone, you look so serious, honey. What's goin' on?"

"Just sit down, Suzanne."

She chose the couch, he his chair. Boone took another sip of his old-fashioned and began to set it on the end table but stopped in midair. "Where's the coaster, Suzanne?"

"Oh, Josephine!" she cursed her housekeeper in absentia. "Just a minute, darlin'. Okay, here's one."

He leaned back in his chair and grabbed the arms in a way Suzanne had never seen him do, as if he were trying to steady himself. "I was gonna surprise you today," he said.

Smiling, Suzanne leaned forward, sitting on the edge of the sofa. "You know I love surprises, sweetie."

"I'd left a message with Mylene to call Dr. Madison and hunt me down another ultrasound picture of Maston. Have him send it to me as an e-mail attachment."

Suzanne's smile began to collapse until she caught it midway down, and it now trembled as it hung there by frayed threads. "Well, did you get one?" she asked.

"What do you think?"

"What are you sayin', Boone?"

"Someone's been eatin' fried chicken behind the curtains, Suzanne. You're not even a patient of his. His office has no record of you."

"Well now that's impossible," she said. "It's probably some stupid secretary's fault."

"No, Suzanne. I talked to him directly. He's never met you. Now, can you kindly tell me what the hell is goin' on here?"

Suzanne shot up to her feet and began twisting her diamond ring with her thumb, as if checking its snugness to make sure it could not come off. She walked over to the curtains at the edge of the window and pulled at a stray thread.

"You're not pregnant, are you, Suzanne?" he asked.

Crying with her back to him, she whipped around to face her husband.

"I wanted to give you a son more than anything else in the world, Boone," she blurted. "I know it's what you want more than anything. And I thought that maybe if I said it then it just might come true . . . and you'd be happy."

"Come off it, Suzanne."

"I know it sounds silly, honey, but you know how women are. I was even thinkin' of goin' off and stealin' me a baby from someplace like that trailer-trash girl did in Macon County . . . just so we could be happy again. And your momma and daddy could be happy. I just wanted things to be right, Boone."

"For God's sake, Suzanne, why did you say you were pregnant in the first place?"

"I don't know why!"

"You're actin' like a crazy woman!"

Boone thought of the visit from the sheriff about the dogs. Partly out of guilt — he'd convinced himself that Suzanne had killed them because he'd been so ugly to her about the problem in the yard — Boone had not mentioned the incident. Instead, he had come home, found the antifreeze and dog food beneath the sink in the utility room and took it all out to the trash.

Suzanne's voice, shaky and thick with mucus, filled the room like the whine of a tornado-alert siren. "But I did it all for you! I'd do anything for you, Boone. Lord knows all this sure proves that."

He slapped his hands on his thighs and stood. "You know, Suzanne, I swore I would never forgive you for marryin' me without tellin' me you couldn't have kids. And I finally got over that and got on with my life, and then I'll be damned if you didn't turn around and do the same thing to me all over again. I can't believe I was so stupid. It's amazin' how you can fool yourself when you want somethin' so bad. Well, fool me once, shame on you. Fool me twice, shame on me."

"What're you sayin', Boone?" Suzanne asked.

"I'm sayin' it's over, Suzanne. I'm sayin' we're through."

"How can you say that? We got the Dogwood party Saturday!"

"And we'll have the goddam Dogwood party because it's too late to back out of that. We need to be good stewards of tradition. But then you're gonna go out of town somewhere and fake a miscarriage and come on back and I'll be sweet and sympathetic."

"And . . ."

"And then you're gonna leave me."

"Boone!"

"I've thought this through, Suzanne. I'll swallow my pride and become the only

Parley to ever get a divorce, and I'll have to bow at my momma's feet and admit that she was right about you all along. And then I'm gonna get married again and have the children I always wanted."

"But Boone!" Suzanne yelled through her tears, stomping her foot on the polished limestone floor. "What'll I do? Where will I go?"

"You'll be just fine, Suzanne. You're as conniving as a cat, and I'll bet my family's name that you're gonna land on your feet every time you get kicked off the roof."

Thirty-three

Dear Chatter: I love how Southerners use the word ugly instead of using the "b" word to describe a woman. B---- has such an unfair permanence to it; a b---- today will be a b---- tomorrow because a b---- is a thing. Ugly, on the other hand, is more forgiving and situation-specific. Ugly has an expiration date: "She was ugly to me." I guess this means that no one can be ugly forever, and I like that.

Michael Kalcheski was dressed in a double-breasted, blue-wool Hugo Boss suit and a maroon tie with green polka dots the shape of kumquats. As he approached Donna, she noticed he was carrying a black-plastic tray of sushi from the fish department. Donna looked at her watch — he was thirty minutes early.

"You want to share my sushi?"

"What kind is it?"

Lord, did this man smell good!

"Dynamite roll — the spicy tuna."

"Sure. That'd be nice."

"Is there someplace quiet we can go?"

Donna looked over her right shoulder. "Well, we could use the employee lounge, but it's against regulation for customers to be in there. There's some benches for the smokers out back on the loading dock. How about that?"

His face crinkled up in disagreement then relaxed again with the arrival of a new idea. "What about that bench in front of the TCBY next door?"

They walked past the cashier stations, toward the front door. Donna saw Koquita look up and give her a wink as she dragged a plastic bag of Wonder Bread over the glowing red window of the scanner.

As they sat down, Michael pulled two pairs of chopsticks from his back pocket and handed one to Donna.

"Oh, I've never used chopsticks," she said.

"They're not hard. You want to learn?"

"Course I do."

He pulled them from the red-paper sheath, which he crumbled in his hand and set on the bench beside them. (Donna quickly grabbed it and shoved it into her pocket. At the employee morning meeting just three days ago Mr. Tom had told them about a growing problem of litter in the parking lot.) The chopsticks were fused together except at their very ends, and he pulled on these until there was a snap of breaking wood.

"Okay," he said, taking Donna's right hand and positioning the sticks in her fingers. She studied them in her hand, pressing them against her thumb as he told her to do, all the while conscious of his warm fingers confidently moving about her hand.

"Okay, now move the top one," he said. "With your middle finger. That's good, that's good. . . . Like a puppet's mouth moving open and shut. Like that. Yes, like that."

Michael held up the tray of sushi rounds. "Okay, now try grabbing one of these."

"There is no way I'm gonna do that," she said, laughing.

"Sure there is."

"They're so big!"

"You can do it. See? That's great!"

It bothered her that he had not yet said her name out loud. Donna cautiously brought the piece of sushi up toward her mouth.

"Now what?" she asked, stopping six inches from her face. "I am not gonna fit this whole thing in my mouth."

"So bite half. Those luscious lips can handle that."

She did so — the compliment warming her inside — but her teeth did not cut through the papery nori, and the piece of sushi was stuck, as the corner of a trench coat gets shut in a car door, and Donna suddenly grew anxious. What was the least embarrassing way to handle this situation? Should she open her mouth and let it all fall into her cupped hand? Should she reach up and twist it with her other hand until the paper tore?

"Here," he said. "Let me help."

Michael brought his fingers to her lips — they gently brushed her mouth as he found a firm hold on the sushi. "Okay," he said. "Bear down on that nori. Cut it with your teeth. Good." Freed from embarrassment, she closed her mouth and chewed.

"Do you like spicy?" he asked. Donna nodded.

He tore open the small packet of soy with his teeth, squeezed it into the clear-plastic lid of the container, and he mixed in a dab of the wasabi, stirring with the blunt end of his chopstick and turning the mixture into a pistachio-chocolate color.

"So tell me about your job," he said. "I

hear you're really good at what you do."

"From who?" she asked.

"Tom Green."

"You know Mr. Tom?"

"We're in the same Sunday school class."

"For real?"

Michael nodded. "Did you always work at Kroger?" he asked.

Donna looked down at the sushi and wished she would have brought a bag of baby carrots with her . . . or some of the precut celery, radish, and cauliflower chunks she faithfully packaged each day for people to buy (though very few did) with their fat-laden cold-cut sandwiches slathered in mayonnaise. (She'd told her boss, "If we can't get 'em to eat low-fat then we can increase their roughage, which'll help push all that poison outta their bodies faster.")

"I used to be a beauty technician for Lancôme at Dillard's."

"No kidding? Then we've got something in common."

"What's that?" she asked.

"I work with faces, too. I'm a reconstructive surgeon."

Donna drew back and looked at him in surprise. "You're a plastic surgeon?" she asked.

"We don't like to call it that, but . . . yeah."

Donna looked away. "No kiddin'," she said.

He looked at her expectantly, but Donna would not meet his eyes. Instead, she focused on the chopsticks in her slowly shifting fingers.

"Tom told me what happened," he said. "He asked me to help you."

She whipped her head in surprise and looked him in the eye. "What?" she snapped.

"He wants to help you."

"Help me what?"

"Repair that gorgeous face of yours."

"What?" Donna shot up to her feet, folding her arms across her chest.

"It wouldn't take much. I rebuild entire noses . . . jaws . . . this is nothing."

"Well, I have certainly been the stupidest girl in the universe."

"Come again?"

"Here I was, thinkin' you were actually likin' me, and I'm just a . . . damn . . . welfare case!" Donna said, already regretting the curse that had escaped her lips. "You feel sorry for me!"

"No, that's not true."

"I can't stand for someone to feel sorry for me!"

"I don't . . ."

"Did you and Mr. Tom ever stop to think that I just might happen to like myself the way I am? I may have a little ol' line across my face and my smile may be messed up a little, but I'm sure not as bad off as Adrian."

"I can see why you're upset, but Tom only wanted to help you. Are you saying you've never considered fixing it?"

Donna reached down and picked a napkin off the bench, which she used to wipe her eyes. She then started to pick at a crusty spot of dried strawberry flesh near the bottom of her uniform top.

She nodded. "Maybe. Used to. I'd be lyin' if I said I didn't."

"Why didn't you do something after the accident?"

"Because . . ."

Donna sat back down, a vacant, defeated look on her face as she watched a new pearl-white Toyota 4-Runner creep by, its female Japanese driver craning her neck toward the sidewalk, looking for her husband who had not yet been disgorged from the electric sliding doors of the grocery store.

Because my daddy didn't want me to . . . because my daddy misses my momma, probably even more than I do, and I just want to keep him happy . . . because my daddy uses

God to hand out guilt like it was an endless roll of paper towels, and I'm just now gettin' around to reachin' up to stop that spinnin' roll and pick up the flood of paper from around my feet and bag it and throw it all away . . . because I didn't have the money myself, and by the time I finally could build some savings — and not spend my whole salary at the mall and Rio Cantina — I'd convinced myself that it was okay, and that I didn't really need a face . . . because I've learned, or maybe I'm just foolin' myself, that I'd rather just be some old, warty, hard turban squash 'cause you don't have to tiptoe through life worryin' about gettin' hurt.

"Because what?" he asked.

Donna sighed, turned toward Michael and looked him in the eyes. "Because I just didn't get around to it, I guess."

Donna knocked on Tom Green's office door. There was a pause and then, "Come in."

On the phone, he motioned for Donna to sit down, giving her an exaggerated look of curiosity because he'd never seen her look so steamed up and red in the neck. She obediently fell into the chrome-and-gray Herculon chair whose seat cushion was stained with pen ink and soda spills.

As Mr. Tom spoke, he tried to diffuse her anger by playing with the plastic Mr. Potato Head on his desk, sticking ears where the eyes should be, a tongue on top of the head, a bow tie for a mouth. Donna did not smile. She rapidly tapped the arms of the chair with her fingers.

Finally, he hung up. "Oh, Donna, what a day," he said, trying to buy more cooldown time because he had never seen her this mad. "You know I'm on the board of the downtown Rotary Club, right? Well, luck has it that we just happen to be the last club in the entire country that is dragging its heels on opening membership to women. And now the national office is threatening to revoke our charter . . . *and* National Public Radio's coming to town to do a story. Not the hacks from Atlanta either. Noah Adams himself. That's the kind of day I'm having.

"So . . . what gives, girl?"

Donna blew: "You wanna know what gives? I'll tell you what gives. I just had lunch with your friend Michael Kalcheski."

"So he finally talked to you."

"Oh, yeah, he talked to me all right . . . and I have never been so embarrassed in all my life."

"What?"

"All that time he spent tryin' to win my trust, and I thought he was sweet on me."

"Oh, no."

"Yep. And boy did I feel stupid today. Thank you soooo much, Mr. Tom."

Tom Green stood up and walked around his desk to sit in the chair next to Donna.

"You've got to know I would never do anything to hurt your feelings," he said. "I have more respect for you than anyone else in this store. Mike was just gonna give you a really good deal. It sounded like a good thing."

Donna stood up, as if they were children playing school, and the roles of pupil and teacher had suddenly been reversed.

"How could you do this to me?" she asked.

"I only wanted to help."

"What makes you think I'm not happy the way I am?"

Tom Green picked up a yellow No. 2 pencil and began tapping it on the desktop. "Donna, you were heartbroken when Robbie dumped you. I was heartbroken to watch it all. Don't you remember crying in the bathroom all those times?"

"But that was a long time ago!" she said. "I'm over that. I'm a different person now, Mr. Tom. I'm way beyond Robbie. Don't you like me the way I am now?"

"Donna . . ."

"Answer me, Mr. Tom."

"Of course I do. God, Donna, if you had any idea . . ."

Donna sat back down, next to him, and when she looked at Tom Green in the eyes he quickly looked down, as if her gaze had burned him, and he stared at his scuffed, black Rockport loafers that were nervously scraping the floor.

Thirty-four

Dear Chatter: I moved out of Orlando twenty years ago because the Yankees ruined it. Then I had to move out of Atlanta for the same reason. Now they're fixin' to ruin Selby. Where am I going to go next? *Anger-management training, perhaps? — Editors*

Randy's head materialized over Margaret's gray cubicle wall.

"Hey," he said. "Let's go to the Forsyth Room for lunch. My treat."

Margaret looked up from her monitor. "I'm not sure I'm talking to you anymore," she said.

Like a puppet whose scene has ended, he suddenly dropped beneath the gray-upholstered wall. Margaret could hear him wheeling Harriet's empty desk chair around the cubicle.

"Knock, knock," he said, pushing the chair to a spot beside hers, then sitting down. "Okay, what gives? You've been increasingly distant and cool."

"The snide little editor's comments you've been putting into Chatter," she answered.

"I thought you'd like those."

"I don't. You know that. It goes against the whole philosophy of the column — to let people speak without fear of retribution."

Randy loosened his tie even though the top button of his pink, oxford-cloth shirt already was undone. He had gained sixteen pounds during his tenure in Selby, thanks largely to Rodney Washington, the new cook in the cafeteria who served Southern specials daily, comfort staples that the tortured soul of Randy Whitestone could not refuse, including fried okra, pork chops, biscuits smothered in bacon gravy, pieces of macaroon pie that were four inches tall, and a breakfast-time egg casserole with canned green chilis and four different versions of cured pork. On average, Randy now drank six glasses of sweet tea a day.

"Listen, Margaret," he said. "Honestly?"

She nodded.

"Chatter's getting flat. It doesn't have the same sparkle that it used to. I'm just trying to make it a little more effervescent."

"What do you mean?"

"I think you've grown sweet on these natives. You're not including the really stupid comments anymore."

"Excuse me?"

"It's not as funny."

"Not as funny?"

"Most of the calls you put in are from Yankees, and you're picking the ones that make them look really bad. Really *ugly*, as they say."

"These people who call *are* ugly."

"And you're cleaning up the language. You're inserting *g*'s now where people don't really say them. You're trying to make these people sound smarter than they really are. I think you're blending in too much, Margaret."

"It's my job to blend in," she said. "I'm an anthropologist."

"You're a journalist. It's your job to be removed and dispassionate."

"Uncaring," she said.

"If necessary to do the job right, then, yes, uncaring."

Margaret took off her headset and set it on her desk, then swiveled in her chair so she faced him. Over his shoulder she noticed that Harriet Toomey had just entered the newsroom, wearing a new spring dress, short-sleeved with a print of pink cherry blossoms on a sky blue background. Much to Randy's surprise, Harriet's Thanks for Askin' column had grown to be one of the most popular features in the *Reflector*, devoured every Thursday by the growing community of Yankees and Japanese hungry to acquaint themselves with Southern fare. Some weeks Harriet received up to fifty inquiries: Can I cut down on sugar in a cobbler without ruining the recipe? Can you reprint that recipe for ham pie? Just where does someone purchase lard?

"You know," she said. "Maybe it's time for a change."

"Just what I've been waiting to hear. You want to go full-time reporting? You're more than ready."

"I was thinking of something else."

"What?"

Margaret's phone chirped. "Let me get this."

"No, wait. Tell me first."

"I have a job to do here, Randy. You're interfering with it." And then, into the phone: "This is Margaret Pinaldi.

"Donna? . . . No, no, that's okay. . . . Yeah, I've got Dewayne's truck today; my car's in the shop. Why? . . . Now? . . . So you specifically need the truck? . . . What's happened? . . . Sure . . . Right now? . . . Okay. . . . At Suzanne's house, right? . . . Okay. . . . Okay. . . . I'll be right there."

Margaret hung up and reached for her Kermit the Frog purse beneath the desk.

"What was that all about?" Randy asked.

"I have to go help a friend."

"Do you need some more help? Want me to come?"

Margaret thought for a few seconds, calculating in her mind: Three women . . . six hands . . . the innate ability women had to cleverly use laws of physics to their advantage . . . What could be so heavy and big that three women could not handle it?

"No," she said. "I'm sure we'll manage."

Though Suzanne's antifreeze-tainted portions of Alpo had killed sixteen dogs in Red Hill Plantation, none of them, fortunately, had taken their last steps on the Parley property. On the Saturday of the Dogwood party, however, Suzanne awoke to find Sonna, the Bentleys' ten-year-old golden retriever, its hair streaked with the white of age, lying dead on her flagstone patio behind the house.

With Boone at his golf game, Suzanne donned her velour navy tracksuit, retrieved a Hefty lawn-and-leaf bag from the kitchen pantry and went out to the patio. Arms akimbo, she stood looking at the dog whose tongue hung out over the moist black gums like an unfurled, pink-red carpet.

She pressed the corpse with the toe of her tennis shoe. It was firm and ungiving, like a newly upholstered leather ottoman. And heavy, very heavy, too heavy for a Hefty, she realized. Suzanne returned inside and came back with the never-worn $1,600 plastic Prada raincoat, which she shook open with a snap and spread on the flagstone beside the corpse.

She went into the garage and looked over the tool rack on the far, inside wall, finally spotting a shovel, which she carried with her back to the patio. Scanning the yard — thank you, Lord, for that new fence! — she then wedged the shovel between the flagstone and the stomach of the animal, pushing and scraping inch by inch until it was well beneath the body of the dog. Using the shovel as a lever, she pushed down on the handle, slowly raising the animal until the handle touched the ground. And then, sitting on the wooden handle to keep it and the dog in place, Suzanne slipped her forearms under the hairy body, leaned into the beast, and rolled her over, onto the raincoat.

"Dear God in heaven!" she exclaimed, breathing heavily and feeling her pulse pounding in her temples and neck. With her clothed forearm, Suzanne wiped the sweat from her forehead. "Lord, tell me," she said to herself. "What have I done to deserve all this?"

Suzanne sat there, catching her breath and plotting what to do next. After a few minutes, she went inside to the master bedroom, rolled up her new gold-and-red Kirman rug, then dragged it outside to the patio.

The doorbell rang; Suzanne could hear it through the open door to the dining room. She looked at her watch. "Donna!" she said to herself between breaths, and she went to let her in.

"Have you got a truck, Donna?" she asked. "You know someone who's got a truck?"

"John David does."

"John David's at the merchandise mart in Atlanta till this afternoon."

"Dewayne has a truck."

"Dewayne?"

"Margaret's boyfriend."

Knowing that Margaret worked at the newspaper, Suzanne was reluctant for

Donna to make the call, but she looked up at the sun as it was climbing higher in the morning sky . . . and there were floral centerpieces to pick up and erection of a white tent to supervise and very soon the breeze would conspire with the swelling heat of the day, and the presence of this dog would be broadcast to all beyond the fence.

Within fifteen minutes, the three women were standing before the dog and the carpet on the patio.

"We should call animal control," Margaret said.

"No," Suzanne replied. "It'll take them three hours to get out here, and I don't have time to spare."

"We should bury it or somethin'," Donna said.

"Don't have time for that either. Please, y'all — I just want some help gettin' this dog to the dump. Y'all gotta put yourselves in my shoes."

Her voice had grown louder, and Donna and Margaret looked at each other.

"I'm puttin' on the biggest party of the year tonight, and then I find out my husband's fixin' to leave me, and this just might be my last chance to show him and the rest of this stupid town that they really do need me!"

"So what do you want us to do?" Donna asked.

Suzanne looked at Margaret. "I want you to go back up that truck of yours into the garage so we can drag this thing through the house and no one sees us loadin' it up. Donna, I need you to help me roll this old dog up in this carpet."

Soon, the three of them were dragging it through the house. Once in the garage, Margaret and Suzanne each took an end of the rug, and Donna got beneath the sagging, heavy middle, and they lugged it into the bed of the truck. "Donna," Margaret said. "You've got muscles, girl."

It was true — Donna was strong. Her trapezius and latissimus dorsi had grown enough that she'd had to move up to a size-eight blouse. Her biceps and deltoids were now full and round, and other young women would sometimes ask her where she worked out. Donna would smile and say, "It's just on-the-job training." Outside of work, she started wearing sleeveless shirts when weather permitted. Even the regional perishables manager, who had misgivings about a woman working in such a physically demanding job, recanted his doubt and sent a letter of praise after coming down from Atlanta one day to watch her work.

The three of them in the cab, they drove the expensively packaged corpse out to the Perry County landfill.

"I just can't believe someone would wanna kill all these dogs," Suzanne said. "Antifreeze. Who would of thought of usin' antifreeze?"

At the intersection of Bradley Street and Parley Road, they passed two black men arguing out loud as they sold watermelons and sweet corn from the trunk of their old Buick. Margaret turned on the radio, which Dewayne had tuned to Cat County 108.5, and as they listened to some song about a woman who couldn't keep secrets from her man Margaret suddenly realized there was no way Suzanne could have known how the dogs had died — unless, of course, she had done the deed herself.

Thirty-five

Dear Chatter: The difference between margarine and Crisco is that margarine's yellow and has salt. You can always add yellow food coloring to Crisco. *And why, pray tell, would we want to dye our Crisco? — Editors*

The hospitality of north Selby did not extend to rain. Though the red clay could absorb the first half-inch or so, it soon became as welcoming to moisture as a wet sponge sitting atop cellophane. And the rain, rejected by the roots and soil and now homeless, would hit the ground running, sheeting off the soggy yards, down the sidewalks, into the gutters, gaining in mass and speed until it dropped through stormwater grates and roared through the round, concrete tunnels beneath the city, cleansing the city of errant cigarette butts and the yellow tree pollen that blanketed Selby like snow this time each year.

The forecast, thanks to an unseasonable tropical storm that had meandered inland, called for two inches, a large amount for this time of year, but by four o'clock more than three had fallen. And with just two hours remaining before her first guests were due to arrive, Suzanne looked out her living room window to see if Red Hill Drive had returned to the landscape. She was pleased to note that the water had receded enough that a single car could now creep down the very middle of the asphalt. Unfortunately, however, as the high waters retreated they left behind a zigzag line of suburban jetsam along the entire length of her property — grass clippings, dog turds, decaying red camellia blossoms, cellophane from packs of cigarettes, last year's obstinate oak leaves that had finally been pushed from their spots by impetuous, green newcomers. Suzanne quickly asked Josephine to call Virgil and ask him to come over and rake it all up before the guests arrived.

In the kitchen, Margaret and Donna toiled over their largest catering job yet, heavy hors d'oeuvres for three hundred and fifty-nine people, including sliced roast beef with mini biscuits and a creamy horseradish sauce, chunks of cantaloupe wrapped in prosciutto, bow-tie pasta tossed in pesto sauce, smothered meatballs made from a recipe served in the Parley family for five generations (which, to Margaret's surprise, called for two cups of sugar), and crudités that Margaret poached so they would better absorb the flavors from her homemade Caesar dip.

Disappointed by Suzanne's reluctance to try anything interesting or different from the normal Selby-black-tie fare, and wanting to put her trademark of creativity on the meal in some way, Margaret took the risk of laying out the smoked salmon, capers, onions, and crackers directly onto the glass of a large mirror with a baroque, gilt frame that she'd found leaning against the wall in the kitchen pantry. When she suggested they use it as a centerpiece, Suzanne was thrilled with the idea, even though she had planned on returning it to Vivian Vaughan's Interiors that next Monday.

Suddenly, John David burst through the kitchen door, holding in his left hand a tinkling crystal tumbler of Knob Creek bourbon on the rocks. His face was flushed, and Margaret wondered if it was alcohol or the neck of his too-small tuxedo shirt. Just as a set designer would for a play on opening night, John David had arrived at two-thirty for three hours of moving and removing and switching and tweaking.

"What did y'all do with that throw rug at the garage door?" he asked.

"We had to move it," Donna answered. "We kept trippin' over it when we went out to the fridge in the garage."

"Well be sure to put it back. That whole entryway looks washed out without that little Oriental."

Boone, as he did in the few hours before every one of Suzanne's parties, had fled the house to the safety of the men's locker room at Sugar Day, where he watched ESPN as he reviewed membership applications for the upcoming year. For the first time ever, there were more names he did not recognize than those he did.

Suzanne, already dressed in her Dogwood-ivory, beaded Badgley Mischka gown, which had been let out to accommodate her third-month prosthesis, walked the house from room to room, praising or condemning herself for improvements she'd made or forgotten to make. In the east guest room, the one in which Boone was sleeping, she admired the mimosa linens with delicate flower sprays and scalloped borders, ordered from Carolina Con's Gracious Style catalog. In the foyer, Suzanne straightened one of the four botanical prints she'd had specially commissioned, all of them roses that would match colors in her reproduction of an early-eighteenth-century Star Ushak rug, including a scarlet Dortmund, a dogwood-colored Alberic Barbier, a chiffon-yellow Climbing Arthur Bell and the white-dipped-in-red Handel.

From there she breezed into the main living room and stopped to look at her new portrait suspended over the mantel, the only portrait in Selby to be painted by Mary Robbins-Hart of Washington, D.C. And on a long, thin table hugging the wall, John David had placed the new basketball-sized Waterford crystal orb, filled three-quarters with water and dogwood blossoms floating on top. For St. Patrick's Day, she would tint the water green. At Easter, pink. For Fourth of July, red or blue. For Christmas, fake snow. "And for baby showers," John David had joked, "y'all can fill it with condoms."

6:20: Ten minutes to party time, as if the sky above were a gray washcloth that had finally been wrung dry, the rain stopped. Neighbors began to arrive. With a string quartet of students from Carollton College playing in the foyer, Boone and Suzanne greeted their guests, though he had not spoken to her since his revelation four days earlier.

"Did y'all swim over here?"

"Come on in and dry off. . . . Josephine, take these umbrellas."

"Well we sure do know who our real friends are, don't we?"

"Motherhood becomes you, Suzanne, you look so pretty."

After welcoming the first wave, fifteen in all, Suzanne stepped out onto the porch and looked over at Jodi and Marc Armbusters' house. She counted three cars, none of which she recognized. Then she turned and went inside, closing the newly varnished door, and again the rain began to fall.

7:30: Josephine walked by with a sterling-silver tray, balancing fresh cocktails and glasses of chardonnay.

"Josephine . . . wait." Suzanne walked up, looked at the contents of the tray and quickly grabbed the pile of pink napkins.

"Where'd you get these?"

"The pantry."

"Well they're the wrong napkins, Josephine! Use the ivory napkins on the kitchen counter. The ones that say 'Dogwood . . . A Parley Tradition.' "

"Those ones with the gold letterin'?"

"Yes."

John David, on his fourth bourbon, stepped up beside Suzanne. "How many are here now?" he asked.

"Thirty-one," she answered. "No. Thirty-three. Jimmy and Reeney Foshay got here."

"And how many are supposed to come?"

"I sent out a hundred and eighty-six invitations. All but ten RSVP'd yes."

"Well looky there," John David said, walking toward the den window that faced the Armbusters' house. "Was the Ivory Princess one of 'em?"

Suzanne joined him at the window and saw two ivory-colored Cadillac sedans at curbside, their wheels completely submerged in water, giving the cars the appearance of small pleasure boats. One by one, the Cadillacs disgorged a collection of people who were greeted with opened, ivory umbrellas imprinted with the International Dogwood Festival logo. Joining Madeline VanDermeter were this year's distinguished guests of the festival, including Ed Nwasu of Botswana, whom Suzanne had decided not to house for the festival after all; Lord Benjamin of Great

Britain; Lonnie Nuckadue, a Perry County commissioner; Hinckley Nasher, the owner of Nasher-Williamson Funeral Home and president of the festival board, who, as all civic and business leaders did for the entire festival week, wore a dogwood-ivory sports jacket with the festival logo on the right breast; and someone Suzanne and John David did not recognize, a woman in a lavender cocktail dress.

"They'll be comin' over," Suzanne assured him. "Her secretary told me to expect 'em. . . . They're just savin' the best for last."

8:30: In the lower, southern half of Selby, rainwater had begun to consume the landscape in a way that had not been seen in ninety-three years. Downtown, the Muscogee River swelled beyond its banks, swallowing every lane of I-75 and creating a backup of cars that stretched for more than thirty miles in each direction.

The bronze statue of Robert E. Lee had been lifted by the waters from its redbrick foundation in Tattnall Park and carried a mile and a half downstream, where it now lay on its side in front of the chained gate of the abandoned Cherokee brick factory.

Sheriff's deputies patrolled neighborhoods in sputtering dinghies, throwing ham sandwiches and bottles of water to those who had sought refuge on their roofs.

Half of the riverside Rosemont Cemetery was submerged. Its resident pack of wild dogs had been chased by water up to the highest point, the Fornley family mausoleum, which they occupied like displaced, defeated gargoyles, lying in the rain on the various, gray-granite terraces.

Not wanting to shatter the buzzing ambience of a perfect party, Suzanne had shut off the ringers on all her telephones, thus unaware of the deluge of regrets that were filling her voice mail every minute.

9:45: Again, the rain stopped. The thirty-five guests at Suzanne and Boone's party lingered because they felt badly about the turnout, and they did not want to further empty a home that already felt cavernous.

Barely touched tray after tray of food had taken on a patina of neglect and decay. The dollops of horseradish sauce no longer shimmered beneath the halogen lights. The heated, brown gravy that once harbored meatballs had evaporated to the point that the orbs of beef were now resting on the bottom of the chrome pan, like the last, dying fish in a desert lake that has all but dried up. Not wanting the caterers and Suzanne to feel badly, some of the women surreptitiously moved the food around so it appeared that more had been eaten. Two different guests found a discreet way to sneak some of the tenderloin into the trash can and toilet.

As the evening progressed, Suzanne seemed to grow increasingly manic, flitting from guest to guest as if to distract them from the emptiness of the party. She'd not had plans to drink that night, but the tensions grew too great, and Suzanne needed help escaping the failure she was watching before her very eyes. So, with help from John David, Suzanne would slip into the butler's pantry, off the dining room, where she quaffed chardonnay like water.

Finally, at ten thirty-five, Madeline VanDermeter and her Dogwood Blossom entourage dashed from the house next door when the downpour subsided for a moment.

Her voice resounded in the marble-floored foyer. "I am so, so sorry, Suzanne . . . Boone. We've been fixin' to come over for an hour now but couldn't because of that awful rain. There will not be a blossom left for all those tour buses comin' in this weekend. This is just a darn shame."

Boone and Josephine took their coats and their dripping umbrellas. "Y'all come on in now and dry off," Boone said. "I was just fixin' to drop that wine and go and get me some bourbon. Any takers here?"

"Yes!" Madeline VanDermeter replied. "I do need to use the ladies room, though. Is it in the same place, Suzanne?"

"Yes, ma'am. It sure is."

Madeline tried the door to the powder room, but it was locked with someone inside. Not wanting to bother the hosts, she went to search on her own for an alternative. She wandered into the master bedroom and into the master bath and chose the toilet that appeared to be Suzanne's, marked by a basket nearly overflowing with decorating catalogs and magazines.

Madeline raised her dress, lowered herself onto the toilet seat, and when her bare butt came in contact with the oily *Shame!* potion that Josephine had smeared onto the cool, doughnut-shaped surface, she slipped off the toilet, toward the wall, hitting her head on the sharp corner of the windowsill and falling into darkness.

Lying on her back on the floor, Madeline

VanDermeter looked up and saw the faces of Boone Parley and Ed Nwasu, and she suddenly realized, mortified, that one of these two men had pulled her panties back into place, and she wasn't certain which one she'd have preferred do such a thing — a strange black man from southern Africa or a handsome neurosurgeon whose mother she played bridge with each Thursday.

Thirty-six

Dear Chatter: The weather is not controlled by God. It is controlled by the jet stream and ocean currents and position of the globe. So please quit blaming the rain and floods on the Almighty.

Though she rarely bought more than an herb plant or two, Margaret stopped by Reeverts' Nursery and Garden Center at least twice a week. Part of the draw was Francine Reeverts herself, a thin, wrinkly, seventy-four-year-old who wore her white hair in a French roll and was comfortable speaking with a smoldering Camel bouncing in her lips. Behind the cash register, Francine would perch upon a chrome stool upholstered in yellow vinyl and snack on fried chicken livers brought from home each day in a Styrofoam cup. Margaret enjoyed Francine's company, and in their talks about Southern culture Francine would often unwittingly toss out interesting horticultural metaphors.

The other thing Margaret enjoyed at Reeverts' was the quirky rock garden Francine and her husband, Robbie, had built adjacent to the nursery to honor their daughter who died of lung cancer. At first glance, the Judy Reeverts Bass Memorial World Garden appeared to be a miniature-golf course in the Flintstone theme with a man-made, concrete-and-flagstone creek connecting large dioramas created from brick and stones and trees and shrubs and a plethora of concrete-cast lawn ornaments.

Each diorama had a sign identifying it. There was the Ngorongoro crater of Tanzania, with concrete lions perched atop a flagstone precipice like the one Margaret remembered from *The Lion King* . . . a miniature re-creation of Arizona's Grand Canyon, complete with Matchbox car–size donkeys whose feet had been pushed into the concrete at the bottom . . . an Asian scene, with a cross-legged Buddha flanked by bonsai cedar trees . . . and in the center, much larger than the others, a re-creation of Jesus' tomb, big enough for a handful of people to come in and sit down. Inside, a painted statue of Mary wept in the dark corner, the tears portrayed on her cheek with red paint that looked like blood. All these scenes and more were connected by the concrete creek that flowed from diorama to diorama.

But today Margaret was here to pick out flowers. For months, Dewayne had been urging her to wrest control of her hairy yard, and suddenly, inexplicably, Margaret found herself obsessed with transforming the weed-choked flower beds in front of her porch.

"Hey, Margaret," Francine said, slowly walking down the aisle of perennials.

"Francine! How are you?"

"Doin' good. And yourself?"

"Doin' real good."

Margaret scanned the greenhouse, breathing in deeply the warm air that smelled of geraniums and new soil and the plastic tarp overhead that was warmed by the sun. "I'm overwhelmed by the beauty of this place," she said. "I always am."

"It's a good time of the year," Francine agreed.

"I'm amazed at the variety of things that grow here. It's such a weird mixture, with the oaks of the north and palms of the subtropics."

"You know what they call it," Francine said.

"Call what?"

"The area that Selby sits in."

"No, ma'am."

"It's called a tension zone."

She took her cigarette from her mouth. "See, the USDA gardenin' zones run east to west. They're these crooked, invisible lines that follow the frost patterns, and wherever two zones meet there's twenty or so miles of schizophrenic weather, and that's where the species from both zones collide and try to intermingle . . . one from the north, and one from the south."

"I love that!" Margaret exclaimed.

"Only the strongest specimens from each zone will survive in a tension zone," Francine said.

She took another draw of her Camel, exhaled, and raised her eyebrows. "Kind of like what's goin' on in Selby right now with another species we know pretty well. Where's your man friend today, Margaret?"

Since Margaret's revelation, Dewayne had called a few times but had not stopped by the house except to pick up a screwdriver from his tool box. Margaret was painting the back bedroom when he came. He peeked through the doorway of the room and, seeing her standing on the ladder, hurried in, lifted her by the armpits and set her gently on the floor.

"What are you doin'?" he said. "Are you crazy?"

"Quit treating me like a little child, Dewayne! That was very demeaning."

"You shouldn't be up there like that."

"Why not?"

Dewayne stood there, silent.

"Was that action based on an assumption I should know about?" Margaret asked.

He turned and walked back outside. Margaret could hear the thud of his heavy boots on the wooden floor of the porch before reaching the concrete steps. And then, the sound of the steps returned, the door opened, and he was inside again.

"If I asked you to marry me," he said, "would you believe it's 'cause I love you?"

He had never said the words, nor had Margaret, and she could sense the weight of them by the way his eyes and lips subtly trembled. She walked toward him and put her hands on his warm, reddened cheeks.

"Oh, Dewayne . . . Dewayne . . . this is not the way it was supposed to turn out. You are so, so sweet. . . . But this is not a path I'd planned on taking. I never have.

It's just never been an option in my mind."

"What path?"

"Motherhood."

His hands crammed into the back pockets of his jeans, Dewayne took a step backward. "You know," he said, "some people actually like bein' mommas."

"Was that a slam on my mother?"

"Yes, it was."

"Dewayne!"

"I'm speakin' my mind here."

"It's about time."

"I've got too much to lose."

"What?"

"My happiness."

"But you won't lose me," Margaret said. "I'll still be there."

"But part of me won't," he said.

"Which part?"

"That part inside you right now."

"I'll ask you again," Margaret said. "Which part?" She took her fist and patted her heart. "Is it part of your heart we're talking about or your sperm? Which do you mean, Dewayne?"

Without answering, Dewayne turned and walked outside, got into his truck, and drove away.

Carrying a plastic flat of perennials,

Margaret returned to her car to find Randy leaning against the hood.

"You can't hide when you drive a car like this," he said. "I was on my way home and spotted you."

"Stalker."

"What do you have there?"

Margaret opened her trunk and set the flowers inside. "Foxglove. Cat's whisker. Black-eyed Susans and shasta daisies."

"I've got some news for you."

"What?"

"The great dying dogs mystery has been solved."

She slammed the trunk and quickly looked at Randy to read his face.

"Turned out to be nothing. At least nothing interesting. Maybe a six-inch story on two-B or a metro brief at best. Sheriff said some dufus's truck at a construction sight was leaking antifreeze. I guess the stuff's sweet and tasty. God knows Southern dogs would lap up something sweet but deadly. Anyway, I knew it wasn't much else — what psycho goes around poisoning dogs? What's with the flowers, Margaret? You been bit by that Southern decorating bug?"

"Actually, Randy, it's called the nesting instinct."

He furrowed his brow. "What are you saying?"

"I'm pregnant."

"What!"

"Yes."

"You are fucking kidding me! Pregnant! The redneck fireman?" he asked.

"His name's Dewayne. Yes."

"I thought this was just a fling, Margaret. Something you'd get over."

"I'm not sure what it is, Randy. I'm not sure where it is either."

"I was patient. I was waiting. Shit! Pregnant? I'm assuming this situation was intentional, then . . . realizing that you probably know more about birth control and the female reproductive system than the entire population of Selby, Georgia, combined."

"It was not intentional, no."

"I know what you want," Randy said. "You want someone who's going to open every damn door for you and take you to the NASCAR races. Jesus, Margaret, I've seen you guys driving around town — you sit right by him. Like some trailer-trash woman."

"I accept your apology."

Randy slumped against the car and looked down at his stomach. With both hands, he grabbed and pinched his roll of fat that had the girth of a baguette. "I used to be lean and mean," he said.

Margaret walked over and gently pinched his right cheek. "You're still mean, Randy. If that's any consolation."

Thirty-seven

Donna's TIP of the Day: Too much fat in your diet? Replace that heavy oil with heart-healthy chicken stock! It's so easy! Just freeze some stock in ice-cube trays, and that way you can just pop out and melt what you need! Keep the other cubes in a baggie in the freezer for future use! Try mixing some fresh herbs (thyme or rosemary!) in with the stock before freezing. Then watch that tummy melt away!

Since five a.m., Donna had been immersed in her newest creation — an end cap display celebrating Cinco de Mayo. In a sea of Italian plum tomatoes she made a giant number five out of dark-green Hass avocados. Using key limes, she spelled out *Mayo* in an arch shape over the five. Still not satisfied, Donna drove back home to get her four margarita glasses, which she filled with green and white jelly beans and a straw and randomly placed them among the tomatoes. Over all of this, taped to a ceiling beam, was a sign she'd made at home the night before with her mother's air-brush gun, featuring giant, smiling jalapeños and the giant word *GuacamOLE!*, with the last three letters exaggerated in size and color.

All that was left was cilantro. As Donna placed bunches of it around the perimeter of the tomatoes, she continued the mental game she'd invented her first week in Kroger — comparing humans to varieties of produce.

In the past, Donna would assign to each person a fruit or vegetable based solely on appearance, yet sometime in the past few months she'd decided that the person no longer had to look like a pear or cucumber but rather had to represent the very essence of that fruit or vegetable. To increase the accuracy of her comparison, Donna would talk with the customer, thus revealing a personality with the sweetness of strawberries or astringent bitterness of rhubarb stalks or the watery, stringy emptiness of celery. A confident walk could denote yucca root. A disheveled, messy person would be a head of garlic. The supreme comparison was the pumpkin — the subject of fantasy and imagination (Cinderella's coach and Peter's prison for his wife) . . . a heavy, substantial, thick-skinned gourd who had no need or desire to be a climber . . . confident in its choice of color that audaciously clashed with most every other . . . a longevity that other produce could only dream of . . . interesting, rippling ridges that were pleasing to run one's hand over.

"Nice display. Very nice."

Mr. Tom's voice caught Donna by surprise. Since their confrontation in his office, he had not been making his hourly swings through Donna's department. The only time he'd spoken with her in the last two days was to confirm the hours on her time card. "You've got to write more legibly, Donna" was all he said.

"Did you get the sprayer heads cleaned?" he asked now.

"Yes, sir. I sure did. I used the pipe cleaner just like you taught me."

"Where's Adrian?" he asked.

"He's corin' pineapples in the back."

"Can you please get him out here to cover for you? I need to see you in my office."

"I'm not still hoppin' mad if that's what you're afraid of. I'm mad, but I'm not hoppin' mad."

"Just get Adrian. Please."

Donna summoned Adrian and followed

Mr. Tom to his office. He shut the door and took the chair on his side of the desk, opposite Donna.

"I don't really wanna talk about it anymore," Donna said.

"Do you think your father would let you move out of Selby?" he asked.

Donna furrowed her brow. "What are you sayin', Mr. Tom?"

Tom Green stood up, picked up his brown briefcase from the floor, set it on the desk, opened it, and retrieved a manila folder. He handed it to Donna.

"What's this?" she asked.

"Just look."

Donna opened the folder and began to read. There were two letters, one from Mr. Tom and the other from Sarilyn Potter, the district manager in Atlanta, both of them suggesting that she be promoted to a new regional merchandising and training position.

"Mr. Tom!"

"It would involve a lot of travel," he said. "And you'd probably have to move to Atlanta."

Donna looked up from the letters, a solemn expression on her face.

"You're supposed to be ecstatic, Donna," he said.

"Did you do this because of what Gary Scalamandre was sayin' about you and me? Are we in trouble here, Mr. Tom?"

He smiled. "They've asked for you specifically. No, Donna. We're not in trouble, though maybe we might get me in trouble if you stuck around any longer."

Donna smiled as the compliment washed over her. She remembered how Mr. Tom complimented Kathy's bleached teeth when all her hair fell out after chemo, and how he took pains to remind seventy-two-year-old Emmett how well he organized groceries in the bags when he suddenly felt old and vulnerable after falling in the parking lot, breaking three dozen eggs and a watermelon. Donna knew that Tom Green was good at telling people what he thought they needed to hear — it's what made him a good boss.

Her throat tightened. "You've taught me everything I know, Mr. Tom. You're really, truly, one of the best friends I've ever had."

"The pleasure's been mine."

"You really think I could do that job?"

"With your eyes closed."

She scanned the plaques on the wall behind him, five that chronicled Tom Green's tenure as perishables manager of the year in the Midwest region.

"I think I'd like somethin' new," she said. "It would be fun livin' in Atlanta. If I go, will you promote Adrian to produce manager?"

"I'm not so sure, Donna. You need two hands for that job."

"But he knows produce better than anybody, Mr. Tom. It wouldn't be fair for anyone else to get that job."

"I don't know."

"Just hire some dumb strong boy to take his place. Adrian's very organized, Mr. Tom. He's been fillin' out my order sheets for a month now."

"I'll think about it."

"Promise me."

"I promise I'll think about it."

"I want one more thing," she said.

"Of course you do."

She hesitated, then said, "I've been wantin' to kiss you for the longest time."

Mr. Tom broke into a smile. "You have?"

"Yes."

"You still work for me, Donna."

"Okay," she said. "I quit."

Tom Green laughed. "You will never go hungry, Donna Kabel."

"That's what my momma always said."

He walked around the side of the desk and stood before her, his arms self-consciously dangling at his side. Donna stood on her toes, resting her hands on his shoulder to steady herself, as if she were preparing to whisper something into his ear, and she leaned into his face and kissed him gently on the cheek.

Thirty-eight

Dear Chatter: I wish y'all would just stop it! *Yeah! — Editors.*

Margaret returned from a long walk in Rosemont Cemetery and found a note taped to her front door: *Got a package for you from UPS. Mr. Ted.*

She walked next door and found her seventy-six-year-old neighbor rocking on the aluminum glider in the shade of his front porch, his gnarly, walnut cane resting between his legs.

"I saw you pull in," he said. "I was waitin' for you. I left a message on your anserin' machine, too."

She sat down beside him and they talked for ten minutes — about Reeva Standish, four houses down, who'd bit into a piece of glass that Sunday in the smothered pork chops she'd ordered at the G&F Cafeteria . . . about Rex, Mr. Ted's terrier mix who treed someone's cat that morning . . . about how the new mayor in Atlanta had changed the recorded warnings on the trains at the Atlanta airport from a Southern gentleman's voice to a Northern male's command.

Finally, as if Margaret had fulfilled her task and would now be rewarded, he reached beneath the glider and pulled out an overnight-letter package. Margaret read the label and saw it was from Freid, Hamblin, Reed & Johnston, the law firm that represented her mother and settled her estate.

"Oh, and this, too," he said, pulling out a square Rubbermaid container with *M. Pinaldi* written on the lid. "Your soups, girl . . . I could eat 'em every day. I poured it over a piece of toast and it made me a real good dinner for myself last night."

Margaret took the container and got up to leave. "I hope I haven't bothered you, Mr. Ted," she said.

"Always a pleasure talkin' with you, darlin'. I haven't seen Dewayne the past few days. Is he okay?"

"We're just spendin' some time apart."

"Dewayne's a nice boy. He fixed my ceiling fan, did you know that?"

"Thank you, Mr. Ted."

"Enjoy the rest of this lovely day, young lady. I think it's fixin' to rain — I can smell the paper mill."

Sitting on the front steps of her house, Margaret opened the package and pulled out a white letter from Sig Hamblin.

Margaret: As directed by your mother, I am forwarding this letter to you exactly one year after her death. Please call me when you want to follow up on this new matter. I hope this finds you in good health. I miss your mother. New York is a much quieter place without her.

Margaret looked into the darkness of the cardboard UPS packet again and this time pulled out what she had missed the first time — one of her mother's trademark red envelopes, sealed and inscribed with *Margaret Pinaldi* in her handwriting. She opened it and began to read:

Margaret: If I were to give you a windfall of cash upon my death, you might have been numbed into a false sense of security and done nothing with your life. You served me well at the clinic, and for that I am forever indebted, but it is my concern that you will hop off into the world, armed with your worthless, esoteric degrees, and fail to define yourself through your work and passions. I trust you are now self-sufficient and successful, and therefore I can leave you this money, which I strongly suggest you invest in an aggressive mixture of stocks (70 percent), bonds (20 percent), and the remainder in liquid cash reserves — at least through your fiftieth birthday, and then the allocations should be revisited.

I hope you're happy, Margaret. Remember that I love you.

There will be no more red envelopes. I am finished.

Ruth

Margaret brought the second page to the top, a bank statement from First Federal Buffalo.

"Oh . . . my . . . Lord," she whispered.

Toward the bottom of the page, Ruth had expressively circled the balance with a red felt-tip marker: $235,812.35.

Margaret set the papers in her lap and looked about her from the parapet of the front stoop. She wanted to share the news with someone, but whom? Dewayne's presence right now made her anxious and confused. Donna was in Atlanta on her interview. There was a time Margaret would have shared such news with Randy, but she had crested that hill months ago. Suddenly, and for the first time since Christmas, Margaret felt acutely alone in this land with soil the color of Mars.

She went inside and returned to the porch with journal in hand. Margaret then uncapped a new, red felt-tip pen and began to write:

Dear Mother: Why did you have me? For the same reason I'm thinking of having mine? Was it because both your parents had died and there was no longer an older generation standing between you and mortality?

Was the ticking of your biological clock so loud and relentless that you gave birth just to shut it up?

Was it because you were so inexperienced with men and love that when someone finally did get you pregnant you were so bewildered and pleased that you just let it happen?

Damn you, Mother — who was/is he? And why did you choose not to marry him? Did you love my father? Did you intentionally get pregnant? What could be so bad about a man that would make you hide him from me for forty years?

There is a man in my own life now, and though he is sweet and gentle I still hold him at arm's length because it seems too easy and comfortable being with him. I think I watched and learned from you that struggle was best and that a state of satisfaction meant you weren't trying and that you were lazy and destined to die ignorant and unfulfilled.

You would not approve of Dewayne — at least I don't think you would. He has taught me to enjoy the light, easy things you scoffed at. (I read the funnies now.) We do not debate the issues as you and I used to do. We argue about the most superficial things. (Who makes the best barbecue sauce in town?)

I am thirty years old. I believe you told me cancer took grandmother when she was fifty-nine. I lost you at fifty-five, and I cannot help but feel a looming deadline here. As I write this I realize how precious life can be and how sweet it is to intertwine one's emotions with another . . . something you never had the pleasure of doing. I think you had me because you did not want to be alone in the world. Yet I realize now you were the loneliest person I've ever known even though we lived in the same house.

Unlike you, I'm going to do it right, Mother. I am going to regard my own feelings and the feelings of others and lap up the love and delights that lie within reach, around me. If that is lazy and Southern, then I am lazy and Southern.

Thanks for the money. I have some plans for it. A new roof, for one. A bed. And then some bigger things.

The last red envelope? I highly doubt it.

Thirty-nine

Dear Chatter: Cheese straws are little finger cookies made from flour and cheese and just a little bit of red pepper. You can fry them in vegetable oil. They are just about the tastiest things in the world.

Dear Chatter: What is it with all the homeowners in north Selby who have a black man doing all their dirty work for them at pitiful wages? Maybe your history books left this part out, but there was this president named Abraham Lincoln? And there was this little war? And you guys lost? And the slaves were freed? Hello out there? Hello?

A grease-spotted white bag of Krystal hamburgers sat open on the seat of Suzanne's black Lexus between her and John David. On their way to Atlanta, at the Locust Grove exit, they'd decided they were hungry and pulled off I-75 long enough to make the drive-through purchase, along with one order of chili-cheese fries and two large Diet Cokes.

As John David drove, Suzanne looked into the bag. "There's just one left, John David," she said in a taunting tone. She reached in and grabbed the little square burger.

"It's not ladylike to take the last of anything, Suzanne. You hand that over. You've eaten most of those anyway."

"John David! I have not!"

He raised his eyebrows. "I'm gonna tell . . ." he threatened in a childish singsong.

"You're gonna hold that over me for the rest of my life, aren't you?"

John David started shaking his head. "Who'd believe me, Suzanne? Who's gonna believe you went around town wearin' strap-on bellies. So what are we gonna do first when we get to Atlanta?" he asked. "I've never faked a miscarriage before."

Knowing very well this most likely was her last sponsored trip to Atlanta, and that Boone would not be changing his mind about the divorce, Suzanne pulled out all the stops for these three days and asked John David to join her. The official line at Sugar Day was that Suzanne was visiting her great-grandmother in Ashville, but instead she'd booked a suite at the Ritz-Carlton Buckhead and then massages for them both at a new spa up at Lake Lanier. Plus, there was a ring she wanted at Tiffany and a new handbag at the Louis Vuitton boutique in Lenox Square.

"I gotta drop by and pick up an urn at Daniel Quincy before we go to the hotel, Suzanne."

"Who's it for?" she asked.

"Mona Beckner. I'm doin' her dinin' room over."

"She just did that dinin' room last year."

"She's still not happy with it. I swear that woman doesn't know what she wants."

Suzanne stopped to picture the Beckners' dining room in her head. "They need a coffered ceilin' in that room," she said. "That room's got too big a feel to it. That high ceilin' probably makes 'em feel like little kids."

As John David visualized the change, they whizzed past a picture of Scarlett O'Hara on a billboard that advertised a new *Gone with the Wind* tour in McDonough, an Atlanta exurb that claimed to be the setting for Margaret Mitchell's novel.

John David began to nod. "You're right,

Suzanne," he said. "A coffered ceiling would add a lot to that room."

"John David!"

"What?"

"Are you actually agreein' with me on a decorating matter?"

"What are you so surprised about? You've got good taste, Suzanne."

"But you always say I'm wrong."

"Sometimes you're a little over the top — like those tacky scallop-shell sconces in the dining room — but you got a good eye, girl. Especially with curtains."

Suzanne shook her head and smiled. "Why on earth did you wait until now to tell me that? I sure would've liked to hear that earlier, John David. I swear I never get a compliment for anything."

"I'm not stupid, Suzanne. You're my biggest account — and now you're fixin' to be a pauper. Woe is me."

As John David took Suzanne's black Lexus past eighty, her mind traveled back down I-75, into Selby and through the front door of 2146 Red Hill Drive, where she began to float from room to room in an exquisite tour of curtains, tassels, and fringe.

Forty

Dear Chatter: I'm calling to complain about a public school bus I saw driving through Red Hill Plantation. There is no reason for that bus to be in this neighborhood. All the kids here go to Canterbury.

Dear Chatter: What has four teeth and is a hundred and sixty-eight years old? Two Waffle House waitresses. Ha, ha! Thought you'd get a chuckle out of that one.

"You outdone yourself tonight, Donna," Frankie Kabel said. "This is the best fried chicken I've ever had — just as good as your momma used to make."

"Thank you!"

"I mean it, girl. Very tasty. Very tasty."

"This is what all chickens used to taste like, Daddy — did you know that? It's a free-range chicken. They taste better 'cause they weren't cooped up in a cage eatin' stale birdseed all day. These chickens run around on a farm eatin' what God wanted 'em to eat."

"Well, all I know is I'm gonna miss your cookin'."

"You're gonna do just fine, Daddy."

In the weeks since she announced her promotion to her father, Donna and Margaret set about teaching Frankie Kabel how to subsist without a woman in the house. They helped him draft shopping lists and shadowed him at Kroger. They taught him how to make turkey chili and chicken soup and squash casserole with low-fat cheddar cheese and how to store all these things in the freezer then resurrect them in the microwave.

What surprised Donna even more than her father's openness to learning all this was his reaction to the news that she was moving out and up to Atlanta.

As a celebratory meal, Donna cooked all her father's favorite foods, including not only the fried chicken but also gravy from the drippings and buttermilk mashed potatoes, collards and corn bread and a peach cobbler. She'd added a single black cardamom pod to the cobbler — something Margaret had taught her — giving it a subtle, mysterious flavor not unlike smoked allspice.

Before they sat down to eat, Frankie and Donna stood behind their chairs for grace.

"Lord, we thank you for these glorious bounties before us," he said, his eyes scrunched tightly closed as if afraid that any intruding light could zap and vaporize the message. "And we ask that you watch over this girl in Atlanta, 'cause she's got a temper and puffed-up pride that can get her in trouble. And, Lord, we wanna say thank you for providin' this opportunity for Donna and helpin' her succeed. In Jesus' name, Amen."

To herself, Donna thought, *This is my doin', Daddy. It's all mine. God didn't scrape me off the floor when Robbie dumped me. God didn't memorize all those produce flash cards. God didn't teach me how to like spendin' time by myself and how to start seein' past a face. God didn't work six days a week and come up with clever cross-merchandising so the produce section of Kroger Store #578 would outperform every single unit in the Atlanta region.*

Instead, she said, simply, "Amen."

They ate their meal, and when it was time for dessert Donna went into the kitchen, pulled the cobbler from the oven, and spooned it into bowls. She watched the steam rise from the piles of flaky crust and peach slices bathed in clear syrup.

"This needs ice cream," she said.

Donna went to the freezer, which was packed with all the single-serving meals she and her father had been making. One by one, as if saving someone from a building that had collapsed on top of them, Donna pulled the bags of spaghetti sauce and soup and casseroles from the freezer and set them on the kitchen table. She came upon the famous heart potato and opened the lid of the Rubbermaid container. It was covered now in fuzzy ice crystals that glittered beneath the light overhead. Donna thought back to the night months ago when she'd awakened with cramps and noticed the kitchen light on, and hiding in the hallway she could see her father sitting at the kitchen table with the tuber, which he had freed from its cryogenic state. His head bowed in prayer, he laid his three fingers, the ones used for the Boy Scout's pledge, on top of the cold skin and held them there as if taking a pulse or bestowing a wish on it. "I know this was your doin', Doris," he said out loud to himself. "She don't listen to me, maybe she'll listen to you now."

After returning the potato to the freezer, Donna then came across the frozen Three Musketeers bar that Billy Ray Cyrus had bitten into and thrown to the crowd. She took it from its container and tossed it in the trash can beside the stove.

And finally, there it was . . . the last of the peach ice cream her mother had made. To prolong its life, Donna had triple-wrapped the two pale-orange scoops in three Ziploc bags before setting them into an airtight plastic container.

With scissors, she now cut away the plastic and set the frozen lumps atop the helpings of cobbler, which were still warm, and in the short time it took Donna to get the dessert to the table the edges of the ice cream had started to melt and run down the slopes of the dessert, pooling at the bottom of the bowl.

Frankie knew immediately what it was. He smiled at his daughter and she at him. At the same time, they picked up their spoons and scooped up a dab of the ice cream and brought it to their mouths. And once the sweet coldness was on their tongues, they closed their eyes and let it sit there for as long as it would last.

Epilogue

(Eleven months later)

Margaret spotted Donna's Saturn from behind the counter, easy to distinguish because of the "VEGGY" vanity license plate.

"Can you please cover the register, Dewayne?" she yelled to the back office. "I'm gonna go meet Donna."

Margaret wiped her hands on her red-and-white-striped apron with *The Casserole Shop* embroidered in thick black letters in an arc across the chest. Dewayne emerged, wearing an identical apron and with a sleeping baby that lay across his forearm in a football hold. Instead of her head nestled in the crook of his arm, however, she lay backward, her legs straddling his bicep and her head in his large hand, his fingers spread open as if he were holding a cantaloupe. At first, this bothered several of their customers — and most all of them were mothers of some age or another — but they soon learned how very comfortable and safe Ruth Case felt in her father's care.

In the early mornings when he cooked, Dewayne slipped Ruth into a blue back-pack carrier. She would bob about though sleep soundly as he worked in the kitchen, manually mashing potatoes and mincing onions and mixing the corn bread batter that would blanket the store's most popular casserole, which he had named Dewayne's Delight. It was a beef and lamb stew with roasted turnips, garlic, carrots, thyme and sage, topped with the corn bread batter that would brown and crisp up real nice after twenty minutes at four twenty-five.

Dewayne did not feel centered unless he was in his daughter's presence, and it was just three weeks after her birth that he resigned from the fire department and went to work with Margaret in their store. Crammed between an expansive Block-buster Video and an L.A. Weight Loss Clinic, The Casserole Shop sold casseroles and only casseroles, albeit a wide variety of them. They ranged from Dewayne's traditional fare to Margaret's ethnic and fusion offerings to the Middle Georgia Celebrity Casserole of the Week, which was by invitation only. Harriet Toomey was a frequent contributor.

"You take your time," he said to his wife.

"I can do this one-handed."

Margaret would not have believed him
had he not proven himself, but she
watched Dewayne time and again as he
pulled casseroles from the display case,
dropped them into their trademark red-
cardboard carrying cases, folded them shut
and conducted a Visa transaction, all while
holding his daughter. At Donna's urging,
they did hire Adrian Braswell part-time to
help carry casseroles out to customers'
cars in the busy afternoons. Though he
was good, reliable help, Margaret occasionally had to chastise him for attempting
to convert their Japanese customers to
Christianity.

Through the glass of the windows and
the door, Dewayne listened to the muffled
squeals and chattering of the two young
women:

"You cut your hair!"

"You like it?"

"I love it — it's so cute! I'm gonna get
mine cut that short!"

"Don't you dare cut that gorgeous hair,
Donna."

The girls had not seen each other for five
months. Though Donna had just been in
her new job in Atlanta for half a year, they
were already using her to train most of the

produce managers from Chattanooga, south. She'd also become their chief perishables troubleshooter. If, say, cruciferous vegetables weren't moving in the central Birmingham locations, they dispatched Donna. She would fax a plan then swoop into town on a direct Delta flight from Atlanta that morning and deliver an hourlong seminar on cross-store merchandising. Three times she'd tried to schedule the surgery for her face and had to cancel because of work.

The bells on the door knocked against the glass, tinkling, as Donna and Margaret came inside.

"Hey, hey!" he welcomed from over the counter.

"What is that attached to your body, Dewayne Case? Bring that little baby over here so she can see her aunt Donna. Oh, my gosh, Margaret — she looks so much like you! Oh, look at those little lips. Those are your lips, Dewayne."

They sat and talked, each of them taking a turn with Ruth, passing her back and forth. The daily rush did not begin for another forty minutes — three o'clock was proving to be the hour in which most north Selby women decided they did not want to cook dinner that night — so Margaret cut them all a small piece of a Greek casserole. Flavored with lamb and feta cheese, fresh mint and roasted fennel bulb, it reminded Donna of the casserole Suzanne Parley so desperately needed to have re-created that one day more than a year ago.

"I almost forgot," Donna said. "I brought you somethin'."

She reached into her purse and pulled out a copy of *Southern Interiors*. "Have y'all seen this?" Both Margaret and Dewayne shook their head. Parents of a new baby and new business, they had read nothing esoteric or recreational in weeks.

"It's Miss Suzanne — look. On page ninety-two."

A frequent customer of The Casserole Shop after the divorce, Suzanne Parley had suddenly, inexplicably disappeared a few months back. Margaret heard rumors that she'd moved out of town. St. Simon's Island, someone said. Brunswick, said another.

"There she is," Dewayne said.

"It's John David!" Margaret added.

Posing in a traditional, mahogany-heavy den, the two of them were dressed all in royal blue, John David in a suit and Suzanne in a simple, scoop-necked sheath dress.

The ad copy said: *Finally, one decorating firm that can do it all — cutting-edge, coastal contemporary, and the traditional look of Dixie . . . BluSouth . . . for drop-dead gorgeous interiors that will be the envy of the Georgia coast and beyond.*

Margaret looked at the picture of Suzanne, deconstructing it in her mind to figure out what exactly it was that made it seem so odd and unreal. She noted the all-blue wardrobe, the new haircut, the lack of the large diamond on her finger. Suzanne had not gained weight; she hadn't lost any either. Plastic surgery? Different eyebrows?

And then, finally, Margaret realized the once-foreign addition to this perplexing image.

"You know," she said, "contentment becomes her."

About the Author

Ad Hudler is a stay-at-home dad and the author of the novel *Househusband*. He lives in Florida and can be reached through his Web site at www.adhudler.com.